YOU ARE MY

reason

DUET

WILLOW WINTERS

YOU ARE MY
reason
WILLOW WINTERS

From *USA Today* best-selling author Willow Winters comes an intense romance with second chances, secrets and a twist.

It's been a long time since I've looked at a man and wanted something more.

Even longer since one has looked at me with a gaze I couldn't tear my eyes from.

No one's perfect, but that's how he felt when I was in his arms.

I started to think everything was going to be all right. That life had finally put the pieces of my broken heart back together.

Fate brought us close.

It's a pretty little thought my poetic mind had.

But there's no doubt that the sins of his past will tear us apart.

You Are My Reason is book 1 in the You Are Mine duet and should be read first.

"Love is more than words;
my heart can tell you that."
—DLS

To Donna, always an inspiration.

YOU ARE MY
reason

one

Mason

"**Y**OU SHOULD BE THANKING ME FOR CLEANING up your mess," my father says snidely from where he's seated in his high-back desk chair. His fingers grip the leather arms and his thumbs rub gently back and forth across the brass studs.

Though the blinds are closed, the tall windows behind my father fill the large office with fading light from the evening sunset.

Looking over my shoulder, I narrow my gaze at him, still holding a random law textbook I've taken from the floor-to-ceiling shelves that line the walls of his office. The room smells like old books. With the dark wood, tan leather and deep red

Beaumont rug, the decor reeks of old money and that's exactly what this room represents.

That and bullshit.

Lies and corruption are what have kept this room in its current state for generations. I've pretended for so long that it wasn't true. But now that I've learned what my father's done to get this "esteemed" position … I can't turn a blind eye to it anymore. His actions are undeniable and unforgivable.

I huff a small laugh, not letting him see how affected I am. "For the last time," I say as I shut the book and smirk at him, "it wasn't my mess."

I'm not admitting to a damn thing. Not even to my own father. In this city, one slipup could send you tumbling into an early grave like my mother. I'm not responsible for the mess my father's referring to and I refuse to take the blame.

I don't trust him. I don't trust anyone any longer.

My father's face reddens before he picks up a cup of hot coffee. He holds the black mug with both hands, blowing across the top and refusing to back down.

"You would have gone through hell—"

"No, I wouldn't have," I say, cutting him off, although my voice doesn't reflect any emotion whatsoever. This is a turning point in our relationship. Instead of his disappointment creeping under my skin, it's the other way around. I look him in the eye as I add, "I would have been just fine."

A moment passes where the only sound is the ticking of the large clock on the right side of the room. "It wasn't my mess you cleaned up, and we both know it." He's the first to look away but instead of showing remorse, his expression only reflects his anger.

"Did you need anything else?" I ask. I just want to get the hell out of here and back to the construction site. This office reminds me of my grandfather, a man I loved and trusted. But he was a man who turned out to be just like all the other powerful men in this city. Ruled by corruption, driven by greed, imperfect. *Devastated* is the word a former therapist would use to describe my reaction when I found out the truth about my family.

"I'm tired of you getting into trouble," my father says and I scoff. This is the first time in my life I've truly been in control of myself. No more fucking around, starting trouble. These recent events have been sobering. When I was a hormone-filled teenager dealing with grief and anger, it was easy to act out and pick fights. Caused first by the death of my grandfather and then later, my mother.

At thirty-three and on my own, I'm not like that anymore. I finally have my life together … all but the ties to my father. It's a tangled mess of lies and offshore bank accounts. Much like the dealings of the elite who rule this city.

The thought makes my gaze fall to the floor before I look back up to the shelves and mindlessly scan the spines of the antique texts.

Being aware of what my father did makes all those old memories of losing my mother surface. My stomach churns and my blood heats, the adrenaline coursing in my veins pushing me to confront the man I no longer know.

I bring a clenched fist to my mouth as I clear my throat and take a few steps toward him. He's the one who called this meeting, demanded it really. But he hasn't even risen from his chair. Lazy prick.

"I don't know what you're talking about," I answer him easily. "I haven't got a single problem on my mind." I give him a polite smile and keep a charming look on my face. It only makes him angrier and I love every second of his pissed-off expression. He thought I'd feel as if I owed him.

I don't owe him a damn thing.

I may be just like him in looks. Tall, dark and handsome, or so I've been told. I've perfected a brilliant smile with an air of ease that's made to fool and seduce the world at large. It makes sense that he's a lawyer. It's the family business but if it wasn't, it'd still be the profession most apt for my father.

"You need to quit this charade and do what you're told, Mason." He stands from his seat quickly, his chair rolling backward until it hits the wall. It disturbs the blinds and streams of dim light flicker into the room.

"I don't need to do anything but breathe and pay taxes."

He could order me around like that all he wanted back when I was a child or before I knew the truth, but now I have no respect for the man in front of me. I'm disgusted by him and caught on the edge of what's right and wrong. I should turn him in to the authorities and let him rot. I grit my teeth as I stare back at him. It's what's right, but I can't bring myself to send my own father to prison.

A low hum of admonishment deep in his throat makes the smirk on my face widen into a smile.

"I have my own company, my own life—" I start but my father cuts me off. Nothing new there.

"You were born a Thatcher, and you'll die a Thatcher." The words leave a chill across my skin. That's the crux of the problem. I was born into this life and I can't run from it. Plus my company is in debt to him. It was a rookie mistake I made back before I knew what I was doing. When I didn't see him for the man he really is.

"Why do you even care what I do?" I finally ask him. His precious reputation is just fine now that I'm an adult and I've moved on from the fuckup I used to be. "I'm not the one coming to you—"

"*She* did," he answers simply with a spark in his eyes and the corners of his lips upturned as if that's all the ammunition he needs. In some respects, he's right. All the people in this city know where I come from and what it means to be a Thatcher. They know I have money and power behind me. That's all anyone here cares about anyway. New York is all about the bottom dollar.

Nonchalantly shrugging my shoulders, I stride closer to the desk, bracing myself by gripping the back of the chair opposite him. "You decided how to deal with her without vetting what she said." I meet his glare easily, willing him to tell me again how he *saved* me. "She didn't have anything on me. She couldn't have done anything." My voice rises toward the end of my statement and I hate that I've shown him this weak side of me. Even if only for a moment.

Control. I thrive with control.

A heavy breath leaves him as he stares back with pure hate but he doesn't say a word. I knew he wouldn't. He's wrong. Dead wrong and ruined if I open my mouth to anyone. He took the initiative so I'd owe him, but in reality we both know that he owes me now.

"It's your fuckup, not mine." I practically spit out the words and shove the chair forward as I turn to leave him. My body's tense and the anger continues to rise. I try not to let it show. I hate that I can't control myself around this prick. Everyone else I can handle, but my own father, not so much.

"Mason!" he calls after me. His voice turns to white noise as the blood rushing in my ears gets louder and louder, drowning out all the bullshit.

The second I open his office door, he goes silent. He'll never let anyone hear us fighting. *Never.* Secrets are always kept behind closed doors. It's a family rule.

The door shuts with a loud *thunk* and as I walk down the empty hall, the thin carpeting muffles the sound of my black leather oxfords smacking against the ground at an incessant pace.

Miss Geist looks up from her spot at her desk. The wrinkles around her eyes deepen as she tilts her head and gives me that familiar smile she always has for me. It's one that says: *Oh, what have you done now?*

Through the years, even after my mother's death, Miss Theresa Geist has given me that look. She's the only one who showed me any genuine regret and kindness when I had to deal with my mother's passing. She's a good person. I have no idea what she's doing here working for a man like my father.

She clutches the small pendant on her thin silver necklace and her forbearing smile changes to something more reserved when I look back at her. It's instantaneous and makes me halt in my steps. I know I must look pissed; I'm beyond furious. It's been two days since my father told me what he'd done all those months ago and my anger hasn't waned one bit. Deep down I think I knew what he'd done back then, even if he never admitted it until now. I wish he hadn't. The whole situation makes me sick.

"He's being a dick," I mutter, waiting for the old lady to be a little more at ease. She doesn't know a thing that goes on outside of the office and I don't owe her an explanation, but I can't help myself.

"Now, now," she says with a bit of playfulness although I can tell she's still shaken. She's not used to seeing me like this. Not in the last decade, at least.

I give her a gentle smile and wink, putting on the act I use so well. Maybe I have a soft spot for her.

"Have a good night, Mr. Thatcher," she tells me as she shuffles the papers on her desk, seeming somewhat less disturbed.

It's enough that it settles me and I push open the double doors leading to the entrance with both hands and keep moving. The sound of my shoes pacing on the granite and the open air of the lobby filled with chatter soothe me.

But only for a moment.

It's not until I leave the building that my true feelings surface. The mask fades, and fear sets in. I didn't know what my father was capable of.

I had an inkling, but I thought I'd always imagined it. I'd thought my memories weren't quite right. It's not that I expected more from him; I just hate that I was right.

What's done is done and I can't stop what's been set in motion.

Julia

BLOODRED LIPS. THE SILVER TUBE IN MY HAND IS labeled Black Honey, my favorite color. I've worn it since my freshman year of college and although I've experimented with other colors at times, it's always been a staple in my beauty bag. Pressing my lips together, I smack them once as I examine myself in the mirror.

My complexion is flawless thanks to the full-coverage foundation I'm wearing. My lashes are thick and long, and I've got just a hint of blush. It's a timeless look, classic and clean. And it hides everything. My reddened skin and the dark circles under my eyes are nowhere to be found.

I don't look like the person I've become. This woman in

the reflection, she's who I used to be. A very large part of me wants *this* woman back. I want to smile like I used to and hear the sound of a genuine laugh from my own lips.

My heart pangs and stops that thought in its place.

He'll never laugh again. It's as if any small moment of time that passes where he's forgotten for even a second is a disgrace. My eyes fall and I slip the cap back on the tube of lipstick, tossing it into the pouch on my vanity.

No matter what I do, every little thing reminds me of him.

Trivial things, like the color of the granite he insisted we purchase when we remodeled this place together. The knobs on the bathroom drawers he hated and never failed to complain about. The change he left in the cup holder in the Bentley. The pile of dimes and pennies that clink together when I drive over speed bumps or a pothole. The same small coins I refuse to touch. He put them there, and I can't bring myself to move them.

Freaking pieces of metal render me useless.

It may seem pathetic, but not to me. From my perspective, I'm being as strong as I can. I face the New York City judgment every day, putting on a brave face and going about my life, my new normal.

All the while I shove everything I'm feeling deep down inside. That's healthy, right?

I won't let them see me crumble. There are those who want to. I could practically hear them licking their lips months ago when my world fell apart.

Julia Summers, born into wealth and raised on the Upper East Side. She always did everything by the book and married young to her high school sweetheart, Jace Anderson. With a loving family, a handsome and doting husband and the social life every young woman in Manhattan dreams of, Jules had a picture-perfect life. Until her husband suddenly passed away at the age of twenty-eight, leaving the twenty-seven-year-old woman widowed and alone for the first time in her life.

Twenty-eight now and numerous months since the tragic accident.

They're waiting to see what I'll do next. Pens to the papers and cameras ready. There's nothing better for the gossipmongers. It's to be expected. Being in Page Six is how I've made my life.

They'd love to see me fall and I have, but not in front of their eyes. I'll keep my hair pinned up and my concealer on thick.

I know what they say, though. This town whispers, especially in the circles I run in. They don't need to see the truth to figure it out themselves. There are rumors of leaning too heavily on alcohol for comfort. I don't command enough loyalty for discretion; every member of my household staff has sold out to the tabloids looking for a hint of what goes on behind these walls. Living on the Upper East Side, every single person who struts in front of my home is looking for a crack in my veneer.

What's ironic is that there's no glamour here, nothing noteworthy. Just a woman who cries herself to sleep at least once a week still. A woman who's struggling to move on because she's never been with anyone else. I suppose it's what I get, though. I loved posing for the cameras and practically lived for regular mentions in the gossip columns. This is what I deserve. They wanted in my life and I let them. I can't expect them to be shut out now.

Days have turned to weeks and weeks to months. Now that my husband's been gone for nearly eight months, I have plenty of cracks in this so-called perfect life. I'm still shattered but I'm working on gluing little pieces back into place.

I glance at myself as I tug down my dress just slightly and smooth out the black lace. *It's time to face the music.*

I clear my throat as I turn off the light and grab my phone, checking the text again.

Are you sure you don't need me to pick you up?

Kat's a sweetheart. She's always looking out for me. Of all my friends, she's the one who still texts me religiously, which is insane because she's constantly working and I have no idea how she finds the time.

My fingers *tap, tap, tap* away an answer. *I've got it. Leaving now.*

The Penrose is only twenty minutes away if there's no traffic. Seeing how it's 9:00 p.m. on a Friday night, I'm prepared to sit in the back of a taxi for half the night.

A light sigh slips past my lips as I bend down to pick up my favorite Louboutins. With a row of spikes up the back and red-lacquered soles, they have exactly the touch of color and attitude I would've worn back then. I almost second-guess the simple black dress I've picked out. It's a nod to Audrey Hepburn. But looking over my shoulder at the darkened bathroom mirror, all I see is one of the options I had for Jace's funeral.

I would've worn this dress last year before it all happened. Back when I was happy and everything was how it was supposed to be. And don't I want to be that girl again? I want to find a way to move forward on a new path.

Holding the heels in one hand and the iron banister in the other, I descend the winding staircase.

I'm not that woman any longer; I've changed. I accept that, but I don't love who I am now. The crying and feeling sorry for myself. I need something. A change and some light in all the darkness. Eight months of a pity party and being stuck in a rut is long enough. I'd like to say that Jace wouldn't want to see me like this, but I don't even know what Jace would want for me. I've quit wearing my wedding ring, although it still sits on my nightstand. I'm ready to find out who I am without him beside me.

Before I open the front door, I glimpse out the large stained glass window in the foyer. It's nothing but gray outside, and the hustle and bustle is only a fraction of what it could be.

Heavy rain greets me when I step onto my small porch. I decided not to bother with an umbrella, simply grabbing a stylish trench coat on my way outside. Quickly taking the steps to the street out front, I hail a cab. My heels click as I wrap the belt around me and tie my coat tight when the first taxi comes to a slow stop in front of me.

I could have called for someone to do this, to order me a cab so it would be waiting. I could ask for help with so many things. I'd rather do it myself, though.

The light breeze and rain feel real. The rain is cold to the touch and I'm sure I'll be regretting my decision soon. But it's something different. I don't want anyone's help. I just need time.

Climbing into the taxi, I shake off the gathered rain from my jacket; the inside of the cab is warm and welcoming. I push the hair out of my face and say, "Penrose, please."

"You got it," the cabby says as he glances over his shoulder to look at me. His thinning black hair is oiled over and he's more than a little overweight. The buttons on his striped shirt are straining to keep it shut.

I can see curiosity in his eyes but just as he opens his mouth to ask something, I don't know what, I turn to look out the closed window and thank him.

Everything outside is wet and dreary. The people walking by move quickly and a couple only about ten feet away are fighting over an umbrella. It's a cute little struggle though and the tall man in a navy blue Henley lets the woman win. She's dressed in formal work clothes, while he's in casual attire. But as soon as she takes full control of the umbrella, she walks closer to him and he wraps his arm around her waist.

I rip my eyes away and pick at my nails. It's little things like what I just witnessed that I find unbearable. I bite the inside of my cheek and hold back the bitterness.

Luckily, the driver gets the picture. I'm not in the mood to talk and the cab moves ahead, taking me away from my sanctuary and toward another test.

That's what these things really are. Tests.

It's only in this moment that I realize I'm really doing it. I've put it off so many times over the last eight months. I've given so many excuses for not meeting up with the girls.

Why today? I don't know. My heart sinks thinking that maybe I'm really getting over my husband's death.

As much as I want to be the woman I once was, happy and carefree, I don't want to forget him.

I lay my head back on the headrest and close my eyes, my clutch in my lap. Jace gave it to me last Christmas. I snort at the thought, running my fingers over the smooth, hot pink leather. More like I picked it out and he paid for it.

I close my eyes and take in a deep breath. It's calming riding in a quiet cab at night in the city. The quiet rumble of the engine and the white noise of the rain are a serene mix.

The last day I saw my husband was when we were watching my nephew Everett, so my sister could have a mother-daughter day with Lexi. It's rare I see my family at all; everyone is so busy with their own lives and my sister is much older than I am… so we're not exactly close. I still love them though.

The thought of my nephew brings a smile to my face. With sandy blond hair that just barely covers his big blue eyes and a wide smile, you can't help but smile back at him. He was only a few months old back then. A brand-new life in this world. That's the way it works, isn't it? Life and death go hand in hand.

I glance forward out the windshield and give a slight start when we stop far away from Second Avenue where the bar is located; a bit of traffic is holding us up.

The cabby notices my reaction in the rearview mirror and shrugs as he says, "We should be out of it soon." He's tense at the wheel, probably expecting me to snap at him, maybe blame him for taking this particular route. More guilt washes over me. I hate spreading negativity simply by being so … gloom and doom with the air surrounding me. I'm not an ice queen, or at least I don't mean to be.

I give him a soft smile, placing my clutch in the middle seat. "I figured we'd run into something," I say easily. My voice comes out even and calm. It's the voice I use with my mother. The kind of tone that says: *I'm okay, just tired.*

The cabby shifts, making the leather seat grumble and he tries to make small chat.

I nod my head and answer politely, but keep everything short and to the point. I can be accommodating with others and I truly want to do so. I'm tired of being alone and pushing others away. It's just harder than I thought it would be after how I've been since Jace passed.

After a moment of quiet, I look out the window again. The rain's nearly stopped, and the sidewalks are instantly crowded as a result. The people were always there, waiting under awnings for protection. Not many people like to venture into weather that washes away your makeup and ruins even the best put-together look.

They were waiting and ready to keep moving just the same. All they needed was a small break before setting out again. The only question is if there will be another awning to save them when the brutal downpour comes back.

The cabby stops and my eyes whip up to the sign on my right, my heart beating faster as I watch dozens of people walking in front of me on the sidewalk. Each going wherever it is that life has taken them. I don't know if I'm ready, but at least I'm here.

"Miss?" the cabby asks after I remain where I am in this cozy seat. I shake my head slightly with quick motions and play off my hesitation, paying him and leaving a big tip as well. He deserves it for having to suffer my company.

"Have a good night," I tell him as I slip out, my heels hitting the slick asphalt and the door shutting behind me with a resounding click.

CHAPTER

three

Mason

IT FIGURES IT WOULD STOP POURING THE SECOND I GET in here. The bar is packed and the cacophony of guests chatting and glasses clinking welcome me. I can get lost in the crowds. I know the people here see me, but they don't know me.

This bar in particular is one of my favorites. It's always full. Its tufted leather seats are constantly filled, and the warm rich tones of the wooden ceiling and brick walls make it feel like home somehow.

My suit is nothing fancy, nothing that will stand out in here. Which is how I want it. I run my fingers through my hair and shake away the rain as I shrug off my jacket and toss it over the barstool at the very end.

It's been a long day and the last thing I need is to go home alone. As soon as my eyes lift, the bartender is on me. I think her name is Patricia. She's in here every weekend.

"Whiskey?" she asks me. She never stops moving, shoveling ice into short glasses and pouring liquor like a pro. Unlike the other women in here, she's not looking for a man with deep pockets. She doesn't do chitchat either, which is another reason I like sitting in this section. The biggest reason is that it's out of the way, somewhere I can simply blend in and watch.

"Double," I answer her with a nod and slip my cell phone out from my jacket pocket. I've only been gone from the office for two hours, but I've got a dozen emails waiting for my attention. A huff of a grunt leaves me as a text from Liam pops up.

You coming out tonight?

Already out, I answer him as the glass hits the polished bar top and Patricia slides it over to me.

My phone pings as I lift the tumbler to my lips and let the cool liquor burn all the way down, warming my chest.

Where at?

I contemplate telling him. I like Liam. A lot. If I had any friends, he'd be one of them. But and after talking to my father today, I don't want to be around a damn soul.

A sarcastic laugh makes me grin as I realize I've come to a crowded bar to be alone. It's the truth, though. You're always surrounded by people in this city; there's never a place to hide unless it's in plain sight.

I down the rest of my drink and tap the heavy glass against the bar top as I consider what to tell him. That's when I hear it. Almost as if daring me to stay alone any longer, it's the gentle sound of a feminine laugh. It's genuine and it rings out clear in the bar even though it's soft.

It's a soothing sound, a calming force in the chaos that surrounds us. Everything around me fades except for the woman who uttered that sweet sound.

The smooth glass stays still as I look down the bar in search of her.

The rest of the crowd doesn't seem to notice as they continue with whatever the hell they're saying and doing, but my eyes are drawn to my left. Through the throng of people, I just barely get a glimpse of her.

Dark brunette hair that's pulled back; pale skin covered in black lace.

A man at the opposite end leans away from the bar, digging in his back pocket for his wallet and giving me a clear view of her.

Those dark red lips attract my gaze first. She licks her bottom lip before picking up a large glass of deep red wine. The color matches her lips perfectly. She smiles at something and her shoulders shake as she laughs, making the dark liquid swirl in her glass and bringing a blush to her high cheekbones.

She tosses her hair to the side and her fingers tease the ends as she brings her tendrils over one shoulder, wrapping them around her finger while she sips her wine.

It's when she looks away from whomever she's been giving her attention to that my curiosity is piqued.

Without their eyes on her, her expression morphs into something else. I finally see her eyes, the lightest of blues, and that's when I really see her. Not just the image of what she's portraying.

Pain is clear as day.

It's the lie though, how fucking good she was at hiding it, that's what really gets me. Even I was fooled.

People can hide behind a smile or a laugh; every soul in here can pretend to be someone and something they're not.

The truth is always there though and I'm damn good at recognizing it. Your eyes can never hide two things: age and emotion. Hers speak to me in a way nothing else can.

But had I never looked just then when she thought no one was watching, she never would have shown me willingly.

She straightens her back and I see her profile, her expression. The corners of my lips turn down. Not only do I know her pain, I know her name. I know everything about her.

Julia Summers.

My blood chills as she turns back to the table, the smile on her face slipping back into position just as the man at the end of the bar steps forward, obscuring her from my vision. As if the moment of clarity and recognition was just for me in that moment. Like fate wanted me to know how close I was to her.

I keep my eyes on the bar, doing my best to listen, but her voice is silent or lost in the mix of chatter throughout the crowded place.

"Another?" Patricia's voice sounds close, closer than she usually is. I lift my head to see her standing right in front of me, both hands on the bar and waiting.

I nod my head with my brows pinched, shaking off the mix of emotions. This city is a small place with worlds always colliding, but I've never seen her in person. Only in a photograph. Only that once. I'm sure it's her, though.

The ice clinks in the glass and I watch as the liquid slips over each cube, cracking them and filling the crevices.

"You okay?" Patricia asks me. It's odd. In the year or so since I've been coming here, she's never bothered to make small talk. It's why I don't mind her.

I give her a tight smile as I reply, "I'm fine." I reach her eyes and widen my smile, relaxing my posture as I lean back slightly.

She eyes me warily as she mutters, "You don't look fine."

It takes me a moment before I shrug it off and say, "I'm all right, just tired."

She nods once and goes back to minding her own business, sliding me the whiskey and moving on to other customers.

I tap my pointer finger against the glass, looking casually down the bar.

She's hidden from view, but I know she's there.

CHAPTER
four

Julia

MY BODY TINGLES WITH ANOTHER SIP OF cabernet.

It's my third glass and it's only tasting sweeter on my lips. The tips of my fingers always feel the turning point first when I drink. That familiar buzz that makes my body feel a bit heavy and my mind light.

"I can't believe your license plate says *Alimony*," Maddie says into her wineglass as she snickers again. She's laughing so hard that the white zinfandel splashes onto her lips, but she doesn't care. She merely smiles and takes a large gulp.

Suzette answers with a shrug and a cocky smirk, "The asshole had it coming to him." Her bright pink lipstick smudges against her glass of Long Island iced tea and she wipes it away with her napkin as Maddie continues to laugh. Sue's given herself a makeover since her divorce is now finalized. Currently she's sporting jet-black hair cut into a blunt bob and bangs to go with her snippy attitude.

"Please tell me he saw it when you left the courthouse today. Please?" Maddie practically begs, still grinning from ear to ear.

Maddie's young and naive and thinks Prince Charming is somewhere out there, so you should always be ready. Sue has a marriage, a divorce, and fifteen years on Maddie, so between the three of us, we have as many opinions on love as we do rounds of drinks.

Sue's plastered-on smile slips and she tries to hide it with a shrug as she takes another sip. Her license plate is just one more way for Sue to make fun of her divorce before anyone else can. Her ex put her through hell and she came out cold as ice to all men. Well, except the ones she likes to sink her claws into after a few Long Islands.

Sue leans back in the white leather booth, keeping the glass in her hand and shrugs again as she says, "What says 'fuck you, motherfucker' better than taking his red Ferrari in the proceedings and getting *that* license plate?"

Kat pipes up from her spot in the booth, rolling her eyes and taking a sip of her Pepsi before she says, "I think it says, 'don't touch this bitch' to every man in the city."

A sly smile slips onto Sue's face. "Thank goodness … that's exactly what I was going for," she says, setting her drink down then stretching her arms over her head. "Maybe all these bastards will finally leave me alone then." The other girls start to howl at that and I join in, although my heart's not in it. My nerves are shot just being out here tonight. Sue's directly across from me and both of us are seated at the ends of the semicircular booth. Kat's to my right, then Maddie.

"Another round?" The waiter startles me and I nearly spill my glass as I gasp and back away. All the poor guy did was offer me another drink and I practically had a heart attack. Several distant gazes turn in our direction as my own table watches me like there's something wrong with me and I do what I do best, I play it off and let out a small laugh. Maybe I'm even more like Sue than I realized.

"Sorry," I say a bit too loud. Exaggerating how tipsy I am, I gently place my hand on the waiter's arm. His starched white shirt feels crisp under my fingers as I lean in and sweetly say, "I'm so sorry, I hope I didn't spill any on you."

That's all it takes for everyone to go about their own business, but my heart's still beating wildly. A few stares linger. I'm aware the people in here recognize me; they probably think I shouldn't be out or that I'm "having a moment." Looking across the room, I'm frozen by a pair of eyes I know all too well.

They belong to a woman in her late sixties, Margo Pierce. She's an heiress and an influential investor in the city. Her large sapphire cocktail rings appear even more over the top as she holds a simple glass of champagne with both hands. For a woman in her sixties, she wears her age well. From her perky breasts to the delicate skin around her eyes, not an inch of her hasn't been through some procedure or another. All the work she's had is very tastefully done, though.

The last time I saw her was at a casino up north, the night I got the phone call. I can still remember the dings and bells of the slot machines and the bright, colorful lights. Still remember the weight of the glass of rosé in my right hand as I sat perched on a barstool in the center of the casino. At the Mohegan Sun, the bar is elevated. I could see nearly a hundred of the other guests playing slots and sitting at the card tables; it was packed that night.

Just like tonight, I was with the girls and we were enjoying ourselves and the atmosphere. We were taking a break from roulette to grab cocktails and Sue was cursing out her soon-to-be ex-husband for prolonging their divorce when my phone rang. I only picked it up because it was odd for my mother to call me so late.

Kat leaned in to order from the bartender as I placed the phone to my ear, turning a bit to my left for a hint of privacy. As much as I could get in such a crowded place, anyway. I didn't show them that anything was unusual, keeping a pleasant smile on my face as I answered.

When I heard my mother's voice on the other end, the smile vanished and the vibrant night life, chatter, and sounds from the machines turned to dead air.

I could barely make out my mother's voice, just a few words here and there, but I knew something was wrong. Very wrong. I needed to hear better, so I stood and started walking. I didn't know where I was going, all I knew was that I needed to find a less noisy location.

My heart raced, and the shock caused my body temperature to drop so low that I was shivering.

He's dead. I heard her words clear as day as I got to the front of the casino. My heels clipped the large rug at the entrance. I stumbled forward, my short dress riding up and one heel nearly falling off. My knees hit the hard granite flooring and the phone fell from my hand.

Jace is dead. That's what she said.

I imagine the people around me at the time thought I was drunk. I would have assumed that if I'd seen someone fall the way I had.

Margo Pierce was there to help me. Those damn cocktail rings were digging painfully into my arm as she helped lift me up. I stood there on wobbly legs just trying to breathe, but when I looked into her eyes, I could tell she knew.

I knew in that moment it was real. I could lie to myself, or I could have hung up and driven home, all the while in denial. But the sympathy in her eyes was damning.

I rip my eyes away from hers at the other side of the bar and return back to the girls, back to tonight, leaving that night in the past right where it belongs. I ignore the way my hand itches to drain the wine and order another cabernet and then another while I push my hair back over my shoulders, trying to relax. Trying to shake off the unwanted memory.

"I think you're flagged," Kat says into her glass even as her eyes meet mine. Her sandy brunette hair is colored with a subtle ombre and she's applied her eyeliner in a cat-eye fashion. I don't know why, but I can't stop looking at it. Like if I can just concentrate on her makeup, everything else will leave me alone.

"No such thing," Sue says, quick to come to my defense, an asymmetric grin gracing her lips. "Drink up, girly." She gives me a wink and it forces a smile to my face. It didn't take long for the girls to come find me that night, crying alone in the back of our limo.

With a burn pricking at the back of my eyes, I blink a few

times to keep the tears at bay. It was months and months ago, but sometimes the pain comes back full force. I don't know that it will ever go away and if it does, surely that would be a tragedy. I don't know where grief and mourning end and my life begins again, but I'd like to find it.

Pushing away the nearly empty glass, I watch the dark liquid pool in the bottom and sigh deeply. I can't seem to keep a smile on my face. The once easy mask isn't slipping into place. Progress is all I need, though. I remind myself of my motto: Aim for progress, not perfection.

"Let's talk about something and someone else," I suggest. "Is anyone getting laid? One of us must be getting laid, right? At least Kat?" I arch a brow in her direction but her forehead creases in response and the action is followed by a huff and, "Yeah right." *Shit.* I forgot she and her husband are going through something.

Way to put my foot in my mouth.

My skin pricks at the back of my neck as I feel another set of eyes on me. The anxiousness comes back and I put on my best fake smile, staring straight ahead as Maddie starts listing off what was wrong with her last rendezvous. This one was some guy she met online.

The nagging feeling doesn't quit. I don't know who it is, but someone's watching me. It could be the paparazzi but typically every time I go out, they approach me before I even notice them. I'm a socialite, after all, and I know the intrusion is part of this life.

Debating on taking a casual look over my shoulder, I shake off the paranoia. *It's all in your head,* I tell myself. I thought I felt someone watching me earlier, but maybe I was wrong.

"You know enough time has passed." Sue's comment from across the table gets my attention. I look up to find her dark eyes twinkling with mischievousness.

"Enough time for what?" Maddie questions Sue. Maddie's the quintessential younger sister of our group and I swear most of Sue's comments go right over her head.

Sue motions toward me and it's only then that I take in her words. I clear my throat and look away, feeling a blush rise to my cheeks. "When I said someone else …" I say playfully and pick up the glass, lifting it high in the air and tilting my head back to get the last few drops.

The girls laugh it off, but there's a certain gravitas in Sue's eyes.

She lowers her voice and looks me in the eye as she says, "We just want you to be happy."

"It's 'we' now?" I ask her, suddenly feeling defensive. They've been talking about me behind my back?

Sue shrugs and Kat's quick to put a hand on top of mine. She twists in her spot and the white leather squeaks under her skinny ass. "We were just making conversation earlier." My brow rises as she takes in a breath and tries to find the right words.

"We want you happy again," Maddie says from her seat next to Kat. Her hands make two sharp motions emphasizing *happy again* as she leans back and looks straight ahead, avoiding my eyes on her.

Oh my God … is this some kind of intervention? I imagine my face reflects exactly what I'm thinking. Judging by the guilty expressions Kat and Maddie are wearing on their faces, I'm sure it does. Sue is shameless though, back to nursing her drink.

Of course they'd talk about me. I can't explain why it feels like a betrayal, though. Why my throat seems to go dry and itch as if I'm going to cry. Why wouldn't they? Everyone else is.

"Hey, Jules." Kat's voice is soft, placating even.

I pull my hand away from her and suck in a breath. "It's fine," I whisper, grabbing my clutch.

Sue's quick to sit forward and say, "Don't go. It wasn't—"

"Just headed to the powder room," I blurt out. "I just need to freshen up," I tell them with a tight smile, standing up and tugging down my dress.

"Do you want company?" Kat asks, already sliding out behind me.

"I just need a minute," I say and shake my head, giving her pleading eyes. I love them. They only want what's best for me. But don't they know how hard this is? How much it took just to come out here.

I can handle this. I just need something although I'm not sure what that something is. A breath of fresh air, maybe. Or a drink of water or something stronger. I don't know what, but I know I need at least a minute to myself to figure it out.

Mason

THE ANXIOUS FEELING DEEP IN MY GUT WON'T QUIT. It only gets more intense as Julia walks behind me, politely maneuvering her small frame amid the crowd of people. Watching her from my periphery, I listen to the rhythmic sound of her heels and watch how her hips sway gently.

She doesn't notice me, which is by design, but still it aggravates me. She passes so close behind me on her way to the restrooms that I catch a hint of her sweet scent. No doubt it's perfume, a gentle floral mixed with citrus of some sort but as it fills my lungs, I can't help but grip the bar top tighter to keep myself from following her.

Ever since I caught a glimpse of her, I haven't been able to move or get her out of my head. For months, I haven't thought twice about her. Each time her picture swept into my head, I pushed it away.

But she's here now, so close that I could touch her.

I can't approach her, though. How fucked up would that be?

I can't cross that line. She doesn't know a damn bit of the truth.

I down the remainder of my whiskey and slide the empty glass forward, pissed off and frustrated.

As I stand abruptly, the stool slides backward and bumps into someone. I turn to look over my shoulder while reaching into my back pocket for my wallet. "Sorry," I say without thinking only to find myself staring directly at Julia.

Her eyes still aren't on me as she waves off my apology, looking at the bottles lining the back of the bar before finally resting her gorgeous blue eyes on me. This close to her I can see they're pale blue with flecks of silver speckled throughout. They're beautiful.

She shakes her head just slightly, making her hair fall off her shoulder and exposing more of her bare skin. "It's fine." Her voice is soft as she walks forward without missing a beat, stepping up to the bar on my right, coming closer. Like a lamb heading into the lion's den, teasing and taunting unknowingly.

She's so close to me, so damn alluring. The black lacy dress clings to her curves. Her hips are seductive and I can just imagine how they'd feel to hold as I took her from behind. I can feel the bartender's eyes flicker to me questioningly as Julia orders, but I can't take my gaze off Julia.

I swallow thickly, leaning my forearms against the bar and attempting to act casual, getting that much closer to her.

She doesn't know anything about how we're linked and she doesn't have to. She'll never know the truth and this is my chance to learn more about who the pretty face in the picture is.

"Julia, right?" My heart pounds, questioning why the hell would I admit that I know anything at all about her. I don't intend to lie to her, though. Nothing but lies of omission. I've heard her name in social circles. Her family is well known so I doubt she'll be surprised that I recognize her.

"Jules," she corrects me warmly, now looking at me differently than she did a moment ago. She seems to do a double take and a hint of playfulness sparkles in her eyes. It's as if I'm suddenly what she's been looking for. Or maybe *who* she's been waiting for.

"Ah, Jules." I tap my fingers on the bar and glance away for a moment. *What the fuck am I doing?* This isn't just playing with fire, this is worse. It's asking to be burned and shoving my fists into the coals.

Patricia sets two shots of what look like chilled tequila in front of Jules. I watch with interest as she throws the first one back without thinking twice. Her slender fingers slip around the second one, ready to down it as well.

The pain comes off her in waves. She's drowning it in alcohol. She's good at hiding her emotions on the surface, but her actions speak so much louder than words.

"For a moment I thought you got two so you could share with me," I say teasingly with a smirk, more to keep her from drinking it than the desire to have it for myself.

She licks her lips and smiles. "You want it?"

Goddamn, does she know how she's coming off right now? She's already testing me, because just hearing those words slip between her lips has my dick straining against my zipper. *Yes, I fucking want it.* She's forbidden. The one woman in this city I should stay far away from.

"If you're offering," I answer her with a flirtatiousness I don't recognize. She blushes and tucks her hair back behind her ear. As she pulls her eyes away from me, she catches a glimpse of something across the room that rips the happiness from her in an instant.

I throw back the shot but keep my eyes on her. The cold liquid burns. I was right about it being tequila. It's strong too. Stronger than I expected and it takes the breath from me, making my chest feel tight, but then it relaxes me all the way down.

I hold up two fingers for Patricia. "Another two," I say and stand, sliding the stool I'd been sitting on over to Jules. "I took your shot so it's only fair," I say. Instantly, her eyes come back to me.

I watch as they swirl with a mix of questions. Vulnerability is clearly present and that only makes her that much more enticing.

"I'm not sure I should," she says softly. Her honesty is so raw, so genuine.

"You really shouldn't," I say with complete honesty as well. She deserves that much. She's Little Red Riding Hood in fuck-me heels and I'm worse than the Big Bad Wolf. I lean forward, knowing I'm breaking every rule I have as I bring my lips just inches from the shell of her ear.

Her fingers tighten on the edge of the stool as I whisper, "But you want to. And this is so much better than whatever you were going to do." I'm not sure if what I said is meant more for her or for me, but either way, I've convinced myself.

My rough voice and hot breath make goosebumps trail down her shoulder. Her nipples pebble under her dress, just barely becoming noticeable beneath the expensive fabric that graces her skin. I pull away from her, offering her space and an out.

She could leave if she wanted to. She could walk away. Fuck, she could call me an asshole and I'd sit here and do my best to pretend I'll never go after her again.

It takes a moment for Jules to pull herself together. She sits there in what seems like a daze. It's only when Patricia sets down the shot glasses, spilling just a touch of the chilled tequila, that she meets my gaze again.

I take the one closest to Jules and hold it out to her. She keeps her eyes on me but accepts it.

"Here's to things we know we shouldn't do," I say with a smile, lifting my glass and extending it for a toast.

Slowly, so very slowly, that bit of happiness comes back to her. Her eyes keep flickering with uncertainty to the floor and across the room.

"Here's to doing what makes us happy," she says, forcing her shoulders back straight as she clinks her glass against mine and then downs every drop. She slams her glass on the bar while I'm left holding mine and watching her every move.

I toss it back as she picks up her clutch, obviously ready to pay for the shots.

"Don't." There's more strength in my voice than I should have used. I soften my tone as I tell her, "It's on me." I hesitate then add, "I was just getting ready to leave."

She watches me cautiously, but I look toward the bartender as I get out my wallet. All the while paying attention to Jules in my periphery.

"Well, thank you … what's your name?" she asks.

"Mason," I answer her hoping she's never heard of me, but she brightens and nods her head.

"Thatcher. Yes, I thought I recognized you." She bites the inside of her cheek as something occurs to her and her expression falls slightly. "I'm sorry to hear—"

"To happiness, right?" I say, cutting off her apology, then pass my card to Patricia. It hurts me to say the words, but I don't bother to hide it.

That only makes her frown, somehow making her appear even more beautiful and alluring. We're both in pain. Both getting over something. Only this shit I did to myself whereas she's collateral damage.

She turns to the bar again, the playfulness gone.

"To happiness, and to the things we want," I tell her as I sign the receipt and leave the pen on the bar. I spear my fingers through my hair, feeling the heat of the moment and the buzz of the liquor starting to affect me.

I glance at her and watch as she closes her eyes. It's affecting her too. She's easy prey—beautiful, naive, innocent. I'm an asshole for doing this, but I can't help that I want her. Her eyes haunt me, but her body tempts me.

"I'm going to get out of here." I let my hungry gaze roam down her sexy curves, not hiding what I want from her in the least. "You want to come with?"

To HAPPINESS, AND TO THE THINGS WE WANT.
Mason's words echo in my ears. I know I'm
buzzed, but the odd mix of anxiety and relaxation
running through me are from something else. It's the realization
that I'm at a crossroads. I'm standing in front of an open door
and I know that going through will change everything. It would
put my world into motion again, moving me forward, shoving
me from the stagnant place I've been in these last few months.

There would be no way to go back, but there's no telling
who I'd be once I'm on the other side. My body is ringing with
desire and adrenaline.

Mason Thatcher. I've heard of the handsome devil. The

pictures I've seen don't do his broad shoulders and muscular frame justice. The rough stubble on his jaw begs me to reach up and brush my fingertips against it. He's tall, dark and handsome … and a notorious player. A man I shouldn't be caught dead talking to. My husband would have killed me for having drinks with a man like Mason.

But Jace has left me all alone. And Mason's so much more than I thought I could want in a man.

I rip my eyes from his hard body. Although he's in a suit, I noticed his hands first, rough and callused. It's clear they're from years of hard work, something the men in here know little about. Actual manual labor.

I try to relax and casually lean against the bar, slipping my pointer finger into one of the empty shot glasses and forcing it onto its side. I don't know why and it probably makes me appear drunker than I am, but I don't care.

"Mason, do you like tequila?" I ask him and this time when I speak, there's a bit of flirtatiousness in my voice. Guilt weighs heavily in my chest, but only briefly before the alcohol drifting into my blood numbs the memories. I've been alone for too long. I can have him for a night. Just one night.

Mason's steel gray eyes roam over the curves of my waist and ass. He's bold, licking his lips and then taking a step forward to lean against the bar with me. He's close enough that the heat of his body makes me that much hotter.

I want to know what it would be like for a man like him to pin me beneath him. To take me how he wants me. I close my eyes as a warm flush rises into my cheeks from the intensity of his stare.

"I do," he replies and his voice is low and rough. It does

bad things to me. I rest my head in my hand, both loving and hating the way the alcohol soothes the pain.

This isn't me moving on, but I'm ready to feel something else. My brow pinches at his response when I look back at him, but then I realize he's just answering my question about whether or not he likes tequila. I'm a bit more than tipsy but I'm still here and present, and I know what I want.

Even if I'll hate myself in the morning, it's one night of not going back to that large, empty house alone.

The tight pull of two small hands at my waist and Sue's loud voice make my heart skip a beat and I swear to God I almost scream. I feel like a child caught with her hand in the cookie jar.

"Jules, Jasper's out front." Sue talks like she has no idea she just scared the shit out of me.

My heart pounds in my chest as I turn to face her fully, my eyes darting from the man candy on my right and then back to her.

Caught red-handed.

It takes a moment for me to realize what Sue said, and a moment for her to catch on to what I was about to do.

She eyes Mason but before she can say a word, I say, "Jasper?"

Although it comes out like a question, it's more of a curse.

Sue gives me a sympathetic look as she says, "The exhibition at Ruppert Park must've ended." Jasper's with the *New York Post*. Every time he sees me he has a question and I know whatever I say will end up misquoted in the paper the next morning. He's not kind like the others.

I blow out a heavy breath, looking through the crowd and toward the entrance. I don't feel like dealing with this shit.

"And what are you doing here?" Sue's question is directed at Mason who's standing behind me, still leaning against the bar and resembling sin incarnate. He doesn't seem to mind the interruption at all. He gives Sue a lazy smile that brings back the heat between my thighs full force.

"Just leaving, actually." Jesus, his voice is as smooth as silk.

One split second passes and a wide grin spreads across Sue's face, her dark hair swaying, brushing against her cheek as she knowingly looks between the two of us. I lean backward, gripping the stool behind me and wanting an escape. It's one thing to flirt with the idea of bringing someone home; it's another thing entirely for everyone to know I was thinking about it.

Sue looks pointedly at Mason's cock and raises a brow, which only makes me want to bury my face in my hands.

"Are you ready to go?" I ask Sue and step away from Mason. Gripping my clutch tighter, I'm ready to get the hell out of here. There's not enough tequila in the world to cancel out the sobriety that the mention of Jasper brings me.

"You two get out of here," Sue says, stopping me in my tracks. That's the last thing I expected her to say.

"What'd you say your name was?" she asks Mason.

"Mason Thatcher." He extends a hand to Sue and she takes his hand coyly with both of hers.

"Mason," Sue says and her voice drips with sex appeal. It always does. She's a cold-hearted bitch to some but just as vivacious and insatiable as she was ten years ago when I first met her during my freshman year of college.

She leans in slightly and I get a good look down her blouse. Her necklace shifts so that the thin gold chain and glittering emerald jewel rest on her perky breasts, but when I look up, Mason's only looking into her eyes. "You take good care of my girl tonight, Mason." Sue looks back at me and that roguish look in her eyes makes me smile.

"I plan on it," Mason tells her and releases her hands.

"You are wicked," I whisper to Sue, my smile widening.

"Just one minute," Sue says. She holds up her pointer finger at Mason and grips my wrist, moving me away from him and closer to the powder room as if he can't hear us a whopping twelve inches away. I keep myself from rolling my eyes.

"It's nothing serious." The words sound defensive even to me. I don't want her to judge me or to hate me. I just want her to understand. Out of all the girls, I think she will. More than anything, I know I want to get out of here with a stranger. It makes me feel dirty and shameful, but right now it's what I want.

"Nothing serious?" she says. "It is for me," Sue says. My lungs stall at her words. She shifts her weight and looks over her shoulder toward our booth. I can't see either Kat or Maddie, although I'm sure they're still there. "You need this." Sue stares into my eyes, the look so serious I'm caught off guard.

"The question is," she says as she lowers her voice and leans into me, "are we telling the others?" Oh, thank the good Lord. I let out a breath I didn't know I was holding. When she pulls away, gripping my elbows in her hands and winking at me, I know everything's going to be okay.

I hesitate, glancing back at Mason and then I bite the

inside of my cheek. "I don't want to lie to them," I tell her honestly.

"Then you two slip out the back. Do it fast before I go tell them and before Jasper can get his scrawny, organic, vegan-eating ass inside."

I snicker at Sue's response, but the reality of what I'm doing is settling in. I lean forward as Sue lets go and I grip her hand before she can turn and leave me alone with my soon-to-be one-night stand.

"Tell me I'm not a bad person." The words slip out before I can think about what I'm saying. I try to keep the smile on my face, but it wavers.

"Getting laid doesn't make anyone a bad person."

I nod my head, willing the emotions to go back to being buried deep inside of me as if they don't deserve to surface in this moment.

"Unless he's married," she adds quickly and I chuckle.

The bit of humor helps me feel a sense of relief, but it's small. Her expression softens. "You just need a little something to kick-start your happiness again."

To happiness.

"I do." I nod my head.

True to her nature, Sue ignores the way my voice cracks as she takes a half step closer to me. "Then get over there already. The sooner you leave, the sooner he can be fucking you with your ankles pinned behind your head—"

A laugh escapes me before she can finish. "Can you even put your legs behind your head?"

"For the right man, I can do a lot of things." She looks at Mason, then to me.

"Just have fun tonight," she says, keeping things light but it's calming.

I nod my head as she turns from me, leaving me alone with Mason.

Alone to do bad things and make bad decisions. But at least I'm doing *something*.

Alcohol helps. I can always blame it on the alcohol.

It's then that I notice a few eyes watching. Including Margo, who's taking covert glances. That's when he wraps his arm around my waist and pulls me into him, bringing my back against his front as he whispers in my ear.

"You ready to go?" he asks, his warm breath traveling down my skin and making my body feel alive for the first time in several months.

I don't care that everyone can see. The city can talk; I'll deny it all.

"Will you hold me afterward?" I whisper my one request before I realize what I've said.

His body stills behind me and I close my eyes, hating that I've ruined this before it's even started. It's a one-night stand, nothing more. No emotions.

"Until the morning?" he asks me. My heart beats again, in rhythm with his.

I nod my head, my hair rubbing against his hard chest and his thumb brushing against the black fabric of my dress.

Just until morning.

CHAPTER

seven

Mason

WILL YOU HOLD ME AFTERWARD? I'm calm on the outside, as if there's not a damn thing wrong with what I'm doing. I don't know what's come over me.

The Mercedes's alarm beeps as I unlock it and open Jules's door for her. Her heels are muted on the wet pavement as she rounds me and slips easily into the luxurious leather seat. Her soft blue eyes look up at me as she tucks her hair behind her ears and settles the clutch in her lap as she murmurs, "Thank you."

I merely smile and close her door, the keys jingling as I walk to the driver side, my pulse racing wildly.

This is a mistake. I don't hold women afterward. Sex is sex and nothing else.

But I'm also a selfish prick, and I'd be a liar if I said I didn't want her. What I want, I get.

I start the car, the purr of the engine and soft classical music filling the cabin.

As I look over my shoulder to back out, Jules clears her throat. "Are we going to …" she starts to ask and then a beautiful blush colors her cheeks.

"Are we going to what?"

With a stronger flush, she shakes her head gently and says, "Never mind … Of course we are."

I can't help the smirk on my face at her shyness or the way my cock jumps in my pants. I peek at her before leaving the tight parking lot and heading down Second Avenue. My fingers itch to rest against her bare thigh as her dress rides up slightly. I place my hand on the gearshift instead, stopping at a red light and looking over to her.

She squirms in her seat under my gaze and I fucking love it. It's easy to forget with her. Maybe that's what it is. Maybe that's why I can't say no and walk away. If I can just have her for tonight, then it'll all be all right. I'm her downfall and she's my savior.

"Where are we headed, sweetheart? My place?" I give her the option but she's free to suggest someplace else. She's quick to nod, glancing at me then looking down at her hands in her lap.

I'm enjoying this way too much. I turn to look out the driver side window and ignore that voice in the back of my head saying I'm a Grade A prick for doing this to her.

"Thank you," she says softly as the light turns green and

traffic starts to move. "For heading out the back and away from all that …" she pauses, waving her hands in the air before falling back against the seat and concluding, "bullshit."

The curse word seems foreign on those sweet lips of hers. I nod my head once, looking back to the windshield and twisting my hand around the leather steering wheel.

"No problem," I say easily but I can feel her need to talk, to tell me everything else that's on her mind. I wait for it, staring straight ahead, but nothing comes. Just silence as we drive to the sounds of Tchaikovsky.

It's only fifteen minutes to my place at this rate, but the time can't pass quickly enough. Every second of silence is a second I consider turning back. There's still time to walk away.

"Do you always do this?" Jules asks, breaking up the quiet.

"What's that?"

"This," she says, her cheek resting against the seat as she looks at me.

"Hmm?" I still don't understand her question.

"Pick up women—" she stops and rolls her eyes. "You know, one-night stands." Tapping my thumbs on the steering wheel, I consider her question. I used to without thinking twice. But that was before Avery. Before my father and this hell I've been thrown into.

"So I'm right, you do this often?" she says and I have to suppress my smile at her brazen demeanor.

"I'm not going to answer that, Jules." My voice comes out a little harder than I wanted and she shrinks back some. *Smooth, real fucking smooth.*

It's tense for a moment and I flick on the turn signal as we head down a deserted street. So close. I can't lose her now.

"I don't take women to my place," I tell her simply. "And it's been a while."

Her brows pinch for a moment and then she struggles to hold back a laugh. It catches me off guard but then I remember how much she drank. I'm still feeling a bit of the tequila myself. My tolerance is high as fuck, so if I'm feeling it, she must be wasted. The realization has me rethinking things again.

"How are you feeling?" I ask her.

"Fine," she says and then covers her mouth with her hand.

"Are you drunk?" She doesn't look like it in the least.

She purses her lips and shakes her head as she says, "Nope. Just right." She stretches in the seat, covering another yawn when I stop at my gates.

I eye her for a moment and then brush it off.

I know Jules comes from money and was born into this lifestyle like me, so I'm surprised to see admiration on her face when we arrive. "Your home is beautiful." Her voice is even and sincere. I'm proud of my home. I built it myself. Liam, my business partner, helped design it for engineering purposes, but it was all based on my ideas and plans.

I pull up in the driveway as her phone starts vibrating.

She doesn't pay attention as I approach the front of the house. Judging by the look on her face and the way she shoves the phone back into her clutch, her friends from the bar are probably giving her hell.

"Everything all right?" I ask, more to make sure I'm getting her ass into my bed than anything else.

For only a moment, I think she received a message from someone who knows what happened. Someone who saw what I did, although I don't think anyone could have possibly seen. My muscles coil and my knuckles turn white as I grip the gearshift, putting the car into park and searching her face for answers.

She blows a bit of hair out of her face and looks anywhere but at me.

"It's fine," she says but I know she's lying.

"Tell me what's wrong." The command comes out easily.

Her eyes go wide and I almost second-guess talking to her like that. *Almost.* But then she caves to me.

"My friends just found out."

I cock a brow at her. "Found out?" She parts her lips slightly and I'm guessing from the way she leans into me, my touch is all she needs to loosen up. I rest my hand on her thigh, just beneath the hem of her dress, caressing her lightly with my thumb.

"I don't do this often or… ever—"

I lean in and press my lips to hers, stopping her explanation. I move my hand to her cheek and then behind her head as she deepens the kiss. Her lips part for me and her hot tongue massages mine in swift, strong strokes.

I groan into her open mouth, our breath mingling as my dick hardens to fucking stone.

"Forget about them," I tell her as I break the kiss and pull away. She's left breathless, her eyes still closed when I open my door and start to get out, taking the keys with me.

I almost close the door and miss her whispering, "I'll forget about it all."

But I heard her. I heard the whisper, the raw vulnerability and truth in her statement.

I wish I hadn't.

CHAPTER

eight

Julia

I'VE NEVER HAD A ONE-NIGHT STAND BEFORE.

Not once.

It's not like I have a thing against them and Lord knows my friends enjoy them, with or without discretion. It's just never happened. My body heats everywhere, one place a bit more than others when Mason touches me, and especially when he cuts through it all with his demanding ways.

My thoughts race as Mason wraps his hand around my waist and leads me to the front door. The chill in the night air is sobering. I can't explain how my nerves are shooting through me. My breathing comes in a little faster now that the alcohol's all but worn off.

I try to focus on how even our footsteps sound but all I can think about is how I've never done this before.

I'm doing it. I'm going to sleep with a stranger. *I'm going to sleep with someone other than Jace.*

Jace and I met as children, paired up in boarding school. I've never been with anyone else. My heel slips on the paved steps at the thought, almost making me fall, but Mason catches me.

He's quick to grab on to my elbow and waist, his hands hot on my body. It's a shock as something inside of me reacts almost violently to his very touch.

Eight months alone … even longer since I've been touched. The idea of moving on has never been such a dominating thought, or so terrifying.

I wrap my arms around myself, fueled by both fear and desire. My pulse quickens as I look back over my shoulder and toward his car. Toward an escape.

Mason straightens his shoulders, squaring them and hitting the keys against his leg once. The jingle catches my attention. It's the only sound in the cold dark night.

I stand frozen as I look into his eyes. I'm a fool for doing this. It's not me. Not the woman I am today and not the woman I was before I lost my husband. Mason's steel gray gaze searches my own and I feel lost all over again.

I part my lips, ready to give an excuse, a lie, or even the truth. Anything to just go back in time and avoid being in this situation.

To run, just like I've been doing for the past eight months. Didn't I say I needed a change? I said I needed something drastic, but that was back when the alcohol was flowing and we were surrounded by a crowd of people.

Mason is so very tempting. He's gorgeous and confident, but I can't handle a man like him. I can't deal with this.

Weak and alone. A low whisper from the self-loathing bitch inside of me resonates in my ears. I slam my lips shut without uttering a word, hating that she's right.

I won't leave. I suck in a breath and force myself to be determined. Whether what I'm doing is right or wrong, it doesn't matter. I need a change.

A moment passes with the two of us standing still in front of his porch. Only a handful of steps are between us and his front door. I just have to get there.

My eyes drift from the deep navy door to Mason. I'm caught in place as he takes a single step closer to me. It's only one step, but with it is something powerful. His height, his scent, and his very dominance overwhelm me when he's this close. He radiates desire and my mind may be questioning things, but my body is pulled to him, magnetized by his presence.

It's soothing. Surprisingly so as I let my body move forward, closing the small space between us. He trails a finger down my collarbone lightly, testing my reaction.

"I want to touch you, Jules," he murmurs, forcing my gaze back to his all-consuming stare. I hadn't imagined it'd be this intense. Not at the bar and not in his Mercedes. He didn't push, and he didn't do anything to make me feel trapped. How odd—now that we're out in the open with no one watching and no enclosed spaces, it's only now that I feel cornered. All because of the way he looks at me.

What's most surprising is that I love it. *I want this.* The way he looks at me is addictive; it's freeing in more ways than one.

I can't wimp out. I won't.

I nod my head once and his fingers trail up my throat. His light touch feels much rougher than he's being with me. I tilt my head as his grip moves to my chin and he just barely brushes his lips against mine. It's a soft kiss that leaves me wanting more. I keep my eyes closed and stay as still as can be when he hovers close and whispers, "I want to kiss you."

"Then kiss me," I whimper, a pathetic plea, or maybe one of strength. My head feels so clouded that it's hard to know what's driving me. Raw, primal instinct or desperation. Perhaps a lethal cocktail of both.

He pulls away just slightly, but I don't let him get far. I take a half step closer to him, my breasts brushing against his shirt and I crash my lips into his. I need him. I need this.

He's quick to wrap his arms around me and pull my body against his. The faint noises of the night surround us and they seem to get louder as my breathing gets heavier. His lips travel down my throat and I throw my head back. I may have been tipsy from the alcohol before but in this moment I'm drunk with lust, and I find it too difficult to care.

"I want to fuck you, Jules," Mason practically growls. He pulls me into him suddenly and forces a gasp from me as he nips my earlobe. "I want to make you cum so hard you forget everything."

I moan as my nipples harden and my back arches. "The only thing you need to worry about is remembering my name," he whispers into my ear, his hands roaming down my waist, stopping at my ass. "Just my name and what I've done to you tonight."

I tilt my head back and everything he's saying is exactly what I need to hear. "Yes," I say into the soft breeze that cools my exposed hot skin.

"Only tonight," he says so low, I nearly miss it. My fingers slip under his shirt so I can feel his bare skin, and it triggers him to pull away from me. Just slightly, only so he can look into my eyes, but I grip him harder. I'm afraid to lose what he's offering me.

I want him. I want his promise.

I want to forget and feel alive again.

"Yes, only tonight," I say in agreement and then press my lips to his, moving a hand to the back of his head. My fingers spear through his thick hair as his tongue strokes mine and he lifts me into his arms by my ass.

I gasp at the sudden movement and wrap my legs around his waist. He takes the opportunity to trail open-mouth kisses down my neck and torture my deprived body.

I'm sure of it now. All I need is to be held by this man. Fucked by him and ruined by him.

With my back against the wall of his porch, he slides a hand up my dress and between my legs. Petting me, testing me until the sudden spike of pleasure hits me harder than I expected. He presses his thumb against me just right and my grip on him tightens.

I come alive for him, every nerve ending on fire, ready to burst into a flame so hot I can't control myself. He doesn't stop, even as I writhe and beg for him to take me inside. My fingers dig into his shoulders, my nails scratching along his shirt and wishing it were skin.

The pleasure is so intense already. It's nearly too much. I want to pull away because the inevitable drop from this high is going to shatter me. I'm all too aware of it, but I can't help myself.

He never stops kissing me as he balances me in one strong arm and unlocks the door. He never sets me down until he has me on his bed.

And he never gives me the chance to think about anything but the desire threatening to destroy me.

He doesn't take his time with my dress, desperate to have me bared to him. I reach behind me, unclasping my bra as he pulls the lace down my body. His fingers loop around my thong and take it along with the black dress.

My heels fall to the floor with a loud thud. I'm given a quick moment to consider what I'm doing as he pulls his shirt over his head. But instead of giving in to self-doubt, I'm mesmerized by the rippling of his muscles and then by the girth and rigidity of his cock as he shoves off his pants.

It happened so fast. Like a whirlwind of chaos that only surrounded the two of us. The mattress groans with his weight as I prop myself up on my elbows. He slides between my legs, spreading my thighs. My body opens up for him as if he was meant to be there all along. As if my movements are controlled by his desires.

My heart feels like it's trying to get away from me. His hard, hot body pushes down against mine and I can barely breathe.

My head turns to one side and then the other, feeling the

cool sheet beneath my cheeks as he brushes against my slick folds.

"You're so wet for me," he says and Mason's voice is a mixture of wonder and reverence. He captures my lips with his and suddenly pushes his cock deep inside of me, all the way to the hilt in one swift stroke.

I scream out, my neck arching and my back bowing as he stills and gives me a moment to adjust to his size. My breath halts in my chest, but then he moves.

Not just moves. He fucks me with a punishing force. The bed slams against the wall with each thrust. He kisses me as though he's breathing the air from my lungs. He pins me down and takes everything from me, forcing me higher and higher, all while giving me everything I never knew I needed.

It's not until I'm left panting and recovering from waves of pleasure that I start to question what I've done. But it's late and I'm so exhausted. I forget it all except his name and what he's done to me, and give in to sleep.

Don't leave me alone, I cried and I screamed.
Don't leave me alone, my whole life demeaned.
You left me unguarded. My heart raw and bleeding.
You left me forever. The pain there left seething.
You left me here weak. Just a stone in the ground.
You left a place beside me, my picture-perfect life unbound.

nine

Mason

L AST NIGHT WAS STUPID. SUCH A JUVENILE WORD but I can't think of anything better. Fucking stupid. I'll blame it on the alcohol. A low exhale travels up my throat as I walk away from the floor-to-ceiling window in my office. The hustle and bustle of the street below is what drives me to keep moving. This city never sleeps and the work never ends.

Last night was about taking a moment to unwind from the shitshow my life has become. From my father, the arrogant prick and criminal that he is. The awareness of just how ruthless my father is has never hurt me more.

That's what it really is. *Pain.* Coming to the realization

that your father's a disgusting excuse for a human being and should be behind bars is … difficult to handle. It's even worse when you're tied to his bullshit.

I sink into my leather desk chair and it protests the movement with a groan until I'm comfortable. Unlike my father's office, traditional and smelling of polished wood and old books, my office is the opposite. It's airy and open, modern and sleek. A model of our newest planned development sits in the very center of the space.

That's what started all this shit. A celebration for my company's first suburban development. No more apartments downtown. We're ready to expand into uncharted territories. I'm an idiot for thinking this would change things between my father and me. I really thought things would be different. I'd attributed the tense relationship with him to my own doing. A rebellious child with pent-up anger over his mother's death. Born into this black-tie bullshit.

I was always supposed to act right. Always supposed to say the right thing, stand the right way, behave and pay attention. Well, I didn't want to. I crack my neck remembering the fights I started. A smile kicks up my lips. Four boarding schools and hefty donations from my father still couldn't keep me in line.

Working in construction was just another way to stick it to my father.

Higher education? Fuck that. I got a job … but it didn't last for long. I'm just not made to work for someone else and I wanted a more physical job. So, I started Gray's Homes with Liam nearly three years ago. He had the schooling and I had the designs. I didn't think it'd be this successful or grow so quickly. So successful, in fact, that I ran out of capital and so did he.

I took out loan after loan, investing in myself and I'd do it all over again. It was worth it to keep growing and taking advantage of the momentum we had. I should have known better when my father came to me and offered to invest in me too.

Clients were eager to sign contracts with his name on them. Having him back me made bids easier to attain and everything run smoother. I knew it was too good to be true.

He just wanted to be able to hold it over my head. He wanted to *own* me. I narrow my eyes at the model in the center of the room. It's all because of this one project. Now I'm in debt. I owe more than I'm worth and everything is hanging in the balance as we move forward with this one project that I'd love to trash just to spite my father. I should cancel it all now that I know the truth, but that would mean bankruptcy and more people than just myself being affected. Liam and all our employees and contractors. At the thought, there's a sick feeling in the pit of my stomach. One even a night of whiskey and great sex can't dissolve.

I pull my eyes back to the computer screen, back to reviewing all the invoices that have been paid. Everything's moving accordingly and on schedule, but only because of my father's loan.

I run a hand over my face knowing I'm just as much of a fucking prick. I don't deserve to breathe the same air as someone as sweet as Jules.

The thought of her shy smile and innocent looks … God, it does something to me. The guilt and anger are minimal compared to the desire. I want to feel her again. I want to get lost in her touch and be the one to do the same for her.

I can make it all better.

She has no idea how screwed up this situation is. If my

father knew who I'd spent last night with, I imagine I'd never hear the end of it. He may be a piece of shit and deserve to be locked away for the rest of his life, but if the world knew what I'd done, they would think the same of me.

I click the mouse to light up my screen as it goes dim once again. I can't think; I can't focus.

As my temples throb and irritation grows, I think back to last night. Back to Jules.

Out of every possible way for this morning to start, I never guessed she'd sneak out.

I imagined how the morning would go over and over again while I watched her sleep, her long hair a messy halo on the pillow. So peaceful and beautiful.

I couldn't get over how fucked up it was. How selfish. But it was everything I wanted and more. *It was fucking worth it.*

As she slept, exhausted and spent from the raw fuck, my fingers longed to travel along her curves. I was still hard for more.

Staring at her lush lips, the vision of her eyes shut tight, her head thrown back, and her mouth parted with soft, strangled moans spilling between them was etched in my memory. It was the sexiest thing I've ever seen. Jules was utterly in rapture from what I was doing to her. She was completely at my mercy and I know she loved every minute.

I tugged the blankets over myself and lay there watching her, debating how I'd end it in the morning. I could crave her more than anything, but it was over. It should never have started to begin with. As I thought up exactly what to say to ease the sting, I watched her steady breathing and my lungs filled with her sweet scent.

Just once more. I should have woken her up, spread her legs wide and taken her again. Had I known that I'd wake up alone, I would have.

I lean back in my seat, letting out the aggravation in a groan as I watch the security footage again. She slipped out just before dawn, leaving only a note behind. I watch in amusement as she keeps looking up from the pad of small sticky notes she'd found on my kitchen counter. The pen never even touched the paper for a full two minutes as she contemplated what to write.

She's lost and confused. She doesn't even know what she wants.

But I do.

I fidget with the yellow sticky note, passing it from my middle finger to my pointer and back again mindlessly.

Thank you.

If last night was more than just last night …

I trace the delicate, feminine script of the letters. She was made to tempt men. I'm convinced of it. Everything from her soft sighs to the way she carries herself.

It's as if she was designed to lure me in unknowingly.

Even the way she's written her phone number calls to me. Each graceful curve makes my fingers itch to punch in the numbers on my phone.

Weakness. Stupidity.

Last night was a one-time thing. I don't have to call her. I don't owe her anything and I'm sure she doesn't expect a damn thing either.

Why does that bother me even more?

The sticky note moves from finger to finger more rapidly

now. I know I shouldn't call her. Nothing good can come from this.

My eyes look back to her message and focus on her phone number.

Selfish. So fucking selfish.

That's the problem, though. I just don't give a damn about anyone else. The thought is what strengthens my resolve. It's all going to come crumbling down around me soon. I deserve to enjoy what little time I have left.

CHAPTER

ten

Julia

WATER DRIPS FROM THE SPOUT OF THE IRON faucet. I grip the side of the claw-foot porcelain tub, the water splashing slightly in the silent room as I get comfortable. Then I rest my cheek against the cool hard porcelain and watch the water as it continues to drip.

The water's nearly lukewarm by now, but I don't want to get out. My wet hair clings to my skin as I sink in deeper, letting the water climb to my neck. My legs sway from side to side and I listen to the steady rhythm of the dripping water.

Part of me wants to pretend like last night didn't happen. And this morning—I close my eyes and bring my hands up to my face, embarrassed by the memory. There's nothing in etiquette class about how to leave your one-night stand.

My throat feels raw as I take in a breath, remembering how last night felt. His hands on my body, his chest against mine as he rocked in and out of me, mercilessly, ruthlessly.

I've never … I swallow thickly, hating that I'm even comparing last night to what I had with my husband. I feel like I've betrayed Jace but I just let myself fall into the water, as if I can wash it all away.

No amount of time spent in this tub will cleanse the sins of last night.

One good thing's come of it, though. The words are flowing through me so easily now. All I've done since I've been home is write. I shouldn't be happy about that; I shouldn't feel like a weight has been lifted, but I do. Every single thing I've written since my husband's passing has been dark and stunted. It's nothing that I would willingly choose to write. My poetry has always been a happy place and now I have a piece of that back.

The pain in my chest though, the way my heart feels tight and my lungs too crushed to breathe, that's because I don't regret it.

I feel guilty that I don't feel guilty. How does that even make sense?

Ping. I groan at the sound, squeezing my eyes tight. I must've been more than a bit tipsy last night to let Sue act as my conscience. She won't leave me alone. There were way too many texts waiting for me this morning for her to have gone home with anyone last night.

I woke up to a myriad of messages.

Please tell me he didn't kill you.

I'm so sorry if he did, though!

Seriously, are you okay? Text me later!

She thinks she's funny. I thought I was doing a good thing by letting her know I was still alive and unharmed, but all that did was open a floodgate of questions.

She's finding more joy in this than I am, which makes me laugh.

I can't help the way my lips beg me to smile and the way my heart flutters. Sue's having a good time teasing me. *Ping.* I turn my head to the right, to where my towel and phone are sitting on the marble bench.

I can only imagine what she wants to know this time.

"I can't hide in here forever," I say under my breath, finally lifting myself out of the comfort of the tub. I lean down and pull the plug, letting the cool air hit my heated skin.

It was nice while it lasted and after last night, it did my body good to relax in here. As I lean over to grab the towel, the sensitive bits between my thighs ache again with slight pain. It's a good kind of hurt though, the kind that lets you know you've been properly laid. I laugh slightly into the towel and dry off my body, then work on patting my hair dry. My feet pad softly against the black-and-white penny tile floor.

The bathroom matches the estate's classic interior. Every accent and piece of decor reflect the timing of when the house was built. There are a few modern pieces, but they only accentuate the charm of the classic architecture. It's expensive to maintain, but the beauty is unmatched.

I continue towel-drying my long hair as the memories of renovating the house come to me one by one. The bit of happiness I'd claimed only moments ago vanishes.

Jace and I got into so many fights over this tile. I can see him standing in front of the mirror, glaring at me for being stubborn. It's my family's house, though. This isn't an Anderson estate. I inherited it when my parents moved from the city. We both knew I was far more well-off than he ever was. The steamy glass doesn't hide the past. I can hear his voice; I can see it all like it was just yesterday.

But the memories are from years ago, and he's never coming back.

Ping. This time when the phone goes off, I can't help but want to cling to whatever Sue's said. She could ask how big he is and I'd give her every detail including the veins. I'd be eternally grateful for a distraction right now. I take a seat on the bench, wincing as my sore bottom rests against the hard marble and pick up the damn phone.

It's not her.

Well, this last message isn't.

I have three from Sue, all wanting to know details about what I did with Mason last night. I roll my eyes and let out a small snort at her question about size. Of course she would ask me. I knew it.

By the looks of him, he should be packing … but I'm going to guess he's only four inches. Am I right?

She cracks me up. She's been sending me these kinds of messages all day. Anything to get me talking.

Nope, only three, I type back just to give her something to laugh about. She deserves it. Without all these messages and prodding, I'm not sure how I would have handled this on my own.

I click over to the other message and my heart does an odd

flip in my chest when I see who it's from. Like it can't function for just a moment. Maybe it's the shock and disbelief, or maybe it's fear? I'm not sure, but either way, I'm struck by the fact that Mason messaged me at all. I was sure that sneaking out would have sealed the deal between the two of us. It was a one-time thing. One I'm grateful for and content with. I knew what I was getting when I went into the arrangement.

I wasn't sure if I should leave my phone number. I imagine he was relieved to find his drunken one-night stand gone and I didn't want him to feel obligated to call me.

At the same time, I hoped he would.

Not because of him. It's not that I'm clinging to having a relationship at all. I just … I liked the way he made me … I don't know what the right word is. The way nothing else mattered when I was with him. How it all slipped away and I didn't have to focus on anything but him. Mostly because he was only focused on me.

There's nothing wrong with wanting more of that, is there? I bite down on my bottom lip and read the message.

It's not a hello or an admonishment for leaving him.

I want to see you again. Blue Hill at 8 p.m. tonight.

My lashes flutter a few times as I reread the message. How very presumptuous. As if I have nothing better to do than meet up with him.

I don't, if I'm being honest with myself. I haven't got a single thing to do other than write, which I fell into earlier and loved every second. I lose a little bit of the fight in me at the thought that I am available tonight, but still. This isn't happening like this. I'm not a booty call or whatever he's used to.

I look down at the message again and the second read-through only pisses me off.

Maybe I want a good lay too, and by maybe, I mean I really do need it, but I'm not a call girl and I don't want to be treated like one. Last night was something out of my realm.

Sorry. Busy. I type in the words and hit send without even thinking, letting my high and mighty attitude lead me. But as soon as the message pops up on the screen, I wish I could take it back.

My eyes close and my head falls back as I groan in aggravation. I should have just said yes. I mean after all, aren't I using him too? I'm so busy staring at the ceiling and cursing myself that when my phone pings in my hand, I jump slightly.

Are you busy now?

A second passes and then another. Is he toying with me? I think he is. I can just imagine the teasing way he would say it. Like he knows exactly why I responded how I did. I smirk and bite the inside of my cheek as I text back.

Maybe I am.

His response is immediate. *No you aren't and I want to see you. Blue Hill at 8 p.m.*

My shoulders stiffen and I can't help but feel like this is some kind of battle of wills. And I have no intention of losing.

I said I was busy.

I wait for his response, a deep crease settling in between my brows.

There's no immediate message back and I start to question my position. I don't want to be alone tonight. I know it's pathetic but I'm so tired of being lonely, lying in bed at night, staring at the other half of the bed where my husband used to sleep.

Maybe I need to take a step back and think this through. Dating isn't exactly an expertise of mine. Neither is hooking up. With a heavy heart I reread the messages and try not to overthink it all, but I'm sure that's exactly what I'm doing.

I contemplate messaging the girls in our group text when minutes go by and I don't hear from Mason. A lot of pride lives in me, but not when it comes to this. I'm out of my element.

Tossing my phone down, I decide it's probably for the best that I don't see Mason tonight anyway. I've never been alone before and I'm too tempted to cling to him already and over-analyze it all. Pushing my hair back, I wonder if I should try to convince Sue to go out tonight. I'm sure she would if only I asked. Any of the girls would and I love them for it.

The phone pings against the porcelain and I'm quick to read what he's said.

You win. Just tell me when. I'm available for you.

The smile on my face isn't stopped by my teeth sinking into my lip and I sway slightly as I compose my response. The warmth that spreads through me is addictive. It makes me a little too happy, but I'm too caught in the moment to overthink anything else right now.

"So, who is she?" Liam asks from his office as I'm on my way out. He leans out the doorway, both hands on the doorframe as he smirks at me.

"Who?" I say, turning my back to him so I can lock up my office. It's a habit I've always had. No one else has a key. I've got fifteen employees working here who come and go throughout the day, but my office is only for me.

"The chick you hooked up with last night." I test the doorknob, making sure it's locked and drop my keys into my pocket. I won't be long since I'm only heading out for lunch, which is good because I want to have all these numbers crunched by the time I need to leave for Blue Hill.

When I turn back around, Liam's got his arms crossed and he's leaning against the door, waiting for me like I owe him some sort of explanation.

"None of your damn business," I say, keeping my tone casual and smirking at him.

"Oh shit," he says then lets out a bark of a laugh with a wide grin. "You really did hook up with someone last night?" he asks me with disbelief. Liam's always been a talker. He doesn't seem to mind my demeanor as much as everyone else does. Give him enough time and he can have an entire conversation by himself, so maybe the two of us were meant to be friends.

Pushing off the doorframe he says, "I was going to give you shit for leaving me hanging last night."

"Just didn't want to be alone last night," I tell him honestly. "Better her company than yours," I joke with a grin, trying to lighten the mood even though I want this conversation to be over.

"So, are we going to go over it tonight then?" he asks me.

"Go over what?"

"What our investor said at the meeting you had without me yesterday." By investor, he means my father.

"It wasn't about Gray's Homes." I take a few steps closer to his office. Mine's the largest and in the very back. Liam's is kitty-corner to mine and the only other office in here. Across from his is the boardroom which is currently empty and only ever used for sales pitches and the end of quarter wrap-ups.

"Oh," Liam says and he seems genuinely taken by surprise. His expression lets me know he wants to ask me a million fucking questions, all of which I'm sure I don't want to hear. *Why was my father so persistent on meeting me? Why did he come in here asking for a conference over and over and demanding I sit down with him?*

"It's been a bit rocky between us for the last few months," I say with my voice low enough that it's just the two of us in this conversation. I know Margaret, our secretary, is right down the hall and close enough to hear if we talk loud enough.

"Few months?"

I stare at him, feeling my expression hardening. It was a necessary evil for me to stop talking to my father a while ago. I'm caught between wanting to do what's right and not knowing for sure that I'd be doing the right thing. So instead of taking action, I avoided him every chance I got.

It worked my entire life up until now. Until he told me what I already knew, confirming it and forcing me to face the truth.

"Don't worry about it." I give him a tight smile. "It's got nothing to do with the business."

"And what about you?" he says, pushing further. "I can't be worried about you?"

The simple answer I give him is bullshit and he knows it. "I'm fine."

"Yeah, you keep saying that," he says then turns like he's going to head back into his office as the phone rings.

"Go get it." I nod toward his office. "I'm just picking up a Reuben from across the street."

"All right." He heads into his office but before I make it

another two steps, he's popping his head outside of the door again to ask, "Will you get me a Coke?"

Glancing over my shoulder, I tell him yes as the sounds of everyone else working get louder and louder.

I don't break my stride as I head down the hall. Our company owns this entire floor of the Rising Falls Building; it's a tall office building that's made for businesses just like ours. The second I stepped in here, I knew this was where I wanted to work. There's clear glass everywhere. So much natural light and impressive views of the city to provide constant inspiration.

Even the cubicles have plexiglass walls.

"Out to lunch?" Margaret asks as I stride past her, needing to shake the nagging feelings that wrestle in the pit of my stomach.

"I'll be right back." I nod, again not slowing my pace and head past all my employees to the elevator.

"Yes, sir," Margaret answers with a light-hearted tone. I've never seen that woman not smile. As if being our secretary is the highlight of her day. She's damn good at what she does too. At first, I was opposed to letting someone step in and take control of scheduling and inventory, but as we grew, I just couldn't handle it all.

Pressing the button for the elevator, I try to think about anything other than my father. With the button lighting up, I'm reminded of Jules's text. The irritation and anger nearly vanish.

Just the thought of what was going through her mind when she messaged back makes me smile. She's a testy little thing. I didn't expect that. There's more to Miss Summers than I thought and I'm definitely intrigued.

I check my Rolex as the elevator dings and the doors slowly open. There's no one inside, so I walk right in and hit the button for the ground floor. Only six hours until dinner.

My chest feels tight and the small smile leaves me. It's fucked up in so many ways, but she'll never know. I'll make sure she never finds out.

CHAPTER
twelve

Julia

T HERE ARE PINK MACARONS AND CRYSTAL chandeliers everywhere I look. I love this place. It's a tiny shop and the treats are far too expensive for what they are, but it's the vibe I truly love. I scoot my silver stool closer to the small round table and unpeel the wrapper on my cupcake as I listen to Suzette.

"I want to know every detail," she says with barely contained joy. Kat glances between the two of us and so far, she hasn't touched a thing on the etched tray in the center of the table. I know there's something there that would make her smile, but she's not interested. I bet she and her husband had another fight. I wish they wouldn't;

they love each other. It's been obvious to me since the day she met him.

Clearing my throat, I avoid replying to Sue's comment. I can feel both sets of their eyes on me, but I don't look up. It's too pretty in here to feel this anxious. My eyes settle on the crystal flute of pink champagne and I take a quick sip, tilting my head up to gaze at the carved tin ceiling. Everything in here is pink, silver, shiny and new. So beautiful to look at, but useless in saving me from this conversation.

"How could you not tell us?" Kat's voice is low but not scolding, more surprised than anything. She's still standing with her purse on a stool and I don't think she has any intention of sitting down in the least. Until she does, plopping down with her eyes boring into me. "I want to know who you're seeing," she adds with a pout.

The disappointment in her voice makes my appetite for all things sweet and scrumptious vanish. I knew this was coming. You can't just take off from Katerina Thompson and not have her chew you out later.

"It wasn't meant as an insult," I start to tell her. It's not like I was trying to upset her, she should at least know that for a fact.

"It's because you would have stopped her," Sue interjects before shoving a tiny cupcake into her mouth and biting it right down the middle. She has no shame and gives Kat the answer as if it's obvious. Which it is. If I'm an overthinker, Kat is a second-guesser.

"Of course I would have stopped her." Her wrath is directed at Sue now and to be honest, I'm grateful. Sue can handle it. She stares Kat right in the eye as she pushes the other half of the cupcake into her mouth with her pointer finger.

Kat justifies her stance. "She was drunk and how many one-night stands have we regretted right after?" She has a point, I'll give her that.

"It's not that I was keeping it from you," I say. There's a small plea in my voice for Kat to calm down. "I was …"

"You were keeping it from me," Kat says, finishing my sentence for me.

"Only until it was over," I say as my face scrunches with guilt and I hide behind my drink.

"Oh hush," Sue says easily and then nods at me. "Good for you for going out and dusting off those cobwebs." I snort a small laugh and my shoulders shake from it. "He's cute too."

"He'd better be," Kat says beneath her breath, pulling out a bottle of water from her oversized leather hobo bag.

Sue rolls her eyes and says, "You going to track him down and beat the crap out of him if he isn't?" A smile forces its way onto my face and I try to make it go away, but it's not happening. Kat side-eyes Sue for a moment before returning to her water and taking a sip. With that, the tension vanishes. Kat gets why I didn't tell her, I know she does. And I get why she's upset. It's a simple squabble that's over the moment Kat reaches for her own cupcake.

"So, your first one-night stand. How does it feel?" Sue asks.

I could write a whole book on the effects I'm feeling right now. The guilt, the anxiety. But the other things, the bit of liveliness and … is it pride? Is that what it is? Knowing that I was wanted and desired like *that* by a man like Mason. And that he still wants me. Yeah, that's a bit of pride, which is odd to be feeling over this.

"He texted me this morning." I sway a little in my seat,

picking at the hem of the tablecloth. "He wants to go out tonight."

Sue's eyes go wide. "Really?" She grins in slow motion and then makes a face as she wipes her fingertips on her napkin.

"What's that for?" I ask her.

Sue shrugs and says, "Nothing."

"That's not a nothing look," I tell her right back. "That's a something look."

Kat reaches for another cupcake, listening intently.

"You must've been good." Sue pops a piece of macaron into her mouth all the while smiling. The tiered tray was filled with an assortment of sugary treats when Sue arrived, but it's almost empty now except for the large cupcakes.

My mouth opens some and I have to force it back shut. By the heat on my cheeks, I imagine I'm beet red. Yeah, it's definitely pride.

"So, what'd you tell him?" Kat says. "Don't worry, I won't try to stop you," she adds with an asymmetric smile.

I'm embarrassed that I first told him I was busy and then suggested the exact time and location he said originally when he told me it was my call, so I just cut to the chase. "I said yes."

"You said yes to a date for tonight that was asked today?" Kat asks with a raised brow. Yup, she's just like me.

"I did," I answer slowly as Sue claps her hands and leans her head back with laughter. She's so loud that a few customers in line at the counter look back at her.

"I love her. This is just too good to be true." Sue's smile just gets bigger and bigger until she spots the last tiny cupcake.

"I know how it sounds but I told him no at first, and then he said he was available whenever I was ready."

"So then you said yes." Kat nods her head and I nod in return. I can see the wheels spinning.

"I want to go out and see him again. It's that simple."

Kat hums, her eyes narrowing like she's thinking far too hard, biting her tongue, or both. She finally settles on her response, asking, "So you like him?"

She's awarded another nod from me as I say, "I do. At least I like the way he makes me feel."

There's another hum from her and Sue shakes her head, opting to finish her drink rather than contribute to the conversation.

"You have fun tonight," Sue says with a wink. I give her a small smile back and kiss her cheek before she leaves us so she can get to her meeting on time.

Maddie's not coming to this little cupcake brunch so it's just me and Kat now. I don't like the feeling that I need armor to have a quick chat with one of my closest friends. I bite the inside of my cheek as I watch Sue leave, the bells hanging above the door ringing as I shift on the stool.

"Kat, look—"

"Nope," she says and holds up her hand. "It's fine. Last night was fine. Tonight is fine." Her eyes are closed as she speaks. She nods her head as if she's convincing herself, moving the purse from on top of her stool to the one Sue was sitting on. She has to shift in her seat to tug down her black pencil skirt. Her white blouse is nearly see-through, but she still resembles the epitome of professionalism. She's always put together and on top of everything.

"I know last night isn't something you would do," I start to say and Kat nods slightly. "I know it upset you for me to leave and not tell you." I lean forward, putting my hand on the table, closer to her.

"I think I overreacted," Kat blurts out before I can say anything else. She doesn't meet my gaze at first, but then she lifts her eyes to mine. "It really is okay, all of it, and I'm not trying to make you feel bad." Her words come out with sincerity and it surprises me how much I needed that. "Or slut-shame you or anything like that. I'm happy that you're happy. I'm just nervous that he's taking advantage of you, or that you're going to get hurt …" I brace for what I know is coming as she lowers her voice and says, "You know, so soon after everything."

"I know. Thank you." My voice cracks some and I look for my glass, but then find it empty. I run my fingertips down the stem, feeling overwhelmed again with a mix of emotions.

Guilt comes out to play more than the rest. It's not her making me feel guilty. It's the thought that I should still be mourning.

"Am I a bad person?" I ask Kat, finally pulling my eyes from the empty flute to her.

"No," she answers with sad eyes, taking my hand in both of hers. "I didn't mean to make you think that—"

"You didn't," I say and wave her off the path she's going down. "I was just thinking this morning … about …" About Jace. I don't say it out loud.

"Just tell me that he's not going to make you miss your deadline." Kat deflects, sidestepping this conversation and creating an out for me. God, I love her. She's my editor and this manuscript is due in two weeks.

A smile grows on my face, but it's not genuine in the least. Not because of Kat or Mason or any of that. It's the use of the word *deadline*. I know for a fact I'm going to miss that deadline. She doesn't need to know that, though. "He won't get in the way of that." I shake my head cheerfully, my hair swishing against my shoulders.

"Okay then," she says as she raises her brows and finally picks up a cupcake. Not the small ones from the tray of random sweets, nope, Kat goes for the largest cupcake with hot pink icing and an Oreo stuck in the center. "Please tell me you're at least using condoms until you get back on the pill or something."

I know she meant for that to be funny, but when I give her a side-eye and a shrug, she practically chokes on that Oreo.

thirteen

Mason

So close you can touch her,

Delicate and sweet.

You need her, you crave her,

To hide your deceit.

Be gentle and coaxing,

You can't let her know.

If she finds out the truth,

Out the door she will go.

Blue Hill dims the lights in the evening at six o'clock sharp. The dinner atmosphere is romantic with lit candles on the tables, combined with the soothing sound of water flowing down the river rock wall next to the kitchen. The chatter from the other guests goes unheard as I sit here alone. The only sound that resonates with me is the clink of silverware and glasses as I wait for Jules to walk through the doors.

My fingertips brush over the silver tines of my salad fork as I stare straight ahead toward the entrance and maître d'. Multiple guests have arrived since I sat down twenty minutes ago, each one catching my attention and disappointing me. I glance down at my watch again. She still has five minutes until she's late.

I make a habit of being early, but I'm regretting it this time. Every minute that passes makes me more eager to leave. Curiosity is the only thing keeping me here in my seat. The door opens and the soft cadence of heels clicking on the slate floor echoes in the large open space.

She's here. Jules slips her gray wool peacoat off her shoulders when she walks in and drapes it in her arms as she strides to the maître d'. I stand and button my suit jacket as I walk toward her. I'm only a few tables away and she sees me as the man asks her if she has a reservation.

"She's with me." My voice comes out deep, confident … possessive even. As she turns toward my voice, the hem of her plum-colored dress sways around her thighs. It's tighter around her ass and waist, showing off her curves and reminding me how she looked beneath me last night.

"Of course," the maître d' says and nods.

"Thank you," Jules answers sweetly, giving him a soft smile and looking back at me. It's only a quick glance before a blush rises to her cheeks and she takes my hand.

She has a shy elegance about her, but there's more to her than that. I want to dig a little deeper, if for nothing more than curiosity's sake.

I gesture toward the table, pulling out her chair for her like a gentleman. It's not in my nature, but I have enough manners to impress a woman at least.

"I'm surprised you wanted to see me again," Jules says as I take my own seat. The confession sits between the two of us for a moment as I consider a response.

Before I can say anything, she adds, "Thank you, by the way." Her eyes flicker from mine to the candle. I don't miss how she takes a few glances around us as if she's searching for someone.

I nod my head easily, setting my napkin in my lap and giving her a moment to get comfortable. The waiter quickly pours her a glass of water from the pitcher he's holding.

"Good evening. May I start you off with something to drink?" The young man squares his shoulders and waits, holding the pitcher at attention. He's dressed in a crisp white button-down and dark gray slacks that match his thin tie.

"A bourbon for me, please," I say and wait for Jules. Her slender neck and shoulders are on display. The way the thin straps of her dress lay across the very edge of her shoulders taunt me to pull them down. A simple thin silver necklace sits right in the dip of her collarbone with the word *happy* etched in the middle. It's the only piece of jewelry she's wearing. No ring on her finger. I didn't notice one last night either.

"A glass of chardonnay, please."

"Right away," the waiter says and nods, leaving us alone. Once again, Jules squirms uncomfortably. I love her nervousness and how she has a habit of tucking her hair behind her ear. It only adds to her innocence.

"No tequila?" I say, playing around with her to break the ice.

She huffs a small laugh and rolls her eyes. "No," she says as she unfolds her napkin and moves it to her lap, smoothing it out. "No tequila tonight."

I shrug, waiting for those soft baby blue eyes to look back up at me. "I didn't mind the tequila." I murmur the confession across the table. There's not a damn thing dirty that I've said but she still blushes. There's an attraction between us that's undeniable. It's easy and carefree. But the air is tense as she looks to her left again and then back to me.

She hesitates to say something, then changes her mind and clears her throat as she picks up the menu. She talks without looking at me. "I've never done anything like this."

"Like what?"

"Like, seeing someone."

"Is that what we're doing?" I ask her. "Seeing each other?"

Jules puts her menu down and looks at me with a serious expression. "I have no idea." The sincere answer and complete honesty in her voice force a rough laugh from my chest. I was only teasing her, but she's too sweet and sincere to get a rise out of her.

"You can laugh all you want, but I have no clue what's going on." She picks her menu back up and says, "I'm just along for the ride, Mr. Thatcher."

"Is that so?" I ask her playfully and reach for my glass of water when the waiter returns, setting down my drink first and then hers.

"It is," she says, smiling into her glass and taking a sip of the white wine. She closes her eyes and lets out the softest moan of satisfaction that's barely audible. My cock hardens as I remember last night, the same sweet sound slipping from her lips as I thrust into her over and over again.

She's completely oblivious. Even with a shiver of desire running down my spine, she doesn't seem to notice what she does to me.

"So, what changed in your plans?" I ask as she eyes the menu again. I don't bother looking at mine. I know exactly what I'll have.

A short, feminine laugh makes her shoulders shake as she pulls her long dark hair over her shoulder and then brushes it back again. "I thought this would be better than what I had planned."

Bullshit. I can tell she's lying from a mile away.

"And what did you have planned before?" I say and smirk, pushing for more and wanting to see her admit to this little game she played this morning.

She takes a sip of wine and then answers, "Writing."

"Writing?"

"I like to go to Central Park to write," she says easily, slipping her hands into her lap and leaning forward.

"Are you a journalist?"

"No," she says and shakes her head, "I'm an author." She takes a sip of wine again and I watch as she fiddles with the stem and continues. "I'm not well known or anything. Just poetry." She tries to wave off her insecurity then adds, "It doesn't really make much money, but it's the career I chose."

She's already justifying herself and I don't like it. She should be proud.

"I think that's wonderful. It takes a lot of work and diligence to write a novel of poetry."

Her eyes light up and she visibly relaxes as she says in a delicate voice, "Thank you."

"Who's your favorite poet?" I ask her.

"Robert Frost," she answers quickly. "Hands down."

"I've read a bit of Frost." It's true, albeit years and years ago in grade school and I'm pretty sure I hated every minute I was forced to read it. It doesn't matter, though; my remark makes her calm and that sweet smile comes back.

I clear my throat, smoothing the napkin on my lap and trying to remember what Mrs. Harper said. "'Poetry is when an emotion has found its thought,'" I say as I look into her eyes and try to say the second part correctly, "'and the thought has found words.' I believe it was Frost who said that." Her entire demeanor changes to one of surprise and ease. I'm shocked that I remembered it myself.

A surprised grin looks back at me. It's amazing how something so small can make her genuinely happy. She nods and says, "Yes, I do believe you're right."

The moment between us is filled with comfortable silence as we each take a sip of our drinks.

"So you're in construction, I believe?"

"I'm a developer," I say, hoping she won't ask too many questions. I don't think she has any idea of the connections. I don't intend to lie to her, but I don't need to give her anything that would help her put the pieces together.

"In the city, right?"

"Brooklyn mostly, although we're currently under contract with the city to renovate and rebuild some properties in Manhattan."

"What's that like?"

"Being a developer?" I've never had anyone ask me before and I take a moment to consider my reply. "It's challenging at times and it pisses me off most days. A lot goes wrong and hardly anything goes the way it's planned." I smirk at her as she laughs into her glass at my answer. "Isn't that what all jobs are like, though?"

She nods her head, setting the glass down but then her expression changes. "I'm not sure I should be doing this," she tells me with her forehead scrunched.

"Doing what?"

"This," she says and gestures between the two of us.

"We're just having dinner."

Her eyes narrow and I ignore the accusatory stare, picking up my bourbon and taking an easy drink of it. It burns just right on the way down, leaving a trail of heat in its wake.

"I just want to feed you," I say in a tone that I hope comes out somewhat innocent.

"And fuck me," she whispers so softly but with a roughness I haven't heard from that sexy voice of hers. I stare into her gorgeous gaze, daring her to blush, to be embarrassed by it, but she only stares back with desire in her baby blue eyes.

"Yes, and fuck you," I say. It doesn't go unnoticed that she clenches her thighs. "You want that, don't you?"

"I'm not sure I should be sleeping with you," she says simply but with a firm resolve in her voice. My heart beats in a way that makes it feel tight. Like there's not quite enough room for it to beat again.

"Are you seeing someone else?" I ask her. My knuckles brush against the white tablecloth as my hands start to fist. I stop them and try to keep my body from showing what I'm really feeling. She better not be fucking anyone else.

She loses the conviction in her voice when she answers, "No."

"Then why shouldn't we?" I say, glancing at the waiter as he makes his way toward us.

"Because—" Jules stops as soon as she notices him. She plasters on a fake smile that doesn't reach her eyes and waits patiently for him to address her.

"Are you ready for me to take your order?" he asks me but I gesture to Jules, taking another sip to settle my irritation.

"For you, miss?"

"May I have the herb-grilled salmon, please?" She passes the menu to him and rests her hands in her lap, giving him her full attention. Meanwhile, I can't take my eyes off her and wondering why the hell she thinks she shouldn't be seeing me.

"Are the grilled vegetables all right with that?" he asks her.

"Yes, they're perfect."

The waiter scribbles on the notepad in his hand then turns toward me.

"Sirloin, medium rare. Vegetables are fine." I preemptively answer his unasked question, still staring at Jules. The waiter takes the hint, nodding once and immediately leaving us.

"You were saying?" I say, picking up my bourbon.

"I—" Again she hesitates, sensing the change in my temperament. "I don't know if I should really be seeing *anyone*."

I wait for more, taking another sip.

"I'm not sure how to," she says, waving her hand in the air, at a loss for words. "I'm still—" She can't put a sentence together.

"I want to fuck you, Jules. Give me one good reason why there's a problem with that." I hold her gaze listing all the reasons in my head, but ignoring every last one of them. She needs someone to fuck, to hold her, someone to make her smile. I can do that; I can be that person.

"It's just sex?" she asks and from the look in her eyes, I don't know what answer she wants in return.

Fuck, I wish it were. I can't explain why I want her this badly. It's more than the physical attraction, but I'll never admit the truth to her.

"Just sex," I lie. "If that's what you want."

She licks her lush lips, peering down at her silverware and then up to me. "I'd be using you," she says as if she's confessing a sin.

A bark of a laugh leaves me and my tense muscles relax.

"Use me, Jules." I stare into her blue eyes flecked with silver, feeling the tension between us morph into something sweeter, something darker and depraved. "I want you to."

CHAPTER

fourteen

Julia

It starts with a kiss.

Then dinners and dates.

It starts with a smile.

Your evenings run late.

It tempts and teases.

And makes you want more.

But it's not how it starts,

When it can only end in war.

THERE'S SOMETHING ABOUT HIM TONIGHT. Something darker that I didn't see before. It's the way he looks at me like I should be running from him. It both scares me and lures me in.

Lifting the glass to my lips, my one and only glass, I finish off the sweet wine.

"Did you write today?" Mason asks. We've made a bit of small talk and light conversation. I'm still feeling him out. I thought I wanted this thing between us but the air changed a bit ago, and the tension is something else now. Like we're at war, although I don't know why.

"I did, yes." Every bit of it was about Jace, though. Something I'd rather not bring up with Mason. I pick up my glass again, finding it empty and cursing internally.

I head off whatever other questions he has for me by saying, "Why dinner tonight and not just drinks after?" My voice is low, nearly accusatory, but unlike what happened earlier, he doesn't seem to mind.

It takes a moment for him to respond, but he does. "Because I had to eat and so did you."

He takes another bite of his steak and then asks, "Would you rather we were just having drinks tonight?"

"Yes." My answer is immediate. He doesn't seem taken aback. He's calm, unmoving and unbothered.

"Why's that?"

I can't look him in the eyes as my fingers nervously move up and down the silverware. I don't know how to put it out there. "How did you know my name?" I ask him.

"From the papers," Mason says and then quickly takes a sip of his drink.

I nod my head. That's how everyone knows me. "The papers?" I say, hoping he'll elaborate.

"I've read a few things."

"Then you may have me at a disadvantage. The papers know far too much about me," I joke, seemingly innocent, but I'm sure he's aware that I'm prodding.

"That's possible, probable even." He smirks at me, his brilliant smile adding to his charm. I try not to let it affect me, but I'm at his mercy whenever he looks at me like that. I consider the facts and list out all the reasons I have to end this. Maybe the conversation with Kat got to me more than I thought.

I'm vulnerable. *Check.*

I've never done this before. *Check.*

I don't know that I'm okay with this. *Check.*

And a man like Mason could crush me. *Check a thousand times.*

"Well, all I know about you is that you're a bit of a player," I say and dare to hold his gaze.

"I used to be, yes."

"Used to?" There's a tension between us. It's hot to the touch and it makes me want to move closer to him, but I know that I need to keep my distance right now.

"Yes, used to. I mean it. I used to be ... more unattached, then I met someone."

"Oh." I'm surprised by his confession and also by the immediate reaction I have to him meeting someone who made him want to settle down. Maybe all the thoughts and emotions are playing on my face, because Mason continues.

"She's not in the picture anymore and it wasn't anything serious at all." He answers my questions before I have to ask them and I'm grateful for that. "It just changed things for me."

I wish I could keep my expression neutral but I've never been very good at hiding what I'm feeling, and this mix of curiosity and even jealousy surely isn't becoming. "So now you want someone to fuck and take to dinners?"

A deep rough chuckle vibrates up his chest and the way he smiles at me does something to me that makes me reconsider my list of reasons.

"Someone, no." His eyes heat and he licks his bottom lip as he adds, "You, yes."

I huff out a small breath and peer down at my nearly empty plate before looking back up to him.

"I want to take you out, bring you back home and lay you down in my bed." He holds my gaze as he says the words so calmly. I fight the urge to look around the room filled with families and couples to make sure no one's heard us. My body is on fire with the thought of him doing just that, over and over. But the part where he talks about taking me out … that makes this seem serious. It practically begs for drama, given my history as a socialite. Whatever this is between us … I don't want that out there for all the judging eyes.

"I feel …" I trail off as I realize I don't know how I feel, and with that frustration I lay down my silverware.

"What's wrong?"

"I don't really like going out anymore." I blurt out the confession and feel sick to my stomach.

"You don't like going out?" He frowns.

"It just makes me anxious because of something that

happened. Something that maybe you read about?" It would be a blessing if he already knew. If he could understand that privacy is an issue for me and this is something I would greatly prefer to keep private.

He stares at me for a moment, although his eyes flash with a knowing look.

I don't want to say it out loud and I wait for him to answer, but he doesn't.

"It's just," I say as my voice gets tight and I choke on the words, but only for a moment, "my husband passed away and it's hard for me to deal with moving on with someone else." I stumble over my next words for a moment when I say, "Because people …"

"Will read about it in the papers?"

"Yes. It's hard going out and not being with him. That's difficult for me." It feels like a massive weight off my chest to just say it out loud. "I don't know how to handle everyone's expectations. It could go over very poorly."

Mason's next words come out hard, a command if I've ever heard one. "Fuck their expectations."

I'm shocked by how blunt Mason is. I don't think he understands. "I just don't want to be judged—"

"Fuck. Them."

I stare back in disbelief, thinking he can't be serious but he is. His eyes hold an intensity and his hard, muscular arms are corded. He clenches his stubbled jaw and then seems to relax slightly, but I'm still caught off guard. Mostly because I want to obey him. I want to eat up every word he's saying as if it's law and bow down to him.

"You're entitled to feel and do whatever you want. It's no

one else's business. Their perception of you is their responsibility. Not yours."

I take a deep breath, hating that he doesn't understand. "Maybe I'm just shallow." I didn't mean to say it out loud, but I did. My breath leaves me and I pick up the empty glass again. Before I have the chance to let out the exasperated sigh begging to choke me, the waiter comes to my rescue, the bottle of chardonnay in his hand.

"Thank you," I say gratefully.

The second the waiter leaves, taking both our plates with him, Mason says, "We can play this however you'd like."

"I don't really want to go out yet. I'm just not ready." I realize he has a point but he doesn't understand that I welcomed these people into my life, and shutting them out now would be like a slap in the face.

"Is it because you loved him?" Mason asks, his forehead wrinkled and his brow furrowed. He can't even look me in the eye. "You loved him and they think you can't move on? Or that you shouldn't?"

"I loved my husband, but that's not why." I take a sip of wine and staring at the glass I answer, "I just don't know how to not feel guilty about being okay and I'm worried because I don't know how it will be taken."

The words came out easier than I thought they would.

"So you're all right?" Mason asks me and he's so genuine with his concern that I could practically cry.

"Some days are better than others, but it's hard because I wasn't much without him."

Mason takes my hand in his at my comment, squeezing it

and opening his mouth to say something, but nothing comes out. I'm surprised at how deep our conversation has gotten.

"I'm sorry," I say, shaking my head and pulling my hand away. "I didn't mean to—"

"Stop apologizing," he tells me in a tone that makes all my worries vanish. "I asked you, remember?"

I nod my head and utter a small response, although I don't remember how the conversation started.

"Tell me something that will make me smile," he says.

A grin plays on my lips at the thought of him smiling and I say, "You're a very handsome man. Very charming. Obviously successful." I lean in slightly and let the tips of my fingers play along his large knuckles as I add, "And I really, really liked last night."

I accomplish my task and sit back in my seat, staring at his handsome face.

"I'm glad you enjoyed it." He keeps his eyes on me as we both sip our drinks. "I would have liked to have had you this morning as well."

I almost choke on my wine but luckily I save myself, swallowing it down and taking a moment to get myself together.

"About that …"

"I imagine you'll make up for it tomorrow morning." He says it like it's a statement but I hear the question.

Another night with Mason Thatcher.

"I did say I was just along for the ride," I say, reminding him and myself.

fifteen

Mason

Pretend it didn't happen.

Don't let the truth show.

Curiosity will lead you.

Just where you should go.

She'll lure you and tempt you.

And bid you farewell.

It's only then you'll realize,

You've wound up in hell.

I COULD BLAME THE FIRST NIGHT ON SHOCK AND alcohol. The second on curiosity. But this pattern of behavior, this deep-seated need to watch her, to touch her, to have her ... there's no fucking excuse for it.

I stare at the computer screen mindlessly. The office is empty; even Liam's gone home, leaving me here alone with simple tasks that should have already been done.

My to-do list consists of analyzing this inventory and comparing the replacement materials Liam thinks will be suitable. It's crucial to our budget that this works and I need to make the decision today. Every penny is accounted for and spent, all except for this last purchase. All of it for one massive project. And all of it I owe to my father.

It's been hours and I'm purposely dragging my feet. I want all this to stop so I can hit pause. Instead I'm falling down a black pit, forced to make a choice of what will happen when I crash at the bottom.

Sitting forward in my chair, elbows on the desk, I nudge the mouse to my computer and it lights up the screen once again. Two gorgeous blue eyes stare back at me. Her long, thick lashes frame them perfectly. Her skin is flawless, with only a hint of color in her cheeks. But it's her expression that had me staring at her picture all morning. Her lips are parted as if she's about to smile. So close to happiness, but the photo caught her before she could have it.

It's only been two days since I've last seen her, but each night I've felt compelled to message her and make sure I knew where she was. The insecure side of me wanted to ensure she wasn't with someone else. That's the truth of the matter. I trust her when she says she's not involved with anyone. However, I know all too well what loneliness can do to a person and I want her completely to myself.

If I pretend like the events that led to meeting Jules didn't happen, then there isn't a damn thing wrong with what's between us. If only it was that easy to forget.

Knock. Knock.

My gaze lifts to the clock and then moves to the door to my office. It's past 8:00 p.m. and almost time to meet Jules.

"Who is it?" I call out, not knowing who the hell it could be. Maintenance, maybe?

"Your partner in crime." Liam's voice comes from the other side of the door and I relax slightly.

"Come in," I yell out to him, checking my cell phone and seeing a text from Jules. She's waiting for me. The very thought spreads a feeling of warmth through my chest.

I set the phone down, giving Liam my full attention although I have no idea why the fuck he's here.

"You seem preoccupied." Although it's meant as a statement, it comes out as a question. Before I can even think about it, Liam's eyes are on my computer screen.

It's an innocent glance, but he doesn't need to see her. More importantly, he doesn't need to know about my new obsession. I'm quick to exit out of the article about Jules. It was about her husband's passing. How she was dealing with the loss, although the picture they used of her was from years before.

I've read dozens of articles about her over the last few days. They're all the same. Every single one of them ooh and ahh over her. Some articles gush about her charity work.

Others are less substantial and concern themselves with her opinion of an event or what clothes she's wearing. They put her on a pedestal and in such a precarious place that it's far too easy for her to crash and burn. And that's just what she did according to the articles that came out after her husband's death.

The sole fucking image I can't get out of my head is one of her crying at her husband's funeral. Maybe they showed mercy by using an older photo for the article I spent the day looking at because on the day she buried him she looked as if she'd died herself.

Inhaling deeply, I will the memory to go away. Wishing I'd never seen that grief on her beautiful face. Wishing I didn't have a hand in causing it.

"Well now," Liam says, ignoring my irritation. "Is this—"

"What are you doing here?" I ask him, cutting him off and leaning back in my chair with my shoulders squared. He's still standing and leaning against the desk casually, but my tone has that arrogant smile on his face vanishing instantly.

He rubs the back of his neck, raising his brow and looking past me out the window as he takes a step back. "I was just wondering if you'd put the final numbers in."

I clear my throat, feeling like an absolute prick. "Sorry, it's been a long day." I rub my shoulders and click on the spreadsheet. "I was just getting ready to put them in."

"So it's all finalized?" Liam asks me with a chipper smile, seeming to forget that I'm an asshole just like that.

"So far, so good." I force a smile and try to shake off the unease flowing through me. I can't explain the dichotomy of how I think of Jules. I want to take her out, impress her and please her in every way, including showing her off and showing off for her. But I also want this thing between us to be my secret. I don't want anyone close to me to have an idea of what's going on.

It's a design for failure. I can't help what I want, though.

Liam claps once and says, "Perfect." He starts to walk away but then looks back at me with an expression asking if he can pry. Curiosity is evident in his eyes. "That's all I wanted to know."

"You don't need anything else?" I ask him, the beating of my heart raging loudly in my chest. I don't know if I should refuse to answer whatever questions he has about Jules. Everything in me is screaming to deny it all. I can never let anyone know.

"So … Julia Summers?" the prick has the balls to ask me.

Not hiding the irritation by audibly exhaling, I nod in confession. I can't help that I feel a sense of pride as his cocky smile widens.

"It all makes sense now. I guess I can forgive you for being such an irritable fuck lately."

"Watch it," I say under my breath but the smile on my face only encourages him.

"Good for you," he says as he looks back at the screen, but it's only a spreadsheet. "Is it serious?" he asks me and I don't know why. He's never asked me before about who I'm fucking, or dating for that matter.

When I don't answer, he adds, "You just seem unusually preoccupied recently."

I move my seat closer to the desk, stretching my back and then shrug, doing my best to come off casual. "I've had a lot on my mind."

He waits for a moment, expecting more, but I return to

the spreadsheet and open the folder of options on my desk. "I'll have it done before I leave," I tell him, giving him a tight smile and ending the conversation.

He leaves quietly, merely waving a goodbye on his way out and letting the door shut with a loud click that fills the empty room.

I look up when he's gone and tap the pen against the desk. I don't know what to deny and what to keep a secret. Confusing the two could be fatal, but the lines are already blurred.

CHAPTER
sixteen

Julia

> *This is not a date.*
>
> *This is not serious.*
>
> *This isn't something that needs to be more.*
>
> *This is for fun.*
>
> *This is pretend.*

My pen stops on the last line. I stare at the words I've scribbled into the notepad, but my mind is blank. I don't know what I intended for this poem to be. Inspirational maybe? It all just looks like lies to me.

I click the end of my pen over and over. *Click. Click. Click. Click.* Debating ripping this sheet out of the notebook and balling it up for the round cabinet … a.k.a. the wastebasket.

The clink of several ceramic mugs being stacked together makes me turn to look over my shoulder. I inhale the rich smell of coffee in the small shop. The floors are checkered and the walls painted plain white, but this place serves the best coffee downtown. It's also right across from Mason's office and I told him I'd meet him here. My eyes drift up, my thumb still on the end of my pen.

The Rising Falls Building is sleek and modern. It looks like a polished black sheet of glass all the way up with a thick steel frame outlining everything in matte black, separating the panels. It's tall and dominating, dwarfing the small buildings across from it.

It's everything Mason is. The clicking stops when I drop the pen.

With both hands wrapped around the mug, I pick up my coffee and take a sip. It's not hot anymore, but it's not room temperature either. The smooth ceramic feels just right in my hand as I take in a deep breath.

I keep telling myself I shouldn't be with him; I don't do casual and never have, but this doesn't feel casual. It's been days of seeing him and I'm already catching feelings. Feelings I'm certain are one sided.

Maybe I'm reading into things too much. It's only been a week and a half. It's just sex … or so I keep telling myself. *Maybe I should add that to the list of lies in my notepad.* I huff at the snide thought.

Luckily, not many people have seemed to notice, other

than Kat checking up on me and gently prodding. That's not atypical for her.

We aren't seeing each other in public, mostly. Not for events anyway.

There are whispers that I'm dating, but nothing that seems malicious or judgmental. Which is better than I'd hoped.

My heart pounds painfully in my chest at the thought and the small air of confidence leaves me. I would care if they said I was a bitch for moving on too soon. Or that I'm no longer the good girl they thought I was. That Jace's death was in some ways my death too. They wouldn't be wrong about that last one.

Most importantly though, I don't want Jace's father seeing that I've moved on. Or my mother. I close my eyes and try to rid myself of the image of her reading about me in the paper as she sips her morning tea. Drunk at a bar with a known player holding me. Yeah, I don't need my mother seeing that.

The bells above the front door jingle and my eyes instinctively open at the sound.

There he is, Mason, taking the breath in my lungs as he strides toward me. I'm stuck as I sit there, pinned to my seat and captivated by the air of confidence he gives off. His steel gray eyes look darker than ever as he grabs the back of the chair across from me and pulls it out. The legs scrape on the floor, announcing to the world that he's going to sit with me. He claims his seat and fixes those eyes on me.

"Jules," he says, my name falling from his gorgeous lips in a rough baritone and I finally breathe.

"Mason." I say then smile, although I don't know why. I simply can't help it. He makes me feel like a little girl caught in a fantasy. It's the way he wears his suits, the way he walks into buildings, the way he looks at me. As if he owns them all.

A small smile plays on his lips as well. I did that. I made him smile. These feelings, this bubbly laugh that erupts from my lips as I take a sip of my coffee … this is where the real problem hides.

He gestures to my cup and asks, "Should I get one as well?"

I sit up straighter and look over my shoulder again at the counter with the one lonely register and stacks and stacks of mugs behind it. It's late but this coffee shop never closes, because this city never sleeps.

"If you'd like to." I don't expect him to reach across the table and tuck a strand of hair behind my ear. His eyes and hands linger on the exposed part of my neck. The tips of his fingers trail down my skin slowly, with purpose. I feel the heat race through me, the desire creeping slowly down my chest and lower … and lower. He confuses me when I'm near him. I can't think of anything but what I want him to do to me and that's a dangerous thing.

I'm mesmerized by the way he looks at me. The steel gray seems softer, the harsh lines of his jaw less intimidating, more vulnerable. Maybe my poetic mind is getting the best of me.

"I think if I do," he finally answers, leaning back in the chair he's claimed as a throne, "I'd like to get it to go."

Nodding vigorously, I make it obvious that I agree and then feel foolish as he lets out a rough laugh. The bells jingle again in the doorway just as he leans across the table for a kiss.

Anxiety shoots through me, and I pull back just as his scorching hot lips touch mine. My back hits the hard plastic of the chair and my eyes whip over to an old man in a tweed suit. His white hair looks ruffled from the wind, but he doesn't seem to care. His light blue eyes gaze through horn-rimmed glasses and up at the menu behind me.

I'm slightly relieved that it wasn't anyone who would recognize us, but that doesn't last long. My heart drops when I see the expression on his face.

It's more than disappointment; this is something else.

"I don't know …" I say but trail off, clearing my throat. I'm still trying to catch my breath and explain when Mason speaks before I can continue.

"If you're with me," he says and the tone Mason gives me is authoritative as his eyes pierce me, pinning me to my seat and stealing my excuses from the tip of my tongue, "then you're *with me.*" He finishes his thought and I can't look away, I can't shake off this guilt.

"You know I prefer discretion," I say and the excuse leaves me in a single breath.

He rises from his seat and buttons his suit jacket. The hold he has on me is finally broken although he doesn't look at me as he walks past me and up to the counter. I stare at the door, wondering if I should just leave. My body feels hot and I don't think I can do this. I still don't even know what *this* is.

It's definitely not "just sex." Going out on dates and coffee meetups aren't in the fuck buddy handbook. Not according to Sue, anyway.

My body stands on its own. Although my legs feel wobbly, my body weak and my head clouded with frustration and confusion, something inside me pushes me forward. It's only four steps, four strides toward him, all the while my heart beats faster.

"I don't know what *this* is." My voice comes out strong, clear and full of a confidence I don't possess.

A shaky breath comes and goes as he faces me, his shoulders squared, to give me his full attention. I try to come up with the right words. "I don't know what I want." The words are so true. "I am not *with* anyone. I'm alone and that's—" I stop midsentence.

I almost say that's how I want it. I almost lie to both him and myself.

From the corner of my eye, I notice the barista who looks away casually as if she wasn't listening. My cheeks flame with embarrassment.

"If you want me to leave you alone, it's done." His statement lacks both conviction and emotion.

"I want you," I whisper, my eyes pleading with his. "I just don't," I say then swallow and force my eyes to meet his. "I don't want people to know."

I feel like an asshole. "I'm not ashamed of you … I'm ashamed of me …" Oh God, even I cringe at my words. It's the truth, but it's so shitty of me. I swallow thickly, searching Mason's face for something. For understanding or anger. For something, anything. Instead there's a coldness that greets me and it hurts. "I don't mean it to come out in a way that is offensive. I've just been thinking a lot about it since the other night and I don't want my family to find out." My voice breaks at the last statement and that's when the barista decides to set down Mason's coffee.

"It's because of your husband?" he finally asks me and I don't waste a second to answer yes. The word is barely a breath.

It's more than just publicity and articles that paint me however they want. It all cuts deeper than that.

"I want to take you home," he says then licks his lips, and instinctively my eyes are drawn toward them. He lets his eyes roam down my body. "We can talk about this in bed."

My lips part and I struggle not to look back at the barista who's no doubt watching us.

"Do you want that, Jules?"

I do. I want him to touch me and hold me and make me feel alive.

Why is this so hard? It's emotions, that's why. Luring me in and then snapping me out of it.

"Jules?" he asks, pushing me and I cave to what I really want, because if I deny him, I may lose this chance at an escape forever.

"Yes." I whisper my response and I hope the tone reflects my gratitude.

I think it does because he places his hand on the small of my back, as if he knows I need support in this, leading me away from the counter and toward my jacket and coffee that I've left on the table.

As I pick up the white jean jacket, focused on calming down and ignoring my overactive brain, Mason leans forward and whispers in the crook of my neck, "I don't know what I want, other than I want you in my bed every night." *Every night.* There's a pang of both fear and desire from his confession. A small wave of relief and arousal flood through my veins. He lifts the jacket over my shoulders, helping me slip it in place and then looks me in the eyes.

"Is that something you want?"

That's what I want, but this seems like more. I choke on the answer, the words colliding together in a jumble and refusing to come out.

It's because I don't know how to separate the two. A relationship versus someone to sleep with at night.

It's going to be a problem for me, I already know it is, but telling Mason that in this moment is something I can't do. If I do, I've lost him.

Silence sits between us for a moment, growing more tense by the second and as though it slows the clock in the room, time stalling and my mind whirling with how this is all going to end.

He's going to crush me. He'll leave me shattered when he's done.

He's not the first though and there's not much of me that can break any more than I already have.

I put a small smile on my face and nod, feeling as though I'm making a death wish. "Yes," I answer, holding his gray eyes, "I want that too."

He doesn't know the truth and I'm too much of a coward to tell him.

I've sealed my own fate in this moment. I know I have.

If only I hadn't said it. If only I could walk away.

seventeen

Mason

What's right and what's wrong are overrated.
The lines are blurred; consequences negated.
I'm left with no truth, only lies that I've built.
I'm left all alone, consumed by the guilt.

SHE'S FIDGETY, QUIET TOO. MY PARKING SPOT IS THE last one on this level in the garage; it's the largest and away from everyone else's. We walk in unison, my hand still on the small of her back. I'm not letting go until I have her in my car. She's running, we both know it, and I won't fucking allow it.

She needs to know that she belongs to me. She wants to hide this and that's fine with me. But only to the extent that she knows not to be ashamed for going after what she wants. Discretion is one thing but I won't be denied.

I'll give her everything she desires; I want to. I want to see her smile, to hear that laugh that drew me to her. I'll do everything I can to make it up to her.

And she'll give me all of her in return. There's no exception to this compromise.

The passenger side door clicks loudly in the empty garage as I open it but then I stop, shutting it before she has a chance to slip in.

My dick is hard; my blood is hot. Glancing at a confused Jules, her doe eyes stare back at me. The same eyes I've been looking at all day. But there's no hint of a smile, only concern and rejection mixed in those soft blue hues.

There's a large cement post to the right of my car. It's square in shape and maybe three feet wide. If someone drove up, it would block us for the moment. Only a moment, but the odds of anyone coming to a commercial parking garage this late at night are slim. Fixing what's between us right now is worth taking the risk of being caught.

My shoulders are tense as I slip off my jacket and lead her to the front of the car, where we'll be blocked from view. Her heels click and her eyes flicker with a knowing want. Although her steps are hesitant, she follows my lead, looking over her shoulder and no doubt wondering what exactly I have planned for her.

"Mason?" The hesitation in her voice comes out as a gasp as her lush ass presses against the car.

My only answer is to grip her hips and back her up to the hood of my car, pinning her down and crushing my lips against hers. Her hands fly to my chest pushing me away at first, caught off guard by the sudden change of plans. But then they travel up my neck ever so slowly, giving in to me and then move to the back of my head, pulling me in for more.

That's a good girl. My good girl. The woman who needs me and I damn well need to show her I need her too.

I break our heated kiss to breathe, her chest touching mine as I look down at her. "Be good for me and be quiet." I murmur the command and she can only nod in response, her warm breath trailing down my neck.

I crush my lips to hers again and she moans into my mouth, but before she can deepen it, I fist her hair in my hands. Pulling her away, I grab her hip and flip her over so her breasts are pressed against the metal.

"Stick your ass out for me," I command her in a rough voice as I palm my dick through my pants and look around the pillar. There's no one in sight and I fucking need her tight pussy coming on my dick.

Her lust-filled whimpers encourage me as I pull her head back by her hair and kiss her neck. She rocks her hips and that small space between her thighs brushes against my dick. Teasing me.

I'm quick to unzip my pants, my pulse racing from the very thought that someone could see us or hear us. I finally let her go to stroke myself once and wait for her reaction now that she's fully aware of what I plan to do. She lets out a gasp, bracing herself and looking over her slender shoulder at me with those gorgeous blue eyes so full of lust ... and trust.

Slipping her lacy panties to the side, I kiss her neck once more before shoving myself deep inside her tight cunt. *Fuck.* She feels too good. With my eyes closed, I give her a moment to adjust. Only for a moment. This has to be quick, no time for playing.

Her back arches and her fingers scrape along the car, but she doesn't scream out. Nothing leaves her lips but a small gasp as her mouth forms a perfect O. Her pussy spasms and feels like heaven as I hold in a groan and place my hand on the small of her back, pressing her down and keeping her in place.

Her eyes are closed tight and her teeth sunk into her bottom lip. I rock out slightly and push back in, forcing the sweetest sound from those beautiful bloodred lips. A moan of pleasure.

I grip her chin in my hand and force her to look at me. I want her to watch me. I want her eyes on mine as I take her just how she needs.

Her eyes slowly open as she lets out a breath and that's when I slam into her again. She bucks forward, a small cry uttering from her lips and I wait again for her to look back at me.

"You need to watch me, sweetheart," I say with an even voice even though it's really a demand.

I'll show her who she belongs to and how good I'll be to her. But she has to watch me, she needs to see it all and know this is exactly what she wanted. *That she wanted me.*

She rests her cheek against the car and keeps her eyes on me as I thrust into her again and again, pulling all the way out and then slamming all the way back in. It's difficult to keep the groans low but I do, and she does what she's told, staying quiet and watching me as I fuck her like she deserves to be fucked.

The sound of tires squealing above us makes her squirm beneath me, but I hush her and lower myself closer to her. Leaning down, I push my chest against her back and kiss her gently on the lips. "They won't see." My hand slips between us and lifts up the front of her dress, lightly running along her clit.

I play with her, teasing and rubbing while watching her writhe under me. "Look at me," I command her and she's quick to turn her eyes to me. They reflect nothing but torturous pleasure and the need to cry out her release. She's gorgeous and I could make this easy for her. I really could. I could fuck her quickly and take her over the edge so she doesn't have to fight the urge for long. I could let her close her eyes and look away.

But I'm not interested in that.

Jules is going to see. I won't let her think this is all pretend and something that it's not.

I'm going to give her everything she needs. I'm going to make it all right again and she's going to love me for it. I couldn't care less if that makes me a prick.

It doesn't matter how it's going to end, just that it happens this way. Right here and right now.

"Mason." She whispers my name as her release takes her gently, her soft folds taking me deeper into her. I have to wait for her to stop trembling, a cold sweat breaking out along my skin before moving my fingers to her lips. I wish she were naked so I could see every inch of her. So I could see the flush that's creeping up her chest.

"Turn around." I give her the simple command and she obeys, her chest rising and falling unsteadily and her legs still trembling slightly.

"This is going to be quick," I tell her and then grab her

hips in both my hands and angle her how I want her. I glance up to make sure she's still watching and just like the good girl she is, those gorgeous pale blue eyes are on me. I piston my hips, surprising her as she braces her limp body against the car. The intensity of the raw fuck makes her bottom lip drop with a silent scream as her body tightens. I fist her hair again and pull her head back.

"Mason." My name is a twisted word of desperation on her lips.

"Come for me," I tell her, moving my other hand to her clit again to strum her swollen nub.

She screams out for the first time and I'm quick to bite her neck. Hard. It's a punishment for not obeying me and it only makes her struggle against me harder. And only makes her impending release that much more intense.

I fucking love it. I love what I do to her and how much pleasure it gives her. How she makes me forget everything when we're together like this.

Her body goes rigid and her pussy tightens around my cock. She struggles to breathe and her head falls back as she looks at the cement ceiling, her climax threatening to crash through her.

I nip her chin and move the hand that was gripping her hair to her face. I stare into her eyes as her body shudders and her neck arches, her hair draping over my shoulder. Her face is the epitome of sinful ecstasy. It's the most beautiful thing I've ever seen.

"Fuck," I groan as she finds her release. It only takes four more thrusts, riding through her orgasm and taking her that much higher until I find my own release. My balls draw up and my spine tingles. I bury my head in her neck as my cock pulses deep inside of her.

The sounds of our heavy breathing surround us for a long moment.

I kiss the side of her neck right where she's marked from my bite, running my nose along her soft skin and breathing in her scent. Her legs are still shaking and a shudder runs down her body as I pull my lips away from her. She's perfectly sated, just as she should be.

"You're mine, Jules," I murmur but make sure it's loud enough for her to hear and watch for her reaction. Her long lashes flutter as she opens her eyes and looks back at me. I pull her panties back into place and fix her dress.

"Mason," she says, whispering my name as her forehead creases and her eyes beg me to take it back.

"No, you want me and I want you. You're mine."

She bites down on her bottom lip and says, "I'm not okay." Her voice hitches and her words crack. She closes her eyes and speaks as if it truly pains her to say the words. "I don't know if I can be good for you."

I rest my forehead against hers and ask her, "Why are you so afraid?"

"I don't think this can just be sex for me," she says. I cup her jaw in my hand and brush my thumb across her cheek. "I think I'm going to want more. I think I already—" she stops as her voice cracks again.

My body feels unbearably tense, each breath hurting my chest. *Why am I doing this to her? Why can't I just let her go?* Because I'm a selfish prick and I can't help myself. "I can give you more," I whisper in the air between us, knowing it's what she wants to hear. "We can see how it works between us in private, and keep things quiet in public?"

I'm giving her exactly what she wants, just to keep her.

I'm an asshole for doing it, knowing I can never be what she really needs and wants.

Her eyes light up and that soft smile reappears on her face. She brightens with hope and my shy girl comes back to me. "Are you sure?" she says, still panting, barely recovered from what I've already done to her. "You aren't going to break my heart?"

She has no idea that she should be running from me. I'm well aware that I should turn her away regardless. Instead I smile down at her and kiss the tip of her nose. "I'm sure," I tell her and hate myself that much more.

THERE'S NO RHYME OR REASON FOR WHEN THE memories come back. There's nothing I can pinpoint that triggers it. Nothing that I can blame.

Lying in Mason's arms, naked and warm, the two of us each working on our laptops in comfortable silence, there's not a damn reason that I should be thinking of Jace, but I am.

I don't want to. Even as I scoot my back close to the sofa, I try to rid myself of the images of him smiling at me. When I'd wake up in the morning, Jace would push the hair from my face and give me a quick kiss. Always on the lips, no matter how much I tried to dodge them. He thought it was cute how I didn't want him to smell my morning breath.

Moments like that, moments we shared together that were easy and fun, where we fit beautifully together, those hurt the most when I remember. I let out an uneasy sigh and try to relax, ignoring Mason's eyes on me.

You'd think I'd be happy that I had that at one point in time. That I had a man who loved me and whom I loved too. It's easy to say: *I'll be glad because it happened and not sad because it's over.* But the truth is I can't say that, because I don't mean it.

"What's wrong?" Mason's deep voice cutting through the silent evening makes me feel even worse. I'm trying to move on, but it's not that easy.

I swallow the lump in my throat and pull the dark gray throw over my legs and up to my shoulders. "Just having a moment," I answer honestly, although I can't look him in the eye. I hope he'll just let it go.

His warm breath surrounds me as he pulls me closer to him and kisses my hair. I don't expect the gentle touch from him. He whispers, "I get it."

He splays his hand on my hip and runs his thumb back and forth over my bare skin. I wait for more, but he doesn't say anything else. Only that he gets it and my treacherous heart thumps in recognition.

My laptop jostles across my legs as I try to get closer to him, loving the warmth, needing more of it. I wonder if it's wrong to be upset over the passing of your husband while in the arms of your lover.

"Sometimes—" Mason starts to speak just as my eyes glaze over and the words on the screen start to blur. I take in a steadying breath and stop that shit. Crying never helped me. It doesn't do any good at all.

Mason clears his throat while I wipe under my eyes.

"When my mom died, sometimes it was the oddest things that set me off." I'm surprised by Mason's confession and grateful to be talking about him and not me.

"I'm sorry about your mom." My condolence is softly spoken; my voice a bit scratchier than I'd like. I stare up into his eyes which appear so much lighter than usual, maybe because it's dark all around us. Only the glow of our laptops and the city lights beyond the large living room window to paint the room in a soft glow.

He tilts his head to the side, tucking my hair behind my ear and I push my cheek into his palm. He has such large hands, rough but warm. They're the perfect size for this.

A coarse hum comes from deep in his chest. It's short, but a sound of approval.

"It's okay to hurt still." His words are comforting. "It's okay to cry and let it out, even if you're already spent."

My heart beats harder and my breathing becomes more difficult with every passing second that I absorb his statement. I search his eyes for something and he must see the panic in mine.

"Or we can do something else?" he says.

"Like what?" I ask him.

He clicks his tongue, his gaze on my face, but not my eyes. Finally, he takes his hand away and types something into the search bar on his computer.

He pulls up a book of poetry. Robert Frost.

I eye him curiously and he pets my hair before pulling my head closer to rest on his shoulder. I get comfortable as he says, "I can read to you?"

My heart hurts so much in this moment. Not the pain of what I've lost, but the pain that I have something so beautiful and something I'm so grateful for, and yet I still have these moments.

I nod against his shoulder and say, "Please."

I could listen to his deep, rugged voice read poetry to me in the dark for hours.

I could rest in his warm embrace for days.

I could stay here with this man forever.

I T WASN'T SUPPOSED TO BE LIKE THIS. IT WASN'T supposed to be this much more. Two weeks have passed and it's all become more and more normal. More and more it feels like I've finally won her over.

I watch Jules as she licks ice cream from her spoon, her tongue flat against the bottom and mindlessly watches the news. Her notepad is in her lap with the pen on top although she was writing when I walked in here. It's 4:00 a.m. and she can't sleep.

My mother used to feed me ice cream every night before bed. I had to be in my room and under the sheets as soon as I was finished, but I got ice cream every night. She made to keep a variety of flavors on hand; I wanted something different every night. Mom always ate strawberry, though. It was her favorite.

Jules glances over at me, a flirtatious look in her eyes. "Do you want some?" she asks, maneuvering her body in catlike motions to crawl over to me.

Even though I shake my head, there's a small smile on my lips as I wrap my arm around her and place my hand on her thigh to scoot her closer to me.

She moans softly as she scoops up a bit of cherry ice cream from the bowl. That move has to be intentional but her gaze stays on the television as if it's not. Maneuvering on the sofa, I readjust myself in my pajama pants.

She peeks at me, blushing and then brushes her arm against my bare chest.

"You're sweet to get me this," she says with that look in her eyes. The look that tells me I've made her happier than she thought she would be. "Thank you," she adds and plants a small kiss on my shoulder.

Staying up to distract her wasn't my intention when I came out here, but I don't mind. Truthfully, I couldn't sleep either. I felt the absence of her warmth the moment she got up. For such a graceful woman, she's not very quiet getting out of bed.

I gave her a few minutes to see what she would do, peeking in the doorway to the living room as she got lost in her words. Watching as she sat cross-legged on the sofa, leaning over her notepad and scribbling like mad. It wasn't until she started to cry that I came into the room. I thought she needed me; I thought it was about him.

But she said they were happy tears, like the kind you cry when you've gotten closure. I don't know why that hurts me more.

"No problem, I wanted to get out anyway."

"Did you go for a run?" she asks me, eating the last of the ice cream and facing me. I shake my head no. I don't have time for that right now. Usually she's in bed when I run early in the morning and then shower before she's gotten up. It's been a week of her staying at my place and that being the routine.

"My fault?" she asks and scrunches her nose, not liking that she's thrown off my schedule.

"It doesn't matter," I tell her. It truly doesn't. "I'll make it up later tonight."

She hums a small sound and then adjusts on the sofa. "Will you come by my place tonight? Instead of here?"

I answer easily, not thinking twice, "Of course. I may be late; I have a lot of things to wrap up at the office."

She straddles me then, a leg on either side of my hips until she settles into my lap. I let my hands rest on her ass as she drops the empty bowl and spoon beside us on the sofa, the spoon clinking as she shoves them farther away.

"Mr. Thatcher," she says as she wraps her arms around my neck and squares her shoulders. "You're going to be late. I need you to stay at the office … and help me …" Her long lashes flutter as she bites down on her lip and continues, "… to file the paperwork."

An asymmetric grin finds its way to my lips as she laughs at her own attempt to be a sultry secretary. I can tell she's holding it in, not taking it too seriously at all. Her straddling me though, that has nothing to do with role play.

Glancing at the clock behind her, I note that I have another hour at least before I need to get going. "I think you may be mistaken, sweetheart," I tell her.

She rocks herself against me and gives me a smoldering look. It's one I don't get often, one full of confidence and determination. But damn, when she does give it to me, it drives me wild. If anything, this woman knows what she wants and with the tension gone between us, she wants me.

"You need your exercise, Mr. Thatcher." She drops her voice low and slides the straps to her silk nightgown off her creamy shoulders, exposing her breasts. They're small but fit perfectly in my hand.

With a groan and another rock of her hips, my dick stirs in my pants and I sit back on the sofa, thrusting my hips once and making her gasp as she reaches out to steady herself by clinging to me.

My hands wrap around her small waist as she kisses my jaw. I don't know when it happened, but my control has waned with Jules. I love it.

This is such a fucking mess. A beautiful mess.

CHAPTER

twenty

Julia

Happy is relative.

An emotion in time.

Guilt waits in shadows,

Makes you pay for your crime.

When push comes to shove,

And the two have to meet.

You'll be judged, never loved.

It's all bittersweet.

I BREATHE IN THE STEAM OF THE HOT COFFEE IN MY hands. It's the most amazing smell this early in the morning. That or Mason's pillow. I don't know what it is about the masculine way he smells that drives me crazy. Each morning I pull his pillow out from under him and take it as his alarm goes off.

I can't stop the smile that spreads across my face remembering this morning how he flipped me over and "punished" me for it. Maybe things are moving along too fast, but for the first time in a long time, I'm happy. Genuinely happy.

"Stop smiling like that," Maddie playfully scolds from across the table as she blows on her latte. She lifts the cup to her lips and eyes me before taking a sip. The smile doesn't fade; her next comment only makes it grow larger. "You're making me jealous."

"That is the power of sex," Sue says as she takes her seat across from me. Her coffee is in a to-go cup in her hand, so I imagine she'll be leaving shortly. She sets her bag on the floor and slips onto the stool easily. "It's about time you girls caught on and decided to get some." A coy smile lifts up the corners of her lips as she adds, "Well, except for Kat since she's married."

Maddie laughs into her cup and Kat gives Sue a cold look for a moment then shrugs. "He's good at what he does," Kat says but we all know there have been some complaints recently in that department. Not the bedroom per se but the lack of anything happening in the bedroom.

Whenever Kat looks at me, it takes me down from this high. She represents what I once had and what I should really be striving for. She has a loving husband, a stable and growing career. Children are in her future. I know they'll get over this hump. She loves him and he loves her. Every marriage goes through ups and downs. That's what everyone told me when Jace and I were working out our problems.

I set the cup down on the table and try to stop being … whatever it is that's come over me.

"Is it different?" Maddie asks me as she crumples the wrapper from Kat's straw. She has both hands on it, balling up the small white paper into a perfect circle. "Like since you were only with Jace before this new guy?" she adds and then peers up at me. Gauging my reaction.

The mention of his name … It still affects me. I think it always will. Maddie has horrible timing, though.

"At first." I take a sip of coffee and try not to let the overthinking and insecurity rule this conversation. Baby steps. "It felt like I was cheating on him," I croak out, my chest feeling tight. "But that was in the beginning and it's been a few weeks now, so …"

"Cheating?" Sue's reaction is complete with a huff. "Um no, that's what he did to you," Sue says with a firm voice that grabs my attention. She rests a hand on my forearm. "Moving on is *not* cheating … But you know you two …" she trails off then purses her lips with her eyes on me as if she doesn't know if she should say what's on her mind.

"Say it." My voice is strong as I speak. I just want to get it out there, like ripping off a bandage. Even if it hurts, I need to hear it. I didn't expect her next statement, though.

"I worry about you and Mason." It's like being thrown into ice water. I thought she had something to say about Jace. She didn't really care for him. She didn't hide it either. I wasn't prepared for her to talk about Mason, though. "It doesn't have anything to do with Jace." She waves her hand through the air as if to thoroughly drive home that message and then continues. "You know I never liked Jace much, especially after he hurt you." *Cheating. After cheating on me.* That's what she means. We'd only ever been with each other, so he said he'd been curious and he swore it was a mistake. I forgave him. We moved past that together. Sue never did but it wasn't her marriage and it wasn't her decision.

"Why are you worried?" I ask cautiously, tapping my nails along the side of the cup and removing the thoughts of that infidelity from my mind. "It's nothing serious." I bite the inside of my cheek; even to me, that sounded like a lie.

"That right there," Sue says as she leans back and points her finger at me. "I worry that you don't know what casual dating is or how to act with a fuck buddy, or whatever this is for Mason."

If they could hear the way my heart protests, she'd be doubly worried.

I clear my throat and spit out my next words. "He said he could give me more so it's not exactly just for fun." The tips of my fingers tingle and then go numb as both Sue and Maddie stare at me for a moment. *Say something.*

"What?" Maddie interjects, scooting her stool closer to the table. Her pink dress is pulled tight across her breasts as she leans forward and says, "What did he mean by 'more?'" She's as giddy as a schoolgirl.

"Yeah, what the fuck did he mean by more?" Sue asks, her skepticism obvious. Even Kat looks up from her phone to listen. She's barely said a word since sitting down other than to apologize for having to work and that she swears she's listening. I suppose now she really is.

"I don't know. I just ..." I stop and focus on Sue, my former cheerleader and the one I know I need to convince. "I was worried too," I say, making sure I'm careful with my words, "and I told him that I didn't know if I could handle 'just sex' because I would probably want more, and he said he could give me that." I think back to that night just two weeks ago, or has it been more now? I'm fairly certain that's what I said and how he answered. "It makes me feel secure, that I can be open about how I'm feeling and that he's receptive to it."

Maddie lets out a small sigh of satisfaction, like a young girl in puppy love. She's the only one obviously happy about what I've said. Sue taps her nails rhythmically on the table and Kat hasn't moved, still watching me like a hawk. Like I'm prey and she's just circling in the skies above, waiting to strike.

"Can I just ask a question?" Kat says, setting down her phone and turning her full attention to me. "Why him? Are you sure you want more ... and with him?"

"Okay ... I didn't expect that as the follow-up question." It takes a moment for me to put my thoughts into words. "Mason is nothing like the man I *should* be with. But that man is gone and I'm not interested in replacing him."

I take another sip of coffee, feeling defensive and like I'm not sure that I really want to even have this conversation.

"Are you wanting to settle down with him?" Kat asks and waits for me to look at her. "Like are you dating, dating?"

"I'm not settling down or replacing—" Jace's name gets caught in my throat.

"Oh no, oh no." Kat's quick to correct herself, reaching out for me even though my hands are now clasped in my lap. "I didn't mean ... I don't know what I mean."

"Maybe he's a rebound," Sue chimes in with a shrug and then looks up at the menu on the other side of the room. The text is fairly large, but she's not reading it. All four of us have that menu memorized. "It doesn't have to be serious," she says and the other two women all nod in agreement, but I'm certain it's to placate me.

"Yeah," I say noncommittally, holding up my coffee and looking back at Kat for her response. "What if he's just a rebound?"

Kat picks up her phone again but she doesn't look at it. She bites her lip and asks, "Can we meet him?"

"For fuck's sake, Kat," Sue says from across the table, practically glaring at her. "You don't introduce a rebound to your friends."

"Is that a rule?" Kat bites back. "He likes drinks, we like drinks, let's all just have drinks."

"It's weird!" Sue's brow is comically raised as she stares back at Kat like she can't be serious. "Just let her do what she wants to do," she says and Sue's last sentence is hushed.

"I'd like to meet him," Maddie says with a sweet, innocent tone. Staring at each one of my friends in turn, I know they're all looking out for me. All nervous like I was weeks ago.

"I've got this," I say to all three of them at once. "It's just sex, but there's a level of respect and understanding." I nod my head. "That's what the *more* is."

A soft sigh leaves me and I feel like I've fixed my nonexistent problem. That's exactly what this is. "It's just a mutually beneficial arrangement with respect, and sex of course."

Both Kat and Sue are silent, each nodding and probably

not convinced with my words. Each for their own reason, and I love them for their concern.

"I have a meeting with my CPA," I say as I glance down at my phone. I was going to walk there but there's no way in hell I'm going to make it on time now. "I have to go," I huff out as I reach down to grab my leather tote off the floor.

"Hey," Kat says. "You're happy?" she asks with all seriousness.

I stand up, slinging the purse over my shoulder and pushing the stool back. "Yeah," I say and that smile comes back. "I'm happy."

I expect some kind of guilt or feeling of inevitable doom, but the girls all smile and Maddie squeals with delight. My chest feels empty, as if I'm lying to myself and afraid that someone will expose it. But I am happy. This is what happiness feels like, isn't it?

"That's what matters," Kat says with finality.

"Damn right," Sue says, adding her two cents as she grabs her purse to join me.

"Want to share a cab?" she asks, the conversation of Mason and whatever the hell I'm doing with him long gone. At least for now.

twenty-one

Julia

THIS OFFICE SUCKS. EVEN AS A WRITER, THERE ISN'T a better word to describe it that comes to mind. For starters, it's always dark. Crossing my ankles and shifting in the chair, I don't understand why Mr. Allen Walker never opens the curtains. I used to joke with Kat that he's really a vampire. The plain white shades aren't thick but they're very good at blocking out what little sunlight would shine through the windows to my right. The office practically brushes against the neighboring building. Through the small gap where the fabric panels meet, I can see the old brick from Parks Towers next door. I'd rather look at that and have some sunlight than stare at closed curtains.

I scoot back on the chair with my purse in my lap, feeling more and more uncomfortable.

"Miss Summers." Allen addresses me as he always has since I was a little girl and even after I was married, but it feels different now. He shuts the door behind him, a smile on his face as he shoves his wire-rimmed glasses up the bridge of his nose. Fine lines and wrinkles crease around his eyes as he holds out a hand for me. I stand up, the lightweight chair scooting back on the thin carpet as I shake his hand.

"It's been too long," he says warmly. I nod my head and smile politely although I disagree.

The last time I was here was a few days after Jace passed away. That day, Allen made sure to call me by my legal name and not the name I grew up with. The memory makes the tiny hairs on the back of my neck stand on edge as I clear my throat and retake my seat. Uncomfortable as it may be, it's the only one I've got.

It seems he's forgotten that Summers still isn't my legal name. I look down at my barren hand and think that's my fault. I took my ring off months ago. That was easy, all things considered, but changing my name is something else entirely. It would be like erasing Jace, and I won't do that.

"It has," I say lightheartedly, pulling down my light gray pencil skirt and readjusting in my seat as he takes his on the other side of the desk.

My chair is small and uncomfortable, while his is large and practically molds to his body.

I shake off the anxiety running through me as I

straighten my back and ask, "What is it that you needed me to sign?"

A rough laugh fills the room as he shakes his head then says, "Not just yet. I need decisions, Miss Summers."

My body tenses at hearing my name but I bite my tongue. "Of course. What kind of decisions?"

"As acting advisor to your estate and investments, I need you to look these over," he says as he pulls out several folders and sets them in front of me. My brow furrows as I open the first and then the second. I don't know a thing about any of these. I've never been involved with investments and stocks.

"I—" I start to say and then let out an uneasy breath as I continue, "Is there a way that I could take your advisement, Mr. Walker?"

He turns his head to the side and raises his brow as if to say I should have done that a long time ago. "I advised your husband when he made these transactions. Unfortunately, the choices now are to stay and keep your money in a losing bet or to withdraw and lose a substantial amount."

My body goes cold as I take in his words. "I don't understand."

"Mr. Anderson was adamant about buying these properties and he assured me that it would be worth the risk, but I've waited over nine months now and there's still no growth since the drop."

"The drop?" I ask him, feeling the blood drain from my face. Jace never mentioned buying any properties. "This was with our personal assets? Not the business?"

He nods at my question, taking in a deep inhale. "They were on the decline when he purchased them. He was a bit surprised that they continued to drop, yes." Mr. Walker leans back, waiting for my reaction.

"How much of a decline?"

"Fourteen million."

I close my eyes, gripping the edge of the seat for a moment. Fourteen million. That's … I can barely think straight. When we married, I know my assets were around twenty million. How could he take such a large chunk and not disclose any of this to me?

"There's still nearly six million invested so you can withdraw if you'd like. I like to say you've never lost money until you sell, but the fact is that I still believe you're not going to see the return your deceased husband was banking on."

My entire body is tense and on edge. Fourteen fucking million dollars. Fourteen million! I want to scream and curse, I want to throw up. It takes me a moment to gather myself to be able to respond.

"Why am I just learning about this now?" I ask him in a voice that's more filled with anger than full of shock and grief. I flip through a few pages with shaking hands, reading through them, but not actually reading a word.

Fourteen million and now I can only sell for six? I'm going to be sick.

"Well, it was stable but it's recently gone up just a touch, and I'm of the opinion that you should take advantage of the current climate."

My mouth hangs open just a bit as I look back at Mr. Walker, eyeing his blue suit and thin red tie. I blink a few times, then fall back into my chair and shut the folder.

"Is this all of the investments?" I ask, realizing how little

I knew of Jace's dealings. For the first time in my life, I'm worried. I've never had to concern myself with income. I've been blessed and grateful, but I wasn't careless. This right here, this feels like careless to a maximum degree and I'm embarrassed. I'm sick to my stomach and mortified.

I swallow thickly and cross my legs, not able to stop my foot from rocking back and forth in the air. It's only as I sit here, my mouth feeling dry and my body like ice, that I realize I know nothing about my current financial situation. I trusted Jace to handle all this.

"Allen," I say as I pick at the clutch in my lap and look up at the man I grew up with. He's an old friend of my father and I do trust him, but right now I feel unsettled.

"Yes, Julia?" he asks.

"Financially speaking," I say then pause, taking in a steadying breath before I continue, "is everything all right?"

He takes a moment to answer me and the time ticks by slowly while I wait for his reply.

He opens his mouth, looking down at the desk but doesn't say a word and dread hits me. "You're going to be fine, Miss Summers. You will be." He puts strength behind his words and looks straight into my eyes as he speaks.

I should be relieved, but he didn't exactly answer my question.

"It's going to be difficult getting this money back, especially considering the amount of debt you went into when remodeling your home."

"What?" I feel struck by his last statement. "We didn't go into debt." I got everything I wanted on that remodel because it was funded by the money I'd made with my first publishing contract. It was my personal reward to myself. "I know how every penny was spent and I know it was paid for with the money I brought in."

I can't help that my voice is full of panic and my tone is accusatory. I sit there on the edge of my seat, waiting for a response from Allen. I swallow the lump in my throat as he clicks on his mouse and takes off his glasses, scrolling through a row of spreadsheets.

"The remodel put you in quite a bit of debt, I'm sorry to say." I shake my head in disbelief as he adds, "If you were to sell the apartment, it could potentially make its money back."

Chills travel down every inch of my body as I take one breath, then two. "What apartment?" I ask him, my voice deathly low.

"The one downtown on Pacific Street. The one that was remodeled this past year."

My world spins on its axis and I grip the arms of the chair. "Mr. Walker? I don't own an apartment on Pacific." I lick my dry lips, my body coiled, my muscles feeling tense and tight.

There's a pause, filled with more ticks of the clock. "Well, your husband did and that was left to you. As was everything else in his will. So you do own an apartment on Pacific."

"Why wasn't I told about this sooner?" I ask, focusing my attention on something other than the fact that my husband bought and remodeled an apartment without me knowing. Betrayal consumes me but oddly, I feel numb to it. As if I'd known all along. As if I'd turned a blind eye. It's not naivety or trustworthiness. It's me being stupid. All the late nights at the office, all the weekend trips … My skin pricks and a numbing tingle goes through me. He told me it was just once when I found him in bed with another woman. I try to breathe in easier, but my throat is closing.

Disbelief is outrageous. He didn't. He wasn't cheating on me. There's no way.

"You were given the paperwork, Julia. You signed everything after the funeral."

I look up at Allen, feeling betrayed by him just as much as my husband. I want to question him, scream at him. But at the same time, I don't care. I had this coming to me.

I didn't know about this debt. I didn't know about the apartment. I didn't know about a damn thing because I trusted them.

"I was mourning," I say and I can barely get out the words. They're cold and stagnant. Just a lame excuse for my ignorance.

"I'm sorry, Mrs. Anderson." He starts to say something else but I rise from my chair, a bitter taste in my mouth as I bite out, "Don't call me that."

He cocks a brow at me as I start to leave. "You need to sign these, Julia," he says matter-of-factly, speaking to me like my father does. Ignoring my emotions and simply telling me what I need to do.

My shoulders shudder as I open the door with my back to him and grip the cold brass knob for dear life.

"Email them to me," I tell him. "Email *everything* to me."

"I suggest you read them quickly," he says to my back as I walk through the door.

I nod my head but I don't verbally respond; I don't trust

myself to speak. I don't look back at him and I don't even breathe until I'm in the elevator. I can't relax though, even in the empty, closed-off space. I want to sag against the wall, gripping the steel handles. I want to hit the emergency button and give in to the pathetic emotions of sadness and betrayal.

More than any of that, I want to see this apartment and I want to see how the hell my money was spent. I need to get myself together and figure out how deep of a hole I'm in and more importantly, how to get out.

twenty-two

Mason

KNOCK. *KNOCK. KNOCK.* MY KNUCKLES RAP against Jules's door quickly. A second passes and I take a look around, shoving my hands into my suit pockets. The Upper East Side screams old money and is far more traditional compared to downtown where I live.

My father's home is only a few blocks from here.

Jules's street is different from where I grew up, though. The cream stone and intricate carvings have history to them. Real history. I glance back at the small iron picket fence and gate in front of her house. The city sidewalk is just beyond it, littered with people walking by.

I rock on my heels and knock again, wondering what they think of this house.

It looks like wealth and with the well-maintained garden, it only adds to the beauty of the old house.

I've been inside Julia's home a handful of times now, and it's odd that I feel nervous about being here now. It's because I'm coming through the front door in daylight. I smirk at the thought, but it's true. My forehead pinches as I knock again, using the large iron door knocker this time.

The door swings open and there's my Jules, but she doesn't stay there long. She leaves the door hanging open and disappears inside, claiming that she has to get something, but I didn't hear what.

"Jules?" I call out after her, placing a hand on the heavy red door and peeking inside after her. The door creaks and I second-guess going inside after her, but she doesn't answer me.

Taking a few steps inside, I flick on the light switch to my right before shutting the front door. A large crystal chandelier lights up the large hallway. The ceilings are taller than they seem at night. Paisley wallpaper in shades of pale blue and cream covers the upper half of the walls with a deeper blue painted below the chair rail.

It's modern and updated with a feminine and elegant touch, definitely not my taste, but it still holds the classic beauty of the home. A mix of modern and traditional. It's all Jules.

"Jules," I call out again, pocketing my keys and wiping my shoes on the mat before stepping onto the plush area rug in the foyer.

"I'm sorry," I hear Jules say through the hall before I see

her. She rounds the corner of what looks like the dining room, both hands on her left ear as she slips an earring into place. She's barefoot, wearing a navy blue dress with white polka dots and a skinny white leather belt at her waist. She's gorgeous as always, but something's off. Something's wrong although I can't tell what.

"Everything okay?" I ask carefully, staying right where I am as she bends down to slip on a pair of navy blue heels.

"Fine, just fine." She shakes out her hair and stands upright, taking a step toward me before turning on her heel and heading back the way she came.

I follow her into the dark dining room. It doesn't look a damn thing like a dining room, though. The furniture is all here, but stacks of papers cover the table, along with a laptop. On top of the buffet is a printer. She's using the room as an office.

"Sorry about the mess." Her voice is dampened as she turns around. "I just need my purse." She starts to walk past me, making her way to the door, but I put my arm out, my palm against the doorway and wait for her to look at me.

When she does, my heart drops. Her eyes are rimmed in red. Although her makeup is flawless, she can't hide that she was crying. Not from me.

"What's wrong?" It comes out as a question, but it's more of a command.

Her lips are the same dark red shade they were when I first met her and as she parts them, my eyes are drawn to them. She doesn't say anything though, she merely licks them and turns away from me. For the first time since we met, she's deliberately disobeying me. Hiding from me.

"I don't want to talk about it." She pushes my arm away, to leave me and deny me again, but I'm not letting this go. I grip her hip tight enough that she stops and looks at me.

"That's not how this works. I told you, if you're with me, you're with me." Her hard expression vanishes as I speak to her, replaced by nothing but hurt.

"You don't own me." She bites out the words meant to make me mad, meant to destroy the ease between us.

"It's not about that, Jules." My voice is low as I release her. She doesn't walk off; she stands there waiting for my next move. She has to know how good this is between us. She knows whatever the hell it is, I'll take the burden from her.

"I don't like seeing you upset." I bring my lips closer to hers. "Tell me what's wrong, so I can fix it." I open my mouth to give her a reason not to push me away, to tell her that she can trust me. That I care for her, to tell her everything I know she wants to hear, but I can't bring myself to do it. Luckily, I don't have to.

She moves her hands to her face for only a moment, her expression crumpling before she falls into my chest. She gives in to me so easily. It's addictive. I wrap my arms around her, feeling her shoulders shake and shudder with a soft sob.

"I didn't want to cry again," she says into my chest, muffled by the suit jacket and her hands still covering her face. She inhales deeply as I bend down, running my hand up and down her back in soothing strokes and kiss her hair repeatedly.

"It's all right, whatever it is, I'll take care of it." I don't know why I promise her something I know I may not be able to accommodate. It's stupid of me to say it and it gets the reaction it should from an independent woman like Jules. She pushes

away from me, wiping under her eyes and taking a shuddering breath.

"It's nothing you—" she stops to close her eyes and calm
herself. "It can't be fixed." She glances at a photograph in a silver frame behind her on the wall and then wipes under her
eyes again, walking to a large mirror on the far side of the dining room.

I only catch a glimpse of the photograph before turning my
back to it. It's from her wedding day and he's in it. Obviously.
He was her husband after all.

Panic races through me and a sick feeling churns my stomach. "It's about your husband?"

She peeks over her shoulder, looking guilty. The fucking
irony. "I'm sorry."

"Don't be." My steps are just as careful as my words as I
walk over to her, placing a hand on her delicate shoulder and
watching her in the mirror. "Is everything okay?"

"No," she answers quickly and sniffles once. She's already
fixed her makeup and looking as though she's back to pretending nothing's wrong, but then her eyes meet mine in the mirror. Her baby blues are filled with anger and an unforgiving
chill. "He had an apartment," she says with certainty. "A place
for his mistresses or one-night stands or whatever they were."

I attempt a look that expresses shock, but none of that is
news to me. I wasn't sure if she knew. For the first time since
meeting her, I feel guilty for not telling her. As if somehow I
could have saved her this heartache if I'd given her a piece of
the truth. Only a piece.

She laughs something wicked and sad, a mix of both as
she shakes her head and says, "You think I'm pathetic, don't

you? A housewife who had no idea what her husband was doing behind her back." Her voice is strained toward the end of the statement and the strength leaves her with each word. I hate how she does this. How she blames herself, belittles herself. She's stronger than she knows. And worth so much more.

"What he did is a reflection of himself, not you." Taking another step closer to her, I stand behind her with her back touching my chest, just barely. "You aren't pathetic, Jules." I kiss the side of her neck, my eyes on hers in the mirror as I say, "I'd never think that."

"I do," she says. "He cheated once. He was so upset. He cried and swore up and down he'd never do it again. And I believed him."

My heart beats erratically and I'm desperate to ask who he cheated with. To see if Jules knows her name. I keep my mouth closed and wait for more from her.

"I believed him." The pain comes through in her words as she turns in my arms, placing her small hands on the lapels of my jacket. Her eyes travel along the buttons of my shirt, her fingers soon following. "I really thought he was good to me."

I pull away slightly, taking her wrists gently in my hands and getting her attention. "I'm sorry," I tell her with true sympathy but it comes out rough and short, shocking her.

She pulls away from me. "I am too," she says to the ground, turning around and brushing the hair out of her face. "I think maybe tonight—"

I can hear the excuse already, I can see her pushing me away and I'm not going to let it happen. There's no way I'm leaving until I know she's still mine.

Each time she questions me or what's going on between us, I feel the need to hold her tighter.

"Come here," I command her. She stops in her tracks, peeking up at me through thick lashes with a question in her eyes. She doesn't ask whatever it is though, she obeys me, taking two small steps back to me in those heels.

"He was a fool to cheat on you." As I speak, I brush my thumb along her delicate jaw.

She huffs a small laugh at me and I didn't expect that. I narrow my eyes as she says, "You're a well-known player, Mason." The humor vanishes and her smile fades to nothing as she adds, "You don't have to pretend to care. I'll be fine."

My chest tightens with anger. She can have an attitude about him all she wants. But there are boundaries when it comes to us. I won't allow her to demean our relationship. "Bend over the table." I grit the words out between my teeth. I don't even think twice about it.

She merely blinks at me, shocked. She should have known better.

"Now, Jules." My voice comes out hard and I almost take it back. But this is the man I am and this is what she's going to get. There's a war brewing between us, causing the air to suffocate me. I need Jules for the woman she truly is, not this version that the memory of her husband brought back.

She holds my gaze for a moment and my pulse flickers, thinking I'm going to lose her, but she caves before I even blink, submitting just like she wants to. *Good girl.*

She presses her hips against the table, slowly leaning down to lay her upper body against the tabletop. That's the beauty of our relationship—she wants to give in. She desperately wants to trust someone and not be hurt.

"Lift up your dress."

I hear her breathing pick up. "Mason—" she starts to say.

"No, no talking. No excuses." I palm my dick but I have no intention of fucking her. This is all about pleasing her and showing her what she means to me. Showing her what I can give her. "Lift up your dress and show me your pussy." I crouch down behind her as she slowly pulls the cotton fabric up her thighs and exposes her black panties.

My fingers trail up her thighs slowly to her ass, then up to the small of her back, pressing her down flat. I carefully push the panties out of my way, taking a languid lick of her pussy. My tongue brushes along the lacy material and I almost rip them as I pull them farther away, but decide to put my fingers to better use.

I play at her clit first, gently running my nail across the swollen nub and then back to her entrance. Goosebumps travel along her body. It doesn't take long before she's glistening for me, her wet folds begging for my attention.

She hums as she relaxes on the table. It's going to be a slow build for her. I don't care about our dinner reservations. She'll have to deal with being late.

I slide my middle finger deep inside her as I stand up behind her, keeping my other hand on her hip. Her eyes are closed as I fuck my finger in and out of her, loosening her up and testing her readiness. Remembering my anger, I pick up my pace and slip another finger into her.

"Come on, Jules," I say and kiss the back of her neck. "Tell me again how I don't care." A strangled cry leaves her as I press against her clit and she whimpers an apology, still struggling to get away from the intense pleasure.

I push three fingers deep inside of her tight pussy, stroking against her front wall right where that sensitive bundle of nerves is and I don't let up as she moans. Her body writhes in an attempt to get away, pulling at the tablecloth and kicking one leg out, but I've got her pinned down to the table with my hip. One hand continues to rub her hard nub ruthlessly, while the other is inside of her dripping wet cunt.

"I would never cheat on you." And then I tell her, "I'd never take advantage of you." She has no idea how true those words are.

"Mason." She cries out my name as she tightens around my fingers. *My. Name.* I want her to come undone screaming my name. To find her release with what I do to her all because she let me. All she has to do is give in to me.

"Tell me you understand, Jules." I'm not letting her get off until I hear her say it. I swear to God I'll stop it all if she doesn't give me that.

I may be holding back the truth, but I'm not lying.

"Yes," she moans out as she thrashes her head.

"Yes what?"

"Yes, Mason."

I smile into her hair, slowing my pace and making her whimper as she desperately rocks her pussy into my hand.

"Yes, Mason what?"

My heart thrums in my chest, but I need to hear her say it. I don't want that shit with her husband having anything to do with what we have with each other.

"You wouldn't do that." She bites her lip looking back at me with a plea for mercy. "You wouldn't hurt me."

I crash my lips into hers and fuck her cunt with my fingers, relentlessly pressing against her swollen nub. She cries into my mouth as her release hits her hard, her head banging on the table as she tries to pull away from the intensity. I don't let up, coaxing out every single bit of her orgasm from her.

Her back bows with tremors still rocking through her. This is how I want her, always.

No worries in her soft blue eyes, only a look of pleasure on her face.

A look that I put there.

My dick's hard as a fucking rock, but this isn't for me. She looks over her shoulder, still panting with her fingers gripping the cream tablecloth. She's waiting for me to take from her. To fuck her right here and now. But that picture of her husband is right there.

Part of me wants to do it. To force that beautiful cunt to spasm on my dick in front of him. To show him how a real man would treat her. But I can't. I need to get the fuck out of here.

I pull her hips back, her ass pressed against my hard cock.

Her lashes flutter and her wide eyes look back at me, waiting for whatever I have to say. "Dinner first, sweetheart." I kiss her gently then brush her clit through her panties and smile as a tremor runs through her body and forces her head back against my shoulder.

I kiss the dip in her neck and whisper in her ear, "Tonight."

CHAPTER
twenty-three

Julia

> *Naive and stupid, this shit has to end.*
>
> *What did I think? I can't comprehend.*
>
> *Mistakes belong where they're made, in the past.*
>
> *I knew better, I knew this wouldn't last.*
>
> *It left me numb, dead in the ditch.*
>
> *Love is wrong and my heart's a bitch.*

I STARE OUT THE WINDOW OF MASON'S CAR AS THE CITY lights flicker on, although it's not even dark yet. Classical music fills the cabin and my body is still humming from the rush of pleasure he gave me moments ago.

But nothing is okay.

I need to end this. What's the saying? Get over one man by getting under another? I'm not interested for two reasons:

1. I'm not over what Jace did to me.

2. I'm not ready for another man to do the same.

That's what I've been telling myself all day ever since I left Mr. Walker's office. I don't have time for fooling around and I'm not ready for anything serious. And that's what this has become; it's staring me right in the eyes.

This is serious. It's too serious. I'm suffocating and what's worse is that the minute I'm with Mason, the very second that he looks at me just right, says all the right things, the moment his lips press against mine and his skin touches mine, I'm done for.

I'm head over heels for Mason. I didn't even hesitate when he told me to bend over my dining room table for him. I didn't hesitate in the parking garage either. He's had me from the very night we met.

There's something about him that makes me weak, and I'm so very tired of being weak.

I can't do this. I need to end it. Just the very thought … it hurts.

"I—" I start to give him the honest truth, my whole truth. I don't know how to be okay on my own and that's my priority right now. That's the bottom line. Pressing my back against the smooth leather and glancing at him in the driver's seat, the words are right there on the tip of my tongue. *I can't do this anymore.* I don't know what's real and where I stand with anything, and I need space to figure it all out, but my phone goes off in my purse, the ringtone loud and obnoxious.

I let out a frustrated sigh, pulling it out and just missing a call from my mother. I almost call her back, but then I see the text messages. Dozens of them.

I hit the first one from Kat.

The last message makes me sick to my stomach. *It's going to be okay.*

What's going to be okay? What now? I scroll up to read the messages starting from the top.

OMG I just saw, are you okay?

Minutes later:

I can't believe he did that to you!

Everything is all right, we're going to get it taken down.

A chill slips like ice down my skin.

I don't have to ask her what she's talking about. Maddie sent me a link to the online article. It's already been taken down, but she screenshotted it.

My heart sinks as I skim it, but my eyes keep flickering to the picture. It shows me and Jace, and right next to it, Jace and some beautiful woman. It's obvious what the article was about and it makes me sick. My throat goes dry and tears prick my eyes.

Really? They posted this now? I think back to who I told and who would have heard about the apartment. It's up for sale as of 4:00 p.m. today, so that was only five hours for someone to dig up the dirt. I can barely breathe.

"Jules?" Mason's voice doesn't stop me from reading. It's not the worst thing that's been said about me but it's not kind, and it's not true. I wasn't turning a blind eye. There's a difference. I truly didn't know.

My anger only increases when I see what they're saying

about me now. I'm not running around town. I'm not spreading my legs … I can't even finish this article. The last paragraph I read is:

Now that her husband is gone, she's letting loose but choosing the same kind of man. The socialite doesn't seem to care about her reputation anymore.

Whoever gave the details to the *Daily Word* knows that I'm seeing Mason but they don't know how often, since they claim he cheated on me two nights ago. I've been with him every single night for weeks now.

Every insecurity in me is replaced by raw rage.

Heat dances along my skin. I'm not this person that they're painting me to be. I'm on the edge of breaking into a million pieces. I told Mason this is why I didn't want us to be public. I knew something like this would happen. *I knew it!*

Is that a stage of grief? Wanting to murder everyone?

I just want to be left alone.

I bite the inside of my cheek and place the phone in my lap as Mason's hand lands on my thigh.

"What's wrong?" he asks, his eyes darting from me to the road.

"Take me home," I say. I don't bother to answer his question and I lick my dry lips. My heart hurts too much.

"What's wrong?" This time his voice is harder. The one he uses right before he turns me into a damn rag doll for his will and then magically fixes everything.

I'm done listening to men and I'm done rolling over for them.

"What's wrong is that this isn't working for me anymore," I finally tell him, although I don't know how, in an even tone that splits my heart right down the center. Guilt consumes the anger immediately. It slices through every emotion with the sharpest knife, the cut clean and quick, but the blood is pouring out and I know it's not going to stop anytime soon.

I lean my head back against the headrest. "I want to go home."

Mason's quiet although his pissed-off expression reads loud and clear as he pushes down his turn signal.

The silence stretches between us and this awkward, horrific dread makes me squirm. I find myself going back to the screenshots. What's really and truly messed up is that I feel safe and happy with Mason. If it were a different time, I could easily fall for him. I *am* easily falling for him. It's as if I'm tumbling down a well in slow motion, giving me enough time as I fall to look up and admire the stonework before crashing to the black bottom of the abyss.

"I can't do this anymore," I say, reaffirming myself and him. "I need to be on my own."

He doesn't look at me and a long moment passes before he says anything at all. Mason's voice is low when he asks, "Because of an article?" He grips the leather steering wheel until his knuckles are white. "I'll take care of it," he says. I'm sure he could fix all my problems. He's so good at that.

But I need to fix myself. I need to be whole before I can give myself so completely to someone.

"It's not the article." The words drop one by one and my eyes burn.

"Is it your prick of a former husband?" he asks with

disgust so apparent, I hate him in this moment. I confided in him about my deceased husband and yes, he may have hurt me, cheated on me and lied to me, but that's not for Mason to judge. I still don't even know how to feel about it all. How dare he speak about him like that?

"That's exactly why this needs to stop." My heart rages in my chest, hating me for being so raw, but I can't stop.

"I'm not okay," I say, feeling a burn in my eyes dampened from tears, but I don't care, let them fall. Let everyone see and call me whatever they want. "I haven't been okay and I've been running from it. You can't just fix me. I can't fall into another man's arms and forget about everything I'm going through."

With shaking hands, I almost throw my phone when it pings again. The absurdity of my entire world crashing down around me feels too overwhelming. I'm too hot, too angry, too miserable.

"I just want to go home." There's a finality in the statement and it feels like razors at the back of my throat.

"Stop," Mason commands me as he slows down at a crosswalk. "Just take it easy." His entire demeanor changes to something placating, as if he's talking to a wounded animal. It only makes me angrier.

"No, I won't stop. What do you want from me, Mason?"

A part of me is hoping he really is my knight in shining armor. Part of me wants to be weak. I want him to solve all my problems and just crawl into his bed every night, moving on to a new life and leaving the old one in shattered pieces behind me.

I know it's wrong. It's giving in and denying my responsibilities. But God, I want it. My heart is suffocating, hoping for him to say just the right things to convince me to be his, to forget everything else. Just like he has from the first night I met him. "What is it that you want from me?" My voice shakes.

"Jules." He says my name and looks at me with a gaze I don't understand.

"Just tell me right now, what do you want?" I swallow the spikes growing in my throat, but they don't move. They only grow larger and sharper and make the words scrape as they leave me. "I can't give myself to you right now unless—"

"Unless what?" Mason asks so quickly he cuts me off. His reaction makes the pain that much deeper because I don't have an answer.

I can't give myself to him unless this is forever. Unless I can trust him but right now I can't trust anyone. The harsh reality is what truly does me in. I don't trust anyone anymore. I don't want to love anyone anymore.

I can't breathe as I take off my seat belt. My townhome is only a few blocks away. My shelter. My sanctuary and my grave. My hands shake as the seat belt pulls back, hissing and hating me just as much as I hate myself.

"I can't," I say. "I'm sorry," I whisper.

I unlock the door and push it open. A car drives by close, but I shut the door quickly, avoiding Mason's reach for me. His fingers brush against my back as I get out.

"Jules!" Mason calls after me. I cross the lane, the other driver beeping and holding down his horn. Go ahead, hate me too.

The sound of a door opening alerts me to the fact that Mason is out of his car, leaving it parked in the middle of the road and already holding up traffic. "Jules!" he screams but I keep running. The horns don't stop and it's not lost on me that what I did was wrong.

I rush past the onlookers and ignore the dirty looks and stares. My shoulders rise with a heavy breath. I need to go home. Tears stream down my face. I need to take care of myself and figure out what the hell I'm doing with my life.

Tires screech and make my head throb as Mason drives alongside me now, slow and causing more traffic to build up.

I ignore Mason as I whip open the iron gate. I don't stop until I'm safe inside my house, my back to the hard door, my body shaking and my heart hammering.

I hate myself for running from Mason.

But this is a reckless distraction.

I cover my mouth as another sob leaves me, slowly falling to my knees on the floor.

He's a good man and he deserves someone better than me.

Someone who doesn't have all these problems.

Someone who can fall for him freely and be with him openly.

I sag against the door, letting it all out, still hoping he'll come bang on the door and plead with me to explain. I can't be this person, though. It's better that he doesn't.

It's the way we both knew it would end. I envisioned it would be him leaving me though, not the other way around. I take a shuddering breath, feeling exactly how I should, like shit. Not that any of it matters.

It was never meant to be. That's all there is to it.

twenty-four

Mason

SEVENTEEN. I CALLED HER SEVENTEEN FUCKING TIMES. It hurts worse knowing she left me for something other than the one reason she should. Knowing that I couldn't keep her on my own. I held on too tight. It's my own fucking mistake.

But I saw what I could do for her.

What I could do *to* her.

And that made me feel … something other than this. This fucking hate that I have brewing inside of me.

What the hell did I expect? I expected to keep her. For her to learn to love me. For that to cancel out what I'd done.

The ice clinks in my glass as I grab a bottle of Macallan single malt.

No reasoning or any amount of logic justifies why I feel betrayed and alone. Not a damn explanation can leave me feeling as though this is something that doesn't need to be mended. The liquor sloshes in the bottle as I read the label, my fingers playing with the seal.

My father gave me this bottle as a gift when I started the company with Liam. When I told him I was going into business for myself, but still doing what I loved. I felt so much pride that day. My breathing quickens and my grip on the bottle tightens.

Relax. I grit my teeth, feeling an uneasy tightness settle through my body.

Jules was a sweet distraction; how fucking ironic. She pulled me away from reality. She made me feel like I had time. Like I had a choice.

I toss the seal onto my sideboard buffet, opening the bottle and not bothering to appreciate the rich scent before pouring it into the glass.

If my father were here, he'd give me hell for drinking it over ice.

"But that bastard's not here," I sneer under my breath. "No one is." The last thought leaves my chest feeling hollow. I take a long drink of the whisky that flows so easily. Burning and traveling through my chest, down deeper and stirring in the pit of my stomach. My head still tipped back I take another and finish the damn thing, the ice frigid against my lips. I slam the glass down a little harder than I should and let the liquor hit me.

It takes too long and I find myself gazing straight ahead to the family portrait sitting on top of the buffet. This room, the dining room, is the only room in the whole place where there's a picture of anyone.

The rest of the house is devoid of anything truly personal. But what do I really have that's personal anyway? My lacrosse stick and all those fucking uniforms stayed at my parents' where they belonged. I'm sure they were thrown away long ago.

I pour more of the whisky into the glass, feeling my breathing slow as my body sways and I remember the first day I walked in here.

I'd just gotten all new clothes, all new furniture, all new everything. This home was the start of the professional version of me. All that was in the cardboard box I was holding were a handful of old tee shirts and a few postcards from a friend of mine in Germany I'd met after I graduated high school and got my first job in construction. We've lost touch since then.

I take a sip, listening to the ice rattle against the glass. The whisky sits on my tongue and I press it against my teeth before swallowing. All the awards I've won are in my office. Framed and arranged just so on the wall.

My gaze drifts back to the portrait of the three of us. I'm standing between the two of them in it. I don't look a damn thing like her, like my mother. I'm the spitting image of my father. Mom's smile is soft, but her eyes are what sparkle. She was so expressive. Soft spoken, but she made what she said count.

She could make an entire room laugh by only speaking once the whole night. I let out a breath, looking at the firm hand my father has on my shoulder in the photograph.

He liked that about her. He told me once she was the perfect example of what a wife should be. That was before he caught her cheating.

I wonder if that man, the one she risked her marriage to sleep with, loved to hear her talk. I wonder if that's why she did it. Because she had more to say than just a single sentence.

I down the whisky, dragging out the chair at the head of the table and taking a seat. I sag and let my head lean back against the crest rail of the antique chair.

This room is so dark. With black textured wallpaper on the longest wall and the other three painted a soft gray, I wanted it to feel masculine. I remember telling the designer that. I told her I wanted it to feel like me.

On the right, centered in the room and next to the dark mahogany buffet, is a long gas fireplace. It's surrounded by a sleek marble hearth. More black. Even the light fixture in the room, a circular pendulum that holds the light inside, is black.

I huff a breath into the short glass and suck an ice cube into my mouth.

This is me.

A heart of fire that's never lit. A dark past that only holds a single moment of time in significance.

I wonder if that bitch designer knew what she was doing.

I kick the leg of the antique chair next to me. It's carved wood that's been stained. The deep brown leather of the chairs has a worn look to it.

What's ironic is how much I loved this room. I loved everything about it when I first laid eyes on it. The only addition I made was that fucking silver picture frame and then I filled that buffet with liquor.

Thank fuck I did that. I raise my glass even though it's empty, save for ice. "To you, you fucking prick," I toast the picture and take another ice cube into my mouth.

I crunch down, wondering if the last three words were for my father or for me.

Pushing the glass across the slick table that I've never sat at for more than a drink or two, I pull out my cell phone from my back pocket.

I fucking want Jules.

She's pure and sweet. Even if she overthinks every last detail, there's so much about her that I want to keep. I really shouldn't have her. I've already been given more than I deserve.

I can't do this anymore.

The screen lights up as I hear her words in my head. She shouldn't get to decide when it's over. Not by herself and not like that. Not because of something so fucking unimportant.

We work together. We make each other happy. I'm tired of living this life with nothing to fight for. I want her back.

My phone rings in my hand, startling me and I drop it on the table. It vibrates, moving slightly as the ringtone goes off again.

Groaning and rubbing my eyes, I feel the heat of the drunken night start to take me in before answering the call.

"Hello?" I think my voice is even. I'm fairly certain it comes out strong.

"Mason, we need to talk." I recognize Liam's voice immediately.

I brace my elbow on the table and rest my head in my hand before pinching the bridge of my nose. We do need to talk; we need to have a long talk about how I can't go through with this.

All the money is spent.

But I can't keep pushing forward.

I need to return it all to my father and cut ties. I need to turn him in.

Every bit of breath in my lungs leaves me, making my body feel light and my stomach sick. We're going to go fucking bankrupt, but I can't be under his thumb any longer.

"We need that investment from your father's firm." A sad, pathetic laugh leaves me as I register what Liam's said.

"We already have it." I stagger to the buffet, placing the phone on speaker, leaving it on the dining room table as I pour another glass. The bottle's already halfway gone. "We've already spent it," I say loud and clear as I bring the amber liquor to my lips.

This time I inhale the sweet scent. Fuck, it smells as good as it tastes.

"We need more." I gulp down the drink, staring at the phone on the table as Liam continues. "We got the estates on the Upper East Side and the committee approved the demolition plans."

As I take a step forward, I start to regret having the last two drinks. My head feels groggy and my body hot. "No, they didn't."

"I got it overturned. We've got everything approved, Mason." I can hear the glee in Liam's voice. Pride even. He claps on the other end of the phone, a rough laugh filling the room as it spins around me. "We just need that last check from your father."

Setting both of my elbows on the table to steady myself, I tell him, "We don't need shit from him."

It takes a moment for Liam to respond, "What?" He took so long I almost forgot he was on the phone.

"Are you drunk?" Liam asks, his annoyance only thinly veiled.

"No." I'm quick to deny it, but I know I am.

"What the hell's wrong with you?" he asks. "What's going on between the two of you?"

I shake my head, not wanting to answer. "We aren't taking shit from my father." It's all I can say.

"We are. We need those funds by Monday." Liam's voice is hard but also panicked.

"We'll find someone else." My eyes narrow as I steady my breathing and steel my resolve. I refuse to owe a man like him. I refuse to play by his rules.

"By Monday?" he says, raising his voice and the disbelief rings through. "Mason, we can't. We'll lose the deal. It's not like no one else was waiting for this property. It took almost a year to get it."

Liam's voice drones on as he lists off every reason why this plan is fucked. How we'll be ruined. How everything will fall around us.

I already knew it, though.

I stand, leaving the glass where it is and the bottle of whisky open, taking the phone and leaving the dining room.

"I don't give a fuck." I take a deep breath, listening to the silence on the other end of the phone. "I'm not taking another cent from him."

I have to face reality. Even if it fucking kills me.

CHAPTER
twenty-five

Julia

> *Nothing is suffocating.*
> *It cuts off the air.*
> *Nothing is drowning,*
> *But nothing is fair.*
> *Nothing to hold and nothing to thrill.*
> *When left with nothing, nothing can kill.*

THE AIR IS CRISP ON THE IRON BALCONY. THE THICK canopy of oak trees just barely blocks the sounds of the city traffic. I've always loved the colors of autumn and the way the dark green leaves thin out and shift to gorgeous reds and burnt oranges.

They'll fall and wither away to nothing. Yet every spring they come back, good as new.

I've always loved their majestic natural beauty in the middle of this concrete jungle. Not today, though.

It's not fair that they come back untarnished. It's not right that life continues after death … only for those deserving.

Bundled in my favorite cashmere throw and sipping tea, I let out a deep breath, calming myself. I twist the cap to my flask and pour a bit of tincture into my tea. A small, faint chuckle leaves me as the liquid mixes with the now lukewarm tea. *Tincture.* Really, it's just vodka.

It used to be a tincture. It used to be just enough to take the pain away.

But sips turned to bottles as I preferred to feel numb.

Today is one of those days.

If I can roll out of bed and have the strength to tuck the sheets in and fluff the pillows, the day will be okay. That's what I'd tell myself over and over again when Jace first died. Sometimes it's true. All you need to do is make your bed and somehow the day is possible. As if simply pulling the sheets tight and smoothing out all the wrinkles is enough to hide the past and put the daily routine into motion.

Some days, it's all a lie.

All the time I spent with Mason … all that time feels like a lie. Some fantasy I forced to convince myself that life could be okay again. That it could somehow mend itself.

I take a sip of the tea, but it only makes my throat feel more parched. Instead of gulping it down like I've been doing, it finds its place on the saucer and I press my palms against my sore eyes.

It's been so long since I've felt this empty. Since my heart has felt as though it's been torn open.

It doesn't make sense in the least. I was over him. I was making progress. True progress in healing by being okay with Jace being gone.

I was okay.

For the first time since his death, I felt like I had a reason to be happy. More importantly, like it was okay to be happy.

Glancing over my shoulder, I rub my tired eyes with the sleeve of my silk blouse. I thought I heard someone. Just for a second, I thought I heard someone behind me.

My first thought is Mason. That he's come back and he isn't taking no for an answer. I roll my eyes feeling my heart squeeze violently in my chest.

I can't make that situation more than what it was. A hookup, a fuck buddy, I don't have a clue. I know what it is now, though. It's over.

Settling back down in the iron chair, I snatch up my note-pad. I haven't written like this in so long, but there are scribbles everywhere. It's all loose poetry, lazy I suppose. It tells the story of how Jace and I met when we were young. How we fit so well together and everyone told us we were meant to be.

My eyes close as I remember the day we first got together. I can still hear how the school bells went off as we walked on the sidewalk to get to class. I brushed my knuckles against his, waiting and hoping. It had to have been obvious to him. Maybe I was the one to make the first move, but he chose me. He threaded his fingers through mine and he didn't let go. He was a good man, not a perfect man. He was good to me. Or so I thought.

"I hate this." I utter the words beneath my breath and it comes out shaky. They say when someone dies, you remember the good times more than the bad. Rose-colored glasses or something like that. I have to keep reminding myself that there were bad times too. With all these articles, I'm not having a difficult time remembering.

There's guilt too, which is something that I don't want. I don't want to be angry at someone who will never again have the chance to defend himself.

How can I move forward when I'm too busy hating everything as I scribble down scenes of our fights in this notepad? I let the words flow and pour out all of it, but mostly his infidelity.

Creak. The creak of the floorboards behind me sends chills sweeping down my body. I stand abruptly from the chair and the iron scrapes on the balcony.

Every emotion that's made me a wreck washes away, quickly cleansed by fear. I turn slowly, my mouth parted but words refuse to come out.

I don't have the strength or courage to ask who's behind me.

But I don't have to.

I let out a breath as a bushy tail comes into view.

"Boots," I say, greeting the neighbor's tabby cat and add, "You scared me," with my hand over my heart.

She must've snuck in while the balcony door was open and I was busy mulling over my wretched married life. There's an archway between my house and the neighbor's, and Boots used to be a regular on this balcony. Taking a few steps inside the bedroom, I scoop up the small cat. Her fur is soft and she purrs with contentment the moment I pet her. I only have a moment, though. She gets fed up with attention quickly and I've been on the wrong end of her claws before.

"You know you're not supposed to be in here," I scold her. Suddenly feeling exhausted, my conviction wanes. I escort Boots back outside, setting her down and move to shut the door just as my phone rings behind me on the bed.

The balcony is at the end of the bedroom so I have to walk quickly to answer in time, but I do on the last ring.

"Hello?"

"Jules, how are you?" Kat's voice asks. "I was just calling to check in."

"A mess," I say and my throat is tight. Is this what a breakup feels like? Or is this what regret feels like? I'm not sure which is which anymore. I suppose the two are one and the same.

"God, I know … it has to be rough." I nod my head but my lips are pressed into a thin line without any words wanting to come and contribute to the conversation.

"Do you want to talk about it?"

Closing my eyes, I shake my head even though I know she can't see; a moment later I'm able to tell her no.

"Hey, it's all going to be okay," Kat says as if it's a fact. "You know that, don't you?"

A small breath of disbelief leaves me. "No, Kat." I lay back on the bed and add, "No, I don't know it's going to be all right. It doesn't feel like it will."

"Stop it. Stop it right now." Although her tone is harsh,

the pain behind her words is undeniable. "Not everything in life is good, but that doesn't mean you don't have a good life."

I lick my dry lips and close my eyes, lying back farther on the bed and trying to absorb my friend's advice.

"You have a great life, Jules. You really do."

"I thought I was okay. I thought I'd be able to move on. I thought I *was* moving on."

"You're going to, Jules."

My exhausted eyes stay shut tight, refusing to feel anymore and I hold my breath. "One day, probably sooner than you know it, it's going to feel normal without him. It's going to feel good without him. And there's not a single thing wrong with that."

"It doesn't feel like it's okay, though. It doesn't feel like it's all right to not be upset."

"It doesn't have to right now. You don't have to do anything right now, except tell me you're going to come to my house to-morrow night."

A sniff is what she gets in response until I'm able to compose myself.

"Of course."

"Good, now … are you all right?"

I answer her honestly. "I'm not, but I think I will be."

"You *definitely* will be," she says with such conviction, I believe her. My body feels lighter as I scoot closer to the edge of the bed, ready to do something.

"Do you want to go out for dinner?" I ask Kat.

Kat takes a deep breath on the other end of the line and I know she's busy and can't. That's her *I wish I could* sigh. She's always busy with work. "I can't—"

"It's fine," I say, cutting her off. "I've got to get out of this house." I speak while looking up at the coffered ceilings in the bedroom. This house has too many memories in it.

"You go out and get some fresh air, maybe get some shopping in and I'll see you tomorrow night."

Nodding in agreement, I answer, "See you tomorrow."

"Love you, Jules." Kat's voice is soft when she tells me she loves me.

"I love you too." It's so true. I'd crumble into a complete mess without her.

As I rise from the bed, it groans slightly and I look back to find it in disarray. I take the time to pull the sheets tight and lay the comforter just right. I even fluff the pillows and place them where they're supposed to be.

As my feet pad against the old wooden floor, it creaks right where I know it should and that chill from earlier comes back to me. I look up at the balcony door and find it unlocked, which is odd. I swear I locked it.

Click. The sound is loud as I stare at the lock, my fingers still on the cold hard metal.

I never did like having a balcony in the bedroom. Jace told me it was a silly fear. I cross my arms, feeling unsteady and colder by the second. I tuck a strand of hair behind my ear, grabbing my phone and clutch then throw on a pair of faded blue jeans.

Unsteady is the feeling that's most recognizable. I'm not sure where I go from here. Worse, I don't know where I want to go.

All I know in this moment, with everything in me, is that I just want to get out of this house.

twenty-six

Mason

Ticktock.

It's a bomb, not a clock.

Ticktock.

It's about time to go off.

Ticktock.

Prepare for the shock.

Ticktock.

It's the truth to unlock.

I STAND FACING THE WINDOW IN MY FATHER'S OFFICE with my hands behind my back and don't bother turning around to greet him as the door opens. I watch as my cold gray eyes narrow in the reflection. The city traffic below is stirring with life, but it's silent up here. So many people surround us, but not one of them can save me. Not one of them would even give a fuck.

Julia would. *My sweetheart.* Or at least she would have days ago before she realized she needed to get away from me.

"Mason," my father says and I turn around, finally facing him and knowing I need to confront him along with everything else I've been running from. As much as I want to hold Jules close and pretend just being with her will make this right, I know it won't.

"Father," I say, greeting him with an icy tone in my voice, hating that I'm even related to this man. I stare into his eyes and see my own. Everything about him reminds me of what I'm becoming. I fucking hate it.

"We need to get over this," my father says and gestures between the two of us.

"We do." I clench my jaw, my pulse rushing faster. I rip my gaze away from his, staring down at my hands. "I don't think there should be any more ties." It pains me to tell him that. Even after all these years and everything he's done, I still feel a gaping hole in my chest at the thought of severing this relationship.

"Ties to what?" he asks.

"Between the two of us."

My father flinches as if I've struck him. But what did he expect?

"Watch your mouth," he says. I'm surprised he has the nerve to admonish me as if what I'm saying is unspeakable.

"I want to walk away. I don't want to be tied to this anymore. I don't want to be associated with you."

"I'm your father, Mason. You can't walk away from that."

The fuck I can't. I bite down on my tongue to stop from blurting out that answer, gritting my teeth as he walks closer to the left side of the desk. I walk to the right, matching his pace, a careful dance of power that escalates the conversation.

"You need to just forgive—"

"I'll never forgive you for what you did to Avery," I say, looking my father in the eye as I say her name for the first time in months. Every muscle in me is wound tightly, waiting for his next move so I can destroy him and let out this rage.

His eyes flash with something—anger, maybe betrayal, I don't know what.

"I did what I had to do to protect you," he says, pushing out the words from between clenched teeth, but his nerve is shaken, unlike mine.

"She didn't deserve to be murdered." My hands ball into fists. Avery was a mistake. A fiery redhead with long legs and a smile that could kill. She had *mistake* written all over her.

I met her late one night at an event and I knew she was trouble. I knew it from the start but I needed a quick fuck. She tempted me and I took the bait. But I could never have imagined how it would all end.

"That's what happens when you blackmail a Thatcher." My father practically spits. "She decided to roll the dice. She's the one who came to me with demands and tried to back us into a corner."

"You could have sent her to me." My muscles twitch with the need to pound my fist into his face as I take a step forward. "I would have told her the baby couldn't have been mine."

"If I'd known then—"

"You didn't have to know!" I shout, unable to control myself any longer. My throat feels raw as the words are ripped from me, screaming up my chest. "She wasn't innocent." I take a step toward my father and grab the edge of the desk to keep from gripping his collar and say, "But she didn't deserve to die."

"She did." My father's voice is hard, his back straight and his gaze full of confidence.

"She was pregnant!" I tell him. Hating how he could so easily dismiss her existence. He had her murdered. He didn't even think twice about ending her life.

"With a married man's child!" my father sneers, his face turning red as he leans in closer to me and I can't take it any longer.

I can't take the arrogance and justification of ending a person's life so easily. I clench my fist until my knuckles are white and punch my father in the jaw. His teeth crack from the weight of the blow. His head whips to the side as he falls to the floor, limp and shocked. My arm stings with the pain of impact.

It feels so fucking good to finally give him a piece of what he deserves.

He lays there for a moment, his hand over his mouth as a trickle of blood leaks from the corner of his lips. I shake out my hand, adrenaline rushing through my veins. I just barely restrain myself from kicking him in the ribs, from letting all this anger and pent-up guilt out on him.

"You ungrateful prick." He spits blood onto the floor and

looks up at me with a menacing glare. "You chose some whore over your own family."

No, I'm choosing what's right. I'm choosing to be better than this life I was born into.

My father doesn't quit with his justification. "Anderson didn't want that kid. Think about what she would have done to him!"

The mention of Jace Anderson makes my gaze break from my father's. The memories come back and make my tense muscles spasm. I can't hear whatever my father's yelling at me. It's all white noise.

I may have been born a Thatcher and I'll die a Thatcher, but I refuse to be anything like my father. Not today, not ever.

"I won't forgive you." I force my body to relax. I've said what I came to say. This ends now. "I never will." I start to walk out, accompanied by the sound of my heart racing.

Just as my hand grips the doorknob, I finally get the balls to ask him.

One last thing to say. One final question.

Walking back to his desk with confident steps, I imagine his answer as if I already know it. He turns slightly from facing the window, still curled up on the floor behind his desk, looking at me as if he doesn't trust me. He shouldn't. Not with how I'm feeling at this moment.

I stop on the opposite side of the desk, my mind racing as I go back years and years. Back to only a boy who lost his mother. Scared, confused … and angry.

"Mom didn't die from an overdose." The statement comes out accusatory and it's meant to. He wipes the blood from his mouth with the bright white sleeve of his dress shirt. He doesn't look me in the eye, doesn't acknowledge what I said in the least.

I take one step toward him, a large step that gets his attention. His gaze whips up to me. "Did you have her killed too?"

"How dare you!" His nostrils flare as he pins me with his gaze. "How dare you, you fucking …" he trails off and doesn't finish. His shoulders are hunched forward as he grips his desk chair for balance to stand.

I'm struck by the powerful way he's affected. I've wondered for so long, months now. If he had Avery killed, maybe he did the same with my mother.

I flex my hand and swallow thickly, feeling the need to explain. My question was prompted by a gut feeling more than anything else. I don't remember much from around the time she died, but I remember how I felt. How the air between them was tense. How scared my mother was that he would find out her dirty little secret. "I know she was cheating—"

"Get out!" My father shouts at me, not holding anything back as he throws his chair to the side, putting all of his weight into it. It crashes against the bookshelf, several of the books tumbling to the floor as he slams his fists against his desk.

I turn my back on him, my fist pulsing in agony from the punch and my chest hurting with a pain I can't explain.

He pounds his fists again and again on the maple desk as I force myself to walk away from him.

Leaving my father alone in his office and promising myself never to see him again, never to speak to him, never to trust him. And never to be like him.

Never again.

twenty-seven

Julia

I STARE DOWN AT THE NEAT PILES OF PAPERS TO MY right in the dining room. My back is killing me and my shoulders are screaming in pain. It's so wrong that now that these contracts and files are sorted out, my first thought is to call Mason, to see if he's free and tell him that I miss him. God, do I miss him.

He could ease my physical pains, but also that sick lonely feeling I have after going through three years of finances.

Three years of hard evidence of Jace cheating. Three long years compiled in black ink on white pages.

I glance at the email still open on my laptop. Mr. Walker will have more for me tomorrow. It makes my stomach lurch because I know I'll see more credit card statements for hotel charges during the day when he was supposed to be working, along with charges for jewelry and everything else he bought the women he kept on the side. I don't need to see it. That's the messed-up part of it all.

Selling the apartment and being done with it is the last of all the problems and loose ends Jace left.

I'll be fine financially; everything is going to be okay on that front. But I want to know how long it went on. I want to know at what point in my life I wasn't good enough for him anymore.

The wine in the glass is almost gone and it's late, but I pour myself another. We all have our vices and it turns out mine are cabernet and Mason Thatcher. My lips curl into a pathetic weak smile and then I take a sip of the sweet wine.

I stare at the open newspaper on the table. The one with a photograph of Mason and someone else. Someone *new*. It's not hard to admit that it hurts to see it, to think that he's moved on already. It hasn't even been two weeks since I saw him last. It has their picture but the accompanying article is about me being used by the playboy bachelor and left brokenhearted. They know nothing and I couldn't care less about what they think happened. What matters is that I am heartbroken.

Mason. I've stared at that photo for far too long praying it isn't true. Mostly because I'm selfish. I'm not ready to commit to him, or to anyone, but I want him all the same.

Sue has assured me it's all made up and the woman in the photo is someone he dated long ago.

I take another gulp of wine and only look up from the

same paragraph I've read five times when I hear my phone go off.

It's a text from Kat wanting my manuscript. Oh God.

It's a good thing I have an apartment up for sale, I suppose. Maybe I should thank my cheating deceased husband for that.

It takes a small sip before I have the courage to text her back, asking for an extension and then open my laptop to write. To let the words flow. If anything, I expect it to be about anger, grief, betrayal. But all that comes are thoughts of Mason's touch. How powerful his physical presence can be. How he can soothe my every pain. How he wants to do just that, and about how much I want it even more.

I let my head fall to the side when I remember him kissing me as he played my body right at this very spot that I'm sitting. My fingers never stop tapping on the keys as I relive the moment. I open my eyes and stare at the grain woven into the wooden table where I bent over for him. I confessed something so real, so painful and he made me feel alive and as though nothing else mattered.

I suck in a deep breath, hating that I left him the way that I did. I'm so damn broken. I don't understand why he wants me when it's obvious that I'm a wreck.

Biting down on my lip, I stare at the phone and think of texting him.

I miss you. I type in the words and then delete them.

I'm sorry. I stare at the two words that are so simple, yet mean so much.

I think I love you. That's what I should send him. Scare him away for good.

I delete the text as Kat messages me back. She's usually

hard on me. Guilting me if I miss a deadline and reminding me about everyone else's schedules involved. It lights a fire under my bottom.

But all she's written this time is that it's okay and to take care of myself.

"Take care of myself," I whisper beneath my breath and let my fingers trail down the stem of the wineglass.

I wish Mason were here, but that's just an easy out.

This is supposed to hurt. It's supposed to be hard.

I want to crawl back to him and beg for forgiveness. Beg him to take away the pain again. It's selfish and I won't do that to him, but I'd be a liar if I said I didn't want to.

twenty-eight

Mason

"I just got an email." I hear Liam's irritation as the door opens. His light gray suit is sharp and crisp, but he looks like shit himself. His dirty blond hair is a mess on top of his head and the dark circles under his eyes prove he hasn't gotten much sleep.

"About what?" I ask. I don't let on that I already know what the email was about as I rest my elbows on the desk. Waiting for him to speak, I make a steeple with my pointer fingers. I know what this is about. My father's pulled the funds.

We're fucked. And I don't have a way out of this.

"What happened, Mason?" His question is drenched with desperation.

I swallow hard, hating that I owe Liam anything. I know I do. At the very least I owe him an explanation, but what can I tell him? My jaw clenches and I look down at my desk as I pick at my hands where a small cut mars my knuckles. I can't turn in my father. I don't have any hard evidence of his misdeeds but more than that, I can't bring myself to do it to my own father. That last part causes me more shame than I'm willing to admit.

I clear my throat and lean forward to face Liam.

"We have to back down or find new investors."

"Back down?" His wide eyes stare at me as though I'm the insane one here. Maybe I am. "We can't fucking back down. We've sunk millions into this!" I can practically see his heart racing out of his chest.

"I'm sorry, but—"

"What the fuck happened?" he shouts as he stands up, throwing the papers on the desk behind him. My blood heats as I glare at Liam.

"Sit down." The words come out harsh and as a demand. It gets his attention, like a child who's been scolded. I'll own up to failing him but I have my limits, and when it comes to business, I demand respect. He's still, almost frozen for a long moment and then he places both his hands flat on the desk and leans over, getting closer to my face. He's still a foot away, but it's too fucking close for my liking.

"Don't tell me what to do, Thatcher," he says low in his throat. "This is going to ruin us. Ruin *me*," he hisses.

"We'll recover." I don't have the confidence my voice reflects. But I'll do whatever I have to in order to make this work.

I have no intention of going anywhere. If I have to start from the bottom again and claw my way back up to the top, so be it.

"You need to get over whatever it is that's going on between you and your father. Whatever the fuck it is, just let it go."

He glares at me long and hard. Waiting for me to comply, but it's not going to happen. I may not be sending my father away to prison for life, but I'm through with him for good. I'm sure as fuck not going to take his money.

"I have a few meetings tomorrow with Marcus Jennings and Austin Hook." I lean back in my seat, daring him to come closer. His body tenses as he turns his head in disbelief, still leaning over my desk.

He shakes his head, looking bewildered. "How could you do this to me?" He barely gets out the words. He pushes off the desk, shaking his head again and walking a few feet away before looking back at me.

I can see each emotion as they flow through him and finally he settles on anger. "Is it because of Anderson?" he asks and my heart stops in my chest.

I stand up straight out of instinct. Out of the need to figure out how much he knows.

"What the fuck does he have to do with this?" My voice is deathly low as my eyes narrow; my muscles are coiled and ready for a fight. *What does he know?*

He gives me a confused look in return. "He?" Liam tilts his head and it's then that I realize he was talking about Jules and using her married name. My heart sinks lower and a cold sweat breaks out over my body. *Fuck!*

"I'm talking about the bitch you've been fucking." My body turns to stone, stuck in place by an anger I can't control.

Everything goes red as he keeps talking, oblivious to my reaction. "Everything's changed since she's come around."

I crack my neck to the side, deciding to ignore it. To give him one chance. That's all he'll get. "It has nothing to do with her."

"Oh yeah? She didn't convince you not to make amends with your father? Or fuck him over or fuck me over?" With each question, his voice gets louder and louder.

"She doesn't know shit about my father and she has no place here or in any of this."

He flashes me a cocky grin. "Really gets you worked up, doesn't it?" He rounds the desk as he talks. "Is it because she dumped your ass on Madison Avenue?" The question comes with a laugh and he closes the space between us. I already know this is going to end badly; I'm only waiting for the right moment to strike at this point. "What'd you do that had her running out of that car, Mason? You fuck her over too? Just like you fucked—"

I can't stop what's started. He shouldn't have brought up Jules. I can't control myself when it comes to her.

My fist comes out of nowhere, hitting him square on the jaw and sending him flying backward. Twice in one week I've hit a man. And for the second time, I don't give a shit.

My knuckle flares where the cut from the last punch is still healing and my shoulder screams with pain from the impact. My vision clouds, anger making it redder by the second. Everything rages inside. The anger of her leaving me, the disappointment of my father, the regret of what I've done all mix into a deadly concoction. I take two steps forward with my hands up, ready to beat the piss out of him, ready for the fight he obviously wants, but he's limp on the floor, blood leaking from his nose.

Crouching down, I grip the lapels of his jacket, pulling harder than I should but I can't stop myself, panic warring against everything else. He's motionless and unresponsive. I fist his jacket in my hands, shaking him. "Liam!" Dread courses through me. What the hell did I do? I slap him lightly across the face, but he doesn't respond.

I hold a hand over his nose just to make sure he's breathing. The warm air confirms that he is. *Thank fuck.* My body aches as I stand, running my hands through my hair and then down my face as I pace the floor.

I look up to the clock and I only have five, maybe ten minutes before everyone arrives at the office. I lean my forearm against the wall of windows, feeling defeated and like a fucking idiot. This isn't who I am now. This isn't the man I wanted to be. I lean all of my weight into the glass. I'm spiraling, all from the mention of her name.

The realization that I just knocked out Liam weighs heavily on my shoulders. The one man I could occasionally refer to as a friend.

I stare at my own reflection as I realize how badly I've fucked up.

It doesn't take long before I decide I need to call an ambulance and I'm very much aware they'll call the police. I clench my jaw and swallow my pride. *It'll be a fucking spectacle.*

He shouldn't have talked about Jules, though.

He had to know this was going to happen.

twenty-nine

Julia

Why do you haunt me so?
You take control of my thoughts,
You consume my sleep.
How do you wound me still?
You need to leave me alone,
I'm not yours to keep.

"IT CAN'T BE TRUE." I ONLY PARTED MY LIPS, BUT the words tumbled out without thinking. Sitting around the same small table in the coffee shop feels surreal as I read the article. We were just here not even a month ago and it's unreal how everything has changed.

"You broke him," Maddie says somewhat jokingly to try to lighten the mood.

His company, his friendships, his father. I know the tabloids make up a good portion of their content, but the mug shot is something that can't be denied.

"It's all dropped and he'll be fine," Sue says airily as if it's no big deal.

The newspaper falls to the table and the faint sound of the paper rustling is all I can hear.

"I don't understand what happened," I say, thinking out loud. "He never said anything to me about his father or about the business."

Sue shrugs. "Sometimes people don't talk about the things that bother them. He'll be fine." How can I not know, though? I shared so much of myself with Mason. I was raw and open and giving of so much of me. I know he did the same. I could feel it between us. It wasn't one sided. I hid the darkest secrets from him … and he did the same with me. A new form of regret wraps itself around my throat. *I should make sure he's all right like he did for me.* That's an excuse I can use to run back to him.

"Coffee?" Kat asks as she sits down and places a hot ceramic mug in front of me. It's been mixed with an almost offensive amount of creamer and the color matches my cream accent pillows at home… just the way I like it.

With a grateful smile, I accept it and blow over the top, inhaling the smell and trying to feel normal. Or as normal as I can, all things considered. Kat's busy reading over the manuscript on her phone, but whether or not it will do is nowhere on my mind. All I can think about is the fact that Mason was there for me, so many times. He needs someone right now. The only question is whether or not he'd let me in.

She murmurs the lines as she opens the book.

> *Sweet lies you told me, beautiful forever.*
> *A dream or a terror, I craved it, whichever.*
> *A taste so sweet, too much to say no,*
> *I couldn't resist and you couldn't let go.*
> *Your healing touch and comforting kiss—*
> *But I never thought it would end like this.*

Kat tilts her head, her lips stopping mid-poem and she gives me a questioning look as she says, "Is this one about Jace?"

The book was supposed to be about mourning and loss. It is, but it's a deceptive cocktail of the two men. I loved and lost both of them.

All I can do is take a sip of coffee and try not to choke on the lie as I say, "I don't remember."

"So have you heard from him?" Maddie asks me, thankfully saving me from Kat's interrogation.

My ponytail swishes along the crook of my neck as I shake my head no. He got the message that we were over after I repeatedly refused his calls. I don't think he'll ever reach out to me again.

"Have you called him?" Maddie asks.

"Not yet," I tell her. "Or, no. No, I haven't." *Thump, thump, thump,* my poor little heart won't stay where it's supposed to and I hide in my coffee cup again.

Her voice is hopeful as she scoots forward, the sound of the stool scratching against the floor making an annoying screech. "You should."

"I don't know … I want to. He was …" I trail off as I run my fingers up and down the cup and stare at a lone muffin in front of me. I haven't eaten since I heard about Mason this morning.

"I think you should," Maddie says softly.

"I think you should shut your mouth and let things happen as they should," Sue bites out and Maddie merely gives her a look of defiance.

"She breaks up with him and he falls apart—" Maddie looks like she's about to go off on Sue, but she doesn't get much out.

"Stop it," Sue says. "That's not her fault." Sue points at the paper and adds, "This has nothing to do with Jules."

"You don't know that." Maddie's response is soft as she looks down to her own blueberry muffin and picks at the top of it. "Everyone's saying he's heartbroken."

"Jesus, Maddie!" Sue snaps. "Jules, this is not your fault and you don't owe him anything. Don't go back to a man because of guilt." Her voice cracks and her eyes hold a warning. "Please. If you want to reach out to him, do it for any other reason than feeling guilty or like you owe him." There's a tear at my chest, an open wound knowing Sue is speaking from experience.

"I wasn't trying to hurt him, Maddie." I can't respond to Sue right now, my throat feels tight. "I didn't think he'd care, to be honest …" I don't know if that's true. I wasn't thinking of him when I ended it. I was only thinking of me. Of my anger. "It just happened so fast and it was too much."

"There's nothing wrong with fast," Kat says, surprising the

three of us. It's then that I notice she hasn't moved past the first page. "Evan and I got engaged in three months."

Their story was a whirlwind romance. Everyone's story is different. Maybe this is regret or guilt pushing me toward Mason, but it's different from what Sue went through. I swear our story has to be different.

My heart begs me to stop, but I have to ask them a question that's kept me up the last three nights I've dreamed of Mason. It's killing me slowly and carefully, destroying everything I thought I knew. "Isn't it wrong to fall for someone *else* so quickly after Jace?"

"No," Kat says and shakes her head. "It's wrong to throw something away because you're afraid of it, though." Her voice is full of regret, but it didn't stop her from telling me exactly what she thinks.

"You guys are giving me whiplash." I swallow thickly and brush the loose locks out of my face, resting my elbows on the table and burying my face in my hands. "I shouldn't be with him, I should be with him. I hurt him by breaking up with him, but I shouldn't be with him if I feel regret. I don't know what to think!" I say, my voice raw and the words tearing their way up my throat.

"What do you want, Jules?" Sue asks me, not missing a beat although my other two friends only stare at me with questions and guilt of their own. "Love isn't about thinking, it's only about what you feel." Of all the women in this group, I'm not sure I should take her advice on love, but she says it with such conviction that I believe it. And I trust her.

"I feel like I've been sad for too long," I say. "I feel like I deserve to be punished for moving on. I feel like I miss Mason.

Like really miss him. And I know I hurt him." I brush my fingers under my eyes and suck in a breath to keep myself from falling to pieces. "I didn't know it would be like this. I feel like life was spinning out of control and he was the one steady thing and I was taking advantage of that." My fingers tremble as I press my palms against my eyes, finally finishing my thoughts. "I don't know if I'm running away from all this hurt or running to him." I swallow and whisper, "Maybe some of both? And it scares me."

It's too much to take in and process, but I need all this mayhem to stop.

"You don't have to know. You don't have to do anything," Kat says. Her phone's flipped over on the table and as soon as I notice that, I also notice all three women staring at me with sympathy. Waiting for me. I don't deserve this. I don't know how I ended up so close with these women but without them, I'd be so lost.

"You can take as much time as you need," Maddie says with a small nod.

That's the problem, though. I wanted things to be slow, but he was a force I couldn't control. My body bowed down to his and I would have been swallowed whole if I gave any more of myself to him.

It doesn't stop me from wanting him and the way I feel when I'm with him. He was right that first night when he said he'd make me forget everything but his name and what he'd done to me.

"Are you sure it's not wrong? Because it feels like the worst kind of wrong." I glance at each of the girls, feeling like whatever they tell me will propel me in the direction I need to go.

"It's scary," Maddie says, shifting in her seat and breaking eye contact.

"Love is terrifying," Kat adds.

"It's not wrong. You haven't done anything wrong and you should do what you want to do. Even if that's breaking every bachelor's heart in New York City." A soft, playful smile greets me as I look at Sue. She nudges me and reaches for the paper. "This wasn't your fault, but I can't say I'm not curious about the gossip … and that I don't think there was something good about you two being together."

thirty

Mason

Anger management. The paper crinkles in my hand as I crumple it.

No charges were pressed, but I'm sure Liam's getting a kick out of the anger management classes the judge ordered me to attend. *Prick.* I know the asshole would have pushed the issue further if it wasn't for the company. He wants to save face and hold this over me so I can do his bidding.

That's not going to fucking happen. I'll take on all the debt if I have to and do it myself. The project is canceled; I'm taking the hit and dissolving the company. It's better that I'm alone. It's as simple as that.

I drop the empty bottle of whisky in the trash can as well

as the notice regarding the anger management course. The glass bottle clinks against the metal frame of the photograph. I stare down into the bin, the shattered glass marring the photo of the picture-perfect family. It's destroyed … but really, it's always been that way.

I'm tired and angry, and tired of being angry too. This isn't what I wanted or planned. I wanted more. For me, that meant Jules. With my fingers pinching the bridge of my nose, I lean back against the kitchen wall.

Call it what you want. Out of everything in life, she's the only thing I know I truly want. That should mean something.

I make my way upstairs, walking slowly and dreading another night alone in this empty house. It never bothered me much before, but I can't fucking stand the silence now.

Someone knocks three times at the front door and I still with my hand on the banister.

I wait a moment, wondering who the fuck would be here this late at night, even though only one name comes to mind. I steel myself for the worst, thinking it's my father. I can't face him right now. Not after what he's done and what I accused him of. It's only after another three knocks that I force myself to face the consequences. I open the door with a swift pull, prepared to turn him away, but my voice is caught in my throat.

Jules's baby blue eyes look at me with a mix of emotions. Fear, sorrow … hope. The chill of the wind spreads goosebumps along her arms and blows her long brunette hair off her shoulders. She looks to her left and then right, pulling her leather jacket tighter around her and taking a small step toward me.

"Mason," she says and licks her lush lips, painted with that same color I've grown to expect from her. "I—" She stops to clear her throat and looks away again as I stand numb in the doorway.

Fate's delivered her to me. I can't let her go this time. I won't.

"I was hoping we could talk?" Her voice is timid and her heels click on the cement porch as she shifts in place. Her tight blue jeans hug her curves, although the loose cream blouse beneath her jacket leaves much to the imagination. I know what's under there, though.

I don't say a word, too afraid of scaring her off. Instead I take a step to the side and open the door wider, waiting for her to walk in.

Her cheeks and the tip of her nose are a beautiful rosy red from the bite of the night air.

She hesitantly steps inside and looks around as if she hasn't been here enough times to have the place memorized. I close the door and stare at the lock a moment too long before turning it.

"Mason, I'm sorry." Jules's voice calls to me as I turn around to face her. I watch her swallow and then bite down on her bottom lip. She's worried and apologetic, but I don't give a fuck about the past. I never did. I care about what she wants now.

"Why are you here, Jules?" I ask her in a deep voice. It's rougher than I intended, but it's all I can manage.

"I heard about what happened," she says. She fidgets as she waits for my response, but I don't give her one. I'm not interested in talking about anything but us. I don't want to taint her with the bullshit. "I just wanted to say I'm sorry for hurting you," she says in a tight voice full of agony.

"Is that all?" I say and it takes all the air I have in my lungs.

Taking a step forward and closing the space between us, my heart thumps chaotically in my chest.

She twists her fingers around one another nervously. "I also," she starts to say and then swallows. "I was wondering if you still … if you were interested …"

"In what?" My eagerness gets the best of me. *Make this easy for me, Jules, and I'll make everything right. I promise you, sweetheart, I'll make it up to you.*

"If you'd like to maybe go out again? If that's what we were doing?" A nervous huff of a laugh accompanies her proposition. I stare at her a moment, thinking it's just too good to be true. She came back to me. There's a saying about that, but it's not meant for real life. It's not meant for men like me.

"If you still want me," Jules adds, the raw vulnerability so thick in her voice.

"I never stopped wanting you," I say, my voice barely a murmur. Her doe eyes never leave mine as I gently push her jacket off her shoulders. If she thinks I don't want her, she'll know better soon enough.

"Mason," she says and gasps as I lean down and kiss her neck. Maybe it's the alcohol or maybe it's just that my body knows hers. But I'm not waiting for apologies or excuses or explanations.

I need to *feel* her.

"Mason, stop." She pushes her hands against my chest, shrugging her jacket back on as I take a step back. "I need you to know that I'm worried we're going too fast. I'm worried that this isn't going to last."

A deep breath steadies me as I stare down at my sweetheart. "I told you, Jules. If you're with me, then you're with me and that's all there is to it." I take her hand in mine and kiss one knuckle, then another.

"Mason," she whimpers as if I've broken her heart. She has no idea. I turn her hand over and kiss her pulse, my heart beating faster.

"No more of this running from me or from us, Jules. Are you with me?" I ask her, feeling more vulnerable than I ever have in my entire life. I whisper, "Are you mine?"

"I don't know that my heart is mine to give, Mason. It's broken and I don't know if it will heal the right way." Jules sniffs and looks ashamed, but she has no idea how much I understand. I truly do.

Grief is a journey and she doesn't have to go it all alone.

I wrap my arm around her waist and pull her into me. "You don't have to be perfect, Jules, in order to be perfect for me." I kiss her hair and hope that she can understand. "I want you how you are today, and tomorrow I'll want you how you are then."

Jules buries her head into my chest, her hair brushing against my chin and I kiss the top of her head. "Why are you so perfect, Mason?" she says and relaxes in my embrace. "How do you know just the right words to say?" Her voice is soft and relaxed as she molds her body to mine and that's when I know I've won her over.

"I'm not perfect, Jules." My heart aches in my chest, knowing just how imperfect I am. And how imperfect I am *for her*. She has no idea. We aren't meant to fit together, but I'll force the pieces to line up and pretend it's meant to be.

For her. Because I owe her that much.

"I can't tell you how happy I am that you came back," I whisper and run my hand in soothing circles along her back.

CHAPTER

thirty-one

Julia

I asked you to leave.

I need to be alone.

But you stayed in my head.

My heart and my home.

I asked you to leave me,

But you won't go away.

When I go to find you tomorrow,

I only hope that you'll stay.

MASON'S BEDROOM IS SO MUCH DARKER THAN mine. Full of deep grays and dark wood. It matches the rest of his home, I suppose. His curtains are thick velvet and shut tight. Even with hardly any light, I can see him, all of him. His muscles ripple in the faint light. It makes Mason seem so much more dominating, which is criminal.

He already owns me, consuming me with his presence. But right now, at this very moment as he towers over me, skimming his fingers over my sensitized skin, I'm weaker for him than I've ever been in my entire life.

"Mason." I murmur his name as he lays me down on his bed. I turn my head to the side and arch my back as he leaves open-mouth kisses down my neck. We're both naked, but it's more than that. So much more. We've been here before plenty of times, but this is different. We're bared to each other.

"If we do this, can you promise me one thing?" My heart is pounding in my chest as I lay back on the bed, because I feel like this is the end. It's putting so much to rest and moving on toward the unknown. I'm terrified that I'll fall and he'll let me shatter when he's done with me.

"What?" He whispers the question between kisses.

"Please don't hurt me," I beg him. "I want you and I want what we have …" I trail off, barely able to breathe. "But promise if you want me to go, you'll do it easy and as soon as you know." He braces his forearms on either side of my head and looks down at me with an intense look in his gray eyes that pierces my lungs, stopping me from breathing.

"You need to stop this." His voice is hard, but it always is when I say something he doesn't like. "Do you understand?"

I nod my head and say, "Yes." I really do. I want this to stop and for *us* to begin.

"Don't hide from me, Jules. Don't run from me," Mason tells me with an authority that can't be denied.

I nod my head in complete agreement. I'm tired of running and denying myself what I really want. "No more secrets," I say into the hot air between us.

Mason pulls away, looking at me as if he's going to tell me something. The silence and tension grow, but no words come. Instead he crashes his lips to mine and pushes his body against me, forcing me to spread my legs for him.

And I do, I let him have all of me.

His fingers trail down between my legs as my core heats. He doesn't stop nipping and kissing all over my heated body, his hands roaming freely, taking in every inch of me. I'm helpless beneath him. Falling deeper and deeper into the darkness and loving how overwhelming it all is.

I missed this. God, how I missed this.

He groans in the crook of my neck, a sexy deep sound that makes my body arch toward him as if drawn even closer to him by an undeniable pull. His heated skin brushes against mine as he pushes himself inside of me.

My mouth opens and I stare up at him, his steel gray eyes holding my gaze as he enters me, slowly stretching me and not stopping until he's fully inside of me.

My heart beats faster, my body numb and on edge, waiting for him to move and take me how he wants me. Rough, raw, and making me his.

His fingers dig into my hips, pinning me down as he pulls out slightly and then slams back in, forcing a whimper from me. My body bucks instinctively, but I never break eye contact. I can't. He holds me captive beneath his gaze.

He does it over and over again until I'm so wet and hot for him that he easily slips in and out, each time forcefully smacking against my clit.

My body writhes and begs me to move away; it's too much, too intense. But that's just how Mason is. I knew it when I met him. More than that, I need him. I need this.

I love you, my heart whispers but I don't say it aloud. Small whimpers of pleasure spill from my lips with each thrust and I swear I'm close to admitting it. So close.

He groans low in his throat as he speeds up his relentless thrusts, resting his forehead against mine and kissing me mercilessly. Our lips barely touch, but they do, kiss after kiss after kiss. A series of slow kisses with our hearts racing fast beg me to confess.

He steals the breath from my lungs. His hot body makes mine burn with desire. I cling to him, wrapping my legs around him and digging my nails into his shoulder.

Higher and higher he pushes me.

The pleasure comes in small waves, dim at first but growing stronger and stronger. They threaten to overwhelm me as my fingers and toes tingle. The crash will shatter me, I know it. I don't beg him to stop. I don't try to pull away. I want it, I crave it, I'm desperate for him to ruin me.

"Mason!" I cry out as the wave consumes me, pulling me under in an intense orgasm that paralyzes my body. It's Mason's cue to devour me and he does, fucking me with no regard for the state I'm in. He's chasing his own release, pounding into me recklessly and extending my pleasure that much longer.

I scream out as he whispers, "Mine," in the crook of my neck again and again. His throaty voice gets louder as he fucks me harder. I can't do a damn thing but take everything he's giving me. And I do, with my nails digging into his skin and his masculine scent surrounding me. His large body suffocating me in the most delicious way.

It's only when he stills deep inside of me as I pant under him, desperately trying to breathe, that I'm able to moan out my pleasure. His thick cock pulses and the wetness between my thighs leaks between us.

He doesn't stop holding me.

He doesn't stop kissing me.

I almost don't tell him. I almost hide from him, but I promised him I wouldn't.

"I love you," I whisper and give that piece of me to him too. He doesn't say it back, but I know he heard it.

He kisses me without mercy, soothing my pain and taking everything I have.

thirty-two

Mason

HOW LONG IS LONG ENOUGH? I KEEP THINKING it with every second that passes. As if I'm not a complete fraud for asking Jules to marry me.

It's been two weeks of things falling perfectly into place. She's still waiting for the other shoe to drop. For this fantasy we're living in together to crumble into pieces. I won't let it, though. I'll give her everything she wants and that includes a ring, a sense of security that will seal us together and truly put our respective pasts behind us.

Financially, with my business in shambles and the money tied up in contracts I'm obligated to fulfill but can't, I'm fucked. I was smart enough to incorporate the business as an LLC, though. Personally, all I have is my house and stocks. It's nothing compared to her bank account. But I'm stable and when the contracts are finalized and the business assets are split, I'll be able to give her even more. I'm surprised she hasn't asked, but I'm prepared if that's a concern for her.

My eyes focus on the deep red petals scattered on every surface. I want her. I don't care about anything else anymore.

The only thing I give a damn about is making Jules mine in every way.

I don't want her to tell me no. I can't stand the thought of her turning me down or worse, if simply asking her to be my wife could push her away.

It doesn't matter how fast she is if she runs though, how quickly she'll turn me down and try to hide. I'll find her, I'll catch her and I'll wait for her. Always.

I close the small black velvet box, making the vision of the four-carat, cushion-cut diamond vanish and shove it into my pocket. Letting a heavy breath leave me, I turn and look at the living room. It's obvious. So damn obvious that I'm going to propose.

The second she walks in here and sees the crystal vases of deep red roses on every surface, she's going to know what I have planned.

I can see her now, standing in the doorway, gripping onto the frame while her beautiful blue eyes go wide and she breathes in the floral scent. The lights are low and the tea lights are scattered.

I'm not a romantic man by nature, but for her and for this ... Hopefully for the start of our lives together, I can do romance. *All for her.* I'll pretend to be someone else until both of us believe it.

At the sound of the doorknob turning, my heart skips in my chest, hammering harder than I anticipated. I take a step back, pulling the box from my pocket and preparing to get down on my knee. My blood heats and anxiety suddenly washes through me. It's really happening. I'm really going to ask her to marry me. The thought itself calms me.

Of course I am. *I love her.*

I run my hand through my hair as she steps forward enough to come through the doors. I thought she'd be astonished by the sight of the room. I imagined her taking it all in, but she's only looking at me.

"Julianna Lynn Summers, I would be honored—" I start and already I've fucked up. I had this damn thing rehearsed. I thought I had it all memorized but having to look up at her, and not knowing what she's going to say … I stumbled over my words.

Jules covers her mouth with a gasp, letting the front door shut slowly behind her. Her shoulders hunch forward some as her purse falls to the ground. I knew she'd be emotional; I just wish the shock would wane so I could see which side of her was winning out. The side that loves me and wants to live in the moment, or the side stuck in the past and afraid to move on.

Jules takes a few steps forward when I don't continue, her thin heels clicking on the polished wood floors as she places her hands on my shoulders and starts to lower herself to the ground, but that's not how I want her. I don't know how I'm able to wrap an arm around her long legs and look up at her, still holding the ring out although she's staring into my eyes. Her skin is soft beneath my touch.

"Jules, I love you and I want to spend every day of my life with you." I hesitate to say the words but I have to, even if she says she can't. "I want you as my wife," I tell her and watch her facial expression crumple with a hint of pain reflected in her eyes as I say the words.

"I love you too, Mason." She barely gets out the words as she covers her face with both her hands and then wipes under her eyes. Her eyes are glossy with tears and her voice is choked as she says it again. "I love you and I didn't know if I could …" Hearing her start her confession breaks my heart and I rise just enough to hold her. She wraps her arms around my shoulders, gripping onto me as though she needs me to stand. And in so many ways, she does. She needs someone there and I'll always be that person for her.

So long as she'll let me.

She pulls away slightly, trying to pull herself together as she brushes her hair out of her face and looks away, taking a calming breath.

"I want all of you, Jules," I tell her as I cup her chin in my hand and force her to look at me. "When you're upset, I want to know so I can make you smile. When you're angry, just tell me. I'll let you take it out on me however you need, then make you come so hard you'll forget you ever felt anything other than bliss. I want the real you. Always. I never want you to hide from me."

Those lush lips part and a soft breath escapes her as she stares into my eyes. She's searching for something. She better not fucking wonder if everything I've just said is true or not.

"I want the same from you, Mason." I'm surprised at her response. I stay still on the ground, wondering how she could think for a second I wouldn't share all of me with her. Not my past, though. She doesn't know shit about that and she never will. None of it. I'm going to fix it all and keep it hidden in the shadows and buried nine feet deep where it all belongs.

She kneels on the floor in front of me and takes my jaw in both her hands, planting a soft sweet kiss on my lips. Her touch calms all my worries. It dispels the demons threatening to surface. She does this to me. She makes me a better person and I desperately want to be that man for her.

She speaks with her eyes closed, her lips close to mine and her hot breath filling the air between us. Her long, thick lashes are damp with her tears as she tells me, "I love you for you. The good and the bad. And I do want to be with you, Mason." Her voice is pained and I can't help but reach out and hold her, pulling her closer to me. "I need you," she whispers.

I kiss the crook of her neck. "All I need is your love."

"You have it, Mason."

She has yet to answer; I need to hear her tell me yes. I want to be good enough to be her husband and if I'm not today, then tomorrow I'll be better. I'm determined and she needs to know that. I put my hands on her shoulders.

"I love you, Jules. Will you marry me?" I ask her, looking deep into her eyes.

She gives me a sweet smile, almost a shy one as she sniffles and finally gives me everything I need by saying, "I love you too. Yes." Her words come out as if it's obvious. As if it's only natural.

I finally breathe a deep sigh of relief, heaving in the air

and holding her close to me. I stand up, still carrying her and swing her in my arms as I rise.

I kiss up her neck and every inch of her exposed skin, making her let out a small, feminine laugh and push away from me slightly. This is the only kind of pushing I ever want her to do again. From this day forward, she's mine.

I only set her down so I can take out the ring from the box. I watch as Jules's eyes widen once again. "Oh my gosh," she says softly, eyeing the ring as though it's the most beautiful thing she's ever seen.

"Do you like it?" I ask her as I slip the box into my pocket and hold the ring out for her.

She bites her bottom lip as she nods vigorously and says, "Mason, it's beautiful." Finally, she looks up at me as I slip the ring onto her finger. "I love it," she whispers.

A small breath leaves her as she rubs her fingers over my five o'clock shadow and gently kisses me. I've never felt anything like what I feel for her. Seeing my ring on her finger makes it seem as though it's all going to be all right.

As long as the past will stay buried where it belongs.

thirty-three

Julia

Lies lies go away,

The sins are all from yesterday.

We tried to run, you tried to beat us.

Now we're ruined, left defeated.

THE FRAME CLICKS INTO PLACE AND I TURN IT OVER in my hands and smile. I straighten my back and hold up the heavy silver frame. This isn't for hanging out here where everyone can see. It's silly really, but I wanted it framed.

My engagement ring clinks against the silver frame as I

hold it up, the sunlight from the large bay window in Mason's house, well our house now, reflecting off the glass as I read the words.

A New Love and New Beginning.

It's a picture of us from the first article about us that was run in the papers. Back when I didn't know how to feel about the two of us. When I was riddled with guilt and pain and not seeing things clearly, I hated that we were in the papers at all. But I loved the candid photo.

I happened to come across it online the other day and when I read it, I lost it. Mason had to come in and find out why I was crying. He's always worried that I'm going to break down. I wish he wasn't so concerned for me. Yes, I'm emotional, but I know what I want. *I want him.* Something as simple as this article shouldn't get me so emotional, especially since half the facts aren't even true. But I love that our story has a beginning that was captured. I love that everyone around us knew.

I would never have thought that this article would give me a sense of pride and bring back a memory I want to be reminded of. A night when two lost souls knew they needed each other, even if we were too blind or stubborn to see it, we felt it.

"Finally," I say. It's framed and perfect. Just how I wanted it.

I hear Mason's rough chuckle as he walks into the kitchen and wraps his hands around my hips then plants a kiss on my shoulder.

I have to close my eyes as he hums and places his hand on my lower belly. He wants a baby. The very thought warms my heart and makes my head fall back against his broad chest. Wedding first, though. I want it all with him.

"Soon," I say softly with my eyes closed.

"What's this?" Mason asks, picking up the frame and reading the article left on the counter from where I cut out the photo. I watch his eyebrows raise as he reads the first few lines and he looks at me questioningly.

"I was going to put it on *my* nightstand," I tell him softly, waiting for his reaction. I'm still adjusting to moving in. I'll never sell my family home but I'm happier here, away from all the reminders of what used to be.

With no response, he sets the frame down and kisses me again. It's soft and sweet, but it lasts. My heart swells each time he kisses me like this. When he pulls away, he grins at me. It's a cocky one that lets me know he thinks he's got me all tied up in knots. And he does.

"Why this one?" he asks me.

Truthfully, I'm not sure I can vocalize why I want this particular one on my nightstand, so I just shrug.

"I just want it," I tell him simply and my easy response makes him smile.

"Well if you want it, then it's all yours."

That right there is why it was so easy to fall for this man. It's simple and natural. No rhyme or reason. It just feels right.

I set the frame down on the counter. It's not at all a lazy weekend; I have to write like crazy to get this manuscript in before the deadline, but I'm doing everything I can to procrastinate.

"You want a drink?" Mason offers, his voice dripping with

sex appeal. He has a sexy grin on his lips and I know he wants to stay in and do bad things tonight.

I can't resist him, so I nod my head and his smile widens, filling me with warmth. I'll never get enough of him and how he makes me feel.

I pick up the envelope on top of the pile of mail sitting to my right as he heads to the fridge. The envelope tears easily and a handwritten letter slips out.

I feel my forehead crease as I unfold the thick cream parchment. Who sends a letter like this in a plain envelope? Before I read it, I check the envelope again. My name is there, but there's no return address.

Dear Julia,

It pains me to tell you this, but I can't stand to watch from a distance as you fall into a trap. Your husband was murdered. I know this is going to shock you, but I have proof. You may not believe me but I pray that you do.

Mason Thatcher murdered him. Don't trust him. Don't let him know that you know. If he finds out, you won't be safe.

My blood runs cold as I stand at the counter, my heart racing out of my chest. There's more written, but I can't read it. A shiver rolls through my body and everything seems to blur.

There's no way this is true. There's no way, yet my fingers tremble and my gaze shifts from the letter to the man accused, standing only feet from me.

My eyes dart from Mason's back as he rummages in the fridge, then back to the paper.

My heart thumps.

Murdered. Jace wasn't murdered. I deny it all, swallowing thickly.

I reread the letter, blinking and taking it in. My lips move with the words, but I can't breathe. I can't focus.

The handwritten letters seem to swirl together into a cloud of distrust. My vision fades and I feel so fucking dizzy. I back up slowly, pushing from the island and letting the feet of the stool scrape against the tile. Mason looks up at the noise and my weak legs barely hold me up as I grip the stool, the paper crinkling in my hand, my bare feet padding against the cold floor.

My head shakes on its own. That's not true. It's not true. It can't be true.

"Jules?" Mason's voice is riddled with concern and something else. Something I never registered before, but I can hear it now. I can see it on his face as I barely breathe and look up at him.

"The—" I can't bring myself to confess what I've just read. It's a lie. It has to be a lie. What a cruel lie it is. But Mason's response is throwing me off.

He's careful as he sets a bottle of beer on the counter, squaring his shoulders, all humor gone from his face and something else, *someone* else, stands in his place.

"Mason?" I barely get out his name.

"What is it?" he asks me in a voice so menacing, fear lights a fire deep in the marrow of my bones. No. I shake my head. "Mason, no," I say as my throat goes dry and my words crack. *He didn't do anything. He didn't even know Jace.*

This isn't real. My fist grips the stool tighter and I struggle to react. This is a nightmare. It has to be.

I'm caught between my need to run to somewhere I can think and the need to know the truth. I need the truth. No more lies; no more secrets.

He promised.

He loves me.

There's just no way.

"Did you do it?" The question leaves me in a single weak breath and in an instant, something snaps into place. As if he's very aware of what I'm saying. As if he's been waiting for this.

No. My body turns to ice; my blood and lungs freeze and I can't believe this is reality. It can't be true.

Mason takes a step forward, around the island and it breaks me from my denial.

It's my cue to run, a natural instinct that takes over. The stool falls hard, crashing to the tiled floor as I take off, but Mason's faster, gripping my waist and making me jerk backward. I cry out from fear and he releases me, only for me to fall onto the floor. His large frame towers over me, his hands up as if he's approaching a wild animal. I feel as if I am just that. My eyes wide, my heart pounds in my chest. *Thump, thump, thump.*

"Did I do what?" he asks, his eyes narrowed and with a coldness I haven't seen before. This isn't the man I know.

My bottom lip wobbles, the small bit of strength vanishing as I take in the raw truth. "Did you kill my husband?"

YOU ARE MY
hope
WILLOW WINTERS

Mason gave me chills when I first laid eyes on him. The good kind. The kind that make your body ache, and your heart hammer.

It's not fair that his touch eased my pain.
That his lips on mine made my worries vanish.
That his love gave me a reason to breathe again.

With him I felt complete, as if fate had given me a second chance.

Then I learned the truth—the sins and secrets of what had really brought us together.
I only hope we can go back. I never could have imagined this.

This is book 2 in the You Are Mine duet.
You Are My Reason should be read first.

Kintsukuroi,
Means to repair with gold.
The once destroyed and shattered,
Repaired with binds to hold.

The bits are mended over time,
The piece stronger than before.
It's more beautiful for being broken.
Different? Yes, but ruined no more.

prologue

Mason

One month ago

DON'T LET THEM SEE.

Her words echo in my head as I stalk toward the quiet bedroom. She whispered them against my lips last night. The cool air slipped between us as she broke our heated kiss and slowly opened her eyes in the dark of night.

The streetlamp shined down around us like a spotlight on the back porch of her place on the Upper East Side. The city life slept quietly so late at night—or early in the morning, depending on how you look at it. Only the sinners like us were left awake.

Don't let them see. She left me with the parting plea and here I am… complying with her wish.

I've never crept through anyone's back door before. Not once in my life have I had to sneak around like this.

I don't want to keep this up, but here I am. What the hell has this woman done to me? *I'm wrapped around her little finger.*

She doesn't want anyone to notice me walking through her door because she's ashamed. I know that's why she doesn't want people to know we're together.

This isn't a fling; this isn't a rebound fuck. There's something more to us now, but she still doesn't want the world to know.

The floorboards creak under my weight and I hesitate in the doorway, the dim lamp from the hall filling the dark room with a hint of light. I'm being careful so her neighbors won't be able to hear anything. I just don't want to disturb her.

It's obvious she's sleeping, but then she stirs beneath the silk duvet until finally she opens her eyes and sees me. She tilts her head to the side as she looks at me, burying her cheek into the pillow, a soft smile playing on her lips as she utters a pleasant feminine hum.

"I missed you," she whispers and her voice is laced with an equal mix of sleep and lust.

If only she knew the real reason I crave her touch. The reason I'm so tempted to break all my rules.

"I'm sorry I'm late," I tell her in a deep, rough voice as I start unbuttoning my shirt. A smirk lifts up the corners of my lips as her eyes sparkle with humor. She doesn't care when I come and go, so long as I lie in her bed at night, or she in mine.

Her doe eyes peer back at me while I slip off my button-up

and let it pool into a puddle at my feet. I yank my tight white undershirt over my head and look back to see those lush lips parted.

My muscles ripple as I let the tank drop to the floor, the moonlight bathing the room and the two of us in a faint glow.

She may want to keep this a secret but she wants me nonetheless, and she can't hide it. I've become addicted to the way she looks at me like she needs my touch to stay grounded, just as she needs to breathe air to survive. I'm conditioned to crave the faint sounds of her quickened breath as she waits for me to come to her. *As if she'd die without me.*

I'm slow to unbuckle my belt as my eyes roam down her luscious curves. She's mine to take. Mine to touch. *Mine to keep.*

I don't want to sneak around anymore and I don't give a shit who knows. I'm tired of all the secrets and politics, all the gossip in this town.

The anger boils in my blood as I grip my leather belt tighter, making it sing in the air as I pull it through the loops. The buckle drops to the floor with a *thunk.* All the while my gaze is on her gorgeous eyes, and she stares back at me with the same desire I have for her.

The past is over and done. No one else will ever know what really happened—not her, not anyone. *So why can't I truly have her?*

"Mason." She practically whimpers my name and it pulls the beast in me closer to her. My knee dips into the bed, making it groan with my weight as I crawl over to her.

Her soft blue eyes pierce through me, cutting through the dark room. More of the soft lighting from the city slips between us as the heat kicks on and the curtains sway. The way the light kisses her skin as she pushes away the blush silk duvet makes her all the more beautiful.

She's laid out for me. *All for me.* She needs me.

I crush my lips to hers and dig my fingers into the flesh of her hips as she spreads her thighs for me. Her soft moans fill the hot air between us.

She's ashamed to be moving on so quickly. Especially with a man like me. I wasn't made for a woman like her. I'm someone who could tarnish her sterling reputation and make the cracks in her picture-perfect life even deeper. To say I'm rough around the edges is putting it lightly, but I have what it takes to keep her.

She thinks she's ruined, but she's perfect. It's my sins and secrets that could destroy us both. I'll never let them come to light. Not now that I have something worth fighting for.

CHAPTER
one

Julia

Present day

I'M CAUGHT BETWEEN MY NEED TO RUN AWAY AND THE need to know the truth. I need the truth from him. No more secrets; no more lies.

He promised.

He loves me.

There's just no way.

"Did you do it?" The question leaves me in a single weak breath and in an instant, something snaps into place. It's as if he's not at all shocked by what I'm saying. As if he's been waiting for this.

No. My body turns to ice; my blood freezes in my veins and I can't believe this is reality. It can't be true.

Mason takes a step forward, starting to move around the island and it breaks me from my denial.

It's my cue to run, a natural instinct that takes over. The stool falls hard, crashing to the floor as I take off, but Mason's faster, grabbing my waist and jerking me backward. I cry out from fear and he releases me, only for me to fall onto the tiles at my feet. His large frame towers over me, and he puts his hands up as though he's approaching a wild animal. I feel like I am just that. Eyes wide as I stare up at him, my heart pounds painfully in my chest. *Thump, thump, thump.*

"Did I do what?" he asks with a coldness I haven't seen before and his eyes narrowed. This isn't the man I know.

My bottom lip trembles, the small bit of strength I had vanishing as I take in the raw truth. "Did you kill my husband?"

The words leave me in agony as they hover in the tense air between us.

I can't believe I even asked him that. *Deny it. Please deny it. Tell me I'm a fool. And this, whatever this is, it's something that's already over and never happened.*

Mason stands up straight, giving me enough space so that my breath can come back to me, but my lungs refuse to fill until he answers me.

"They think they can do whatever they want," Mason says, still standing over me as he snatches the paper from where it lays on the floor. I didn't even realize I'd dropped it.

No. That's not what he should be saying right now.

"Your husband wasn't a good man," Mason adds lowly, his

eyes piercing me before flicking back to the paper. He crumples it in his fist as a cold sweat spreads across my skin.

"No." It's all I can say. "You didn't." I try to say more but it's in vain as my throat dries up and constricts. I don't know if it's the shock or if I'm just that pathetic. I didn't fall for a murderer. Mason couldn't—

"I did." Mason's confession makes me light-headed, and a sickness churns in my gut.

My heart twists with a pain that's unbearable as I crawl away quickly, trying to escape. I slip against the ground, crashing hard to the cold, unforgiving floor.

"No!" I scream at him, leaving a strangled cry to linger between us. It's only then that I even register I'm crying.

I try again to run, managing to get to my feet this time and the foyer is so close as I stumble out of the kitchen. I call out for help, although I doubt anyone could hear us. Not here inside Mason's home. I practically slam into the front door, but Mason's right behind me.

With one hand on the door and one on the knob, his hard body presses against mine, trapping me between him and my only escape.

His large body cages me in. I'm left facing the door, barely able to stand or breathe. "You were never supposed to know," he whispers. I shrink beneath him, the weight of the reality crashing down on me. "I'm sorry."

I've fallen in love with my husband's killer. I've slept with him and given him everything.

"I'm not going to hurt you, Jules." His warm breath sends shivers down my back as he adds, "But I can't let you leave."

CHAPTER

two

Julia

*T*HE ONLY THING YOU NEED TO WORRY ABOUT IS *remembering my name. Just my name and what I've done to you tonight.*

Mason whispered those words so close to my ear, sending a shiver of want through my body. It was everything I desired when I met him. He made that promise to me the first night, and I so easily fell into his bed.

I'd been so desperate to feel *anything* but the heartache and misery I'd succumbed to.

If only I could take it back.

If only I'd known this man was the cause of my pain.

Anger seethes inside me as I stare at him across the other

side of his bedroom, where he's sitting in the corner. His elbows rest on his thighs as he hunches over the edge of the reading chair with his head in his hands. His fingers run back and forth along the back of his head as if there's a thought inside his mind he can't quite reach.

He won't look at me; he merely stares at the ground in complete silence. All the while I'm shattered, and with every minute that passes I feel the broken pieces more and more.

My body is restless and my eyes burn with a desperate need to cry, but I have nothing left.

I try to scoot my exhausted body up the bed to soothe my sore arms, but the rope tied around my wrists tightens with the sudden pull, chafing me. I wince and suck in a breath through clenched teeth; my shoulders are screaming in pain.

Hours have passed since I found out the truth. Hours spent restrained to this bed. When I wouldn't stop screaming and fighting him, clawing at him and trying to escape his strong grip, he tied me up.

It's been only minutes since he's come back into the room, though. Minutes since he's opened that door and let his eyes rest on me. I'm pathetic, weak and completely at his mercy. Captive to a man I loved who hid a secret so dark and corrupt it's ruined me. I'll never be the same. There's no way to recover.

Ticktock. Ticktock.

It's only been minutes since he lowered himself into the chair without speaking a word to me, I remind myself. He sits in a chair I brought from my home to his. A chair I'd cried countless tears in after my husband died.

And yet he says nothing. It's the silence that kills me.

"I hate you." The words slowly scrape their way up my sore

throat. They're barely audible, since my voice is so raspy and weak from all the screaming.

He slowly lifts his head, his corded muscles rippling. For the first time since I've been with Mason, after months spent falling in love with him, I feel real agony. The small involuntary shudder my body makes proves there's a bit of fear present too.

The sharp lines of his jaw look more intense in the dim light, the shadows only making them seem more severe. His steel gray eyes are like daggers as he captures my gaze.

I can't breathe; I can't look away. I hate him for what he did then and I hate him for how he's making me feel now.

"You don't," he says and his voice is rough and deep. He sounds stronger than before. But it's a lie. All lies.

I do. I hate him more than I could ever express.

Finally, I gasp for air rather than crying any more tears, breaking his gaze to stare up at the ceiling. Even that minor movement makes the raw wounds at my wrists hurt. I try to hide it, though.

I gave this man everything. How could I have been so foolish? "I hate you more than you'll ever know," I murmur to the ceiling in an eerily calm voice although my heart is anything but.

The creaking of the floorboards grabs my attention, and my gaze whips to Mason as he stands. Goosebumps spread slowly over every inch of my skin as he rises.

His muscular frame seems so much larger in this moment, and a hint of a lethal concoction gives a low stir in the pit of my stomach. He's always been dominating and intimidating, but this is something darker… something more.

I have nothing to protect me, not even a sheet. He stripped

the linens off the bed before tying me up and I was left in only the underwear and baggy, thin cotton T-shirt I slipped on this morning. The chill is getting to me.

The bed dips and groans as he places a knee on it only inches away from me. I would struggle to pull away, but I'm stuck here. Both of us know that.

"I love you, Jules," he murmurs and his words are a mix of strangled pain and determination. He's a broken man with a tortured soul.

I don't know how I could possibly look at a man who's done this to me and feel any kind of sorrow for him, but I do.

I've met men before who've been wound tight, waiting to go off like a bomb. They were always constantly on edge and ready for a fight at a moment's notice. Mason's not like that. Instead he's like thread loosely wrapped around a spindle, nothing but a mess of tangles. It's not soft string; this thread's sharp to the touch and there's no hope at unraveling it without cutting yourself.

I never knew how deeply he'd wounded me. I had no idea that while I was busy mending myself and leaning on him for support, he was watching me bleed out, saying nothing. The closer he got, the deeper the inevitable betrayal, but that didn't stop him. He had so many chances to tell me what he'd done.

I let my head drop to look him in the eyes. It makes my heart swell with an unbearable pain to have him so close to me. To see how injured he is, but knowing it's nothing compared to what he's done to me.

I truly loved him. I thought fate had given me a second chance at love and happiness. I knew it was too good to be true.

"How could you do that?" The aching question isn't what

I'd planned to say when I narrowed my eyes. "You're sick," I add and the words are gritted out somehow, bearing the strength I was aiming for and I wait for him to strike back with the same venom I've given him.

His steady breathing is somehow calming and it irritates me as I watch his chest rise and fall. "Maybe," he says before rising off the bed and turning away from me. My heart plummets at the sight of his back to me and my expression crumples. It physically hurts me to know he's hurting too. I thought I knew agony before. My God.

Why did this happen? How could it happen?

Tears threaten and I shove them back, hating all of this and praying to just wake up and find it's merely a bad dream. *Please! Please, I would give anything for this to only be a nightmare.* My silent prayers are disrupted by the wood floors creaking as Mason heads toward the door, leaving me here and not giving me any indication of what's to come.

"Aren't you going to say you're sorry?" I whisper the ragged question. Maybe that's what's most shocking; he hasn't said he's sorry. Not for tying me up and keeping me here… not for murdering my husband almost a year ago.

His tall frame pauses in the partially opened doorway, stopping in his tracks as he registers what I've said. He turns his head slowly to look back at me over his shoulder, his hand still on the carved glass doorknob.

"I already told you that I'm sorry. You were never supposed to know the truth."

"You're only sorry that I found out?" I ask with equal amounts of disbelief and hurt.

His eyes dart to the floor and the bedroom door groans as it opens slightly wider.

He glances up at me hesitantly, as if debating on telling me something. It would be the truth; I can see it, can feel the intensity. Instead he says nothing, walking out of the bedroom with even strides before slamming the door shut behind him.

three

Mason

The past is dark,
And filled with pain.
Mistakes were made,
And nothing gained.

If I had known,
I'd have found a way.
But what's done is done,
The past never goes away.

SOMEONE KNOWS. THE KNOWLEDGE BRINGS A CHILL that prickles down my shoulders to the base of my spine. Someone knows what I've done. It's been nearly a year. So much time has passed and yet they've said and done nothing until now. All the possibilities of who it could possibly be are jumbled in the forefront of my mind. For hours I've been focused on this rather than what I've done to Jules. My poor Jules.

I didn't think anyone knew until Jules received that letter.

It destroys me that I couldn't lie to her. I couldn't hide what I'd done. Some sick, twisted part of me is relieved that now she knows.

But then I see the way she looks at me. I deserve the hate… I knew it would come to this and still I want to fix it. I don't have any other choice but to make this right. I can't let her go.

I won't.

They say if you love someone, you should let them go.

That's bullshit.

I didn't know it until I lost her, but I had nothing to live for without Jules. There's no possibility in this life that I'm going back to what I was before her.

The idea that she could turn me in has barely even registered. It's merely a passing thought that intrudes upon the images replaying in my head of seeing her walk away from me. The memories of her pushing against my chest, violently scratching and kicking me. Her screams that she hates me echo in my ears over and over.

She doesn't mean it. She can't hate me. Not for that.

I swallow thickly as I descend the stairs, gripping the

railing and matching the pounding of my heart with the heavy thud of my bare feet.

I can make it right. I can and I will. My palm is clammy as I hold the railing tighter.

It's a priority to figure out how to make her forget the past and remember her future is with me. I nod, envisioning how this was *supposed* to be. How it could have ended so beautifully.

I check to make sure the front door's locked as I pass the foyer, still completely trashed from our earlier struggle and head for the dining room, ignoring the mess.

More importantly, I need to find out who the fuck knows what I did and if they have any evidence. That's first. Jules needs time to cool off and while she does, I need to work out who sent that letter and why.

Jules is angry, and I get that. Saying it was a shock is obviously an understatement. I flick on the light and my eyes are instantly drawn to the bar. To a vice I desperately need to lean on while I process my lack of grace at what I did to her.

She was never meant to find out what happened. I was a different man then. If I'd known her at the time, I would have handled it differently. I would have ripped her away from that piece of shit and taken her for myself. In another life, perhaps it happened that way.

But that's not our reality.

Picking up a glass from the rack on the edge of the bar, I remember the haunting look in her eyes; the glass clinks as the adrenaline in my blood begins to wane for the first time since seeing her face as she read the letter.

I don't know how to fix this. Every other trouble Jules has had has been easy to remedy. This… I know it's unforgivable, but what she wants isn't an option for us. I can't go back to what I once had and who I used to be.

I need her and she may not want to admit it right now, but she needs me. Deep down, she knows it's true. This doesn't change anything.

She just needs time and so do I. I'll figure out a way to keep her and make her happy again. *It's not the first time I've destroyed her*, I think as the bottom of the heavy glass hits the bar top.

I crack my neck to the side as I hear her cry out again, sharp profanity echoing down the stairway and hall. Her voice is raw and hoarse, and I know the regret plagues her.

A smirk lifts up my lips. She's right, I must be sick. The thought that lingers is that she has to regret moving in with me. My house is on the edges of the city and in a secluded, remote location. If we were at her place, the neighbors would have heard everything, and the cops would have already been called. I'd be fucked.

I give a small grin as I twist off the cap to the whiskey and slowly pour it into the tumbler. No one can hear her but me while we're in here.

I'm the only knight in shining armor she's going to get.

I bring the glass to my lips and the smile vanishes, my eyes drifting to the lit fireplace. She turned it on earlier, claiming it brings a warmth to the darkness in the dining room.

Downing my whiskey and then raking my fingers through my hair, I let out a frustrated sigh over the sound of her screaming.

She's going to be sore and angry, and the marks on her wrists will need time to fade, but she'll survive. She'll get over it.

Whoever wrote that note though, whoever tried to tear

my sweetheart from me, that fucker won't survive this. I grit my teeth as I slam the glass down and feel the burn of the liquor spread through my chest.

The thought prompts me to head to the entryway. The rug is crooked from when I dragged Jules up the stairs, and the lamp on the hall table is on its side, but at least it's not broken. My keys and wallet are still on the floor from when she knocked them off the table in her frantic attempt to hold on to something, anything to keep her from being taken upstairs.

My eyes dart up to the wall behind the iron banister. A low hum of admonishment leaves me as I bend down to pick up the scattered items.

The dents and scrapes on the walls are going to be a bit more difficult to fix. Recalling the feel of her struggling against me stirs an unrecognizable emotion inside my gut. I close my eyes and picture how I held her tight against me, forcing her still and pushing her against the wall, trapping her. She never stopped fighting, though. I count every little mark. Her nails scratched against the drywall, desperate for something to save her. It's *evidence* that's not so easy to clean up.

I did what I had to do, I think although the justification sounds hollow in the back of my mind.

The keys jingle as I toss them onto the table, scooting it back into place and then I snatch up the crumpled piece of thick cream parchment.

The note that destroyed what I had.

I clear my throat, willing the images and memories to go away as my chest tightens with unbearable pain. I had her. I had my sweetheart and she loved me, I know she did.

The letter crinkles as I focus my eyes on it and turn my

back to the staircase, resting my shoulder against the doorframe of the dining room and listening to the crackling of the fire.

It's handwritten and leans more toward feminine penmanship. My eyes narrow as I look over every inch of the paper attempting to recognize the curve of a letter, something, anything. Not a damn memory comes to mind. There's no name. No way to identify who it came from.

Dear Julia,

It pains me to tell you this, but I can't stand to watch from a distance as you fall into a trap. Your husband was murdered. I know this is going to shock you, but I have proof. You may not believe me, but I pray that you do.

Mason Thatcher murdered him. Don't trust him. Don't let him know that you know. If he finds out, you won't be safe.

All I can tell you is that you need to run. Stay far away.

I can't say any more. I hope this letter finds you safe and you take every word for what it is, the truth.

Truly yours,

X

Proof. My narrowed gaze focuses on the single word, my heart racing faster and faster. There's not a single possibility that someone has proof.

There were no cameras around. There's no fucking way anyone saw. Her prick of a husband was leaving his apartment after screwing his mistress, and on his way back home. Back to Jules, his wife he didn't deserve. My chest rumbles with a low murmur of anger at the memory. His arrogance was one of the things I hated most about him.

My eyes whip to the stairs as I hear Jules call out again. Her voice is cracked and so uneven I can't make out a damn word she's saying. I grit my teeth and resist the urge to burn the note. I need it and the envelope it came in.

This is a fucking mess. But I make a solemn promise to Jules: I'll fix this.

Gripping the banister, I wait a moment for her cries to cease and then slowly ascend the staircase. A tic in my jaw starts to twitch as I formulate a plan. I need to explain why I did it and calm her down. I need time or a fucking miracle. It's too late to deny any of it. I was too rash, too caught up in the moment when she confronted me. All I could see was red.

The door opens with a gentle push. I didn't bother to lock it since she's tied to the bed.

My eyes latch onto her the second I step into our bedroom. She's barely clothed, her gorgeous pale skin on full display, although most of it is flushed from her struggling and screaming.

"What do you need, sweetheart?" I ask her calmly, completely ignoring the current situation.

Her eyes narrow as she sucks in a breath, and I can feel the anger rolling off of her in waves. I nearly let out a sigh of relief. *Anger I can deal with.* The thought almost makes me smile.

"Let me out," she says although her eyes flicker down and her voice wavers with the demand.

"I can't do that if you're going to run."

"Just let me go, Mason," she pleads with a soft whimper. She licks her lips and attempts to push herself upright. Jules winces from the binds cutting into her wrists, and I can't fucking stand it.

My hands ball into fists, but I stay put. I can't risk her trying to escape.

"You need to stay here, with me, until we figure this out," I say to her in a placating tone as I step forward, rounding the bed to get closer to her. Her breathing quickens and I'm not sure if it's due to anger or fear from me getting closer to her. My blood runs cold at the second possibility.

"We need to talk about this," I tell her gently as I sit down carefully and attempt to ease whatever worry I can. I don't want to tell her anything, and everything in me is screaming to lie and let it all be forgotten. But she's mine, and I won't do that to her. It was one thing to withhold the truth about the past, but it's another to outright lie about it.

She should know the truth, even if she doesn't like it.

"Ask me anything." My gaze is struck by hers as I speak. Her baby blues are rimmed in red, and her cheeks tearstained. She's gorgeous even like this, but not when she misbehaves. She presses her lips into a thin line, even though the bottom one trembles, and shakes her head. It seems fear is the dominant emotion. A vise tightens over my chest.

I look past her as the thick gray velvet curtain sways slightly when the heater turns on with a click. I watch it for a moment, steadying my breath and quickly come up with a solution.

"For every question," I start to say and then pause to look back at her. She's wary and when she realizes I'm offering her something, her entire body noticeably stiffens. "Every question you ask, I'll answer you honestly and untie you a bit."

It's not the best solution, seeing as how there are only four knots total keeping the rope in place. One on each wrist, and two tying her to the bed.

"You can't fight me, Jules." I harden my voice just before she can answer. "I'll let you go, but I won't let you run. Do you understand?"

She swallows and then licks her lips. "Yes," she says, the answer just above a murmur. I can tell it hurts her to speak at all, because she withdraws the moment the word slips into the tense air between us, a look of pain evident on her face.

She needs tea and to be held. She needs a gentle hand.

The bed groans as I sit, resting my hand on her bare thigh. Like a good girl she doesn't move, but she does close her eyes as if she can't stand my touch. I gently rub my thumb in soothing circles and I stare down at where our skin meets as I wait for her.

She'll forgive me, I know she will. It's only a matter of time and I'll let her lead. But only if she moves in the right direction. Closer to the two of us regaining what we had only hours ago. I just need time and given the fact my development company is now dissolved, I have plenty of it.

"Why did you do it?" she asks.

My head lifts at her question, and I meet her gaze head-on. There's nothing but sadness in those gorgeous doe eyes. "He was responsible for a woman's death."

Before I've even finished saying the words, she's already shaking her head. Already in denial. "No, I don't believe you." Her voice cracks, a telltale sign of her refusal to accept the truth as she rips her gaze from me and stares straight ahead at the door.

"I'm not lying to you, Jules." It's a struggle to keep my voice tender, thinking back on what came over me when I decided Jace Anderson deserved to die.

"You lied," she practically hisses at me, taking me by surprise. She screams with outrage, "You're a liar!"

"I never lied to you," I answer evenly, correcting her and ignoring her outburst while I tighten my grip on the edge of the bed. I have to wait a moment for her to calm down before reaching up and slowly untying the knot on her left wrist. A deal is a deal. Even if I fucking hate her response. Her tender skin is bright pink, and it makes my chest feel tight with guilt. I never wanted to hurt her. Never. I retake my seat as she whispers, "You didn't tell the truth."

My throat dries and a rawness takes over, dampening every nerve ending along my skin. I don't have many memories of my mother, but the ones I do, the ones that are clear, are the ones where she calls my father a liar. The images flash in front of me, and my body goes cold. "I'm not a liar. I did what I had to do."

"I could never do what you did," she says.

Everyone can kill. I keep the thought to myself, hating how true it is. It's only a matter of what would push someone to do it.

"Do you have any other questions?"

"Are you going to kill me?" she asks as if it's a real possibility. Her breathing is hesitant and then hitches when she closes her eyes tight.

Waiting for those doe eyes to look back at me, desperate for an answer, the one word I give her is filled with a promise. "Never." It makes my heart hurt that she thinks it's even an option. "I told you I'd never hurt you." Of all the things today that have me on edge, that right there is the most distressing. The thought in her head that I'm someone who would hurt her is unacceptable.

My hand rests gently against her thigh and she's quick to pull away, as if I've scorched her skin. I still at the sobering sight of her.

Her blue eyes have never looked so cold as she looks up at me and says, "No." Her next words carry so much conviction, so much hate. "Don't touch me… please."

I clench my jaw and hesitate. This is too much. Too far, and too much. I'm quick to untie all the remaining binds, blood rushing in my ears and my fingers seemingly going numb. I drop the thin rope and it pools into a puddle around her, but she doesn't move to get up. She doesn't do anything but lean farther away from me.

Her mouth opens as I push off the bed and stand to leave, but she doesn't say anything. There's only silence.

"You may hate me now, Jules, but I still love you, and you're not going anywhere until you know that and until you understand why it had to happen."

The door closes behind me with a loud click and I don't stop walking until I get to the office to retrieve the house keys. I'll lock the door. I'll keep her here until she understands.

There's no fucking way I'm letting her leave. She'll figure it out eventually; she's always been mine. It was only a matter of me finding her.

CHAPTER

four

Julia

ALTHOUGH MY EYES ARE TIRED AND MY HEAD AND limbs ache, I don't move. Not an inch. Not since I took the engagement ring off my finger and flung it across the room.

I'm far too aware of every event that led to this. It's as if I've lived my life under the warm silk sheets of the most welcoming bed, only to be kicked out, landing face-first on the cold, cracked concrete floor.

More than anything, one word keeps coming to mind. *Unprepared.* I have no idea what to do, or even what to think. It's all a mess. My life is a jumbled mess of chaos and tragedy.

It's hard enough to grasp the fact that Jace was murdered. Much harder still to think that I fell in love with his murderer.

I need to get away. Far away from Mason just so I can think straight.

I can't focus on anything else other than that one truth: I need to get the hell out of this room.

The bedroom door's locked from the outside; the telltale jingle of keys and then the loud click of the lock a few moments ago alerted me to that. I already know it's the case without even trying to turn the knob. I suppose that's better than having to face him. To my left, the curtain sways and draws my eyes.

My throat closes at the thought of seeing him again. I loved him. My heart feels like a vise is clamped around it, squeezing tighter each time I think about who Mason really is and what I've done. I fell in love with my husband's killer.

The shock is still there, but it's not enough to keep the sickness of my reality at bay.

My head feels dizzy—from exhaustion maybe, I'm not sure, but I don't have time to think. I don't have time for anything until I'm far away from here.

I stare at the lone window in this room. I know it's an idiotic notion to think I can climb down from the second story and land safely below, but I have no other choice and I refuse not to try.

If there's one thing the recollection of the events leading up to this have screamed at me, it's that I need to take action and stop allowing life to railroad me.

I don't have my keys, my phone or wallet. With the groan of the bed seemingly chiding me as I stand up and make my way to the window, I peek outside to see there's already a thin layer of snow on the ground. Given its late November in New York, I'm not shocked but it's still frustrating. If I make it down there alive without breaking my neck, he'll be able to see where I've gone. A part of me huffs at the thought, knowing this is foolish, trying to escape.

But I only need to flag someone down on the road or bang on a neighbor's door. *I have to try, and I'm not waiting another second.*

The floor in the bedroom is creaky and every little sound forces me to check that the door is still closed. I know he'll be able to hear me from downstairs if he's listening. I'm careful with each step and do my best to limit the noise as I move around. I inhale deeply through clenched teeth as I open the dresser as quietly as I can but it's loud just the same as I slowly pull on the drawer. I've never noticed it before, but right now every single noise is far too loud.

My heart rampages in protest at each squeak and groan from the wooden floors. *I'm only getting dressed*, I tell myself over and over. If he comes up now, if he hears me and storms into the room to check on me, I'm only getting dressed. Surely that's what he must think.

My eyes burn with unshed tears thinking about Mason coming up here. Realizing the fear I now have for a man I once loved makes my chest feel unbearably tight.

What if he catches me?

What will he do when he's realized I've left?

Even worse: *What would he do to me?*

I swallow down the insecurity and fear; I can't be

paralyzed by them. I can't wait here in this damn room for him to decide what to do with me. I'm stronger than that.

The first shirt and pair of leggings I pull out are good enough and then from the drawer below, I grab a pair of jeans to pull over top of the leggings. It's freezing outside. I don't have a coat because they're all downstairs in the hall closet, but I layer a sweater and then another one over my long-sleeved shirt. It's hard to tell if the burning heat is from the fabrics or from the anxiety that rages through me.

My fingers shake as I pull down the long cashmere sleeves. If he came up now, he'd know for sure that this is more than me just getting dressed. I'm dressed to leave. The thoughts don't slow me, they only push me to be faster; I'm fueled by nerves and the desperation to save myself.

I can barely breathe as I kneel and tie the shoelaces on a pair of sneakers I grabbed from the walk-in closet. My hands don't stop trembling and my vision keeps going in and out as the dull pain behind my eyes gets worse. I sway as my light-headedness becomes too much, and I have to close my eyes and breathe. Just breathe.

I stand on wobbly legs and walk as quietly as I can to the window, which is just as unhelpful as it was a moment ago. Staring over my shoulder at the closed door, I lick my dry, cracked lips as I unlock the window. The lock on the left turns easily but the one on the right is tight, and I need both hands and all my focus to loosen it. Each second that passes seems too long, as if this small moment is enough time for him to stop me.

Tick, tick, tick.

The sound of my heavy breathing and the blood rushing in my ears are all I hear as I push the window up as high as

I can. I manage to lift the heavy thing about two feet, and I hope it'll be enough. I know there's a way to somehow angle the window and get the screen out, but in my haste and nervousness, I can't figure it out.

The heater clicks on again and I nearly have a heart attack, my scream barely contained as it tries to escape from my throat.

Tick, tick, tick.

I can't wait any longer. As the heat drifts up from the vent and mixes with the frigid November air that blows across my face, I panic.

My only thought is to rip out the screen. Without wasting another tick of the internal clock, I snatch a shirt from the hamper to my right and wrap it around my hand. My footsteps were far too loud, but time is more important.

I take one more look back at the door before punching through the screen. It breaks surprisingly easily and I nearly fall forward, the torn mesh scraping against my forearm. I contain my gasp and ignore how my heart seems to leap up my throat as I look down two stories to the cold hard ground below. It's a sobering sight.

There's a thin layer of white snow coating the grass and although the weather has let up, the air is sharp from the biting wind. I take a deep breath, pulling the ripped screen back and tearing it open more, protecting my hand with the clothing. Somehow ripping it wider is more difficult than making the initial tear.

My breathing comes in faster, and the light-headed sensation returns when the hole is large enough for me to climb through.

All the spiked edges of the broken screen are going to

catch on my sweater, I already know. Once I get footing out on the sill, I'll have to try to grip onto the pillar to my right and slowly climb down while balancing myself on the stones that line the house. It's practically impossible. My head shakes of its own accord at the thought, refusing to feel defeated. I have to do this. I have no other choice.

The threads of my sweater snag like I knew they would the moment I climb through the window and brush against the screen, but I press forward. As my left foot finds purchase on the windowsill, the wind blows so forcefully that I cling to the frame with my right hand and consider abandoning the idea completely. *I've gone absolutely mad.* My nose and cheeks burn from the biting cold, and I have to close my eyes.

Breathe. Just breathe.

I refuse to go back in there. The second the wind stops, I finish crawling out and balance on the ledge, my knuckles bright white from holding on so tightly. Each time I have to readjust my grip, I'm filled with a renewed sense of terror. Only the balls of my feet are balanced on the thin ledge, and my hands already ache from clutching the window in the bitter cold.

I make the mistake of looking down and seeing how far I'd drop and how there's nothing to break my fall if the wind were to blow too hard. Or if my grip gives out, or if something else happens and I fail. *I don't want to die.*

A few moments pass and I simply can't move. The wind whips my hair around my face and I shut my eyes tight, frozen by the vision of me plummeting to my death.

This is taking too much time. I need to get going. My left

foot moves first, all the way to the edge of the sill and as far as I can get with both of my hands still gripping the window frame.

I have to let go in order to lean over, and I do it so quickly and with so much force that I nearly push myself off. My head spins from the height, but I keep moving. My right hand grips the window and my left reaches for the brick closest to the pillar. My nails scratch at the rough stone, but my grip is solid.

I feel stuck for the longest time. The cold makes my hands numb and the wind is coming and going so frequently that I'm afraid the second I move, it will violently rip me away from the pillar, but I manage the motion in a single leap.

A scream is torn from my throat as I fall an inch or two until my sneaker hits the decorative carving on the pillar and I'm able to wrap my arms around it. Adrenaline roars inside of me and I pray Mason didn't hear. And then I make another silent prayer: that this foolish plan will work.

Slowly, ever so slowly, I climb down inch by inch. The only places I dare to look are directly in front of me and up to the open window. I watch the curtains sway inside of the bedroom as I slip down the pillar at a snail's pace, relying on the tread of my sneakers against the carved marble pillar for purchase.

I don't even realize I've made it safely until I try to slide farther down and can't. There's ground beneath my feet.

Astonished and still very much consumed by fear, I note my sweater is torn with pulls everywhere, and I'm so cold I can hardly move my limbs. I look up once more at the open window and realize it's only a matter of time before he realizes I'm gone.

Run. I don't hesitate one more second. My sore limbs come to life as I take off down Mason's driveway and I don't look back.

CHAPTER

five

Mason

NEED TO MAKE TWO THINGS CLEAR TO HER.

1. I love her, and I always will.
2. She's not leaving me.

We're going to work through this one way or another. Even if I have to drug her. I know the chances of a roofie working at this point are slim to none, but depending on her reaction, it's the only thing I can think of and the only easy out to make things right again. If only she would forget.

As I draw closer to the top of the stairs, a cold draft wraps itself around me. At first, I'm confused, then furious. She didn't. She wouldn't… my denial is pointless. I already know she did.

My pace picks up and I bang on the bedroom door. My knuckles slam against the hard wood door and I yell out, "Jules!"

How long has it been, maybe a half hour at most since I locked her in there? My heart hammers in my chest. She's gone. *She's left me.*

It's no use. I can already feel the cold air seeping into the hall from under the door. The keys are already in my hand as I pound my fist against the door again like a fucking fool, nearly breaking down the door. They rattle as I find the right one and shove it into the lock before throwing open the door. I'm greeted with an empty bed and the biting cold blowing in through a torn window screen.

I stare at the window for only a second before taking long strides across the room, pulling the curtain back to look down at the ground outside. I half expect to see her lying dead on the grass.

She'd rather risk this than deal with me.

My throat closes at the bitter thought, and the harsh wind whispers, taunting me that she simply jumped to end it all. Relief is unexpected but welcome when I peer out and trace the footsteps in the snow. She hasn't been gone long judging by how clean and clear the prints are.

My lungs threaten to fail me as I take off out the room and down the stairs, and I don't stop moving as I snatch my car keys and phone off the front hall table. She's out there with a head start and I only have so much time to catch her. My coat's in the living room, but I don't bother with it. I don't bother with anything other than climbing into my Mercedes and reversing out of the driveway as quickly as I can.

A thin layer of sweat covers my skin and only adds to the freezing effect of the air.

If she tells anyone… I'm fucked.

"She can't," I say under my breath and curse, the vision of her testifying against me flashing in front of my eyes. There's hardly any snow on the asphalt, and her footprints disappear in less than a quarter mile. With my hands gripping and twisting the leather steering wheel, I continue to drive ahead. I glance down every small gap I pass, although the main road is vacant. It's early morning and I know there are plenty of cars that drive by here on their way to work. She could have flagged someone down.

She's gone. My throat tightens with the realization and I pound my fist against the window.

She doesn't have any evidence. My thoughts take over. She has no proof, and there's nothing the police would ever find. She couldn't possibly go to them. There's no fucking way. But if not to the police, then where?

My heart's racing as I pull over, and I don't know what the hell she's thinking.

That you're a murderer. That you'll hurt her.

I ignore the damning truth and keep pushing down the ache that takes over.

It doesn't take long before I decide my next move should be to search her home. If not there, then I need to find her friend's addresses. My tires squeal as I pull back onto the road, intent on finding her and bringing her back here. I don't need anyone else trying to keep her away from me.

I lean over and click the radio off, only just now realizing it's on and then turn the heat all the way up. I'm numb from the combination of the wintry air and the thoughts that won't quit yelling in my head that I'm fucked. Turning on my blinker to head onto a busier street, I struggle to take in an easy breath.

Act normal. Come up with a plan.

There was a nasty rumor going around that Jules has had issues with alcohol ever since Jace's death. I'd never talk about her as if she were a drunk, but I have to use something that would make people question why she'd accuse me of murder.

I tap my thumb against the steering wheel.

I don't know if it would work. It'd be her word against mine. And there's no real evidence.

But if I went down that route, I'd definitely lose her and everyone in this city would question if there was any truth to what she claimed.

My family name would be called into question.

My business reputation would be ruined.

More than that, the only person I ever loved would be my downfall.

A bitter huff of a humorless laugh leaves me as I look to my left and turn down the street.

I could go away for life if the police do believe her and look into it. If they find something, or if the person who sent that note comes forward with their proof. I don't give a fuck about that, though. I haven't known what love is since my mother died. But I know it's what I feel for Jules.

I've given her the power to ruin me. That's what true love is.

If I let her get away, she'll do it.

She'll destroy every piece of me.

As I struggle to come to terms with the realization, my

phone rings from the passenger seat where I'd thrown it earlier. I lean over and pick it up, answering without looking to see who it is while I drive down Jules's street.

"Hello," I answer, hoping it's her. Hoping she's only asking for time or space. I won't give her either, but at least then I'll know we have a chance.

"Mason," my father says.

"Father," I say, feeling disappointment that it's not her, followed by distrust. We haven't spoken since I knocked him out in his office. What the hell does he want?

His voice is full of confidence but more than that, imperiousness. "I have a little something I think you want." I pull up alongside Jules's street but the only parking space available is a few doors down from her place, and I slow down to lean forward and look out the windshield. It's starting to get light outside, but not so much that I wouldn't see lights on inside her house. I scan the windows as I absently say, "And what would that be?"

"I got a call from Commissioner Haynes." My body stills as my father continues.

His words snap my attention to him. *Commissioner.* "It seems your recent love interest has something urgent to confess."

If my father thinks she's a threat, that's a much more concerning issue.

"She doesn't know anything." I'm quick to respond. I speed down the street, cutting someone off and they lean on their horn. I have to weave through the few cars out this early in the morning to get down to Fourth Street. I need to get to her. "Don't touch her," I say.

"I wouldn't dare," my father says, and I can practically see the smug smile on his face. *Jules.* I grit my teeth in anger.

"I imagine you'll be here soon?" he asks with a thin veil of arrogance.

"I'm ten minutes from the station," I answer grudgingly. I hate that he's involved and interfering, but if he wasn't, she would have talked. She has no idea what she's done. She's put herself in danger.

My foot presses down harder on the gas pedal with each passing thought. I need to get to Jules before she says a fucking word.

CHAPTER

six

Julia

I'VE BEEN PICKING AT THE SAME SNARLED THREAD ON my sweater for nearly fifteen minutes now.

My sneaker taps nervously against the leg of the simple wooden table; they're still damp from the snow. Something feels off and wrong. Crossing my arms, I look away from the mirror. Anywhere but the mirror.

The stranger in the car kept asking me over and over what was wrong, but I could barely speak. I was so cold, and nothing would come out except that I needed the police. I was lucky he pulled over and offered me a ride. The concern in his pale blue eyes was comforting but only so much that it allowed me to get in the car. His checkered sweater slid down his bony arms as he drove, and he kept looking over at me in the passenger seat. He had to be in his fifties, or maybe sixties. The wrinkles around his eyes told me he was at least my father's age.

That comfort is long gone and a different sensation took over the second he stopped in front of the station. I have no proof, no evidence. I don't know if anyone is going to believe me. I need to tell someone, though. I swallow thickly, realizing I don't know where to begin or if a soul will believe me or do anything at all.

The old man stayed with me while a young officer gave me a blanket and told me it was all right. *Whatever it is, you're safe now.* Dressed in his blues, the man was maybe in his mid-twenties and didn't have a clue what I was there for. It was such a spectacle, but even though they were kind and open I still couldn't spit out the words.

Then I was handed over to Detective Myer.

He's much too young for someone in his position, clean-shaven and tall with dark brown eyes. He has to be around the same age as the officer who greeted me warmly. There's no warmth to Myer, though; he's all corded muscle, although he doesn't have the broad shoulders or height to him to balance out his body. Even with his badge and prying stare, he doesn't have an air around him that commands authority.

There's something else as well, something about the way he looks at me that makes me feel as though I'm not safe. Like I should have changed my mind and headed back out into the snow and never stopped running. I don't trust the detective. I didn't when he told me to sit in here and twenty minutes later, what little hope and faith I had has faded.

Maybe I'm being paranoid and it's all in my head, but it

seems wrong he never asked any questions. He simply told me to follow him back here and sat me down while he went to talk to the commissioner. I'm alone and left wondering what the hell I'm doing here at all.

Guilt worms its way through every bone in my body. Every tick of the clock tempts me to get up from this table. I'm going to choke on my words. I can't do this. They'll never believe me and I can't say the truth out loud.

Just as the notion hits me, the door opens and I stand mostly out of instinct, but also possibly fear. The need to run is overwhelming, but when my eyes catch sight of the imposing man walking in behind Detective Myer and another man who I assume is the commissioner, my knees go weak.

I don't need to be told he's Mason's father. I don't need to be introduced. His gray eyes and sharp cheekbones give it away. He even clears his throat like Mason as he unbuttons his suit jacket and sits in the empty chair across from me.

My eyes flicker to Detective Myer's, who simply crosses his arms and leans against the wall in the far left corner. His dark eyes bore into me and send a chill down my spine. The commissioner makes a show of closing the door and then taking a seat at the far end of the table.

"Sit, sit," Mason's father insists. "Jules, isn't it?" he says with a smile that doesn't reach his eyes.

My knees are so weak that I obey him, falling into my seat and staring at the commissioner who isn't looking at me at all. He casually picks at his nails instead. I glance back to the mirror and pray there's a camera recording or someone behind it watching this. Someone else. God, please help me.

I'm not safe here. That's the only thing I'm sure of. *What have I gotten myself into?*

"Good girl," Mason's father says approvingly, and it sickens me to my core. There's something about the air of ownership he projects. Something about the way his words roll off his tongue. The fear is only partially brushed aside by my disgust, but I'm at least able to look him in the eye.

"Where's Mason?" I ask evenly, although I don't know how I got the courage to speak.

His father's eyes twinkle with something that brightens the gray. Something that makes my stomach churn.

"Don't worry, he's coming shortly." Mr. Thatcher looks over his shoulder at the detective. As his mouth parts to say something his straight white teeth peek out from behind his thin lips, but he's interrupted by the door banging open.

"I'm sorry, Detective Myer," a young woman says from the hallway as Mason stands in the doorway, hovering in the opening with an authority that's incomparable.

And he's pissed.

The way his steel gray eyes seem to turn a sharp silver and pierce through me makes every tiny hair on my body stand on end. Every inch of my skin chills and then heats so quickly I can't move. All I can do is stare into his eyes, caught in his gaze.

He breaks it before I can relax, and only then can I breathe.

My eyes drop to the floor as the shock withdraws, and my reality strikes me across the face. The emotions that swarm me are confusing to say the least. I'm relieved to see the very man I fled from only hours ago.

"Jules," he says and Mason's voice isn't cold like I imagined it would be. I lift my eyes to his, and my heart beats in rhythm with the seconds that tick by ever so slowly. *Tick, tick, tick.* The room is silent as the other men wait for my reaction. I can't give them anything, though. I'm numb and useless with exhaustion and a thread of fear so easily broken. My throat is dry, and I can barely manage to make eye contact with Mason. I pick at my sleeve and look back at the table, feeling defeated, foolish and guilty.

How is it possible that guilt is what consumes me most?

"Sweetheart, what are you doing here?" Mason asks me with sympathy in his voice as he pulls out the chair next to me. The legs scrape on the floor and Mason wraps his arm around the back of my chair as he sits close to me, but not an inch of him touches me. Not his arm, not his knee to mine. He's so close I can feel the heat of his body, but he's distant all the same.

"Is something wrong?" he asks me, and I immediately shake my head no.

I'm retreating like a coward. "I want to go home," I say, whispering the plea just above a murmur, still not looking any of the men in the eye.

"What's that?" Detective Myer says from the corner of the room, pushing off the wall and uncrossing his arms for the first time since he's been in here. He starts to walk over.

I clear my throat and ignore how scratchy my voice is as I repeat myself. "I want to go home."

The detective leans against the table, his palms flat as he waits for me to look up at him. His voice is strong and hard, filled with contempt as he says, "Issuing a false report and taking up the time—"

"What false report?" Mason asks at the same time that I refute the detective.

"No one has taken a statement from me. I haven't said anything," I say and my voice is stronger than I imagined it would be.

Mason rises from his chair abruptly, leaning over the table and bracing his forearms in front of me as he gets in Myer's face. "Don't you dare," Mason says, speaking with a tone of malice that makes me flinch. "Don't you dare threaten her."

Mason's chiseled jaw is covered with stubble and the way it clenches while his hands fist on the table takes the commissioner by surprise. He visibly balks, and it's then that Mason's father pipes up.

"Now, now. Miss Summers had something she wanted to say, Mason." Mason's head tilts slowly, daring his father to speak again and the old man does just that, the glint in his eye ever present.

He looks past Mason and asks me, "What was it that brought you here, Julia?"

"Nothing," I say and my voice croaks.

"Oh, come now," he says. Mr. Thatcher's voice is light-hearted, but it's never been more apparent how dark the situation has become. Do they already know? *They must.*

And now they know that I know.

My throat tightens instantly, as if a strong hand has gripped it to choke me. "You can come to me with anything, Miss Summers," Mason's father says, staring me straight in the eyes as he continues, "I know everyone, Jules, and I'll be sure you're taken care of—"

"Enough," Mason practically growls at his father.

His father finally takes his assessing stare from me to give

Mason his attention. "Just out of curiosity, Mason, what little secret did you tell our Jules?"

Mason ignores his father, taking my hand in his with a bruising force and leading me to the door. My legs are weak but I keep up with him. He rips the door open so violently I swear he nearly pulls it off the hinges.

"Go," Mason commands me, sweeping his arm forward and I listen immediately, grateful to be getting the fuck out of here mostly unscathed.

"Bye for now, Jules," Mr. Thatcher says to my back as I leave, and I'm grateful Mason is between us. I can't breathe or do anything other than follow Mason's lead until we've left the station. I can feel everyone watching us and my face blazes with the awareness, but fear is what keeps me moving and my eyes staring straight ahead.

"Mason," I whimper as he braces his hand against the small of my back and leads me across the street to where he's parked. I stare at his car, feeling as though I'm so close to safety, but knowing I'm going back to a cell.

Mason doesn't respond but he pulls me in close, wrapping his arm around my waist as we cross the street to the parking lot. Without knowing what to think or feel, my head spins. I have to walk quickly to keep up with his purposeful strides, but I feel comforted just from his arm wrapped around me, needing his embrace.

For a moment, as Mason opens my door and waits for me to get in his car, I think there's hope. I think I can repair the damage I've caused even though I'm not sure why I'm even considering it.

I'm so confused, so conflicted. The only thing I'm certain of is that if Mason hadn't come to get me, something bad would have happened. Something to make sure I was silenced.

Foolish. I'm so damn foolish. At the thought, I struggle to breathe and I lay my head back against the seat, feeling the weight of what just happened flow through every limb. Heat flows around my skin, uncomfortably and unbearably so.

Mason shuts his door with a loud thud as he gets in and starts the car, all without sparing me a glance while he backs out and merges into traffic.

With tension pulled through every inch of me, I wait for something, for a moment to speak or for him to say something, but I'm given nothing.

"Mason?" I take a chance and say his name as the car stops at a red light. His fingers flex on the steering wheel and then his knuckles turn white as he grips it and slowly turns to look at me.

His eyes are cold, ice cold, and I instantly regret speaking at all.

"We'll talk when we get home," he says beneath his breath. I nod once, feeling alone and abandoned and utterly hopeless.

CHAPTER

seven

Mason

Forever doesn't end,
But it also doesn't last.
What you feel right now,
Will soon be the past.

Left only with the memories,
And the desire to hold.
But time doesn't wait,
And even love grows old.

I WOULD HAVE KILLED THEM. BOTH THE DETECTIVE AND the commissioner. Possibly even my father. I've never been so close to snapping, never. I've never come close to feeling that pull. Pure anger and hatred are fueling my thoughts. I'm barely contained, on the edge of something dangerous, something so dark I've never confronted it before. Not even that fateful day I destroyed Jules's life. Even that wasn't like this.

Dragging my hand down my face, I listen as my shoes smack against the hardwood floors, but then the sound is muted on the rug in front of the gray suede sofa in my living room.

"What were you going to tell them?" I ask as I pace in front of her, my gaze still focused downward.

It's never felt colder or darker in this house before. Not to me. Even with the bright white snow reflecting light through the large modern windows on the back wall, there's not an ounce of warmth in the room.

Ice courses through my blood, but even that's not cold enough to take the heat from my anger.

I can't stop moving; every muscle is coiled and ready to fight. She doesn't know what she does to me. She has no fucking idea what she's done. What kind of danger she's put herself in.

"How could you?" I say. The question is menacing and it stops me in my tracks. It holds a vicious tone I can't contain. I take a single glance up and regret it. With her beautiful blue eyes widened, Jules looks as though I've slapped her, flinching and her mouth dropping open, but she doesn't answer.

"I—" she tries to speak, but can't finish her sentence. It's fucking infuriating. I don't know what's worse, how she's impulsively made everything worse for us, or the fact that she left to turn me in. My jaw clenches so hard I nearly crack my teeth. I have to stare past her at the blanket of snow as she squirms on the sofa. "Mason, I—"

"You what?" My voice booms from my chest as my heart pounds. She would be dead if my father hadn't called me. He could have killed her. Or have had her killed rather, so he wouldn't have blood on his own hands. He'd have done it too, if he hadn't wanted to toy with me. If he hadn't wanted something to hold over my head. If he hadn't wanted me to know that I owe him now. "You have no idea what you've done."

I can only imagine my father is under the impression that she knows about his involvement with Avery's death. That I told her. That she was there to rat *him* out and not me.

"Fuck." The curse lays under my breath as my pacing continues. It takes every ounce of self-control not to destroy this place.

He doesn't know a damn thing about Jace's murder. No one does but the anonymous stranger who sent Jules that note.

My father won't let Jules live. I take in a ragged breath, but it doesn't calm me.

There's no fucking way I'll let him touch her. She's mine, and she'll be my wife and mother to my children. If he dares try any of that shit with her again, I'll destroy him. I'll end his life so fucking miserably that he'll be thankful when I finally slide the edge of a knife across his throat.

"Mason," she says and fear clings to the single whispered word.

"They would have killed you, Jules." I swallow the ball of spikes in my throat and finally look down at her glassed-over eyes. Her baby blues are full of so much emotion. "They would have killed you," I repeat in a whisper and it's that sickening thought that breaks the rage. It shatters into something else. Something that feels like weakness.

Jules holds my gaze, but she doesn't answer me. Tears leak from the corner of her eyes, but Jules doesn't acknowledge them. Her face displays an expression of sincerity. "I'm scared," she says. She gently shakes her head and looks past me, down the hallway and avoiding eye contact. My heart clenches in my chest.

"I didn't want any of this," she says and her voice is raw with emotion.

I swallow thickly and tell her the simple truth, "You never should have left."

She looks up at me with daggers in her eyes as she hisses at me without a second passing between us, "You never should have killed my husband."

It catches me off guard for a moment, but the pure venom and hate she had only hours ago is dimmed, the stark reality of the situation taking its toll on her. I keep my eyes on hers as I tell her, "Your husband deserved to die for what he did."

Jules's lips part as she takes in a heavy breath, looking as if she's going to respond, but no words come out. After a moment she looks away, finally wiping the tears from her reddened cheeks with the sleeve of her ruined sweater and sniffling.

"I don't want to die, Mason," she says weakly. Her chest rises and falls with her steady breathing. "I just want to go home and I'll never say a word."

"You can't go home." My voice is hard and leaves no room for negotiation. I won't risk putting her in danger. I don't know what my father's told the commissioner. I need to make it clear to him that she knows nothing about what happened. I'll lie. I'll tell him I hit her.

He's always seen through my lies, though. He's a damn good liar, and the challenge of outsmarting him has never seemed so daunting.

I could tell him the truth. I'll tell him anything I need to in order to make him believe she's not a threat.

"If you leave me, you're putting yourself at risk—" I can't finish because it's at that moment that Jules finally breaks down. Her always composed demeanor cracks and her shoulders hunch forward as a sob wracks her body.

Any explanation dies at the back of my throat. All of my anger dissipates. She's broken because of me. This happened because of me. I fucking hate myself.

"I'll protect you," I tell her. I only hesitate for a moment before taking the seat next to her. My weight causes her small body to lean into mine, and I'm surprised when she doesn't resist. She lets me hold her for a moment as her cries get softer and she wipes the tears from beneath her eyes. I've craved this warmth since she found out the truth. "I promise."

I lean forward and kiss her hair, taking in her sweet scent but it makes her withdraw. She doesn't look at me, and the moment she has her composure back she pulls away from me.

"Is it really that bad to stay with me?"

Her body stiffens at the question, and she doesn't answer.

"You have no other options but to stay where I tell you and do what I say. You need to convince everyone in this city that you're mine, that everything between us is better than it's ever been."

"I just want to go home." She'll never know how much that desire damages me in the worst way. How empty and hollow her confession leaves me. "I won't tell anyone," she adds, peeking up through her thick lashes.

"You don't have a choice," I tell her as I cup her cheek in my hand. I run the rough pad of my thumb along her lush lips, and they beg me to kiss her. Her pale skin is flushed a beautiful shade of pink and everything in me wants to hold her close. I want to take her pain away; I want to remind her who she belongs to.

"You're mine, Jules. There's no changing that."

CHAPTER
eight

Julia

Pressed against a hard wall,
No choices, no way out.
Without the air to breathe,
And only left with doubt.

There's no way to move forward,
No will to make amends.
Nothing but what he gives me,
Trapped and at dead ends.

I'M DESPERATE FOR MY MOTHER, OF ALL THINGS. Desperate to call her, to confess what's happened, to plead with her to protect me. As if something so simple could save me.

I pick at the comforter on the bed and wish I had my computer or my phone. Or any way at all to contact someone.

Not a single soul has come up Mason's driveway since he brought me back here. There are no neighbors close enough to just drop by, not that Mason's the neighborly type. Even the mailbox is all the way at the end of the long driveway. I'm trapped in this house that's practically a gilded cage without a damn thing to do other than write down every forsaken emotion and thought that comes to me. Time is moving slowly; the past three days have felt like a year, and all I can do is be consumed by the thoughts of how I got here. *How did this become my life?*

The moment I look out a window or walk toward a door, Mason's there. Watching me, waiting to see what I'll do. He went from being my lover and my hope, to a prison warden. Every time he enters the room, I can *feel* him.

Yet he's pretending he's not monitoring me, that he trusts I'll behave because I'm afraid. Part of that's true, but mostly I'm waiting, simply biding my time. I'll be quiet and listen until I have a chance to leave him. He can't keep me here forever.

The bathroom door opens with a soft creak, stealing me away from my thoughts as Mason steps into the bedroom from the en suite. He's bare-chested, his tanned skin on display as he strides toward the dresser with only a towel wrapped around his waist. His demeanor is casual, as if nothing happened. As if I can live with the fact that he's a murderer, and my life is in danger because of him and his father. If I'd known he was tied to anything at all like this, I'd never have gone home with him that first night. I'd never have flirted, I'd never have touched him, let alone fallen in love with him.

I have to bite my cheek to keep from screaming, to keep from doing something stupid as Mason turns his back to me, letting the towel drop as he selects a pair of boxers from the top drawer of his dresser. Between the multiple heartaches and chaos, loss is there. Loss of someone I thought I loved who didn't exist. Loss of the independence I was so sure I had.

"I bought you a dress for Saturday," he informs me matter-of-factly as he unzips a garment bag with his back to me.

My eyes flicker to the beautiful evening gown hanging on the back of the closet door. Its jewels sparkle as the light hits it; they're sparser on top, just a faint pattern that forms the outline of an hourglass, overlaying the darker gray on the sides and absent on the light gray inlay. From the hips down, the gown is completely covered in the dazzling Swarovski crystals.

It's stunning. I'm sure it would impress everyone at the charity event. I don't remember which one this is; I only know that Mason wants to attend to discuss business with a number of investors and it's an annual charity gala I've gone to without fail for years.

For a moment, I can only watch Mason continue with the business of getting dressed, wondering how he could even consider the two of us attending an event together. "I don't see how I could possibly go." I can't imagine standing in a room smiling and playing nice when I feel like this. When I'm trapped and cornered. When I'm literally scared for my life.

Mason's steel gray eyes pierce through me as if he heard

every one of my thoughts when I look at his reflection in the cheval mirror.

"You've had a couple of nights to think about things. You'll have another handful of days to come around," he says confidently and breaks my gaze to shut a drawer, holding a pair of socks in his right hand.

"Where are you going?" I ask him, feeling a touch of hope rise in my chest at the prospect of him leaving. *I just want to go home.* The thought plays in my head on a loop like a broken record.

His lips press into a thin line and he turns slowly to face me, leaning back against the dresser. "Do you think it would be wise?" he asks. He hasn't moved but somehow he seems much closer than he was a moment ago.

I feel the blood drain from my face. "What do you mean?"

"Jules, my sweetheart," he says as he sets the clothes on top of the dresser and strides toward me. The bed dips as he sits on the edge, my heart racing from the proximity even though he doesn't touch me. "I'm still the man I was," he says calmly; his voice is soft and it breaks something inside of me. The smile he gives me is sad and doesn't reach his eyes. Leaning forward, he adds, "I can practically hear what you're thinking."

Thud, my heart pauses, caught in a trap that snaps shut around it. I swallow and focus on calming down to pry it free from the steel bars, attempting to pretend I don't know what he's talking about.

My head shakes to deny the truth but he reaches out, grabbing me by the nape of the neck and my hip, holding me in place and forcing me to look at him. It's possessive, it's dominating and it steals my breath. He hasn't been this close to me in days. His lips are so very close to mine. Just like my heart, I'm trapped.

"I'm not going to lose you, Jules." He speaks with an intensity that makes the world blur around him.

"I'm not leaving," I whisper with a shaky breath, although even I can tell it's a lie. My words are just as weak as I am when it comes to him. The corner of his lips twitch as if he wants to smile and pretend I'm telling the truth, but he doesn't.

"I'm the same man you fell in love with." The steel gray gaze softens, begging me to understand and believe him, but I can't. The tension is thick between us, but how can he expect me to simply forget? When I look at him, I see it all play out, over and over again.

I refuse to believe I ever knew this man, but the very thought splits my heart down the center.

I could never love a murderer. I could never be with the person who killed Jace. Pain lances through my chest, and I have to look away. As much as I wish I could turn it off and stop loving him entirely, I know that's not a possibility either. A piece of my heart is his forever, but that only makes me hate him more.

A question begs to be asked. One I've thought every night since he confessed. "You knew when you saw me that first night?" I ask him with a raw voice. That's what I simply can't wrap my head around. He knew who I was. He knew how much he'd hurt me and ruined me. Yet it didn't stop him.

"Knew what?" he asks, sitting easily across from me and I look him in the eyes to confront him as I say, "You knew who I was? Jace's widow."

He nods once.

"How could you?" I ask as my blood races and whatever took over a moment ago vanishes. It's yet again another betrayal. "Was I a prize to you? A reward for getting away with it?" I say out of spite.

His expression changes to one I'm growing familiar with. To distaste and anger. Apparently we both feel it. "Don't you dare." His nostrils flare as he adds, "Don't you dare do that to us. To what we have."

"Had," I say and my throat hurts as the word leaves my lips. I don't see how I could ever forgive him or how he can expect that I would. He may be the only thing keeping me alive and standing in the way of his father silencing me, but he'll forever be my husband's murderer. A liar, a sinner, and ultimately someone who used me.

"You were only Jules to me. Only a woman who was hurt and broken." His words hang in the air between us and my conviction sways. Mason hesitates then adds, "I knew your pain was because of what I'd done. I knew it was my fault, and I wanted to make it better."

My lips part with disbelief. "Make it better?"

"I don't know what to say, Jules." He lets his hands fall to the bed beside me, his fingers resting against my thigh. "I don't know what to tell you."

"There's nothing to say." I'm certain of that at least. I stare at the comforter and avoid the hurt look in his eyes. He has no right to be saddened or angered. He has no right to expect anything from me. He's the one who put all of this into motion. He could have stopped it.

"There is more to say. And in time you'll want to know more."

My shoulders rise with a heavy breath. I know it's true. I need to know if my husband did have a woman murdered. How could he? Mason must be wrong.

I just can't imagine it. I can't believe I was married to a man who would have someone killed. He was living with me, sharing my bed and kissing me every morning. I can't see it. What's worse, I don't want to see it. Just like I didn't want to see the other lies that came out after he died. *I didn't know the man I once loved.* I look up into Mason's gray eyes and I don't know which man that thought was for. Jace or Mason.

I suppose both.

"I just want to go home," I tell Mason one last time. One last plea.

"No, you're staying here. Don't try to run, Jules," he tells me and his voice is so low. He leans forward, resting his forehead against mine. "I would kill for you. I'd die for you. I love you."

His words send a chill through me, not because of the intensity, but because I feel with everything in me that each word is utterly and completely true.

Mason

I CAN'T FUCKING STAND THIS. EVERY TIME SHE PASSES me, every time I look at her there's a look in her eyes that warns me to stay away. To not touch her, to not approach her, to not say a damn word to her.

I'm the same man I was when I slipped that ring around her finger. The one that lays in the drawer of my nightstand now. The one I picked up off the floor when she left me. I figured it'd be better to hide it from her than give it back and risk her flushing it.

With the ring between two of my fingers, I twist it back and forth, the cushion-cut diamond moving from side to side with moonlight glinting off it as it pours in through the gap in the curtains. I turn my gaze to the window, knowing just beyond the thick velvet fabric is a ripped screen that still needs to be replaced.

This bedroom has become a cage. A prison of her own making. I've given her time. I've been gentle, given her space, but it's only pissing me off when she glares at me. She's a stubborn woman and I understand her needs, but it feels like I'm slowly snapping, not bending.

It's time for a change. I don't know how long it takes to mourn or forgive, but I also don't give a fuck. There's too much on my mind for me to be worried about where we are with each other. I need her. More importantly, I need to know she won't run so I can keep her safe.

I can't have anyone else questioning it either. They need to be very aware that we're still in love. Every. Single. Person.

With a particular person in mind, I glance at the phone on my nightstand. My father isn't answering my calls.

I'm tempted to go to his office to make sure he backs off, but that means either leaving Jules alone or taking her with me. Between those two options of course I'd be bringing her along, but I don't want him anywhere near her. Just walking into the station, knowing he was with her, toying with her, and hearing him threaten her was almost too much for me. I take in a heavy breath, staring at the diamond to calm myself again.

He has one more chance. One meeting on Saturday to treat her the way she deserves and apologize for what happened at the station. She's everything to me, and I won't let him frighten her. It's bad enough as it is. Otherwise… I'll have no choice but to kill him. My plan at this charity, the only plan I have, is to make that promise very clear to my father.

We're in the eye of the storm, I know it. Chaos is lurking in the shadows surrounding us, and I need my sweetheart by my side. I need her clinging to me and letting me protect her.

Right now, with her on the other side of the bed, she's hardly speaking to me let alone capable of trusting me. I can't sleep at night until she does, because I don't trust her either, and it's a battle of wills. Neither of us sleeping, neither of us giving an inch. And that's exactly what will happen tonight if I don't do something.

The diamond sparkles brilliantly, the light shining from one facet to the other.

This belongs on her fucking finger.

I stand abruptly, wanting nothing more than to tell her it's never parting from her again. But the moment I see her, she's running her fingers along her wrists. At the faint bruises and small cuts left from when I tied her up days ago.

My anger leaves slowly, like a leak, leaving me empty and hollow with regret.

"I can't take it back." I clear my throat and give her the words as they come to me. "You need to stop this, Jules. We can't continue like this."

Her posture changes, the bed creaking along with the slow movements as she grips the comforter and pulls it closer to her. Her expression shifts, and she's not pretending anymore. She's not hiding her anger; she glares at me, leaning forward. It thrills me. *Give me that anger, sweetheart. Fight me, slam your fists into my chest, take it out on me. I'll show you I can take it. I can let you get it all out and then soothe it away and fuck you so hard and so thoroughly you won't remember a damn thing except for how much you love my cock inside of you.*

"Did you like it?" I ask her as my dick twitches with the need to push her and make her angrier.

A moment passes and she simply stares at me, refusing to answer.

"Did you like it when I tied you up?" I ask and this time, she can't ignore my question.

"Fuck you," she says, jumping off the bed and making her way toward the door to leave me again. She's not fucking leaving me, though. I'm quicker than her and she knows it. I slam the door shut before she can walk through. With both my palms above her pressed firmly against the door, I cage her in with my arms as she spins to face me with a gasp of shock. My arms are long and her body's small, so there's still nearly a foot of space between us, but it feels as if we're closer than we've been in so long.

Because it's real. This tension and this moment are more real than the lifeless days we've spent together living like ghosts of ourselves since I told her she wasn't leaving.

She slowly takes an inch forward, waiting for me to stop her from leaving, but I don't. By this point, she should know I'm not going to hurt her. I meant what I said. I will never hurt her.

"Just forget it all, Jules." She tries to walk around me and under my arm, ignoring me and I can't stand it. My forearms press against the door and close the space between us, trapping her there and forcing her to talk to me.

"What do you want from me?" she screams out, her lips close to mine and her anger tangible.

"Forgiveness," I answer lowly, but with a rawness I pray she can feel.

"I can't forgive you."

"I had to do it."

Her brow pinches and she looks like she's going to argue, but she stays silent, biting her tongue and attempting to go back to the version of her I've dealt with for days. She stares at anything except me, as if ignoring me will free her from this moment.

I'm not going to let her get off that easy. She has to say something; I need to force her to confront me, because I know she won't say something on her own. "You have to get over it."

"Never," she says, finally looking back at me and staring me in the eyes. "You're a monster."

"Is that what you want?" I ask her as I take a half step forward to force her back against the door, both of my hands pinning her hips in place. "For me to turn into some kind of monster so you can justify hating me?" My grip's not so strong that it hurts her, but it's forceful enough to get her attention. Her head comes forward and I crash my lips against hers, stealing a quick kiss before she can move away. I move my lips to her ear, pinning her whole body against the wall as my right hand travels up her side while my left grips the hair at the nape of her neck. She's trapped.

"There's a difference between what you've been thinking I'd do and what I've really been doing, sweetheart." I speak just above a murmur. My breathing picks up along with hers, and her nails dig into the shirt on my chest. She's not pushing me away; she's holding me right where I am. I'm just as close to her as I wanted to be.

"You think I'm a bad man in that pretty little head of yours, but you fell in love with me. With the real me and there's no hiding from that." I run the tip of my nose from her cheek to her temple, breathing in her scent. Her small body is so hot against mine. Her rapid pants only aid in making me hard as fuck for her.

"I'll never stop loving you." I speak so low, I'm not sure she hears. I open my eyes and stare at the wall, realizing how fucked up this is, aching over it, but unable to let her go. I'm too afraid of losing her forever. I won't let it happen.

"Just do it, Mason." Jules nearly chokes on her words, and I have to look down into her eyes to see the defiance there. She's pushing me. She knows I'll never hurt her. It's so fucking obvious, and the realization makes me smile slightly.

"Do what?" I ask.

"Whatever you want with me," she says, although her gaze drops to my chest with nothing but defeat in her eyes. "Or let your father kill me."

"Is that what you want?"

"You won't let me leave," is the only answer she gives me.

"That doesn't answer my question." My heart pounds in protest at the question: Would she really rather die than love me again?

Jules looks away, turning her head to the side even as I grip her nape tighter. I pull back slightly, forcing her to look at me.

"That would make it easy for you, wouldn't it?" I ask, hearing my own voice crack. I nip her earlobe with my teeth and wait a moment for her to answer, but all I can hear is the combined sound of our heavy breathing. "It would be so easy to hate me if I were the monster you want to believe I am." I struggle with how true my words are. "If I wasn't the man you fell in love with, but I am."

I kiss the side of her neck, my fingers trailing along her

skin and pulling her sleep shirt up slowly. My body's so close to hers but I don't touch her, because I want her to feel my absence. I want her to crave how I make her feel.

I trail the words down her neck, whispering against her skin. "All I want is for you to remember how much I love you and how much you love me."

I want her to beg for my touch again, just like she did when we first met. I know she will. She needs me just as much as I need her. "Give me one month." I speak without thinking, desperate for a change between us. "One month of just pretending. Of trying to forget or forgive and going back to what we once had."

She peers up at me with a brightness in her eyes, but they narrow with distrust. I add, "If you hate me still at the end of the month, I'll let you go." I can barely speak the pained words, but I push out the offering.

My heart beats hard in my chest, knowing it's a lie. But it's something she can hold on to. It's a deal with the devil for her, and I'm sure she knows it.

She doesn't reply, and I couldn't give a fuck so long as tomorrow things have changed for us.

My strides are heavy as I leave her to grab the ring from where it lays, once again on the floor. She stares at it rather than at me when I take her hand. "I'm the same man I was when I first put this ring on your finger." I slide the diamond on her ring finger and hold it there, waiting for her eyes to reach mine.

I lean in and breathe in her scent, closing my eyes and forcing myself to let go of her. "Don't take it off, Jules. That ring will stay on your finger." I watch as her eyes close and her chest rises. "I'll make sure of it."

CHAPTER

ten

Julia

The mind plays tricks,
It likes to deceive.
What once brought you joy,
Will now make you grieve.
What to think, what to do,
When there's no easy way out.
When your heart's torn and broken,
And all you know is doubt.

I WISH A HOT SHOWER COULD WASH IT ALL AWAY. AS IF the steam and heat could cleanse the burden of knowing what Mason did nearly a year ago. So long ago, when we were both two different people. When we were both strangers to each other.

I don't know what to think, and I don't know how to react or which emotion is coming through the strongest. It makes me feel crazy. It's like the sway of the ocean. As soon as one wave comes and crashes over me, another is already waiting to drown me. It's making me weak.

It's late, but I don't want to sleep.

I move to my dresser and sift through the nightgowns mindlessly, remembering how even last night, I questioned if I should refuse him. When Mason laid his arm across my belly, turning on his side to be closer to me, I hesitated before asking him to move and let me be like I have been. It comes down to one truth: I wanted him to take the pain away. The pain he caused. Only him. He's responsible for it all. *Just the same, only he could take it away.*

Glancing down in the drawer I trail my fingers across a nightgown; it's all silk and fine lace. Tempting, luxurious and expensive. I bought new lingerie a few weeks back, for Mason of course. The shine of the navy blue silk catches my eye, but I can't bring myself to pick it up.

I don't want to tempt him anymore. I don't want to try to look beautiful for him. My heart aches with a pain that feels as if it will strangle the life from me. I wish Mason were done with me, because I already feel myself needing his touch again.

It makes me feel pathetic, but what choice do I have? I have no one and nothing, and I've been forced into a corner I can't escape.

I shut my mouth tightly, gritting my teeth as I ball up the

silk gown's matching thong in my hand and slam the drawer closed.

He's not a good man. He planned my husband's murder in cold blood.

But he's damn good to me in ways my husband wasn't. If what he said was true… I take in a ragged breath before sitting on the edge of the bed, still only covered by the towel from my shower. The mattress groans as my eyes close and I lean back, collapsing on the bed.

A thought has taken over, one I least expected. I'm still angry with Jace and the more I want to believe Mason, the more I think Jace really did it. He had a woman killed.

How could I not have known what kind of man Jace was? I already know he lied to me, that he stole from me. I have evidence of that from bank account statements and the deed to the apartment he took his mistress to. *Or mistresses.* I'll never know.

If you'll lie, you'll cheat. If you'll cheat, you'll steal. If you'll steal, you'll kill.

I know for a fact Jace did two of those things. Three, technically, since he used my money and not his to buy that property.

I'm disgusted in every way possible. What's worse is that if Jace hadn't passed, maybe I never would have known. We'd still be together and I'd still be living a lie, completely blind to it all. Utterly naïve.

The reality is sickening. I do believe Mason. I believe my husband had a woman killed. But that doesn't mean moving forward I choose to be with a murderer. How could I ever trust Mason again? How could I ever look at him the same?

If only the shower could rinse it all away. Or a pill could erase my memory.

But then I'd be back to the life I once had, not knowing a thing about the lies and corruption, all the sins I've been blind to.

Defeated but still moving forward, I mumble, "To hell with going back to that." I stretch my back as I stand up, knowing I need to get dressed for bed before Mason barges in here. I don't have the luxury of being lost in my thoughts.

One month, and then what? It's pointless to truly consider the question because I don't believe Mason will let me go. Besides, what would I do if in one month he lets me walk out the door?

I pretend that I don't know how that scenario plays out. I go back to being alone, but never trust anyone again? That's really what hurts the most, the lies and secrets make me feel as though no one is truthful. The two men I gave everything I ever had to turned out to be liars and murderers. I huff a pathetic and humorless laugh.

My girlfriends were right, I really do pick winners.

I'm only able to take two steps to the bathroom door before hearing the door at the end of the hall open. I stare at my closed door, waiting for Mason to enter, but then I hear another door open and shut only a moment later with a click that echoes down the hall.

My forehead pinches with confusion as I hear it again. It's as if someone is checking inside of each room in the hallway. I almost call out to tell Mason that I'm in here and I'm not hiding, but something eerie stops me. A chill I've never felt before, like a grave warning from someone or something watching over me, runs down every inch of my skin and my heart races with sudden fear.

Another door opens, then closes. And this last one was closer.

All I can hear is my heart pounding in my chest as I get down on my knees as quietly as I can and crawl under the bed. *Something's wrong.* I hear the door next to the master bedroom close as I try to turn onto my side, but I can't. I'm stuck, wedged between the floor and the bed frame, but it's enough. My heart beats wildly and I try to convince myself it's just Mason and I'm being stupidly foolish again. Keeping as still as possible, I watch the door only six feet or so away, the light from the hallway faintly pouring in through the crack and shining against the gleaming hardwood.

Click. It opens softly, and two shiny black shoes walk in softly. *It's not Mason.* I know it's not. Fear fills my veins. Violently and with a chill that's paralyzing.

I can't stop the adrenaline from pumping through my blood as the shoes leave my periphery. The footsteps thud to my right, but I can't see him. I hear the bathroom door open and terror runs through me, wondering if I've left the light on. If whoever it is that's come up here will know I'm in this room.

Steam will still be on the bathroom mirror and he's going to see where I've messed the bed up from lying there just a moment ago. My heart rages so hard that I swear it's trying to leave my body. If he touches the comforter, he'll feel that it's warm. He'll know I was here only moments ago.

"Jules?" My eyes widen and flash to the open doorway as I hear Mason call for me from downstairs. I can faintly hear him walking to the bottom of the staircase, and I can practically see him standing down there. Given his casual tone, he's completely unaware there's someone else in the house.

God help me; I want to scream.

The black shoes quickly leave the bedroom but not so quick that the man ran. His steps were silent. He gently closes the door and the click is barely heard. I'm caught between wanting to scream out to warn Mason and saving myself.

Whoever it is that was in this room a moment ago doesn't answer Mason and he doesn't go down the stairs; instead he goes to the left, farther into the house.

I didn't think it possible, but my heart slams harder as I hear Mason start to climb the stairs.

Move! my inner voice begs me. My palms are clammy against the wooden floors as I drag myself across the floor. *Do something!* I don't know who's here, I don't know what they've come for. But I can't stay here and let Mason walk into what could be his death sentence.

I crawl out as quickly as I can, the rug beside the bed burning against my forearms and the metal from the bed frame scraping against my back, but I'm out with time enough to open the door just as Mason reaches the top of the stairs. I swing the door open prepared to scream and when I do, the man is standing right there, staring at the stairwell with a gun in his hand. The thin silencer on the end is pointed straight ahead, right at where Mason should be in only a moment.

"Mason!" I yell out his name, or at least I think I do. I can't hear anything but a loud ringing and my body is so numb from fear and the heat coursing through my body that I can barely feel a thing. As if I'm not even here. As if I've left my body, yet I'm still standing where I was.

The end of the gun points straight at me, only feet away with nothing in between us.

My head spins, and my vision nearly goes black from fear. I never imagined what it would be like to know that you're dying. That you only have a precious second or two left to live.

How time would slow and my body would sway, yet be utterly still.

As I stare at the man's cold dark eyes, it feels as if I don't even exist anymore. They're so brown, they're nearly black. His skin is a beautiful tan, but it looks pale against the black turtleneck and leather jacket he's wearing.

He doesn't look like a killer; he's too handsome, his clothes too expensive.

But that's just what he is.

I'd think this was all a nightmare, if it wasn't for the way Mason screams out and snaps me from this moment, bringing me right back as my own scream pierces my ears.

But the man doesn't shoot, and instead he turns and runs.

eleven

Mason

"**N**o!" The word is ripped from my throat as my body moves forward purely out of instinct. My muscles scream as I move as fast as I can, watching the end of the silencer swing toward Jules.

Not my Jules. Not my sweetheart. *Take me instead.*

I lunge forward to block her, but I already know it's too late. The strike of a bullet doesn't hit me and I can barely stand to open my eyes, my body pressed to Jules, expecting the bullet to have already found her. It's her wide eyes and heavy breathing that hammer the message into my thick skull that she's all right. I search her body for any sign of an injury, but she pushes my hands away. "He's running!" she screams in my face.

He could have killed her. I saw it happen. In that split second, she was dead. It takes more than a moment to come to grips with the fact that she's still here. She's alive. She's okay. And the prick who pointed a gun at her is getting away. With his back to us, he sprints toward the end of the hall and into the last bedroom.

My muscles coil as I stand up, hell-bent on killing the bastard. "Stay there!" I scream at Jules as I chase after him, my heart pounding.

He slams the door behind him, but the palms of my hands smack against it and my shoulder shoves the door open.

It all happens so fast, I can't think, I can't control what I do. With my hands still on the door, a fist crashes into my face, catching me off guard.

My jaw cracks as my head snaps back and he lands another blow before I've recovered from the first.

I bring my fists up, ready to fight, but he shoves me back, even as I strike him hard in the shoulder. He yells out in agony but doesn't stop. The push gives him enough room to get by me. I can't let him go. He's fucking dead.

Fisting his jacket, I grab him with everything I've got, ripping at it and ignoring the shit that falls from his pocket. My nails scratch at his slacks, ripping down the fabric but I get ahold of him, tripping up his right leg and the man falls hard to the ground.

Adrenaline courses through my veins and all I can see is my fist pounding into him over and over. But then I hear her scream.

Jules cries out, terrified, and I stop to look at her, my heart leaping up my throat. I stare at her and search for the threat, the danger that's scared her. There's no threat that I can place. She stands there in the doorway, her hands over her mouth, pale with fright and looking so frail. It's only when I feel the man beneath me buck his hips, lunging with all of his strength and moving so fucking fast I can't pin him down that my attention leaves her.

"Stay in the room!" I shout at her, hating that I can't be in two places at once. Torn between protecting her by staying close, and eliminating the danger. I launch myself forward, grabbing at him once again but failing to find purchase. My muscles scream in pain as I lunge at full speed after the man I don't recognize. He swings around the banister and gets ahead of me, but I take the stairs two at a time, feeling my blood get colder and colder as I leave her behind.

Someone else could be here.

The thought makes my foot slip on the last stair. My heel catches the edge and I fall forward. I'm so close to him though that when I reach out for him, I pull him back by closing my fist around his sweater. I reach up with my other hand, ready to wrap my arm around his throat, ready to pull his body to my chest and hold him there until the struggling stops.

I'll strangle him until he has no life left.

But he's quicker and has better balance than I do, slipping the thin leather jacket off and tearing for the door.

It's unlocked. It's never unlocked. It wasn't earlier. Not a damn soul has a key other than me.

The door stays wide open as he disappears from view. The

jacket flies behind me as I follow after him. The harsh and brutal wind wraps around every inch of my heated skin.

I'm only a few feet behind him, but he's running faster and with every step I'm reminded that I'm leaving her farther and farther behind.

Someone else could be there. You can't leave her alone.

The man darts to the right, gaining ground and slipping from my vision behind the row of trees. *Fuck!* I can't think straight with thoughts of her.

Closer to the street, the sound of cars passing parallel to us surround me as I sprint after him, but it's useless. I can't see a damn thing through the pine trees. I keep running even though I don't see him. I don't stop even when the cars flying by lay on their horns.

Where the fuck did he go? There's nowhere to hide. I stand on the curb, listening to the cars whizzing by only feet away and searching everywhere. I spin around to my right and left trying to find the man, but he's vanished.

Another car beeps several times as the cold sinks in, and I realize I'm not even wearing shoes. My bare feet sink into the thin layer of snow and my heavy breath fogs in front of my face.

Jules.

Her name echoes in my head as I race back to the house, breathing in the cold air and letting it soothe my tired lungs.

The vision of her staring down the silencer of the gun is the only thing I can see as I ignore the harsh weather, and the screaming of my aching muscles as I run with everything I have back to the house.

The warmth of the house is anything but calming. It's too eerie. Too quiet. I barely hold onto the banister as I fly up the stairs, terrified I've played into this fucker's hand. That he out-smarted me. That he came back for her. I don't know who he is. I don't know how he got in here. All I know is that he was here, and he was going to kill her.

I don't stop moving until I'm upstairs. I just need her here, I need her to be safe.

"Jules!" I cry out before I shove the bedroom door open.

"Mason," she whimpers. She's worried and terrified, but she runs straight to me, burying her head in my chest and clinging to me.

"Thank fuck," I whisper into her hair, holding on to her just as tight. Her chest meets mine and she's pressed against me like she can't get close enough. I stroke her damp hair with my cheek, leaving soft kisses and rubbing her back over and over.

She's okay. Thank fuck she's here. I close my eyes, but the moment I do, the fucker's face flashes into my mind.

Who is he? And why the fuck was he here?

The answers come easily, making my grip on Jules tighten.

A hitman. Here to kill. Because he was hired to do just that.

"My father is a dead man." It's all I can say. "I'll kill him for this." My throat scratches with a rawness of pain that touches the very marrow of my bones. Jules pulls away from me, snif-fling and looking up at me with a look I can't make out in her eyes.

She doesn't answer for the longest time, just staring back at me as I slowly catch my breath. *I'm so sorry, Jules.* The apol-ogy is trapped at the back of my throat.

"He had this." Jules breaks the moment with her weakly spoken words. She holds out what she found and a chill sweeps over me. A syringe. "It fell on the floor when," she says and pauses, clearing her throat, then tucks her hair behind her ears, looking past me to the last bedroom. She swallows, wrapping her arms around her shoulders and taking a step away before finishing her statement. "When you were on him."

She doesn't look at me, she continues to back away, moving farther into the master bedroom and I follow until the back of her knees hit the bed and she sits on the edge. Is she angry with me? I miss her warmth immediately, my knuckles pulsing with pain at the memory of beating the piss out of the man who would have killed her.

"I had to, Jules."

Her eyes rip away from the ground and she stares into my own. "I know," she whispers, but the pain and sadness in her eyes won't go away. My chest rises with a heavy breath. I don't understand her reaction.

I close my fist around the syringe as I take a step closer to her. She doesn't pull away, not even when I cup her chin in my hand. "Are you okay?" I ask, staring deep into her eyes.

She nods her head and pushes her cheek into my palm. My worry leaves me when she leans into me, covering my hand with her own and closing her eyes.

"Mason," she whispers in a pained voice and it breaks my heart.

I bend down to hold her, to embrace her and tell her that everything's going to be all right. It'll never happen again.

As I get closer to her, my cell phone goes off in my back pocket.

She bites down on her lip as I rest my forehead against hers, hating that I'm being pulled away from her. I take it out from my back pocket only to silence it, to give her my full attention and make sure she knows she's safe, but I see it's my father.

"Stay here," I tell her softly.

"Where are you going?" she asks as she reaches out for me, grabbing my hand as if I'm leaving her alone in hell.

"Just downstairs," I say, letting go of her hand but not before kissing her knuckles. They're soft and undamaged, unlike my own. I look over my shoulder at her as I answer the phone and pass through the bedroom door.

"Hello," I say coldly as I shut the door and take each step of the stairs carefully. The thuds of my feet are in time with the beating of my heart, slow and meticulous.

"Mason, I have the numbers and it's going to be rough," my father says and doesn't wait for me to reply. He's in full-on business mode. As if I would buy that and this isn't damage control.

The click is loud as I lock the front door. I'm barely listening to the man ramble on the other end. He's an idiot if he thinks for one moment this call will fool me.

Dragging out the chair at the head of my dining room table, I stare at the front door, my eyes focused on the lock before flicking over to the stairs.

I can't fucking calm down being so far away from her.

She's safe, I tell myself repeatedly.

"Stop," I say into the phone, halting my father midsentence. "Do you think I don't know it was you?" My tone is menacing.

"What was me? Are you still on about the… incident?"

Rage pushes down the accusations.

"You have something and I have something. I'll be damned if you're going to screw me on this deal, Mason. Think with your fucking head for once!" He scolds me like he used to, his anger on full display. "I thought we had a deal after I let her walk out with you. Was the understanding not clear?" There's silence after the unspoken threat.

"Attempting to have her murdered is a part of your deal?" I ask him evenly, although my pulse betrays any calmness I attempt to maintain.

"Jesus Christ, Mason! Why won't you get over it?"

"So you wouldn't hurt her? You wouldn't threaten her life?" The recent events play in my vision as the syringe in my hand taps back and forth on the table.

He snuck in. He had a syringe. He had a gun but didn't use it.

"I meant to scare her. But I..." he trails off and the strength leaves my father's voice. "I made a mistake before and maybe I am a little heavy handed, but whatever she was going to say, she didn't. You can't be angry with me for that."

"The hell I can't. And if you ever hurt her, I'll kill you." I don't bother mincing my words; we're well past thinly veiled threats. "If anything happens to her," I say as my blood runs cold as I swallow thickly before continuing, "I'll kill you myself."

All I can hear on the other line is a long exhale. "You control her, Mason," my father says and continues with business. He carries on like this conversation didn't include a threat to his life. All the while, I stare at the sharp silver needle of the syringe.

If my father didn't do this, who did?

"Something happened." My throat dries up and I lean

forward, hating that I'm relying on him. Hating that I'm in such deep shit I can't get out myself. I take in a heavy breath before saying, "Someone came here."

There's a pause on the other end of the line. "Where's here? Your home?"

"Yes, someone broke in; I don't know how. Someone with a gun and he tried—"

"Are you all right?" my father asks, not letting me finish, and he sounds genuinely concerned.

"I'll be all right when he's dead," I answer him coldly, and it's the truth. "And if I find out you had anything to do with it—"

"I didn't," he says, his sharp tone meant to assure me.

I don't respond, not knowing any longer what to believe.

"Are you sure you want to discuss this over the phone?" he asks after a moment of quiet, and I already know I shouldn't. I pause, and he continues.

"Do you know who it was?" my father asks, but there's something in his voice that's off. Something that makes my blood turn cold. "Was there anything on him?" he asks me with a hint of desperation. The line is silent as I look at the syringe on the table.

"No," I say, my voice falling flat.

"Where is he?" he asks me.

I clear my throat and say, "There wasn't anything on him."

"Tell me his location, I'll take care of this. You don't have to worry—"

"He's gone!" I scream into the phone, feeling increasingly angrier.

A hitman. I only know one man who's ever hired a hitman, and he's on the other end of the phone.

The front door was locked. Someone made that bastard a key. I was only downstairs in the office to talk to my lawyers about the separation of the business. I was preoccupied as he crept up the stairs.

My father knew about the call. He knew. My vision turns to red and even though, for a small moment, I questioned if it could be him, it has to be.

It was my father. All the logical pieces click together, fitting nice and pretty as my father's voice comes through the phone. He just happens to call when the bastard got away? I don't fucking believe in coincidences.

I stare at the syringe on my desk. An overdose of something. That's why there was no gunshot. Too messy. The gun was for protection only.

He was here to murder Jules in a clean way so that no one would know, not even me.

My father set me up. I grip the phone tighter. He tried to kill her. A dark whisper deep in the back of my head hisses, *Just like he killed your mother.*

"It was you." The words come out of my mouth as an accusation. "You're fucking dead."

"Me?" My father's voice echoes with disbelief. "You can't be serious, Mason!"

My skin feels like it's on fire; I try to contain my rage, but it's useless.

"Never," he says on the other end. "I would never hurt her. She's yours, Mason. I'm very aware of that," he tells me, and he sounds so sincere.

I don't respond, thinking. Trying to think who would want to hurt her. Or maybe me. Maybe the asshole was after me. He didn't shoot her. He could have, but he didn't. Maybe the syringe was meant for me. Maybe the man was hired by whomever left the note. For all I know, that man is the one who left the note.

"Scare her, yes. Yes I would and if she ever did anything to hurt you, she'd be there on my list, Mason. But I would tell you. It would be your call."

My father disgusts me. Just the thought of what he's done and what he's willing to do is sickening. But he's saying this wasn't his doing. If it wasn't him, I have no clue where to look next. Nothing but a note with no name and this syringe.

"Who then?" I finally say and as I do, I hear Jules's faint steps as she comes down the stairs. I turn in my seat in the dining room to watch as she walks down slowly and then freezes when she sees me.

Her large eyes plead with me, and I instantly rise to meet her.

"Upstairs, sweetheart," I tell her as my father speaks.

"Has she upset anyone? What was she at the station for? You need to be honest with me."

I place my hand on the small of her back and lead her up the stairs. Her eyes dart to the phone as my father talks, and I know she can hear.

"No, she hasn't upset anyone," I tell him. "Her going to the station was a mistake."

"Well, someone knows something, Mason." He says it like it's obvious. "What about Liam?" he asks me. "He knew we'd be having the conference about the division of the assets. He has a motive." Jules nearly trips on the stairs. She shouldn't be listening to this shit.

I grab her hip to keep her from falling and almost drop the phone.

"I have to call you back," I tell him, content with the fact that it wasn't my father.

Someone knows what I did, and they're after me. They may also be after Jules. Especially now that she's seen this. We both saw his face. She's woven so deeply into my mess.

My father continues speaking into the phone but his words turn to white noise, and I simply end the call. My focus is entirely on Jules.

Her grip on me is tight, and she lets me hold her as I drop the phone to the ground and simply pull her into my lap to sit on the stairs.

Maybe it's the shock, maybe it's something else.

But I don't want to let go of her.

I don't want her to let go of me either.

"I'll find out who did this, Jules," I whisper. "I'll find them, and I'll kill them."

CHAPTER
twelve

Julia

The stars are always present,
Even though we cannot see.
The clouds will block them out,
And leave us with a plea.

Sometimes it takes the darkness,
And the coldest, purest lights.
To see what's always been there,
And cherish those stars at night.

"MASON."

He's silent as he sits on the chair in the corner of the bedroom. It's a reading chair that I bought a while back and tucked into the corner of the master when I moved in with Mason. He seems to prefer it now when he's thinking about what to do. Or maybe it's when life is breaking him down to the point where he can't stand on his own any longer.

"Mason?" I call out his name, my voice soft and again he doesn't seem to hear it. There's a comfortable groove and warmth that surrounds me since I haven't moved from my spot on the bed since we came back in here after he talked with his father. Silence sits between us, with both of us letting our thoughts run wild. His chin rests in his hand and his eyes are staring straight ahead at the armoire, unblinking.

Someone attempted to kill one of us. Or at the very least, inject whatever is in that syringe… Closing my eyes, I calmly breathe out, my fingers tightening on the blanket huddled in my lap.

"Mason, please talk to me," I say, raising my voice even louder. I want to know what he knows. I can't be left in the dark. This time his gray eyes look back at me, smoldering the moment he sees me. As if I've lit a fire, and the intensity of it stops me right where I am.

The only thing I can think in this moment is that he's going to eliminate the distance between us, to push me back on the bed, to take me like he used to with that look. My breath halts and my body stays frozen, but not with fear or denial. *This is lust.* I want him to take me, to feel my body and for me to feel his. Right now I need to be held. Just like I did all those months ago when Mason first took me home.

I want to forget it all.

Mason doesn't do any of that. The chair scoots back against the hardwood floor as he rises from the corner. He walks past me leaving a trail of coldness in his wake as he stands in front of his dresser, his back to me for a long moment.

Leaning back on the bed, I attempt to push down the wave of rejection that flows through every inch of my body. A hollowness presses against my chest. Does he no longer want me?

Isn't this what I wanted not so long ago? Why does it hurt so much, why does it hurt even worse?

Mason drops to a crouch in front of the dresser, pulling out the third drawer down and not stopping until it's completely removed from the dresser.

"What are you doing?"

"You need protection when I can't be here." It takes a moment to register what he said, but only until he reaches inside the dresser where the drawer was and pulls out a case. It's thin and silver, obviously a gun case. My gaze never leaves the brushed satin metal as he carries it to the bed.

A numbness pricks its way to my fingers at the very thought of touching it. I've never shot a gun before. I haven't ever even seen one in person until today. Until the sight of one was trained on me.

I scoot back slightly and keep my eyes on Mason, ridding myself of the thoughts of the gun that was here only hours ago.

"If someone ever comes in here again, you're going to shoot them. Do you understand me?" Mason asks.

My heart races and my body heats with an anxiety that's nearly paralyzing. I don't know if I can kill someone.

"Who was that man?" I ask Mason rather than answer, but he merely flicks his eyes to mine before turning the case around and ignoring my question.

"The combination is my mother's birthday: ten, fifteen, fifty-seven." I blink up at him, waiting for more, but he simply pushes the box closer to me, rattling it to get my attention until my fingertips slide to the cold silver metal of the combination lock.

Ten. Fifteen. Fifty-seven. *Click*. The loud noise of the case opening doesn't startle me as much as I thought it would; I'm still waiting to learn who the man was and why he was here. I need to know what he was searching for and what was in that syringe.

Mason swallows thickly, opening the case and revealing a shiny handgun.

"It's a nine millimeter. It—"

"Mason," I say, cutting him off, waiting for his eyes to meet mine. "Who was that?" I ask him when I have his full attention.

"I don't know," he answers lowly, holding my gaze.

"Why..." I can't finish my sentence, my blood rushing in my ears and my body heating.

My throat goes dry as Mason gives me nothing. His expression is unchanging, and I know right then he's not going to tell me a damn thing.

I lick my lips and push the case away from me. I didn't choose this, and I don't want it.

"You need to know how to use this, Jules," Mason says, grabbing the gun by the barrel and passing it to me handle out, insisting I take it. I stare at it, but I don't really see it. Everything's a blur.

"I can't describe how absolutely terrified I was," I say, swallowing down every fear as I rush to get it all out. "Not for my own life or what was going to happen to me, or what could have happened…" Chancing a look in his eyes, I know he hears me. I know he understands what I'm saying.

I was worried he'd never come back. I was worried Mason was going to die.

"I need you to talk to me," I tell him as my eyes burn with the emotions finally surfacing. Scooting closer to him on the bed, I lean closer and plead, "I need to know what's going on." I take a steadying breath, surprised at how even my cadence is. At how strong my voice sounds although I feel as if I'm on the verge of collapsing with hopelessness.

"I don't want to tell you more than you need to know, Jules," Mason says and looks up at me with sympathy, his strength and dominance ever present. He reaches out to cup my jaw but I flinch and move away, scooting backward slightly as I shake my head.

"No, you don't get to decide that," I tell him with a voice much louder than I anticipated. A small bit of anger seeps into the firm statement.

Mason's gaze narrows, but he doesn't respond.

"I need to know." My voice cracks, and I hate that it does, but I am truly desperate and there's no way to hide that. "You need to tell me." Without a response, I lick my dry lips and shamefully look away, down at the patterned rug on the floor.

I wish my voice held the strength I feel. I wish I were stronger overall. I'm trying, I'm truly giving everything I can not to be the meek woman I was raised to be and praised for being.

"You don't need to know." His answer is short but he keeps my gaze as if he's ready to cave to me, to give me what I want. I know that look well. I only need to ask.

"I want to know, Mason," I tell him honestly. "Please," I add as I lean forward slightly, almost reaching for his hand. Almost.

With a heavy sigh, he puts the gun back into the case. He shoves it to the side and finally tells me, "I think he was a hitman. I think there's a hit out—"

"A hit?" I blurt out, not quite picking up what he's saying at first, but then the realization floods through me, along with a coldness that cracks my composure. "Someone wants to kill you?" How I have any voice at all is beyond me.

His expression softens as he shakes his head once. "It could be either of us. But I would think that the killer knew I was downstairs in the office."

"Someone tried to kill me?" I manage to get out, but then immediately have to fight back the need to vomit. The shock is just too much. "Why?" My hands shake without my conscious consent. *Someone's trying to kill me.*

"Your father?" I can only surmise it's him. "He warned me. He… he—"

"I don't think so. I think he'd rather use you to get to me than kill you."

"Then who?" The question is torn from me. "Who the hell would try to kill me if not him?"

Mason doesn't answer me.

"Mason." I whisper his name, my face crumpling with pain

as I beg him, "I don't want to die." I've thought about death so much this past year, ever since Jace died. It often occurred to me that it would be so easy to just end the pain. But I don't want that. I want to live. I want to be happy. Like I was with Mason, before I found out all the lies.

"No one's going to hurt you," Mason states with finality in a voice so full of confidence, I believe him. His white T-shirt is pulled snug across his broad shoulders and as he leans forward, looking me deep in my eyes, my heart flips and everything else but him blurs around me. "I'll always protect you, Jules. I promise," he tells me. I think he's going to reach out and touch me, that he's going to kiss me and hold me in that comforting way I've grown used to. But he doesn't. He's only inches away, so close I could touch him, but the distance between us is still there and I know I only need to give my consent to let him in. To let his touch soothe the pain that's suffocating me.

"Please hold me." I hate myself in this moment for needing Mason, for forgiving him enough to give in to my own weakness and desires. I close my eyes tight, willing my conscience to go away so he can comfort me. It's not the first time I've had to do this. And the last time sent me spiraling into a darkness I couldn't control.

"I need more than that, Jules." Mason's voice is full of raw emotion for the first time since coming back in here. My eyes open slowly, feeling the sting of tears subside and something else forcing its way through me. His cold gray eyes soften and fill with vulnerability.

Mason reaches across the bed and grips the back of my head in his hand. It's large and strong and his fingers spear through my hair with a strength that forces my lips up to his. He crashes his own against mine and pushes my body back.

I don't know how to describe the rush of desire that sparks to life between us. It's like thunder and lightning all at once, right before a downpour in the middle of an open field with no shelter in sight. It's hot and drenched between us. That's what his kiss does to me. It's a natural storm that I can't stay away from.

"Mason." I moan his name as he breaks our kiss, resting his forehead against mine and breathing heavily. His warm breath fills the small space between us, but when I look up there's nothing but pain etched on his face. Does he not feel it like I do? If I could have anything right now, I'd have him in the field with me, letting the rain soak our skin.

Wordlessly, I reach up and trail my fingers along the stubble of his strong jaw.

"I thought I'd lost you," he whispers and his voice is low and carries the same agony I'm feeling. I almost tell him I know what it feels like, I almost let the tears come back, but then his lips meet mine in a soft, slow kiss that makes my heart race.

I thought I'd lost him. I thought I was going to die before that. "Just hold me," I whimper, my voice a strangled plea.

"Always," Mason murmurs before kissing me long and deep. My back hits the bed and my legs part for him. The tension blisters between us with a passion I thought was long gone. Its intensity refuses to be denied as I cling to him, every bit of me wanting to be pressed against him. He breaks the kiss and I have to tilt my head back to breathe in the cool air as he kisses down my body. Each one takes time, leaving a cool sensation behind as his hot kisses move on to the next spot. It's too slow, yet it's just right.

He takes off my clothes as he goes, slowly stripping me for him. With every moment I'm conscious of what I'm allowing him to do. Watching myself give in to baser needs and allow a man I despised to crawl down my body, holding me as if he owns me, but he does it so gently, as if I'm precious to him. I love every second of it and I know I still love him. The swarm of emotions rages, but only one wins out.

My head digs into the mattress as my neck arches and I lift my hips for him.

I may be a fool, but I know what I want and need.

He kisses just below my belly, sending goosebumps to flow across my bare skin before moving lower. I'm hot for him; my body aches for him. His heated breath causes a sweet sensation of desire to travel up my body and harden my nipples.

I let my hands slowly travel from my breasts to his hair, running my fingernails down his scalp as he pulls off the rest of my clothes and lets them drop to the floor. They fall into a crumpled heap and make the only sound that fills the room besides our breathing and the pounding of my heart.

Mason places his hands on my inner thighs and he doesn't have to push; I immediately spread them wider for him. He stares between my legs and even though my cheeks heat with a violent blush, I can't tear my eyes away from his as he leans forward and gently sucks on my clit.

I cry out my pleasure. It's instant and forceful, just as Mason is.

My legs try to close together to force him away, my fingers gripping onto his muscular shoulders and nails digging into his skin, but he doesn't let up until a wave of my orgasm rises slowly through my toes and fingers. It moves higher and higher and then crashes hard, rocking through my body without any mercy. My head thrashes to the side as I cry out, and I'm only vaguely aware as Mason kisses back up my body with purpose and need this time. He buries his head in the crook of my neck, biting down slightly as he slams himself deep inside of me. He doesn't wait for me to adjust. He only takes his pleasure from me as easily as he gave me my own, ruthlessly riding through my release.

He groans deep and low as he pounds into me over and over again. My body begs me to move, but I'm paralyzed by pleasure. By Mason.

It's fitting really. I'm held beneath him with a passion I can't fight. With a love I can't deny. I can try to fight it, but it's useless.

He braces himself on his forearms to look down at me, never relenting his powerful thrusts. My arousal leaks between us as he lowers his lips to mine.

The dim waves rise again through me, making my body shiver and the rest of me tense. It's coming fast and strong and it's inevitable, I know it is. I hold on to Mason for dear life, letting him take from me and crashing my lips into his.

She's broken,
Shattered,
Ruined beyond repair.
The truth has destroyed her,
And left her
Choking on the air.

My mother died of an overdose.

This can't be a coincidence. It's all I keep thinking as I remember the syringe. I threw it into the fireplace and watched it burn, the thick plastic slowly melting and the liquid boiling into nothing, leaving only a thin needle in the ashes.

I couldn't take it to the police. It only took an opioid test to prove what I thought. It was heroin. It's been two days and I only have one answer to all the questions. The syringe was filled with an opioid and I imagine if the killer had done his job, I would have gone upstairs to find Jules dead of an overdose.

I readjust in my seat in the corner of the bedroom, my laptop on the nightstand I've pulled over to the chair. The dim light from the screen provides the only illumination in the dark room. My tumbler of whiskey sits next to it, but I can't drink. I can't do anything but read the report of my mother's death and let the doubt and anxiety wash through me.

For years I blamed my father.

The therapist he sent me to was under the impression she took her own life because all they did was fight and there were concerns about my mother's sudden erratic behavior. Concerns that wound themselves around whispers of drug use.

I blamed my father because I thought he did it.

He wasn't home when it happened, but that was nothing new. He was never around on the weekends. I was in my bed, but the house was so cold. The air conditioner was turned down far too low.

I remember thinking it was odd that the heat had been turned off. Our house became an icebox.

The moment I clicked it on, I heard the shower upstairs. Maybe I was waiting for the telltale sound of the heater, but until then I hadn't realized I could hear the shower.

I remember how I knocked on the bathroom door, but

didn't go in at first. I waited and waited, wondering why she'd be in there so late. Wondering if she was crying again.

I only opened the door an hour later because I'd convinced myself she couldn't still be in there. Not after so long. The water had to be cold by then.

My parents' bathroom door wasn't locked. The knob turned easily and when the door opened and I didn't see a shadow behind the curtain, I was confused but relieved to discover the water had just been left on. Everything felt so off that night, like something was horribly wrong. I was genuinely relieved.

It wasn't until I pulled back the curtain that I saw her.

I slam the computer shut, willing the memory to leave me.

The vision of my mother dead, her body at an unnatural angle. The water was freezing, and it'd turned her lips blue. It didn't stop me from shaking her. From trying to make her wake up.

I screamed and cried out helplessly even though I knew we were alone. There was no one to help. I had to leave her to call the police. I couldn't though, not for a long time. I was shivering in my wet clothes by the time I ran down the stairs to call the cops. I couldn't believe she was gone, but she was limp and heavy and so cold.

It didn't take long for the police to come. Commissioner Haynes was there first.

My father took hours to arrive, though. Hours of sitting on my bed, being questioned over and over until I wasn't sure anymore what had happened.

I only knew I felt completely alone in the world.

The first thing my father said to me was, "I thought you

were staying over at your friend's this weekend." No sorrow was evident. No sympathy that I'd found my mother dead in the shower.

His tone carried an accusation even. I remember staring up at him. The police moved around the house, blurring my vision as my father came into focus and the pieces clicked into place.

For years I've felt he was responsible and even now, even after he'd managed to convince me on the phone that it wasn't him, I imagine he's somehow involved.

I can't shake my gut feeling.

I want to murder him.

The thought makes me close my eyes, trying to rein in the anger from today and from all the years of second-guessing what happened to my mother.

When I open them, they've adjusted to the darkness and I stare at my phone.

I've asked him, but he's a liar. I already know he's capable of murder.

Everything in me is telling me it's my father who hired that man and possibly left the note to scare Jules off before deciding to kill her. I have no other leads.

The person who left a note had different handwriting than his though, more feminine. Perhaps he has a partner or maybe he hired someone but who would he trust?

The only other enemy I have is Liam. He's married, but I can't see it being him and having his wife involved. And Liam wasn't around when my mother died.

I run my hand down my face, feeling exhaustion weighing down on me, but not wanting to sleep. I can't. I'm too afraid to take my eyes away from Jules. My guard refuses to go down for even a second.

I know she hasn't forgotten everything and that maybe the other night, the moment we shared, was a mistake in her eyes. It kills me just to imagine her thinking of it as if that's all it was. A mistake.

The sound of her stirring on the bed and the accompanying slow movements catch my attention. A soft sound of pain carries through the air, and I rise to see if she's all right.

She turns on her side, pulling the sheet between her legs and letting it fall off her gorgeous curves. I brush her hair from her face, leaning down to kiss her gently on the cheek, loving how she can't fight me in her sleep.

When I pull back, her long lashes flutter open and she looks up at me. At first there's a softness to her expression, like the way she used to look at me. But it quickly changes, the trace of a smile dimming as her memories come back to her.

Her shoulders tense and she turns her head, but she doesn't push me away, even as I run my hand down to her waist and sit next to her on the bed.

The bed protests as I climb in under the sheet, still in my white undershirt and flannel pajama pants. I sigh heavily, feeling exhaustion desperately try to force me to sleep as I rest my head on the pillow and pull Jules close to me.

Just like earlier this week, she lets me hold her. She doesn't hold me back, though. Her hand merely rests against my chest, her head on my shoulder. Still, I'll take it. The feel of her small body pressed to mine, the faint sounds of her breathing and the way she nestles her head down against me, brushing the hair from her face is everything to me.

"Talk to me, Jules," I say softly. I miss her. I miss the banter and her optimistic energy. I miss her stories and the sweet sound of her laughter. "I miss you," I confess.

"I'm not sure if we're okay," she says quietly, as if it's a reminder to herself. "There are parts of you that scare me."

I tell her, "But not all of me."

Her eyes are wide open but staring across the room. I readjust my shoulders on the pillow, keeping my arm around her and debating what to tell her. She's quiet for a long time but then she asks, "You said Jace had a woman killed?"

I can only nod.

She's silent, obviously waiting for me to continue.

"I didn't know him well, but he was…" I pause to take a deep breath and stare at the mirror across the room. In the reflection I can see the top of Jules's head resting on my chest. Her eyes are vacant, as if she's broken. Not the woman I once knew, not the Jules I fell in love with. She's not running from me, as if this new woman has become resigned to her fate.

"I saw him for a meeting, and it was the only time I met him," I tell her. I want to explain and I pray she understands.

She shifts on my chest and I splay my hand on her back to keep her close to me, to keep her from moving away, but I don't have to. She's only readjusting and she stays with her cheek pressed against my chest as she pulls the sheet up higher.

"I did it," I say, feeling the words dying to come out of me. To tell her the truth. To tell her how angry he made me. How Jace was so sure of himself, so happy with what he'd done. "Her life was meaningless to him."

"Whose? Whose life?" Jules brings her hand back toward herself, retreating slightly but I reach out to grab it. I bring her fingers to my lips and slowly kiss each knuckle. She doesn't look at me while I do, but when I set her hand back down, she leaves it there.

I don't know what to make of her in this moment. Maybe she's numb, but she's receptive. She's lost her fight to deny it all.

"Her name was Avery."

Jules shifts uncomfortably as she says the words before I can. "She was his mistress?"

I nod my head as I say, "I knew her as well." It's the gentlest way I can put it.

"You *knew* her?" Jules asks in a tight voice. It's the loudest she's spoken for this conversation.

"I did," I answer honestly. "Obviously it was before we met. Before I knew you."

She nods her head into my chest and whispers, "Why?"

"Why did he want to kill her?"

My question forces her expression to fall even farther, but she nods.

"She was pregnant," I tell her and that's the last straw for Jules's composure. I hold her close as she tries to turn away. I kiss her shoulder as she hunches over and tries to hide her face from me.

"It's okay," I whisper into the tense air between us. The hurt and betrayal are echoed in her ragged breaths. I can only imagine how much it shredded her to hear the words, because it killed me to say them to her.

She pushes her hands against my chest slightly, and I let her go for a moment.

Sitting up as if searching for more air, she pushes the thick sheet off of her and pulls her long brunette hair over her shoulder as she scoots up the bed and readjusts herself to lean against the headboard. All the while I can see her reining in the emotions, hiding it all and shoving it down. But she's swallowed the truth of it all: her husband wanted his mistress dead because she was pregnant. It will stay with her forever.

"Was the baby..." she starts to ask in a choked voice as she lies back next to me and instantly places her head on my chest. "Whose was it?" she asks.

My heart clenches in my chest, hating that I have to answer her and knowing it's going to torture her. "His," I finally answer.

She nods once, letting me know she acknowledges what I've just told her, but she's silent. A long time passes with neither of us saying anything. My fingers trail up and down her arm, moving to the dip in her waist and back up her body again. Her breathing becomes steadier, deeper and so does mine. Slowly, she gets comfortable alongside me again, resting down in bed, but neither of us sleeping.

"Did you love her?" she asks just as my eyelids feel so heavy I could fall asleep, her fingers gripping onto my shirt but still she doesn't look at me.

"No. I've never loved anyone like I love you," I tell her and then realize she may not believe me. It's true, though. I'd never planned on spending my life with someone. I didn't think it possible for someone who carries the demons that drag me down. But now I can't see my life without Jules in it. She's a bright light to my darkness. The only hope I've ever had is in her hands.

Again, she acknowledges me with only a small nod.

"Can you forgive me?" I ask her quietly, almost too afraid of her answer to even utter the word *forgiveness*.

Time passes and I think she may have fallen asleep, but then her shoulders shake with a small sob.

"No," she says and my chest sinks from her admission but also from the raw pain in her voice. "You didn't have to murder him." She adds, nearly choking on her words, "But I believe you." She sniffles once and it's then I feel her tears soaking into my shirt. She brushes her cheek against my shirt and settles back down against me.

She believes me, and that's a start.

She needs me, and she's clinging to me because she has nowhere else to go.

At least I can hold her for a little while, but even with her so close to me, even with this progress, I feel farther away from her than I've ever been.

CHAPTER
fourteen

Julia

It's absurd to move through life,
When there's nothing left inside.
When you're hollow and unfeeling,
When all you know has died.

Numb to touch, numb to move,
And silent with no voice.
But strength comes in the darkest times,
When you no longer have a choice.

FRAUD. I KEEP HEARING THE WORD OVER AND over in my head. There's no way I can do this. No way I can stand in front of a room full of people, this hollow shell of a woman, and smile as if nothing has changed. There's no way I can laugh and play along with the façade of a happy couple deeply in love.

They'll see through me; I know they will.

I've always been acutely aware of my public persona. My mother used to tell me it was important for the family name. All my life I've known how to hide behind a beautiful face and stay polite even when offended. I know just what to say, and how to act.

But right now? This moment? No. I can't go through with it. I can't pretend anymore. Pretending's what got me into this mess.

"You look beautiful." Mason's deep baritone voice sends a thrill through my body. His approval always has, and my natural instinct is to cling to him right now. I want to hide behind him. He could make everything all right or at least that's the way it would feel.

Even more than that, I so desperately care for him despite everything that's happened, and that's what's breaking me.

"Thank you," I whisper and then clear my throat, turning my gaze back to the entrance of the Regency Auditorium as the limo stops in front of the building, my fingertips haphazardly grazing the crystals on my dress with nerves that won't be tamed.

I used to live for this. All the gorgeous gowns and flowing champagne, the photographs and mingling. Now instead of desire and excitement and anticipation, all I feel is dread.

I turn back to Mason just as he places his large hand over mine, and in that moment I remember who he is and what he's done and why everything has changed. I want to pull away. My body and mind are confused. I feel attacked and cornered, but I don't know who to blame other than myself.

"It's going to be all right. You're fine," Mason tells me. His voice is a soothing balm, but it's a lie. A sweet, pretty lie meant to calm me down so I can do as I'm told and act appropriately.

Pulling my hand away from him, I watch his face fall and the divider rolls down slowly; it's the only sound in the cabin.

"Is this all right, Mr. Thatcher?" Marcus, the driver, asks. I can't look him in the eye. I swallow thickly, watching the sparkling gowns flow by as women walk past. I know many of them, or at least recognize their faces. Tonight is a fundraiser for diabetic children. Nearly three hundred people will be in the grand ballroom, bidding on donations lined with spotlights and making small talk while sipping champagne and gossiping or bragging.

It's how these functions run. Who you know and who you talk to can be different, so long as you're seen with each group of individuals accordingly.

My role has changed from socialite sweetheart who brings the press to that of devoted arm candy. The to-do list hasn't changed, though: look pretty, smile and be charming. It didn't seem so bad all these years I've been doing this. Even my father used to bring me to events like this as a teen. I loved it. I was proud to come and be a part of the social scene especially when they involved causes like this one.

"This is fine," Mason answers Marcus and I grip my

Chanel clutch as if it will protect me and save me from having to walk out there. "I'll open her door; thank you."

"I don't know that I'm ready," I whisper to Mason, turning to him and leaning in, acutely aware that Marcus is watching. I don't have to look up to see his eyes in the rearview mirror assessing the situation to know he's taking it all in. Everyone is always watching.

Mason searches my face for something, and then the corners of his lips twitch as he reaches his arm around my waist and pulls me in closer to him.

His strength and heat and proximity all make my blood temperature rise, and the anxiety and fear are replaced with something else entirely.

"You're definitely ready," Mason says before leaning into me for a kiss. A split second passes before I even question it. It feels so natural, as if I'm the one who intended for it to happen.

As if nothing ever happened. As if the envelope had never been opened and this part of the tale ceased to exist.

I pull away suddenly, sucking in the hot air and pushing back against the leather seat. My eyes flicker to the mirror as I regain my composure, to Marcus's ever-prying view and immediately the divider begins to move back into place, granting us privacy.

Mason's hand splays on my back before I can move any farther. "Please stop," I say. He must know what he's doing to me.

"Stop what?" he asks as if he doesn't know that his kindness is worse than anything else. That craving his affection only makes me hate myself more.

I look up through my lashes, not bothering to face him as I hold the clutch tighter with both hands.

"I can't do this, Mason," I blurt out with my voice low and pleading. "I can't pretend."

He rests his hand on the back of my neck, gripping my nape but running his thumb back and forth ever so gently. Each action sends mixed signals, and that's the very crux of my position.

"You could ignore me all night," he suggests with a sad smile. "It would be better if you did that… if we were to split in a month anyway. Wouldn't it?"

His words are accompanied by a shadow, the night already darkening. Three weeks. I don't correct him, but it's three weeks that are left, not a month. Swallowing thickly, I glance at the entrance rather than entertaining his suggestion.

"Either way," he continues, "we have to attend. We can't appear to be hiding and no one is going to hurt you here."

The lights from the massive crystal chandelier just inside the auditorium's foyer sparkle and blur in a beautiful dance as two more couples enter. I ignore it and stare at the shrubbery that's barely visible.

It hurts to hear him plan a split between us. I didn't think his compromise, promise, whatever it was, was even a real possibility. Yet here he is, speaking it into existence.

Mason opens his door and leaves me without another word. I simultaneously fear him and love him, but worse, I hate myself for having any emotion toward him other than revulsion knowing he's a murderer. That's what I can't get past. It's easy to put a smile on your face and be what everyone else wants you to be when you know who you are and you're happy as that person. When you have faith in yourself.

I've lost that. It's a new low that's left me shattered and

scattered into small pieces on the floor. I don't even know where to start picking them up. I only know the sharp edges will leave me bleeding out as I do.

Cool air drifts into the limo and the light shines just a bit brighter as Mason opens my door. With the wind comes his scent, a natural masculine scent mixed with a clean fragrance from his cologne.

"Don't deny me, sweetheart," Mason says just under his breath as I stare at his outstretched hand. His statement makes my eyes lift to his and I get lost in his swirls of gray and silver. I never had a chance with this man. A tortured soul lies behind those eyes that makes me weak for him. He needs love so desperately; he needs someone, and my very soul craves his.

He was my downfall. Created to destroy me. I slip my hand into his, comforted by the warmth as he wraps his fingers slowly around mine and supports me as I rise from the limo. I keep my eyes down and don't look forward. I can hardly focus on breathing as my heels click on the pavement and Mason leads me forward.

I pull my black bolero shrug tighter around my shoulders and attempt to hide from the harsh weather while ignoring everyone around me.

The doors open and the mix of chatter and the soft melody of an orchestra carry through the air and envelop me as though it's home, as though it's safe. But I'm very much aware that I'm in danger. I scan every face for the one I saw only days ago. The man holding a gun.

At the thought I grip Mason's hand tighter and he pulls me in closer to him, walking in time with me, our steps in unison as the lights get brighter and the air warmer. A small smile slips onto my face, although inside I'm screaming.

I'm dying from the hypocrisy, but intensely aware it's my only chance of survival.

"Mason," I hear a man call out and my smile falters only slightly as my steps are halted. We're to be seen. Unwaveringly present.

"Father," Mason says tightly and I stand there with a sweetness in my composure, tilting my head slightly as the breeze from the doors being opened again sends a chill up my back. My shoulders shudder and Mason wraps his hand around my hip, pulling me in closer.

I don't flinch when his father looks at me. In a crisp suit complete with a charming smile, he appears to be an entirely different man than the one I met before.

"Miss Summers, you look utterly breathtaking this evening," his father says and naturally my smile widens. It's a shame a man like him can possess such poise and charm. I suppose everyone needs some way to survive and thrive.

My heart beats faster and my limbs scream at me to run, or worse, slap the bastard across the face for what he did only days ago, but instead I part my lips and respond sweetly, "I'm so sorry for the other day. I'm afraid I wasn't well."

He falters, the real emotions showing through and just when I think he's going to hide it, when I think the mask that slipped will be forced back into place, he leans in slightly and says, "I do apologize as well," and I swear it seems sincere. "I had no right to come between you two."

Mason stiffens beside me, and my own composure threatens to dissolve. I've never faced this kind of mastery of manipulation before. I don't know whether to react sincerely or how to play this game.

"I only want what's best for my son."

It's only then that I realize our games are different. I'm no match for him, but in the same vein, he's no match for me.

"Champagne?" a server asks on my right, breaking the moment and I instantly turn to her.

"No, thank you," spills from my mouth easily and she's quick to move on after the men each shake their heads.

I watch from my periphery as she leaves, walking easily without a care and holding the tray just so. The champagne doesn't even seem to move; she's learned to do her job well.

"Excuse me a moment, Mason," I tell him, patting his forearm and waiting for him to release my hand. He doesn't, though.

He holds me a moment longer than he should, quietly watching me and waiting for a reason. "I need to use the restroom," I whisper to him as softly and flirtatiously as I can, feeling the number of eyes on us grow. It may all be in my head, because for all I know I'm losing it, and with every second my anxiety grows.

"Of course," he says although the reflection in his eyes is something else. Something far more vulnerable and unwilling. He kisses my hand, bringing it to his lips and then releasing me without another word.

I force a smile to stay in place although it begs to fall. Everything in me is screaming that something is wrong. I walk as quickly as I can to the back of the room, deeper and deeper through the crowd of beautiful guests. I turn my body slightly when needed and ignore the conversations around me as I head to the restrooms.

I could just run. I could run away.

Away from all of this, and never stop.

I'll find myself again, but not here. Not when I know I want the very thing that will bury me.

fifteen

Mason

So close to having everything,
So close to nothing at all.
The teeter-totter rocks back and forth,
While knowing you will fall.

It's all there within your grasp,
But the life has turned to stone.
You should have known, you foolish man,
You were meant to live alone.

"I APPRECIATE THE APOLOGY," I TELL MY FATHER, although my gaze isn't on him at all. My eyes are on Jules's back as her hips sway and she leaves me. When I first laid eyes on her, she blended in so easily. Each small motion was seemingly genuine. Not tonight.

My sweetheart is obviously full of hurt and pain and insecurity. In a room full of fake assholes brimming with confidence and arrogance, my Jules doesn't belong.

I wonder if everyone else in this room can see it as clearly as I do. I was wrong to bring her. I could have found another way. My father's voice interrupts my thoughts. "Miss Harrington will be there, and she made it clear she's interested."

Marcy Harrington's an investor who likes to get close with her clients and "know" them before writing a check with her family inheritance. Promiscuous would be a kind word to use. In addition, she's practically untouchable, and always gets what and who she wants.

"This is about appearances, not business. I couldn't give two shits about business right now."

"Appearances?" my father asks, and I feel my hands clench at my sides. He knows damn well what the papers are saying.

"I'd like the world to know that I'm not beating her behind closed doors."

My father shrugs as if the rumor swirling around the city isn't a concern in the least. "I'd like to know what you are doing behind closed doors. Or more importantly… what's being said between you two," he says, turning his body to follow my gaze. She's vanished though, wherever she's gone.

As my eyes drift back to him, I feel the accusations rise. *Now's not the time or place*, I think over and over as my forehead furrows and I shove my hands into my pockets to keep from grabbing him. My muscles are tense, and the words are on the tip of my tongue.

There's no use in letting them out though, because I know he'll just lie. He's damn good at it and so used to it, I doubt he knows the truth from a lie anymore.

"We should have a meeting soon," I say easily, completely at odds with my true feelings. "Business and otherwise."

My father's brows raise slightly, and he looks genuinely surprised. "Of course," he says, patting me on the back. "I trust it's about the matter from the other night?" he asks although it's said as a statement.

"It is," I say, feeling the ball of rage grow larger, getting harder to contain. I clear my throat and glance back to where Jules disappeared, only to see her good friend and editor Katerina striding toward me.

My face stays neutral, with no emotions expressed whatsoever as she approaches.

"I'll talk to you soon," my father says beneath his breath, turning his back to Kat and walking away without waiting for me to acknowledge him.

Kat approaches me with an expression of distrust, an air about her that makes it obvious she's here because she hasn't heard from Jules. I thought about responding to her messages myself. Jules received texts from so many people feigning concern, but really wanting gossip. And then her friends, who seem genuinely worried.

Before she stops in front of me, I force a small smile to my lips, one that's welcoming. I'm already losing my sweetheart; I need to play this right.

"Mason." Kat states my name as if she's ready for a fight, but that's not how this is going to go down. She just doesn't know it yet.

"I'm so happy you're here, Kat," I say and nod my head slightly. "Have you seen Jules already?" I play up the concern in my own voice and expression, and watch as her anger slips and her forehead pinches. She finally looks behind her for only a moment before turning her attention back to me.

"We just got here. She's here?"

"You came with Evan?" I ask her. Her husband is well known in the public relations industry, although he travels with an entirely different sort of social circle. The industry has treated him well, but he's rarely home. That's the angle I have. Two couples; the men friends, the women friends. She'll trust me. She'll help me. At least I pray she will.

"I did," she says and peers to her right, closer to the entrance before clearing her throat and adding, "He's here somewhere." She licks her lips and squares her shoulders, remembering what she's come here to yell at me about.

I cut her off before she can begin by saying, "I'd really like it if you could talk to Jules." Jules's name on my lips and the thought of someone talking to her privately makes apprehension creep into my veins at the possibility of her spilling the truth. I shrug it off and use the intensity of the truth to help create the lie. "She's taking the wedding situation a little bit hard."

Kat watches me for a moment, her eyes narrowing as

she assesses my words. I lean forward, dropping my voice and letting the insecurity that is all too real show. "She's not okay," I tell her. "She could really use a friend right now."

"I haven't spoken to her in over a week," Kat says, confiding in me and I don't let on that I know it's uncommon for Jules not to return a call. I play my emotions as I should.

"I'm not sure she *wants* to talk about it"—I can see Kat's objection on the tip of her tongue and I say it before she can—"but she needs to."

Kat's mouth stays parted and she tilts her head, still judging my request as her husband walks up behind her.

"Evan." I pull back from Kat and press my lips into an acceptable smile. One that reflects my unease for what Jules is going through. At least that's what it shows Kat. A part of me feels like a prick, like the manipulative asshole I am, undeserving of Jules. But I already knew I wasn't good enough for her, and this show, this front, is all to save us. To save what we have.

"Thatcher, how are you, man?"

A huff of a grunt leaves me as I rock back on my heels and shove my hands in my suit pockets. "That's my father's name," I say jokingly and Evan laughs deep from his chest, raising a tumbler of amber liquid to his lips. The ice clinks in his glass as he wraps his arm around his wife's waist.

"You two make quite the couple," I say, complimenting them. They have definitely been the talk of the city on more than one occasion.

"Speaking of couples," Evan says, and his cuff slips back over his wrist as he lowers the whiskey, hiding the sleeve tattoo. His left arm is covered in tattoos. His background is perfect for his profession. He's from Brooklyn with the reputation of a man who grew up on the wrong side of the law. He made a name for himself, but only in the best of ways for his job.

He never got caught. Never had a conviction, and he knows the ins and outs of the press.

That's the kind of man the industry wants representing their clients when they're out of the spotlight. Someone to party with and respect and be genuine friends with. But someone who knows when to leave the scene before it gets too rough, what to tell the press and who to go to when shit goes down.

He's damn good at what he does, but how the two of them have stayed married, I have no idea.

"Where did Jules go?" Kat interjects before her husband can finish his thought. He glances at her from the corner of his eye and then releases her, taking a sip of whiskey and looking past me as Kat steps forward. She has no idea how she's affected him.

"Just to the restroom," I say and motion to the back with my chin.

"How's she been?"

"I think she's really taking this transition hard… moving on and getting married again." I could choke on the words.

"I'm sorry to hear that." Evan's condolences are sincere, but I'm more than certain he doesn't want a part in this conversation.

"You better be good to her," Kat says, the declaration sounding like a threat.

I turn my attention back to her. "I'll take care of her, I

promise," I assure her, meeting her prying gaze. I can see the moment my lies slip into place and Kat reaches up to give me a quick hug.

"I'll talk to her," she says firmly, nodding her head and giving me a sympathetic look.

"Thank you," I say and hide the fact that dread is slowly consuming me. Jules was willing to tell the police before. Her dear friend who's concerned for her well-being… I'm certain she'll tell her something.

CHAPTER
sixteen

Julia

MY BODY GETS HOTTER AND HOTTER WITH EACH step I take. Leaning against the counter, I listen to the water rushing from the faucet; it fills the empty restroom with white noise. *Just breathe. Just breathe.* I've never wanted to run so badly. That's all I can think about.

My heels click as I walk casually out of the side exit, smiling as best as I can although I'm not meeting the eyes of any of the guests who are having quiet conversations in the hall. As they sip on their cocktails and throw their heads back in jovial laughter, I want to walk faster; my body begs me to run. It takes great effort to keep my pace easy and pretend that nothing's wrong as I tuck my hair back and say thank you to the doorman when I head outside.

Goosebumps prickle along my skin as the bitter cold greets me. I pull the shrug tighter and maintain my composure when the look from the young man holding the door is riddled with questions.

It's too cold for me to be outside without a coat; I'm certain that's what he's thinking. But I cling to my clutch, the beaded fabric nearly slipping from the sweat on my hands.

My heart races and all I can hear is the blood rushing in my ears as the door closes behind me. The dark night lays before me, the busy street only a block away and through a small alley.

This exit isn't meant for departing guests. It's meant for smoking and the faint smell gets stronger as I take a few steps farther out into the night. Away from the gala, from the spotlight and from Mason.

Glancing to my left purely out of instinct from knowing someone's there incites shock and fear both. Liam Olsen stares back at me. He pushes off of the wall, exhaling a puff of smoke that mixes with the fog of his breath. The bright red and orange embers of the cigarette travel through the air as he walks toward me. His oxford shoes crunch the snow beneath his heavy steps.

I turn to face him, my eyes flitting between him and the exit I've just left. I'm not sure anyone can see me from here. There's no light, only darkness where I've gone.

The moonlight makes Liam's skin look pale and his eyes dark as he walks closer to me. I swallow the dread in my throat and greet him accordingly. "How are you, Mr. Olsen?" My skin feels numb with the cold, yet alive with fear. I've never actually met the man, but I know the business he had with Mason dissolving has left its mark on him.

"Where's Mason?" Liam asks harshly, tossing his cigarette to the side where it's instantly extinguished by the wet snow. Smoke billows from his nostrils as he comes closer, close enough to get a glimpse of his eyes. They're nearly bloodshot and his walk uneven, but his question is forceful. I'm not sure if he's drunk or angry. Maybe both.

"Whatever happened between you two…" I can't finish the thought.

My voice is caught in my throat for a moment, my eyes going back to the exit where I can clearly see the guests. My heart pounds once then twice as time seems to pass in slow motion and I have to think quick. Liam takes a large step forward, closing the distance between us and I instantly take one back, although it's on the edge of the sidewalk and my heel slips. I almost fall backward, and he catches me.

He chuckles and reeks of liquor. I push my hands against his chest as I find purchase on the sidewalk, turning my body so he's no longer between me and the exit.

He's drunk and he's angry, so I'm careful as I pry his hands off me as respectfully as possible and desperately try to put more space between us.

"He's coming," I tell Liam breathlessly. I have to clear my throat and repeat myself to sound surer of what I'm saying, but it doesn't fool Liam. Either that, or he doesn't care.

"You really want a man like that?" he asks me. "After what he's done?" he says and squints his eyes, and my throat closes with fear with the tone he takes. *What does he know?*

"What?" I say, licking my lips although in the cold air it

only makes them feel chapped. "What exactly did he do?" I ask Liam, taking another step back. I watch as he looks toward the door and then takes another step closer to me, his hands slipping into the pockets of his slacks. "Business partnerships don't always—"

"I'm going to make him pay," he says, cutting me off and raising his brow as he reaches in his pocket for something. I involuntarily tense up, but it's only a pack of cigarettes. He takes one out, then offers the pack to me as he slips a cig between his lips and tilts his head back.

"No thank you," I tell him, "I was just heading inside."

"No you weren't," he says as he lights the cigarette, the tiny flame illuminating his face. He takes the cigarette out of his mouth, pinching it between his forefinger and thumb as he says, "You just came out here."

"I made a mistake." I'm quick to answer and it only makes him smile.

"Yeah you did," he says and the smile morphs from cocky to something else. Something sinister.

"I have to go," I say and turn my back to him, heading for the door. But I only take a single step before his hand is wrapped around my hip, pulling me backward and into his hard chest.

"Get off me!" I yell out and drop my clutch as I try to pry his fingers away from me. He's holding me with a bruising force, the tips of his fingers digging into the flesh at my hips.

"Hey now," Liam says, nearly laughing the words as he spits out the cigarette and covers my mouth with his other hand. "Hush, hush, it's okay," he whispers against the shell of my ear.

The cocktail of smoke and lingering alcohol mixes and fills my lungs as I heave in a breath. This is not happening.

I yank my elbow back with everything I have and shove it into Liam's gut. He releases me and I don't waste a second, I run for the door straight in front of me. My shrug falls off and I've already lost my clutch, but as far as I'm concerned, it can stay wherever it is forever.

My palms slap against the glass door, forcing my body to come to a halt and the doorman looks at me with complete surprise as I stand there doubled over and desperate for air.

I'm shaking and completely wrecked. I've dealt with drunken men and roaming hands before. But never from a man angry with my supposed fiancé. I can barely wrap my head around what happened. He grabbed me. He held his hand over my mouth.

The door opens and even though I feel like I'm going to be sick, I walk in, trying to hide what's happened, but completely unable to compose myself. My legs are shaky and I still struggle to come to terms with being grabbed like that. I don't know what to do. I grip onto the man's arm and try to clear my head from the fog of shock, but I'm not given long before a strong grip pulls me away from him.

I yell out in surprise and fear until I realize it's Mason. He holds my forearms and forces me to look at him, and I lose it.

"Jules?" He says my name, compassion and worry evident. I shake my head, and say the only thing I can think of. "Liam—" I say but then my voice croaks, unable to get out the rest of the words. Unable to express what just happened moments ago.

Tears leak from the corners of my eyes, and his concern

turns to anger. I can't say for certain what he was going to do, but there's not a chance he didn't know I was scared. He knew he crossed a boundary. "He… he—"

Mason releases me quickly, slamming his arm into the door and forcing it to fly open as I nearly fall to the gleaming marble floor.

"Jules!" I hear Kat call my name from behind me. I hear the commotion around us. I can see from the reflection in the glass a crowd's come to watch.

I can't respond, I can't even turn to her or form a single thought concerning all of them.

Even as she pulls me to stand straighter and puts her face close to mine, grabbing onto me and trying to get my attention, I can't give it to her. All I can do is watch Mason disappear and wish he'd just come back. *I need him.*

Kat grips my face with both her hands and forces me to look at her. I stare into her worried eyes and confess in a ragged breath, "I'm not okay."

CHAPTER

seventeen

Mason

Anger cannot be denied,

It cannot be contained.

Carnal sins and violent ways,

Its brutality cannot be chained.

It's passion that drives the fist,

It's fear that leaves the cage.

Every movement desperate,

Pain seeping through the rage.

EVERY HOT BREATH TURNS TO WHITE FOG IN FRONT of my face, and it pisses me off. It obstructs my view of the bastard standing right in front of me. His back is to me as he taps a carton of cigarettes against his palm.

He should have run while he had the chance.

"Liam," I call out, my chest rising and falling, my lungs filling with ice-cold air.

Knowing him, he'd fucking love for me to make a scene. I'm sure I'm playing right into his hand, and I don't give a damn.

He's drunk and looks high. His suit's disheveled as he turns to me with a half-cocked smile on his lips.

"Don't you ever fucking touch her!" I say as I walk forward and get closer to him. I have no intention of talking. I don't need to find out what happened or why. All I know is that she was terrified. And the only thing she could say was his name.

He's a dead man.

"How do you know what she came out here for?" he asks with a smirk, and I swing my fist as hard as I can into his pretty-boy smile.

I grab his collar, using it to hold him still as I hammer my fist into his face over and over again.

I smash my knuckles against his cheekbones, his nose, his mouth, the skin splitting open on contact. At first he shoved against me, a pathetic attempt to push me away. He doesn't stand a chance.

I can feel her slipping away, and I'm so fucking desperate to hold on to her. I clutch his throat, forcing him still.

My teeth grit against one another as adrenaline pumps in my blood. *Crack!* His nose breaks as my knuckles collide with his face and I lose my hold on him. The back of his head slams into the ground. I don't stop, I can't. All I can see is red. I lower myself to the ground but he gets in a punch, surprising me. His fist crashes against my cheek and whips my head to the side.

I barely feel it. The taste of metallic hot blood fills my mouth, but that doesn't stop me either. All it does is fuel me.

"She's mine!" I scream out and Liam's eyes widen with fear. I must sound crazy. Even to my own ears, the words I yell out are those of a madman. The worst part, the most sickening, is that I don't care. Maybe I have lost it. Maybe I am crazy when it comes to Jules. I'm perfectly fucking fine with that.

I yank him up by the collar, my knees sinking into the freezing snow and the thick silk fabric of my suit pants slowly absorbing the melting snow. He slams another fist into my face, so low on my chin he nearly catches my throat, and I return the blow by headbutting his nose.

He screams out in pain and I drop him to the ground.

My breathing is erratic, my vision blurred. I know I've won, but I can't stop because never in my life has it been more apparent than seeing Jules quaking with fear that I'm losing. I'm losing it all.

I pull back to smash my fist against his jaw again. To hear the satisfying crack, but two arms wrap around my chest and pull my back into a hard wall of muscle.

"It's just me. Just calm down," someone says from behind me. An angry growl rumbles through my chest as I throw my head back to smash the fucker's nose in. He leans away and I buck him off of me, ready to beat the piss out of him too.

Until I see who it is. It's Evan, and I can hear Kat screaming at him to break us up. They need to stay out of it.

"He tried to hurt her! He put his fucking hands on her!"

All the boiling rage rises to the surface and I take it out on Evan. Everyone needs to stay the fuck away.

Liam deserves everything that's coming to him.

I get one more punch in when Liam lurches for me, and his head snaps back from the blow. It lands square on his chin, and my knuckles scream from the sharp impact against his jaw. His lip splits, but it throws him off. As I lunge forward, Evan's hand grabs my fist and he twists his body to the side, making me fall forward. He pins my arm behind my back and again grabs me, my back to his chest.

My breath comes in heavy pants and I struggle harder when I hear Jules cry out. I can't see her, and I can't see Liam. I shove backward, but Evan's a strong bastard.

"Knock it off," I hear him grit through his teeth as the sound of a car pulling up catches my attention. I lift my eyes and see the headlights, but no one gets out. No sirens. It's not the cops… yet.

"Think about Jules," he tells me, his breath close to the back of my neck as I push back against his grip. "It's only about Jules, all right?" he says as I stop struggling.

I stare down at the ground, at Liam laying in the snow that's speckled with red. He's propped up on an elbow and on his side. In the bright streaks of light from the limo headlights, the blood shines a bright red against the pure white snow.

Liam spits, and another splash of red paints the ground.

"Mason," Jules calls out as she runs over to me, and the second my attention goes to her, Evan releases me.

My muscles are still wound tight and ready to go off. My fists still clenched even as she runs into my chest. I kiss her hair as I hear the limo door open and far too many people—too many witnesses—gather around.

"Leave," Evan tells me in a low voice. "It's mine, I'll take yours." He nods behind me and I glance at the white stretch limo before nodding my head. The rough stubble on my chin brushes against Jules's hair. I meet his crystal blue eyes as he says through clenched teeth, "Go! Just get the fuck out of here."

CHAPTER
eighteen

Julia

Intentions—cruel, helpless, hopeful,
They come in different shades.
They leave the nights with bright light,
And sharpen the dullest blades.

They bend your will and change your plans,
And make you do bad things.
They don't change the outcome,
Nor stop what justice brings.

Y THUMBNAIL NERVOUSLY SCRAPES AGAINST MY fingernails one at a time. I don't have polish on, although I wish I did so I could pick it off. I've always done this. A nervous habit, I suppose.

My eyes drift back to Mason. His head is back against the headrest and it jostles as the limo drives over a speed bump. His hands are clasped in his lap, the knuckles torn and bloodied and his eyes are focused on the roof of the cabin.

His cheek is already bruised. There's a split on the left side of his lips. My fingers itch to touch it. To comfort him.

He hasn't said a word. Silence is the only thing that accompanies us.

I swallow thickly as his head turns to the side and he stares at me. A burning sensation prickles over my skin and begs me to look away, but I can't. It's hopeless.

He licks his lower lip, the tip of his tongue sliding down the cut as he sets his hand on my thigh. I watch as he swallows and then breathes in heavily, all the while holding my gaze. Even blind eyes could see he is a damaged man.

"Are you okay?" he asks in a low voice, deep and heavy and riddled with pain.

"Are you?" I question back with just as much sincerity, but Mason presses on.

"I mean after Liam grabbed you?"

The lump in my throat expands as the memory comes flooding back.

I shake my head immediately, closing my eyes only to recall the unhinged look in Liam's eyes. I shudder and wrap my arms around myself. Mason immediately pulls me into him, holding me. He never fails to comfort me. I breathe easier enveloped in his warmth and resting my head on his chest. I love that he comforts me but just this once, I want to be the one comforting him.

He rocks me softly back and forth for a moment. As I calm down, the guilt weighs heavily on me. Both times now that I've tried to leave Mason, I've come to face regret and remorse for my actions.

"I shouldn't have gone outside," I say, letting the confession drift between us.

"Why were you out there?" Mason asks me, and it only solidifies the offense. I don't answer. Instead I look away, my cheek still resting on his shoulder and his arms still around me.

I hear him swallow and let out a strangled breath before rocking me again ever so slightly. He doesn't let go of me though, and he doesn't question me again. I'm grateful for both.

"I'm sorry," I whisper as I watch the lights of the city slip past us in a blur on our way back to his home.

His deep voice rumbles, "Are you?" There's no animosity there, no curiosity either. Simply a flat question devoid of all the emotion he just gave me a moment ago.

"I am."

A moment passes in silence and the limo rocks us as it passes over another speed bump before Mason kisses my hair and moves me to settle in his lap.

"It's okay," Mason says, running his hand down my hair to my back as he consoles me. He plants a soft kiss on my shoulder and my neck, and then a sweet kiss on my lips before looking me in the eyes. He gives me a sad smile and then kisses me once more before saying, "It's okay, I understand."

His forgiveness is what shatters me. His love and devotion to my happiness are what will ruin me entirely.

"Are you okay?" I ask him genuinely once again, desperate to put the attention and comfort on him. I'll never forget the look in his eyes when he left me. The primal man he became. The way he fought Liam… because of me. My voice catches in my throat as I finally lean toward him and let the tips of my fingers trail over the faint bruise. "I'm sorry," I whisper.

He turns his head, capturing my fingers with his hand and kissing their tips before looking at me. "You have nothing to be sorry for, Jules." His eyes brim with sincerity. "You never did," he says.

Tears prick my eyes, and I don't know which cause is in the forefront. The fear of what happened tonight? The desire to run away from what my life has become?

Or the love I feel for this man.

Maybe it's something instinctual for a woman to want to stay with someone who would fight to protect them. Maybe I feel I owe him for what he's done. All I know is that I can't deny what I feel.

His cold gray eyes stare deep into my own as he cups my chin in his hand and his gaze falls to my lips. He says softly, "I need you, Jules. Even if it's not real…" his voice chokes at the word but he continues with a pained look in his eyes, "Right now, I just need to feel like you love me again."

His hand slips behind my head, holding me still as his fingers tangle in my locks and his hot lips press against mine. I mold my lips to his and part them when he traces the seam with his tongue. My body obeys his and he takes full advantage, pushing against me until my back hits the seat and he settles his hips between my legs. He pins my hips down as he rocks against me, all the while stealing kisses and deepening the intensity. I break away to breathe.

My chest rises as he nibbles along my neck, desire shooting through me and making my nipples pebble.

"I love you, Jules," he whispers into the crook of my neck.

My heart aches. I want to love this man, not because of him, not because of his actions, but because of how I feel about him. A true love-hate relationship. Hot and cold.

I can see myself falling into his arms while simultaneously making plans to sneak out of his bed late at night. I'm ruined beyond repair, and I only blame myself.

It slips through my fingers,
That which I cannot hold.
I cry for it, would die for it,
This love I can't control.

THE ONLY FRIEND I EVER HAD IS DEAD TO ME. The woman I love tried again to leave me, and only came back because she was threatened.

My father may be trying to kill the woman I love. If not him, then someone else.

I've run my business into the ground and with my reputation in the shitter, I don't think I'll ever come back from it.

Last, a secret is out there that could destroy me, evidence that I murdered a man, and I haven't a clue who it is that knows or what they have on me. I'm waiting in the dark, and I can feel my sanity slipping away.

I imagine this is what they mean when they say rock bottom. I slip the heavy law textbook back into its place on the bookshelf as I hear my father's office door open and then close. I don't turn around to face him. I don't have to in order to know it's him.

My father's voice bellows from behind me. "You need to relax, Mason. That shit you pulled—"

"What does it matter?" I say, cutting him off and turning to face him as his forehead creases with anger.

"You look like you've lost it," he hisses at me, slapping the newspaper in his hand down onto his desk as he takes his seat.

"I have though, haven't I?" It's the conclusion I come to, knowing Jules was going to leave me. Again. That's what did me in this time. I take in a heavy breath.

It's all the lies too. Keeping track of them has pulled its weight in bringing me down.

I don't even know what's the truth anymore or who to trust. I only know that I hate everyone I'm surrounded by except for the one person who's desperate to leave me.

"I need the truth," I say, getting straight to the point as I stare my father in the eyes. Although I know it doesn't matter, I add, "Don't lie to me."

"I wouldn't lie to you, Ma—" my father starts, intent on saying something else, but I cut him off.

"You lie to everyone; why would I be any different?" I shrug my shoulders and stride closer to his desk, my pace quick and careless.

"What's on your mind then?" he asks, his eyes narrowed and his frustration barely contained. He must see how on edge I am. I can practically smell the fear coming off of him. The fear of not knowing what I'm going to ask, or maybe of what I'm going to do. "You called this meeting," he adds as he sits back in his cognac leather chair. He unbuttons his suit jacket and adopts a casual posture.

"Did you kill her?" I ask him in a whisper.

He cocks a brow at me before answering in a deathly low voice, "I've never killed anyone."

I don't know why his answer makes my lips tip up into a smile. It's sickening that he doesn't take responsibility. I nod my head, and a rough laugh spills from my lips. "I do apologize," I say as I pace in front of his desk, letting my fingers run over the edges of the leather chair opposite his and then the next. "You *had* her killed."

"You'll have to be more specific as to whom you're referring," my father says as he flicks a switch.

"You think I'm wearing a wire?" I ask incredulously. As if the police could help. As if I wouldn't be completely ruined if I turned to them.

"I don't know what to think about you right now."

I stop in my tracks and face him, bracing a hand on each chair. "I don't either," I say barely above a murmur.

"You were saying?" he says before his eyes shift to the door. This time I know why the smile comes. It's because he wants to get rid of me. He's done with me. It's about fucking time.

"You killed my mother," I say, getting the accusation out into the open once and for all.

"I didn't. I can't believe you'd think that." I stare at him, hearing how false his words sound as they ring in my ears. "There's a difference between killing your own and protecting your own." My father's voice turns hard and at first I think he's justifying having her murdered, but then I realize he's talking about Avery. "Your mother hurt me," he says and leans forward, placing his hand against his chest as he adds, "but I loved her. I would have never done that to her. Or to you."

"I don't believe you," I tell him. "I think you murdered her, and I think you want Jules dead too."

"You have her under control, don't you?" my father says although he knows damn well I don't. After last night, the whole city is talking and now Liam is the topic of the day, not her or me. But three people know what really happened last night.

Jules. Myself. And my father. He knows she wants to leave me. He just doesn't know why.

He doesn't wait for an answer, instead he pulls out a desk drawer and reaches in, rifling through paperwork while he talks. "I looked into Liam's books and subsequent finances." A thick stack of papers lands on his desk with a thud and then he slams the drawer closed. "Would you sit down, Mason? You're going to kill me with this," he says and waves his hands in the air. "Just calm down."

"Calm down?" I ask him before swallowing down the pain, pinching the bridge of my nose as I close my eyes. I've never felt quite like this. Only because the harsh reality has never been so clear to me.

"Mason," my father says my name as if it's a plea, "I promise you, I will protect you with everything I have. If that includes protecting her, I will. You're my son. My one and only, and the only thing I have to live for anymore.

"Whatever it is that's gotten into you," my father continues as he breaks eye contact and shakes his head. "I said I'm sorry about Avery," he adds and presses his lips into a thin line. "You weren't here when she came in." He turns in his chair and looks out of the window. "Or Anderson." He runs a hand down his face and stares out at the city skyline.

"There are choices we make that have to be done quickly." He swallows thickly. "I was only trying to protect you."

I finally take the seat opposite him slowly and wait for him to face me. "No. Stop protecting me." I shake my head slowly and hold his gaze. "I don't want your idea of protection."

"Well maybe this will help," he says as he slides the papers over to me. "Liam Olsen is in the hole, and his life is falling apart."

I hesitantly look through the stack, lifting the corner of the top sheet to look at the next and the one after that. They're all copies of bill after bill he's racked up over the last year.

"We need to talk about what happened the other night before the gala."

It takes me a moment before I realize he's talking about the man with the gun. The intruder with a syringe. An obvious fucking hit. "Someone was hired to kill Jules. I don't know who or why, but it was a hit."

"Are you sure?" my father asks me.

"He could have killed me, he could have turned when I was chasing him and shot me. But then again he could have killed Jules too."

"Then why didn't he?"

I remember the syringe, the heroin. I shift in my seat, staring at my father as I tell him, "He had a syringe on him. He didn't want the hit to be obvious."

My father's expression doesn't change; he doesn't give anything away. "A syringe?"

"Filled with heroin," I tell him and this time he breaks eye contact. He pulls his jacket down and clears his throat, obviously uncomfortable.

"Your mother," he starts to say but doesn't finish. I give him a moment, again remembering the way my mother lay there on the tiled bathroom floor. "So, this is where that shit is coming from?" His question is laced with feigned anger. More than anything, it's a veil over his sadness.

I nod once, not trusting myself to respond verbally.

He nods, although he doesn't look me in the eyes. "Your mother…" he starts to say again and then stops. He waves the thought away, shaking his head and dropping the discussion entirely. I've never seen my father so visibly shaken.

"I don't see why anyone would want you or Jules dead other than Olsen. Even then, it would have to be because of money and I've made it clear to him that the debt owed to me is void. So killing you would most likely be related to some sort of quarrel between the two of you." He finally looks me in the eyes again before adding, "After last night, there must be something between you two… Undoubtedly."

I don't know what possessed Liam to go after Jules last night. I didn't take him for that kind of a man. An arrogant ass, yes. A man who'd hurt a woman? I huff at the thought. Any man who would do something like that isn't a man.

"If not Olsen, who else?"

Every hair stands on end and a chill flows down my skin. I question telling my father about Anderson, the entire truth. I have no one else, my back's against a wall, and this is for Jules. I would do anything for Jules. If that means confessing murder to a murderer, so be it.

I look my father in the eye as I tell him, "I killed Jace Anderson and someone knows."

I wait for a reaction and the only one I get is that his brows raise slightly and he tilts his head to the side, considering.

"I see," he says after a moment and again turns away from his seat. His foot taps against the desk as he thinks. "Over Avery, I assume?" he says.

I nod once. He has the dignity to look ashamed for a split second.

"You didn't love her. You didn't want her. You told me that much."

"That doesn't make it right," I say and grip the armrests, feeling the anger rise, but he holds up his hands in both defense and understanding.

It's quiet for a moment, with only the ticking of the clock counting the seconds to keep us company as my father takes in the truth of what happened.

Finally, he looks up and says, "You could have come to me."

"I was angry at you too," I say and his eyes spark with indignation at my admission.

As if just now putting the pieces together, his expression changes and he asks, "That's why Jules went to the police? She knows?"

"Yes." I swallow the spiked lump in my throat.

"Who is it who knows?" he asks me, thankfully leaving the difficulties with Jules out of the conversation. "And what exactly do they know?"

"I don't know," I say and he clicks his tongue against the roof of his mouth. "Jules received an anonymous letter." The paper lays in my wallet as we speak, but I don't present it to him. "It was a warning to get away from me with no evidence."

"Someone knows you killed Jace, warned her to get away from you… but then tried to kill her?" he asks me with confusion.

I nod my head, fully comprehending the lack of logic.

"I don't think they were planning on doing anything when it came to Anderson. They only told Jules to get back at me. And then tried to kill her to keep the secret silenced."

"Who would do that?" he asks me.

You, I think, but I don't say it. I don't have to, though.

His face contorts with disbelief before he turns completely in his chair and opens a cabinet door. I watch in the reflection of the glass, clearly seeing a safe and what's more, the numbers of the combination to open it.

It's the same combination he had on the garage when I was a child. I rip my eyes away from the reflection when he peers back up, holding a stack of photographs in his hand and shutting the door to the safe and then the cabinet with a kick of his foot.

"I wasn't sure if I should show you this or not," he says and lets out an uneasy breath. "It would have complicated things between you and Liam."

I glance down at the photographs and then immediately

back up to my father's gaze. *Jace Anderson and Liam's wife, Cecile?*

"No," I say and the word leaves me without my consent.

"They're getting a divorce, so I imagine Liam found out about the affair somehow," my father says absently.

"Maybe Liam? Maybe his wife?" my father says, shrugging. "Either way, I'm sure now that the hit failed, I doubt they'll attempt it again."

His last statement catches me by surprise, and I tear my eyes away from the evidence of Cecile's affair to gauge my father's reaction.

"I'm keeping my ear to the ground and waiting to hear back from a certain someone," he says then shakes his head slightly, "but no one knows anything according to my source."

I can't imagine how deep my father's depravity goes that he has contacts in such low places.

My father continues without looking at me. "I talked to the commissioner." I've been waiting for this. I know there are consequences to what happened the other night. Liam's gunning for me.

"You may have to go in for questioning. You won't be charged with anything, of course. But they have to make it seem like they've done their due diligence." *Thatchers belong on only one side of the courtroom.* It's a saying the men in my family have carried for years.

"I need to go," my father tells me, rising from his seat and gesturing to the door. "If you need help this time, let me know."

CHAPTER

twenty

Julia

It's not the anger toward him,
It's not the dimming fire.
It's not the love I feel for him,
Or how my heart bleeds with desire.
My soul is broken, torn and bent,
Never to repair.
To truly hate oneself,
The sin leaves me in despair.

SEVENTEEN DAYS HAVE PASSED SINCE I GOT THE anonymous letter in the mail.

Each day, Mason looks at me differently. It's like

he knows I'm leaving. I'm not convinced leaving is the answer; I'm not convinced I should stay though either.

The bedroom door creaks open as I brush my hair, getting ready for bed. There's no doubt in my mind that he'll be sleeping in bed with me tonight. He walks into the room quietly, shutting the door behind him. The left side of his face is bruised and cut, but somehow it only adds to his beauty. A prince, wounded in battle saving his princess.

I almost laugh. A hint of it must have escaped at the thought, because he turns to look at me as the door clicks shut. The only light in the room is from the small lamp on the nightstand and the way the shadows sharpen his features does the worst things to me.

There's an odd dynamic between the two of us. He wants to touch me, he keeps coming close to doing just that, circling me and waiting, but he doesn't.

The part that's truly insane is that it disappoints me, every single time. I'm crazy for feeling any attraction to him at all, but I'm drawn like a moth to a flame.

He picked me up when I fell.

He protected me when I was weak.

And even though I hate him for what he's done, he's the only reason I'm still alive.

"You can't hide in here forever, Jules," Mason comments half-heartedly with a small smile on his lips that doesn't reach his eyes. He closes the space between us easily, and I let him. His lips brush against mine in what I presume will be a gentle kiss, but he deepens it and without my conscious consent, I lean into it. I didn't realize how much I missed his touch.

He moans into my mouth as he kisses me deeply, not

holding back a damn thing. I wish I could do the same, but all I find myself doing is forcing myself to stay away, to keep my guard up around him. I can't let myself fall again. I won't. I utterly refuse to give him that chance or else I know he'll keep me forever. And I don't know who exactly I'll be if I let that happen.

I break the kiss before he's finished with me, but he only pushes harder into me, wanting more and letting me know exactly what he needs.

I turn away from him, shame filling every piece of me. Ashamed to be kissing him. Ashamed that I *want* to kiss him.

"Is that how you want it, Jules?" he asks and his deep voice comes out rough as I look into his eyes. The passion is still there. The desire that ignites mine stares back at me.

"You want to hate me." He brings his lips to my ear, making a burning ache flow down every inch of my skin. "Try hating me while you cum on my dick, sweetheart," he tells me and I know I'm done for. My head falls back, hitting the wall as his hands trail over my sides, slowly making their way down my curves.

He rakes his teeth down my collarbone, the sensation directly linked to both my sensitive nipples and needy clit. I'm desperate for more. Aching for him to take me and own my body like I know only he can. His teeth sink into the crook of my neck as his hands pin my hips down, holding me in place as I cry out in sheer frustration.

His large body towers over me, the heat from his body suffocating me as his hard erection digs into my lower belly.

"Fight me, Jules," he says, gripping the hair at the nape of my neck and twisting it around his wrist. "Fight me like you want to."

I slap him, his rough stubble scraping against my hand. A low growl rumbles up his chest; it's just as filthy and perverted as I feel, keenly aware of how much he turns me on. I press both of my hands against his chest, a weak and helpless attempt at pushing him away and he just chuckles at me, his gray eyes flickering to life with a heat I've missed. Nothing but wanting moans escape my lips.

He grabs the nape of my neck, forcing my head to tilt and claiming a cry from me as he steals a kiss along my jaw. I shove my weight forward, attempting to push him away with more vigor, but he merely uses my attempt to push and twist me down onto the bed.

My belly presses against the mattress, my back arching as he stands behind me, leaning against me and pinning me down as his fingertips slide up my outer thighs.

My heart squeezes too tightly without being able to see him and feel him. I don't know why, but I don't want this, not like this.

"Mason," I call out for him, and his name is nothing more than a plea with the frantic need I feel.

He instantly braces his forearms around me, no longer touching me and no longer pinning me to the bed. He breathes heavily, panting as I turn slowly, still caged under him. It's an awkward way to lie, with my bottom barely on the edge of the bed.

His eyes are closed, shut tight and his plump lips parted as I lie beneath him. A caged animal, hurt and tortured and needing a way out is all I see. "Mason," I whisper his name and he opens his eyes.

I gently press my lips to his, taking a sweet kiss before

nipping his bottom lip. I brush the tip of my nose against his, and the spark ignites again. He attempts a soft kiss, but it quickly turns into something else. Something primal and filled with lust.

He kisses down my neck, over the small bite marks still red on my skin and aching for attention. He strips my underwear from me and kicks off his own as we slowly climb deeper into the bed. Slowly parting from our clothes and the worries that wait beyond the heavy sheets.

I don't stop whispering his name, I don't stop pushing and pulling against him until he slams into me, filling me and stretching my walls in one swift thrust. My back arches, and a silent scream rips up my throat.

The pleasure he gives me is unmatched, indescribable and something only for us. It's sinful and wrong, but it feels like heaven.

A strangled moan is torn from me and he almost stops when I push against his cheek yet again. I can see the hesitation, the worry in his eyes. I arch my neck and rock my hips, letting him know that I'm his. That I want this and him just the same. My head thrashes from side to side as my throbbing clit brushes against his rough pubic hair as he stills deep inside of me, buried to the hilt and hovering over me, watching my expression. "More," I whimper, desperate for whatever he will give me. I'm deprived without his touch. He should know that; he's done this to me.

Crashing his lips against mine, he moves his hand to my hip, positioning me how he wants me and tilting my ass up just slightly so he can thrust deeper into me. He slams himself harder and deeper into me, unrelenting and unmerciful. "Fuck," I moan, and he's quick to echo my pleasure.

From him, it's a groan of awe filled with gratitude and devotion, fueling him to push me farther and farther as he races for his release. He whispers the word over and over in the crook of my neck, his hot breath sending chills over my body.

From me, it's a strangled cry as my nails scratch down his back and my body pleads for more and also to run from the intensity. It's a mix of pleasure and pain, a cocktail strong enough to kill me and I don't know which one it will be that finally brings me to my death.

twenty-one

Mason

IT'S DIFFICULT TO CONFRONT A PERSON WHEN THEY have a restraining order against you. Regardless, I consider driving by Liam's house, knocking on the door and beating the fucking piss out of him all over again. A week has passed, and not a damn thing has changed. The air is stagnant and I don't know what to do but I won't sit and wait for the next onslaught.

The once sought-after developer and bachelor has taken a fall.

The excerpt of the news article lays above my mug shot. At least I knew it was coming; the journalist was decent enough to give me a heads-up. Evan could only do so much to hold me back from Liam, but he worked as much magic as he could with the press.

It's only a mug shot. No charges pressed and nothing on my record, but the city has a way of talking. The most shocking thing in the article is the information concerning Liam. Apparently he has a criminal record from college for assault and battery, and attempts at much worse. Divorce papers have already been signed between him and his now ex-wife, and the article compares that to the supposed breakup between Jules and myself.

I'm not sure what is true concerning Liam. I'm grateful the spotlight is on him in the article. The article got my father and Jules all worked up. I can only imagine how they'd react if they knew about the letter that arrived today too.

The paper in my hands rustles in the quiet office as I read it again.

I was mad at you for what you did, and I'm sorry.
It's not what you think.
The gentleman was only there to find something, but I found it elsewhere.

I'm sorry for what I've done.
And I forgive you for what you did; I hope you can forgive me as well.

Sincerely,
X

It's the same feminine writing as the other note. This one sits in my wallet, and it's been here for hours, refusing to allow me to think of anything else.

Whoever it was is damn good at concealing their identity. Not a single fingerprint on the envelope or the paper itself. The security footage shows it was delivered by the mailman, but has no return address. I'm lost, and I have absolutely no leads.

I finally crumple the letter, hating it and the fucker more now than ever. The hopeless feeling weighs down on me. I can't fix it. I can't fix anything without knowing who to blame.

They fucked with me, ruined something so precious and perfect, tearing Jules from my life. And now they're just backing away? They wanted to destroy me. Mission fucking accomplished.

I don't know who to trust anymore or what to live for. My only hope is to pretend it's all right. To move through life like nothing's wrong, and pray that Jules can one day do the same. The rough edges of the letter rub harshly against my skin as I close my eyes and tighten my fist around it. It's never going to happen.

She's never going to forgive me.

She loves me deep down. She has to. I can't feel this strongly about her without her feeling something for me.

Tossing the letter into the small trash can beneath my desk, I rise from my seat and wonder about my father, about Liam's wife and how she plays into this. But this game is so much different than any other I've played before.

Too many pieces and moving parts, but I can't see a damn one of them.

It feels a lot like giving up. A lot like losing. But sometimes you need to keep going through the motions, stay on your guard, and just let them think you've lost.

I flick off the light switch as I open the office door and stand there in the hall, contemplating where Jules is most likely to be in the house. My hand tightens on the doorknob, as I wonder if she'll talk to me like we used to. If she'll let me hold her. If those moments when she forgets and looks at me with those gorgeous blue eyes will last longer than seconds tonight.

I'll leave it be, if only to let them think I've lost and given up. I nod my head as I leave; that's what I tell myself.

As I shut the door behind me, it feels like I truly have lost everything already.

twenty-two

Julia

I T'S NEARLY PICTURE PERFECT.

To anyone looking in, we're a couple sitting on the sofa in front of a roaring fire.

There's plenty of lighting for the scene in Mason's living room. The light's brighter and has been all winter with the curtains open and the snow covering the grounds. The white reflects the sunshine into the room, no matter how dim it is. I watch the flames lick along the log. This fireplace is different from the one in the dining room. It's odd they don't match. I would've changed that if it were up to me. But it wasn't. Because this isn't where I belong.

I'm trapped here. I've made up my mind and I'm done.

I swallow thickly, moving more of the blanket over my chest as Mason shifts on the other end of the sofa. I came down here to write and to get this tale out of my head. To put an ending on it and hoping I could get a different perspective, but these words that stare back at me make me want to scream. Scratching out the lines over and over, I attempt to change them and deny it, but it is what it is. There's no changing this ending.

My foot brushes against the pad of paper on the ottoman as I turn to face Mason.

He's working, too, but completely unaffected. If I had to pinpoint what's caused the finality and resentment, it's the way he continues; I hate how easily he can move forward.

I've heard of that psychological condition where the woman falls for her captor. Stockholm syndrome. That's not what this is. I loved this man with my whole heart before. I can feel myself falling, slipping back into that place and I refuse to go there.

He brought me into this hell, and I want out. I need to get out.

I'm scared, and I don't know what to do. But I know I need to be alone. That's what it comes down to. I'm destroyed, and I need to be okay alone.

I'll never stop loving him, but I need to stop hating myself and I can't do that if I'm with him. "This isn't a life," I blurt out and then look up at Mason. "I want to leave, Mason."

He doesn't look at me at first, but he stops typing. The quiet clacking of the keys turns to nothing, leaving the room silent but for the crackling of the fire.

When he turns to look at me, I can see the fight in him is

almost gone. He's almost given up as well. It shouldn't crush me the way it does. It shouldn't cause this pain. This hole in my chest, but it does.

Taking a moment to swallow, the cords in his neck tighten before he answers, "You told me that you'd give me a month."

A sadistic laugh leaves me—one that's terrifying and rude, one that I should feel apologetic for letting slip out, but I can't keep up with all the lies like he does. "You and I both know it's never going to happen." The words come out like a knife—knives, really. They cut us both, each in different ways.

"You can't leave," he tells me simply and I can't help but feel enraged.

"I'm not staying," I state with finality and narrow my eyes at him, and I feel a side of me that wants to fight. Not like the other night. I want to fight for my life. For my freedom and for a happiness I don't ever see myself having with Mason. Not ever again.

"There's someone—"

"I don't care," I spit at him. "I can take care of myself."

His voice holds a note of admonishment as he says, "Don't be stupid, Jules."

"Fuck you," I hiss, gripping the sofa as I lean closer to him. "I was fine before I met you." I'm on edge, and violence brews inside of me. "How dare you!" I yell at him. I hold on to the anger. It's the only sane part of me anymore. "How dare you start this when you knew from the very beginning—" My voice gets so tight I can't finish.

Mason stares at me, judging how to handle me. It's what he does, but this is too much for either of us. High and mighty with his tone, he pushes back, "You were lonely, and don't pretend—"

"Because of you!" I scream the interruption, my voice and throat raw and full of pain. "You did this to me!" I yell. "I'm not okay, and it's because I'm fucking you!" All of my pent-up rage, all the boiling anger spills over and I kick out, throwing the blanket off and getting away from him. There's not enough distance between us, only feet from where he sits and where I stand. I can't leave though, not until he lets me go. Our stares are locked, brutalized with both sadness and anger.

It's quiet for a moment, with only the sounds of my heavy breathing and the fire.

"You need me to fix it," Mason says with confidence.

"You can't fix this," I say dully and my heart hurts as I answer him. I wish he could. I so desperately wish he could fix this. Because I want him. I want to love him, and have him forever. But that isn't our ending. I swallow and say, "You can't fix this."

"You need me—"

"I don't need anyone." I cut him off, letting out a deep breath and slowly lifting my head to look him in the eyes. The silver specks pierce through me as I say, "Mason, I'm done with all this. I'm done." The last two words of my confession are only whispers.

His expression softens as he leans back and I take the seat on the far end of the sofa, wanting the tension to leave us both. "Do you hate me?" he asks, his eyes turning glossy but I know he won't cry. That's not the man Mason is. I already know he loves me. I know he wants me. I know I want him too, but that's not in our cards. He decided that long ago, before he even met me.

"No." My voice croaks as I answer him and that hurts so much worse, telling him and confessing. "I don't hate you, it's not you."

He huffs a sarcastic and defensive sound. "It's not you, it's me," he says as he slams his laptop shut and pushes it off of him.

I lick my dry lips, feeling the cracks with the tip of my tongue. "You know it's what you've done, Mason." I wait for him to look at me again and I sniffle, wiping my tears and nose with my sleeve. "It's who you used to be that I can't get over.

"It's not about you, or what you want. It's about me being okay with this, and I never will be. How can I?" I shrug, wiping the tears as they come carelessly.

"Let me hold you," Mason says although it sounds like a demand, reaching out for me, but I move away, taking the throw with me in haste and then letting it fall to the floor.

"I can't," I say with my back to him. I tell him, "If you touch me, I don't think I'll be able to go."

"Then don't," he says with desperation, but he doesn't move.

"I can't forget, I can't pretend. And I hate myself for loving you." It's the hate I can't live with. I turn to face him, pleading with him to understand and accept it. "I hate myself."

I watch as Mason stands and leaves, as the first tear rolls down his cheek and he brushes it away angrily.

I can't let him walk away like this. I reach out to him, gripping onto his arm and he stops but doesn't look at me.

"Mason, please," I say, begging him, but I don't know what for. "I don't want to hurt you."

He shakes his head as he tells me, "It's my fault." That's all he says as I stand there waiting for more. My body wars with me, wanting to cave and let him hold me. I haven't realized it until now, but all this time, holding me has been his only way to be held in return.

"I need to give you your gun," Mason says in a tight voice, looking past me and toward the stairs.

"You're giving me the gun?" I ask him more as a distraction from standing there so numb and full of despair than anything else.

He nods once.

"And you'll leave me alone?" I ask him, both wanting him to tell me yes and give in to my wishes, and also to tell me no and say he'll love me forever.

"Yes," he says and my heart breaks into two. "I'll watch over you," he says as he nods his head and I nod in return, reflexively. "When you're safe," he says and swallows thickly before continuing, "I'll leave you alone. I promise."

twenty-three

Mason

Time be still,
Show me a way
To turn back what's done,
And change our yesterday.
I'm so damn sorry,
I would repent,
Alas, that time is already spent.

THERE'S NO WAY I'M LEAVING HER ALONE. In time, she'll forgive me. I'm sure she will. It's easier to ask for forgiveness, isn't it? That's how the saying goes.

A heavy sigh leaves me as I climb back into my car and double-check every window of her place. I've got a security system in place so she can be alone during the day, but at night, I'm slipping in through the back like I used to. I'll be quiet. I won't let anyone see. Not even her if she doesn't want to.

It wouldn't be right to leave her alone, but I can still let her leave.

The leather behind me protests as I close my eyes, leaning my head back with an overwhelmingly pathetic feeling consuming me. Everything I've done is to protect her, yes. But I can't let her go. I'm holding on to the last bit of her that I can. She's slipping, running away from me and I'd be a liar to say it doesn't shred me.

It's been weeks of nothing. Weeks of waiting. I don't believe for a moment whoever wrote that note and sent that man is done with me. Or with her.

I press the button on my phone for the security feed. I have it all here. I'll keep her safe.

I'll know the second anyone enters. The locks are all new. The alarms are set. Every door that opens in that house, I'll be alerted—same with every window.

She doesn't want to stay with me, and I can't force her to love me enough to stay. But I'll protect her and care for her. I have nothing and no one else. I have no choice.

The keys jingle as I start my car and the heater blows out cold air while the radio plays soft music. I turn them both off and listen to the hum of the engine. Taking another look over my shoulder and then another glance at the feed on my phone, I make a promise to let her go one day, just not today.

I'll leave her alone like she wants. I'll let her move on and live a normal life.

I can never give her that, I know that. Not with the way our worlds collided. She deserves that with someone else.

My throat feels tight as I gently press the pedal down and pull away from her row of condos on the Upper East Side. There's still a chance if I just hold on… I won't have to let her go. She'll forgive me.

My warring thoughts storm through me. Let her go or hold on to hope.

Even knowing how wrong it is, I'll be back tonight. I can't leave her alone. I can't let her go. That truth always wins out.

twenty-four

Julia

When did life become like this?
When did I lose it all?
When did my will to move on,
Become my wish to fall?
When was it that I gave up?
I'm a hollow, empty shell.
There's no answer that I know of,
And no way out of this hell.

EVERYWHERE I LOOK, I SEE MY DEAD HUSBAND. Lying in bed, sitting on a chair. He haunts this house in a way he never has before. It's not fear I'm feeling when the ghost of him appears as distant memories. It's anger.

I shouldn't have come back here.

I ran away from a man I love, only to come back to a past I hate.

My reflection is pale in the mirror. The bags under my eyes are back, and I look like shit. I wipe the fog from the shiny surface. The steam of the shower still lingers. It's late and I'm drained, both physically and emotionally, but I can't sleep.

Not without Mason next to me. I'm cold without him and feel weaker than I do when I'm with him. Maybe that's the way I trained myself. To be brave when there's someone to lean on. *What kind of bravery is that?*

I swallow the lump in my throat and close my eyes. I tell myself that I was wrong to love him, and somehow fooled into thinking it was real. If I convince myself it was never real, it will be so much easier to let go.

Opening my eyes only reveals the men of my past surrounding me in the mirror. Mason on my right, and Jace on my left, standing next to me in the reflection.

I blink once, and they're gone.

Leaving me alone, and isn't that what I wanted?

A chill runs through my blood as I focus on just breathing and calming myself. Bottles of perfume are lined up so neatly on the shelf. Chanel Chance is the first one in the row of expensive and elegant bottles. My breathing comes in harsh pants as I stare at it. It's nearly halfway empty. It was a Christmas gift.

I wonder if he gave his mistresses the same kind of

gifts? What about the woman he had killed? *The one pregnant with his child?*

The last thought snaps my last bit of control. A wretched cry echoes in the bathroom, burning my throat as I whip my hand across the shelf. The tinkling, crashing and shattering of glass fills the room as I stand there heaving. I grip the edge of the bathroom door, tears blurring my vision and stare back at myself. I fucking hate who I was. Naïve and stupid. "So fucking stupid!" I scream at myself. "I hate you!" I yell out. "I hate what you did to me!"

My body sways as I harshly wipe under my eyes, turning from the mirror before I shatter it as well. The overwhelming scent of the perfumes mix in the air and I slam the door shut behind me, hating how it reeks and how the mess from my outburst, reckless and yet again stupid, will stay there until I clean it up. I'll be the one picking up the tiny pieces of shattered glass. That's how it works when these men storm in, destroying everything and demanding I follow their lead.

Jace's closet is across from the bathroom. It was untouchable before when he passed. I couldn't bear to open it and see all of his clothes. Suits he would never wear again. Shirts that held memories.

I rip the doors open chaotically, but then pause and walk in ever so slowly, flicking on the light. The U-shaped closet is lined with crisp white dress shirts and a myriad of colors on the left. Suits on the right. In the very back is his collection of soccer jerseys. He started buying them all the way back in high school. I remember the first one he ever got. I spot it as the memory comes flooding back.

I told him the red brought out his eyes.

I clench my teeth as I tear the shirt down. The fabric feels like nothing in my fisted hand.

I told him how handsome he looked in it.

A scream I don't recognize as my own joins me when I grab the others, tearing them off the hangers and tossing them onto the floor.

He whispered that he wanted to see me in nothing but the jersey.

I kick the pile of jerseys aside and then dump the suits onto the floor, screaming as the memory washes over me.

I smiled, I wore it just for him and made love to him for the first time in that fucking jersey.

"I hate you!"

I blushed with innocence and handed everything I had right over to him. "I'll never forgive you!"

I don't stop until every last garment is littered on the floor. I take a shaky breath, not knowing if it's him I hate or myself.

My gaze searches the closet for something, anything to validate my rage. I tear open shoeboxes looking for little black books. Ripping through the drawers of a small watch armoire I tear them all out, flinging the cold metal behind me.

Each is a moment I wish I could take back.

Support that I'd given him blindly. The trust. Our marriage vows that meant nothing to him.

There's nothing that overtly makes him a *bad man* in this closet. No evidence that he deserved to die. There's nothing here. Nothing but ghosts of the past and memories I haven't suffered through in a year.

My shoulders rise and fall heavily as I move from one post to the next, focusing on taking it all down. I can't stand to see his things hanging there.

It's all the memories and the details he hid from me. They don't deserve their place anymore. I can't stand it and I want them gone.

I know deep in my gut that everything Mason told me is true. I always go with my gut, and it led me here. Crying in the middle of a trashed closet, with my prick of a dead hus-band's clothes scattered around me.

I'm searching for anything. Anything at all that would tell me it's okay to hate Jace and be done with him forever. That everything Mason said is true, and therefore it's okay to love him. That it's okay… for him to have murdered Jace.

I use the sleeve of a suit to bury my face. The cool mate-rial makes my heated face feel even hotter. I've finally lost it.

"I'll hate you forever, Jace Anderson." Exhaustion makes my legs shaky and I just want to lie down. I want to wake up and forget it all. I push the hair out of my face, taking in a deep breath.

My eyes close, and I see Mason. His gorgeous smile, and those deep gray eyes full of so much emotion.

I wish I could smile. I wish I could go to him and beg him to take me back. That's how far gone I am. I open my eyes, promising myself to be strong, but I can't walk another step.

My body tingles with awareness and fear as I look straight ahead.

The balcony doors are closed, but unlocked.

I know they were locked. My body feels frozen as I look to my left, the gun still in plain sight on my nightstand.

I look back to the balcony, staring at the lock and knowing without a doubt that someone else is in this house.

twenty-five

Mason

D RESSED IN ALL BLACK, I'M CERTAIN I'LL SLIP INTO the night for most people as I casually stroll along the sidewalk to William Street Towers, my father's office building. It's late and although the building is unlocked, the offices inside are locked up and most of the lights are off.

Opening the main door, my blood heats with anxiety as it swings open. The cameras are on, I don't have to look up at the little red lights to know they're recording.

My posture is relaxed, and I'll act like I belong. I won't appear out of place in the least. It's silent in the building as I rock on my heels and hit the button for the elevator. Someone coughs to my right, and I chance a look at a woman in a pencil skirt walking quickly to the narrow hallway where the restrooms are. A lone soul, working late.

This is how men go to prison for life for crimes they committed, but didn't get caught for.

This is how you fuck up and drown in your past mistakes for something so damn stupid.

An arrest for trespassing, or breaking and entering? They could charge me with that, and it wouldn't be the worst thing to have happened to me.

But they won't stop there. If I get caught, then my father will find out. He'll know what I was doing. He can push, and the powers that be will sentence me harsher than justice would allow.

This is how men are taken down. For doing stupid shit, rather than keeping their noses clean. But I don't give a damn. I need to know what's in that safe. I need answers.

It's been itching at me, an irritating thought in the back of my head, over and over ever since I left. A nagging that won't stop and a whisper that tells me everything is there, right there.

He had information on Liam… what else does he have in that safe?

The elevator dings as it arrives, the doors parting for me and sealing my fate.

Miss Theresa Geist has a bad habit. I'm not sure if anyone else knows, but growing up so close to her, spending so much time with her, I've learned that she sometimes forgets her keys. She takes the subway to work, and it's happened more than a time or two.

Because of this, she leaves the main office key tucked in the drawer of the reception desk in the hallway. It's hidden in a false bottom to the drawer. Or at least she used to hide it there. I swing the large glass door open and my heart races as I commit the first crime tonight, knowing it's being recorded. Knowing it's capturing my face.

It doesn't matter. It won't matter unless the cops or security have to pull up the tapes for a reason.

I swallow thickly, picking up the tray of paper clips and collection of pens and thumbtacks.

A small smile curves my lips up as I find the key. I stare at it a moment, watching it gleam in the lights from the hallway. It'll only get me into his practice's section of the building, but his office lock can be picked now that I'll be completely out of sight.

Open from 7:00 a.m. to 6:00 p.m. The white letters look back at me as I slip in the key and unlock the door.

With the soft click, all I can think is that I should have done this weeks ago. I prop the door open with a desk chair and return the key to where it belongs. No one will be the wiser. I should have come in here the moment I knew about the safe and the combination to its secrets.

But Jules was still with me.

She was still in my house and in my bed. Still a target if something were to happen to me. Everyone knows she's left me, thanks to the article in the morning paper.

Everyone is very aware that she left me after the incident that occurred at the gala. Or at least that's what's being read in black and white.

My heart clenches and I grit my teeth, kicking the chair back as I head straight for my father's door in the back. I slip my hand into my pocket, feeling the bent paper clips there. My fingers travel up and down the thin metal.

She would never do something like this. Jules isn't capable of it. I smile and a rough laugh slips through my lips as I stop at his door and slide the paper clips into the lock. Back in the day, I was damn good at this.

Jules would hate to know all the shit I did years ago. My pulse slows at the thought, turning cold, beating in time with the lock clicking and then the knob turns. I push open the door slowly, ignoring the memories.

The room is brighter than the hall was. The city lights pour through the blinds, creating alternating stripes of light and shadow throughout the room.

I don't waste any time, letting the door shut behind me and moving to his desk, to the cabinet. It swings open easily as if there's no challenge at all presenting itself.

I hesitate only for a moment, realizing whatever's in the safe may tell me more than I ever wanted to know.

There may be evidence of him murdering my mother. It's the first thought that comes to mind, and inwardly I curse myself. It's been twenty years.

Slipping on leather gloves first, I press the buttons slowly, mimicking my father's movements although the safe itself looks typical and ordinary. My lungs still, and my blood rushes in my ears as I wait for the light to flash and the small click that tells me it's unlocked.

It was far too easy.

Piles of paper lay in the safe. Stacks of photographs are the first that I remove, right where he kept the ones of Liam's wife and Jace Anderson. The photos are still on top. I flip through them, still in disbelief. How the hell did she even know him?

The stack directly underneath the one my father showed me makes me do a double take. I grab the photo of Jace and Cecile together and hold it next to a photo of Cecile alone. As I compare the two, my anger rises.

I've always known he was a liar.

It's altered. The photo is faked. My shoulders rise and fall with a tense breath.

Why set her up? They're already getting a divorce. *It's for you*, a soft voice whispers in the back of my head. *It was all to convince you it wasn't him. He'd let anyone else take the fall.*

I slip the photo back into place and scan through the others, searching for shots of Jules or myself, or anything else that proves what a conniving bastard my father is.

The next print is of someone I don't know. I'm confused at first because I have no idea why it was even taken. There's nothing remotely scandalous about it. I stare at the man in question and try to place him. It takes me a moment before I realize it's Jules's CPA, her financial advisor. The prick she went to go see months and months ago. I make it a habit to know who she interacts with. Why him? It doesn't make sense. Maybe he blackmailed him into doing something. I'm not sure.

I stop short at the next stack. It's a letter.

I stare at the photograph of Avery's blackmail letter. Her signature is there. I remember how she used to sign her name. Her handwriting was distinct when she signed documents. All I ever saw was her signature. The curves though, the curves of her writing are so familiar.

My blood runs cold. It's not possible.

It's her handwriting in the notes. I turn to the next photograph and it's another letter from Avery. No it's not. It's just a list of what looks like groceries.

I flip to the next, and that's when I realize what these are. Photographs of her handwriting. My skin pricks with an unforgiving chill. I set the photographs down after searching through several more stacks, but not finding anything at all that makes sense.

I lay them on the seat of the leather chair before looking back into the safe.

There's cash stuffed in the bottom. I take a stack of bound hundred-dollar bills and look behind them, shuffling the money to be sure that's all that's at the bottom. There must be over a million here. Although the safe is small, most of it is stacked with nothing but the bundled hundreds. So much money, it reeks of wealth.

I shove it back into place, not giving two shits about it, and that's when my eyes are drawn up to the top shelf. A thin, brown leather-bound notebook leans against the upper compartment of the safe where the photos were. I take it out, wondering what he'd confess in a bound journal, or if it's even his. I expect to find names and dollar amounts. Or names and account numbers, something of that nature. Information that's irrelevant to what I'm after.

The list of addresses I see first, I recognize immediately. They're ones Anderson bought, the ones my company wanted. But next to them are columns of figures. Dollar amounts of what they sold for at the time of purchase, and what they're projected to be worth after the surrounding properties are developed.

My forehead pinches not understanding why he'd give a shit. He doesn't own them, and they aren't for sale. They never were. Next to the dollar amounts are dates. A word has been repeatedly scribbled in tiny cursive next to some of them, but it's hard to make it out. I squint, my lips moving as I try to figure it out.

Acquired.

He bought them. They're investments. He had a plan, and everyone played a role. But Anderson had no intention of selling. He'd made that clear in the single meeting I had with him. Maybe he knew the properties would go up in value. Or maybe he wanted more money.

I run my fingers over the list of numbers as I try to piece together what corrupt business transaction the two men had together, but that's when I come across something familiar. Something I've become intimately acquainted with these past few weeks.

In the back of the notebook, there are several sheets of paper. Paper I'd consider elegant under other circumstances.

But this paper almost made me lose everything.

The thick cream parchment is unmistakable. My hand clenches into a fist as I fall onto my ass. My back hits the cabinet door as I picture my father writing the letters.

Practicing Avery's handwriting. Planning his next move. I was a target, and so was she.

It was him. It was always him. It's that moment when an alert sounds on my phone. *Jules.*

twenty-six

Julia

Emotions will trap you,
You have no choice.
Those bitter words?
That's not your voice.
They play with your mind,
And take over your will.
Anger is deadly, and
Fear can kill.

THE GUN IS HEAVY AND IT SLIPS IN MY HANDS AS I slowly walk down the steps, careful not to make too much noise. I cringe each time the stairs creak. So much noise. My hands are sweaty and my heart races as I move down the stairs with my back against the wall.

Thud, thud, thud, my heartbeat is loud in my ears. Too loud; I can barely hear anything else beyond the constant rhythm.

Barely breathing, my gaze flickers to the front door and then back up the staircase as light creeps in through the stained glass. I hold my breath until my feet land on the cold tile of the foyer. The front door is only feet away but as I get there, footsteps sound from the other side. The knob rattles, and my heart attempts to climb up my throat.

Whoever it is doesn't knock or ring the bell. I wait for a moment, trembling as I grip the gun for dear life, praying they'll prove to be someone I know, but there's only silence on the other side.

My heart is pounding harder now as I quietly race down the hallway, looking ahead and checking behind me every few seconds. *I need to escape out the back.*

The closed-in backyard won't do me any good, but I can climb the fence and slip through the thin veil of a forest straight to the crowded sidewalks of the city.

So close to protection, so close to safety. *Just run.*

I pause, my back pressed firmly against the wall as I get to the edge and peek around the corner and into the living room.

It's empty, and only fifteen or so feet to the sliding doors.

I'll run. The moment the thought occurs, I take off. But a sudden clatter in the kitchen startles me and I scream out, fumbling the gun and falling on my ass. I cover my mouth and turn quickly to face whoever's there. My pulse races and my body trembles.

The gun landed behind me and I struggle to reach it, my

arms propping me up. I keep my eyes forward, though. I'm shocked to find I'm staring at Liam Olsen.

"Whoa," he says easily, a smile on his face. "There you are," he says like he's been waiting for me. Like he's been expecting me. He takes two steps forward and my fear intensifies as he bends down, picking up a magnet that was on the fridge.

"It fell," he says with a shrug.

"What are you doing here?" I barely get out the question as I stand slowly, bringing the gun up behind my back and placing my finger next to the trigger.

"I was told you wanted to talk about something very important?" Liam's tone is playful, teasing and with a grin, he starts loosening the tie around his neck. "That you wanted—"

I bring the gun out in front of me slowly and steady my hands.

Liam's hands go up instantly, his eyes wide with shock.

"I don't want to talk about anything," I tell him and my voice shakes. My body is on fire, and the only thing pumping in my blood other than adrenaline is fear. The memories of the other night come back full force. His hands on me, his lips so close to my neck. "Stay away from me!" I scream at him, and the force of my emotions makes me tremble.

"All right now, you need to put that down," he says with more authority than he has, although his expression is still riddled with worry. He takes a step forward, arms still raised.

"I said stay away!" I cry out as if I'm scared and powerless, because that's how I feel. "Get the fuck out!"

"I'm going, I'm going," Liam says quickly. "I came in through the front and I'm headed out the front door, okay?" He says the words quickly, his own breathing ragged. "There must've been a misunderstanding," he tells me quickly, rushing out the words. Just then, his gaze rises just a touch higher, his focus no longer on me, but instead trained on something behind me. I didn't hear the back door sliding open until it was too late, and my skin pricks with the realization that I'm trapped. *There's someone behind me.*

I scream and as I do, the gun slips again in my sweaty grip and goes off. My eyes dart to it and it's like I'm watching in slow motion as it happens.

The sound of the bang.

The kick of the gun, making my arms jerk.

Large hands settle on my shoulders as the scream tears up my throat.

The bang still resonates in my ears as my body shakes and I try to push the man behind me away, but he holds me close as he says, "It's okay!"

I can hardly breathe, let alone recognize the voice.

Fear is what guided everything. I swear. I didn't mean for any of it to happen.

I look up and into the eyes of Mason, only it's not him. It's his father, looking down at me with sympathy, with sadness and horror.

Only when I see it's him do I look back at Liam.

The blood drains from my body when I see he's not moving. He's face-down, his arm at an awkward angle. "Liam," I call out, but he doesn't answer.

The gun is hot in my hands. A sickness grows in my stomach.

I shake my head over and over. What happened? I didn't. I swear I didn't shoot him.

Mason's father grips me again and I stumble backward, desperate to get away from him. My legs kick out as I scramble across the floor.

"Leave me alone!" I yell at him, still holding the gun, but pointing it toward the ground. *He isn't dead. I didn't kill him. I didn't mean to pull the trigger.*

He lets me go and says with nothing but compassion, "I saw what happened. It was an accident." He almost whispers the words. His eyes are wide as he nods. "It's okay, I saw it."

His words are comforting.

It was an accident. I swear it was. I look back at the body on the floor, my vision blurred from tears. *It was an accident. How did this happen? Why are they here?*

Too many questions scream in my head. Too many things are so very wrong. I look up at him with desperation and say, "Please, help me." My face crumples as the sobs start. "Save him."

What have I done?

twenty-seven

Mason

T HE DOOR IS ALREADY OPEN AS I STORM INTO THE house. Everything rages inside of me. I drove as fast as I could. But it's not fast enough. I've never prayed so much in my life as I did on my way to her place.

Bang! I swear I heard a gunshot, and I've never felt so cold in my life. The only thing keeping me from dying inside as I race through the first floor of her place, is hearing her cry. It means she's still alive.

"Jules!" I call out her name just as I get to her living room, all the way in the back of the townhouse.

My world spins as I stop short in the room. My father's hands are on Jules's shoulders, and Liam is dead on the floor.

"It was an accident," she whimpers over and over and Jules's hands shake as the gun falls to the floor.

"It's all right," my father whispers into her ear. "I saw it," he says and looks up at me, "it was an accident." His statement is firm. Just like his grip on her. He nods and I can already see the wheels spinning. He set this up. It's the ending he wrote. Liam the villain, and he gets to be the hero. Liam's wife gets his properties, then my father can buy them. Jules and I have our villain and he's in the clear.

Everything clicks into place. Each event, everything he's done and how he's played each piece.

I take a careful step forward, so aware of how close he is to her and the gun. *Too close.*

"Mason," Jules cries out. God I want to go to her, I desperately want to hold her, but as I take another step closer, my only goal is to get between the two of them. To keep him away from her.

This all ends tonight. I won't let him live to breathe the same air as us. His greed is deadly. If he did it once, he'll do it again.

"Stay behind me," I say as I rip Jules away from my father, grabbing her hand and forcing her behind me. I kick the gun behind me as well as I keep my gaze on him. His cold gray eyes darken and narrow at me.

"You can't pin this on me," he huffs. Naturally he'd think I was trying to save her and destroy him. It's all he's ever thought. Everyone's always out to get him. This time I am.

"Stay away from her." I swallow and say, "It was you."

My father's eyes dart to the gun behind me and I take a step to the right, keeping my arms out as Jules grips onto me.

"Mason," she whispers desperately, her cries waning as she realizes there's still reason to be afraid. That this isn't over.

"Jules," I say although I stare straight ahead, keeping my eyes right where they belong. "He's the one who wrote the note. The one who set me up to meet your husband. He set Liam up and used all of us. All for a fucking payout."

All over a chunk of property in New York City that Anderson bought out from under him. One corrupt man upping the ante in a game he couldn't afford.

"Now, now, let's not get ahead of ourselves," my father says easily. "It wasn't meant to turn into this, Mason."

Jules releases me, letting out a gasp from behind me. I can't feel her, I can't see her, but I can't turn around. I have to keep my eyes on him. On the liar and murderer and sinner I was born from.

He raises his hands defensively, as if giving up the fight and says, "I swear to you, it wasn't supposed to end like this." All the lies, the spinning of a delicate web woven with manipulation and deceit.

"I don't believe you," I tell him. "I think you didn't care how many people had to be sacrificed."

The corner of his lips twist into a wry smile. "I certainly didn't intend for this, Mason." He shakes his head and adds, "Never."

"And Mom?" I ask, feeling the rage come back to me. Knowing this isn't the first time. I don't know how many lies he's told, or how many people he's killed. "Did you intend for her to die, or was she just a casualty of your games?"

The mention of my mother gets a rise from him, his eyes

heating and his expression morphing into a snarl. "Your mother was a whore," he sneers. It's all I can take.

I heave in a breath as my body lunges for him. No punches, no hits. I wrap both of my hands around his throat. The weight of my body makes us topple over, both of us crashing to the ground as my blunt nails dig into the thin skin around his neck. I grip him with everything I have in me. My teeth clench and every muscle in my body is tight as I squeeze the life from him.

He tries to slam his fist into me at first, but he's not the young man he once was. I lean forward, balancing my weight as he tries to buck me off. I have him pinned.

Finally, he reaches up to his throat, desperate to pry away my fingers. His nails scratch at my skin, but I have no intention of letting go. All the desire in me focuses on leaning my weight into his throat. But the victory is stolen from me.

Bang! Bang!

My body tenses with the shock and fear. Two bullets have been fired. The noise rings in my ears as my father stills beneath me. His eyes are wide and lifeless, staring at nothing. His nails no longer digging into my hands.

Jules shot him. Once in the forehead, the other just an inch from his nose on his left cheek.

I stare at his face, the vision distorted by the blood dripping from the bullet holes down his weathered face and onto the carpet. Even knowing he's dead, I can't relax my grip around his throat.

Tell me! I scream in my head as tears prick the back of my eyes. I just want to hear him admit it. I want him to tell me to my face how he plotted my mother's death. How he hired someone to make it look like a suicide. My body trembles as I come to terms with the fact that it will never happen. His secrets will never be told, and my fingers loosen as I take in an unsteady breath.

It takes a long moment for me to glance up at Jules, who's eerily quiet only to see that she has the gun still pointed at him.

"He's dead. It's over, Jules."

Something in her seems to snap at my words, and she drops the gun as if it's burned her hands. She backs away, shaking and covering her mouth with horror.

The blood drains from her as the realization sets in. "Don't scream," I tell her.

"Look at me," I tell her and she does as I command. "It's okay." I swallow down every insecurity. For her, I'll be strong. I'll take care of this. "It's okay," I repeat and hold her gaze until she nods back although she's still on edge and drenched in terror.

I wipe the gun off on my shirt, getting rid of her prints and trying to think straight. The cops will be here soon. There's no doubt in my mind. She needs an alibi. "Run, Jules." I set the gun back down where it fell and rise to take a step closer to her. She's still trembling and can't take her eyes from the bodies on the ground. I reach out, grabbing her shoulders and shaking her slightly to get her attention. "Go to the Westin. You left me last night. Everyone knows that. I came here to get you, but you weren't here. I'll call the owner of the Westin." I nod as I speak, as if reassuring myself and her. I know for a fact the owner was in my father's back pocket and now he'll be in mine since I have my father's little black book. "He'll do what I tell him to if anyone asks. You checked in last night and that's where you've been."

Jules shakes her head, the implication of what I'm saying setting in. "Mason," she says and sucks in a breath. "No. You can't."

"I can and I am," I tell her, staring deep into her eyes. My beautiful Jules, my sweetheart. I should have known it would end like this. It's how it should have started. With me killing my father and letting everything else go.

"I love you," I tell her, "even if you can't be with me. I love you."

She stares deep into my eyes, and I can see how much it tortures her. We were never meant to be. It was my mistake. I deserve this pain. She parts her lips, I'm sure to explain, I know her so well and I'm certain that's what's coming. But I don't need it. She doesn't have to explain it to me; I already know. I press my finger to her lips, silencing her and then giving her one last kiss.

She leans into me as I pull away and it makes the pain in my chest grow that much deeper. I look down at her with the tears soaking her lashes until she finally peeks up at me.

We share a look, but it only makes her cry harder. We both know it's over.

I hold her, wrapping my arms around her and kissing her hair until she's able to calm herself down. The clock is ticking, and the time we have is already up.

She gives me the saddest smile when I pull away again for the last time, and says, "You're always cleaning up my messes, aren't you?"

"It was never your mess, Jules." She can't stop the tears flowing freely down her face as I tell her, "I'm so fucking sorry." I drop her hand and take a step backward as she covers her face with her hand. I say, "Know that I'm sorry. Know that I love you."

She nods once, licking the tears from her lips as I tell her to go, listening to the sirens getting louder and louder.

I watch her disappear, and I don't regret it.

She needed me to let her go. I know that now. I'm only capable of destroying her. She deserves so much more than that.

CHAPTER
twenty-eight

Julia

The truth is, everyone can kill.
Some born to defend, others for thrill.
What would it take? It's not that hard.
Threaten you? Or leave you scarred?
How much can they push you,
How much can they take?
Until you pull the trigger,
And you finally break.

I'VE NEVER HURT LIKE THIS BEFORE. LIKE MY SOUL'S been gutted.

I can't get the look in Mason's eyes out of my head.

A darkness sets in around me as I close my eyes. The vision of his handsome face displaying nothing but hopelessness is only replaced with something more morbid.

I killed a man. Two.

The first I could convince myself was an accident. I was terrified; I felt threatened. I swear it was an accident.

The second, though… I shot his father out of anger. I wonder if this is what Mason felt like almost a year ago when he killed Jace. If that rage that consumed me was the same for him. I shot his father because I wanted to. That is the only explanation.

I shift on the sofa and pull the chenille throw closer up to my neck. My shoulders brush against the armrest until I get my head right on the pillow. I can't go to the bedroom. I can't go anywhere in this hotel room without feeling like the cops will burst through the doors at any minute. I've only spoken to them on the phone. I can't imagine they believed my lies. Even as I said them, I could tell they sounded nothing like the truth. *Because I'm a liar now. I'm a murderer.*

I'm not the woman people think I am. I don't belong here and I don't deserve to get away without punishment. There's no denying that.

It's one thing to mourn the loss of a loved one. It's only natural, much like a breakup, but you have no way of going back, no way to mend the broken pieces. They simply don't exist anymore except in memories. Consuming your thoughts with no way to recover, other than to move on. Which, in itself, is a tragedy.

It's quite a different thing to mourn the loss of yourself. To realize you're no longer who you once were or who you wanted to be. Your identity has vanished, and staring back at you in the mirror is someone else entirely.

The faint sounds of the TV get louder as a commercial comes on and it makes my skin prick. I turn to face the lights, but I'm not watching it. I don't even know what's showing, it's all blurred. I wanted to turn something on to try to fill the hollowness in me. As if simply hearing something and someone else would make me feel less alone. As if I could somehow ignore my own reality by getting lost in a movie.

When Jace died, this method worked well. I'd turn on a heart-wrenching chick flick just to convince myself that the movie was the reason I was crying. The movie was why I felt the way I did and I could turn it off, if only I wanted to.

It's not working today, though. I'm all too aware of my current state. I bite down on my thumbnail, looking past the television and over at the curtains, hiding the view from the only window in the living room of the hotel penthouse.

I'm not the sweet good girl I was brought up to be.

And I never will be again. My stomach churns and I roll over to my side, trying to ignore the overwhelming guilt.

I try to convince myself that it'll be okay, that it was all a mistake or an accident or someone else's fault, but I've never been a good liar.

My throat dries and seems to close as I try to take a breath of air. It's all too much, this burden, this truth. Mostly the fact that I'm going to get away with it.

I wonder if Jace felt like this back when he sentenced that woman to death? I think back to each morning in his last days with me. But nothing was different. He was the same as any other day. The same smile, the same kiss. The same lightheartedness about him.

He had no remorse. I bite the inside of my cheek

wondering how he could go about his days as if everything was all right. Nothing is. And nothing has been for so long.

I can't hide that any longer. I can't run from it.

When did I become this woman? One willing to kill. Eager to, even.

I can't answer that, because I'd never been in this position until Jace died. All of my life, I've been handed everything easily. Even if I was grateful, it wasn't right.

I've never had to fight for a damn thing. I've never felt the need to defend myself. Maybe this woman, the one who kills out of anger, the one who's quick to end what threatens her… maybe I've always been her. I just didn't know it, because she was dormant deep down inside of me, comforted by the fact that she didn't need to act.

Life was kind to her, but not anymore.

My phone goes off by my thigh, making me jump as it rips me from my thoughts. Instinctively, I look to the door first. Where the cops should be coming any minute. They had to know I was the one who really did it. All the evidence is there in my home. *I should confess.*

They'll take me away and force me to pay for my crimes.

I'm expecting it. *I want it.* I want this all-consuming dread to leave me. I want the guilt to wash away. I want to be tried for my sins and sentenced as I should be.

Even if I sat on a jury and heard my story, I don't know how I'd find myself.

I'm guilty of so much, been baptized in the blood of other people's victims.

Maybe at this point, I'm insane. Maybe that will be my plea. It doesn't make me any less guilty.

I'm just as much of a murderer as Mason is.

And even more so than Jace, in a way.

I answer the phone on the last ring.

"Hello." I expect it to be the police, but it's Kat.

"Are you all right?" I close my eyes. It's good to hear her voice.

"How could I be?" I ask her with a pain she can't even imagine. She has no idea.

"It's going to be okay. I just got a call."

"From who?" I ask as I sit up straighter and pull my knees into my chest. "About Mason?" I need to know. "Is he going to be okay? Mason's going to be okay, is that what—"

"Calm down," she says, cutting me off. I sit uneasily, waiting for her to speak.

"What did you hear?"

She's quiet a second longer than I can stand. "He's in interrogation," she says. "They can charge him with obstruction now though, but that's it." My throat tightens and makes my words come out in a higher pitch than I intended.

"Obstruction?" I blink over and over, feeling light-headed.

Kat continues, "That's what I've heard. Nothing is set in stone yet."

My heart races erratically.

"It's not… I can't." I struggle to speak, to breathe even. "Kat, you have to help him. You have to help me." It's my chance to confess. To tell her everything. I throw my head back and I rock with the need to let it all out.

"It's okay, he didn't do it."

"I know he didn't. They can't keep him. They can't charge

him with anything," I say, pleading with her as if I know how this all works. But I have no idea.

"Kat," I say as my voice cracks again and the words are right there, threatening to come out.

He's taking the fall for me, because he loves me.

And I'm letting him. God, it hurts. It's so wrong. I bury my face between my knees, hating my reality.

He said he loves me; he's taking the fall for me. I didn't even have the balls to tell him how I feel in return. He said I love you, and I said nothing. He must know. He has to. What we have is real and tangible. But I need to tell him.

"Is he going to get off?" I ask her and wait with bated breath. The other line is filled with the sound of her breathing deeply and I find myself hunching forward, my lungs squeezing with the need to breathe.

"Jules, they have some evidence."

Her words make my blood run cold. *Evidence?*

"He didn't do it," I say and the words leave me without my consent. I know they're from me, I know I said it, but I'm somewhere else. Not here, safe in a luxurious hotel penthouse while Mason sits in jail for a crime I committed.

"I know he didn't," she says and I'm not sure if she speaks with certainty for my benefit or if she really believes he didn't. She continues, "But for them to be holding him this long, it means they have something on him, Jules. Evan says they have something. There's something going on."

I swallow thickly, not responding as Kat repeats my name over and over again. The flashes of what happened haunt me. The blood, the heat, the kick of the gun in my hands.

"What can I do?" My voice is eerily calm as I stare straight ahead, although I see nothing but his father's lifeless eyes.

"There's nothing we can do, Jules," Kat says and I shake my head even though she can't see.

I could tell them everything.

"I'm coming over to the hotel," Kat says just as I say, "I'm going to the station."

"Why the hell would you do that?" she says as if it's absurd. "Don't you dare move.

"Trust me, Jules. Mason's going to get out of this. It's just a matter of time before we find out why he's still in holding." I run a hand through my hair, feeling desperate to do something.

"I can't just stay here," I tell her with the desperation apparent in my voice. "I have to do something."

"Not yet," she says. "Don't worry, he's going to be okay. I promise you. You need to stay where you are. Evan is going to keep his ear to the ground. I'll tell you everything as we know it. Right now, they could charge him with obstruction but they aren't… we're waiting to see what they have. Just wait."

My teeth pinch the inside of my cheek as I debate on waiting. It's what Mason told me to do too. I'm so tired of waiting. Waiting to feel again, waiting for the truth, waiting for vengeance, waiting for the guilt to leave.

"I can't—" I start to say but my voice cracks, and I close my eyes. I swallow before firming my resolve to tell Kat, but she cuts me off.

"Just wait one more day. They can't hold him more than that."

The guilt seeps into my veins as I nod my head once as I end the call. One day. One more day.

I learned to live without Jace. And I was better off for it. I was happily living a lie. A false life that was devoid of real meaning.

I don't know that I can live without Mason, and I don't want to find out.

If I confess, we're apart.

If he takes the fall, we're apart.

I have to wait. I have no patience for fate. I don't know what's to come, but I won't let him do this.

As I walk to the large window watching the snow fall from the sky, I listen to the ticking of the clock, waiting to strike.

twenty-nine

Mason

"I DON'T HAVE ANYTHING ELSE TO SAY," I TELL THE detective who's questioning me, the one who refuses to leave. The commissioner is across the room, waiting, eyeing me and probably wondering what his best move to make is. Now that my father's gone, the balance of power has shifted, so it's just a question as to where it's gone and how I play into this game.

Cracking my knuckles one by one, I watch as the skin tightens and turns white before settling into a bright red as I flex my hand.

I don't want anything to do with this shit. I never did, and I never will.

My eyes lift as Commissioner Haynes strides across the room, pulling out his chair slowly and letting the steel drag across the floor.

He leans back, crossing his arms and looking at me as if he's sizing me up. I'm sure this is an act, a game, something that he's done before. I merely look back to my hands. The ones I wrapped around my father's throat right before he died.

It's an odd sense of calm that washes over me at the thought. It shouldn't comfort me. It's not right to be grateful for another's death. I carried the weight and burden of Anderson's death for months. It was only after meeting Jules and knowing I could make her happy that made it all disappear. Maybe if I told her that, it would make it better, but I can't bring myself to do it. I don't want her to know how selfish I was.

I wish I could take it back. I wish I'd murdered my father instead. The rage was meant for him, it always was. I was too much of a coward to do it.

"We have the residue from your shirt, Thatcher." The commissioner finally speaks. I don't look up, I merely pick under my nails, ignoring him and the heat that makes every inch of my skin tingle. He leans across the table, moving closer to me with his hands clasped as he says matter-of-factly, "We know you didn't shoot him, but you're covering for someone. You wiped that gun clean."

Stupid. I grit my teeth, realizing just how stupid I was for doing that shit. I was so desperate to save her, I wasn't thinking. My heart pounds over and over again. But I don't show them a damn thing. I won't give them anything they can use against her.

It doesn't escape me that she could tell them everything.

She could speak the truth and knowing my Jules, my sweetheart, I can see her doing it.

I could see her admitting it all, every last detail of the past year that's brought us to this moment. I'd still love her. I'd love her for it.

"I requested my lawyer," I remind them as I lift my head to look him in the eyes.

He clenches his jaw and the cop on my right shifts his stance, gaining my attention. He's pissed. He's young and naïve and thought he was going to break me. He thought that little bit of evidence would do something to scare me into talking.

But my father and grandfather taught me well. When the lies are too big to weave together, you stay silent. You wait for the right story to come along and slowly the pieces will snake in between the crevices. Those around you will create something that will hide them. Silence will kill the evidence. It only needs time.

"Your money can't save you this time," the young detective says. I don't even know his name, nor do I give a fuck. His dark eyes shine with conviction as he squares his shoulders and nods his head. He's clean-shaven, which only makes him appear younger, but of all the men I've met in this building, he's the only one I have respect for. He believes in justice.

"It never could," I speak without thinking, saying the first thing that came to mind.

"What's that mean?" Haynes questions from across the table. He's desperate for me to give him something.

I don't spare him a glance as the young cop responds, "You're going away. There's no negotiating, no lesser sentence for talking." His eyes narrow as he nods his head once and walks closer to the table, bracing himself on it with both of his fists. "We're going to find who really did it. And you're both going down."

My unaffected façade falters at the thought of them learning that Jules did it. My hands flex and ball into fists, and I have to look away. Not Jules. I already ruined her life enough. I destroyed a pure and beautiful soul.

Piece by piece I tore her down before I even knew what I was doing. I can't let her go down for this.

"Not talking is only making it worse for you."

I open my mouth to do what I do best, to be true to my heritage and lie. I have to think of something good, a reason for changing my shirt before cleaning the gun. I lick my lips, trying to come up with the right scenario, something believable. Something the evidence will prove is true. It doesn't have to be factual, only enough that will convince them I'm guilty.

This is what I deserve, even if it's a fucked-up way of going about it. I murdered a man. I tried and convicted him without thinking twice. It's only fair the same is done to me.

"Let's not get ahead of ourselves, Mickey," the commissioner says from across from me. "You already know that's not going to happen."

His last words catch my attention and I turn to him, ignoring how the detective's back straightens and he stalks toward Haynes. "Sir," the cop says and straightens, waiting for the commissioner to explain, maybe? I'm not sure. There's a duel between them with a thick tension that's suffocating.

The commissioner cocks a brow as if not understanding what Mickey is after.

"He's a witness, he tampered with the crime scene—"

"No judge is going to allow charges with that little evidence."

"Bullshit—"

"It's done," he says and the sharp words strike the young man, leaving him standing frozen, staring down the commissioner with his eyes flicking between the two of us. I don't know about legalities. I don't know how much is enough evidence. More importantly, I refuse to believe anything said by a man my father considered a friend.

"Find more evidence or let him go. It's that simple. We're not taking anything to trial unless we can ensure a conviction, get that through your head."

"You're as corrupt as they are," the detective says with contempt before turning his back to the commissioner and storming out of the room.

Before he can slam the door, I see a familiar face in the doorway, eyebrows raised as he's escorted in by a young female cop with a ponytail. She's looking between the cop who's just left and at Commissioner Haynes.

"I trust my client is free to go?" Mr. Millard asks as he shifts the leather handle of his black briefcase from one hand to the other and watches the female cop close the door to the room. "I'm sure you're aware—" Mr. Millard begins, but doesn't finish.

"I've already spoken to the judge," Commissioner Haynes says, once again leaning back in his chair and eyeing me, as if considering who I am and whether or not my existence even matters to him. "He's free to go," he says with finality as my family lawyer nods once and quickly reopens the door to the interrogation room. "We want the murderer and only him. Evidence proves Mason is not our suspect."

I don't need another invitation to leave. Standing abruptly, I take one last look at the commissioner, who's still staring straight ahead, but no longer at me. Only an empty chair, although the same look is in his eyes.

My pulse quickens as I walk through the station, feeling everyone's eyes on me and listening to the sound of our shoes smacking against the floor as we walk out.

"Just like that?" I say beneath my breath as Mr. Millard opens the large front glass door for me. His brow raises as I walk through, still looking at him and waiting for the other shoe to drop. For whatever deal was made and figuring out who I owe now.

He nods his head once, appearing uncomfortable but not adding any more.

This isn't the first time I've gotten away with things. A slap on the wrist for vandalism, shit like that. *But this?*

I stare at my lawyer, wondering what he knows and what he thinks of me as we leave, no charges pressed. The air is bitter cold and the snow on the street is blackened, but on the sidewalks it's still a brilliant white and makes the late evening seem lighter than it should.

"Just like that," Millard says, repeating my words and looking back over his shoulder before walking across the street. I follow him and wait. Always waiting for what's next.

He opens his car's passenger door and says, "Home, Mr. Thatcher?"

I shake my head no. A gust of wind blows by and the air seeps through my clothes, chilling me to the bone. Mr. Millard waits, as if expecting me to change my mind. But I'm not interested. I shake my head again, shoving my hands in my pockets.

My lawyer clears his throat and looks toward the station before shutting the door with a click and walking toward me. His oxford shoes crunch the snow beneath him as he leans in closer to me and says, "Don't tell anyone anything." He lets out a breath and it turns to fog in the air as he looks behind him one last time.

"It's going to take a couple of months for this to die down, of course. But the evidence found on the scene that could tie you to murder has been dismissed already. It's a matter of finding motive and suspects now. The judge is never going to charge a Thatcher, and he doesn't want any digging around the circumstances of your father's death." For the first time, Mr. Millard looks at me as if he thinks I may have done it, but there's no contempt, no disgust, only curiosity behind his eyes.

"For you, it's over. A few months, and it's all buried. Just stay quiet and don't talk to anyone. Don't give them a reason to come back to you. As far as they know, they followed you there, there was an altercation but a fourth unknown individual shot them both. Evidence proves you didn't fire a gun. They can't change that; they can only hunt down a fourth… and you have no idea of that person's identity. If anyone asks, you're only grateful he didn't shoot you too."

I nod my head, feeling the weight of everything and how it all seems heavier for some reason. Knowing how unjust it is. That a select few have already decided the fate of the case.

I'm a hypocrite, because it's what I did when I saw that look in Anderson's eyes. The smile on his face as I left his office. I did the same. His fate was sealed. Even a glance at the photograph on his desk didn't stop me.

I saw her. I knew he was married. I knew she was his. I told myself I didn't care and that it didn't matter. He had to die.

It's that overwhelming feeling of power that made the first domino tip as I turned my back on him, knowing his fate was decided.

"Thank you, Mr. Millard," I say and turn away from the station, away from him and toward the crowded streets of the city.

I didn't know how the other dominoes would fall. And the judge and the lawyers, they have no idea either. So many pieces tumbled over. So many lives affected.

There's only one who matters to me.

Only one I need to keep safe.

Her piece is bound to fall if I touch her. I almost ruined her once. I won't do it again.

I was never any good for her. I should have stayed away if I loved her, and I think I did even all that time ago. I think I loved her before I ever heard that sweet laugh. Before I saw her gorgeous lips and that sadness in her beautiful doe eyes that she hid from everyone but me. I think I loved her even then.

And I should have stayed far away.

thirty

Julia

T HEY SAY IF YOU LOVE SOMEONE, YOU SHOULD LET them go.

That's all I keep thinking over and over as I stare out the windows of the penthouse, staring blankly at the city skyline. Mason's been out for over twenty-four hours now. I knew the second he walked out, and I waited. And waited. I owe him and all I can think is that if I send him a message, I'm going to beg him for even more. That's not fair and that's not right.

I swallow thickly, and my dry throat sends a spike of pain running through me. Or maybe it's my heart. I'm not sure which. I shake my head, turning abruptly and walk over to the kitchen to fix myself some coffee. If he wanted to speak to me, he would have come or he would have called. The fact is, he doesn't want me. Why did it take me this long to realize that wanting him and loving him wasn't enough?

He hasn't called, hasn't sent a text. I take a steadying breath, balancing myself on a padded barstool at the island counter and then gripping the hot mug of coffee with both hands. The ceramic mug has veins of gold running through the thick cream pottery. I focus on it and drift my finger over the raised texture remembering how he used to trail his fingers down my lips before kissing me.

Everything is a reminder of him and it hurts. I let my head fall back to exhale before taking a slow sip of the coffee. It's worse than death because I could have him. It could be different… He's right there.

I keep thinking he's merely let me go because he loves me. They say if you love someone, you should let them go. Maybe that's what I should do. I should let him go.

But isn't it done with? Isn't it over? The ending is so much different from what I envisioned. I will take this one where there is hope, over anything else. I want a chance.

The truth is, if Mason loved me, he'd be here. If he wanted me, he'd take me. That's the kind of man he is.

"If you want to go to his house…" Maddie says gently from the seat next to me, moving her hand to my thigh. She hasn't left my side since last night when the girls came over. When Kat told me Mason had been released from custody and I had waited for him to show, and he never did. After the first hour, I started to worry. After several hours, it was hard not to assume the worst. I'm glad my friends were here with me instead. I still don't know when I'll be able to return to my condo. The police say it's a crime scene, and that means it's off-limits in the meantime. I should message him… I should message Mason and let him know that. Shouldn't I? He should know that I'm still here in this penthouse when he's the one who's footing the bill.

"Maddie, please." Kat's patience is waning thin with a restless Maddie who won't stop asking questions. I'm grateful for the distraction, though.

Kat's sitting at the dining room table and Sue went to work. She didn't want to, but I insisted.

"There's nothing wrong with going after what you want," Maddie says, finishing her suggestion.

I glance from her to Kat, who's gently nodding her head. "That's true," she whispers. Both of them stare at me as if I'm broken. Like this is the one thing over the last year that has managed to finally destroy me.

I've lost a husband, then fell in love with his murderer. I've been held against my will, killed a man out of anger and another out of fear for my life.

Yet here I sit, worried about the man who brought all of this chaos in my life.

Worried he doesn't want me. Worried I can never have him again. Worried I'll never love anyone or be loved by anyone like him.

The mug clinks as I set it down on the counter, pushing it away to rest my face in my hands. The granite's cold on my elbows, but everything today has been brutally cold. I should be used to it by now.

Shifting on the stool next to me, Maddie gently rubs my

back in soothing strokes, making the cotton blouse travel slightly up and down my back as she shushes me.

The padding of Kat's feet are muted by her socks when she gets up to sit by us too. She takes a seat alongside us at the island with me sitting between her and Maddie.

"Hey, it's okay. He didn't do it," Kat says in such a tender voice. It only makes the pain in my chest grow.

I didn't tell them a word, and I never will. They'll never know any of this truth. Not if I can help it.

"I know," I say and my voice cracks as I agree. I clear my throat and stare straight ahead, pushing the hair out of my face and ignoring both sets of their questioning eyes on me.

I can see myself in the reflection of the steel fridge, but it's not quite me, it's something else. Some different version that stares back, distorted. Perception is what's changed my life. It could have gone on and on with me not knowing a damn thing, only seeing what they wanted me to, and then none of this would have ever happened.

"He didn't do it," I say in a stronger voice, swallowing the lump in my throat.

"Why don't you call him maybe?" Maddie offers.

I have to drop my gaze. I can't look them in the eyes and lie. "I don't think he wants me to," I answer honestly, staring fixedly at the granite countertops.

"You're wrong, Jules." Kat's voice comes out harsher than I expected as she speaks, and I grip the edge of the counter to turn my body on the stool and face her. "Of course he loves you. That's more than obvious."

"You don't understand," I tell her even though I already know there's no convincing her. Kat's stubborn. She stares at me, waiting for an explanation. My eyes flicker to Maddie's, both of them waiting impatiently. I settle for a partial truth. "He said he loves me." I clear my throat and look past Kat. "I didn't say it back," I add. "The last time I saw him, I didn't say it back."

"Why?" Maddie sounds horrified, and it only makes me feel worse.

"It's just that he did something," I say haltingly, and my stomach churns as I look back to the gold flecks on the mug in front of me.

"Something like what?" Kat seems hesitant.

"It was something from a while ago, but it hurt me," I say then close my eyes, wishing they could just know. Wishing I didn't have to say it for them to understand.

"Did he mean to hurt you?" Kat asks and there's a pain in her gaze. I know it's because of what she and Evan are going through right now. I wish she'd talk to me about that, rather than feeling like I'm prying when I try to ask how she's holding up.

"I'm sure he didn't," Maddie says softly, but her brow is furrowed with sympathy as she waits for my response.

"It wasn't meant to, no, but it was meant to hurt someone else and it wasn't right." I see Maddie and Kat exchange glances.

"What did he do?" Maddie asks.

"Maybe he's not here because he thinks you want to keep your distance for now since he was arrested?" Kat says, delicately hinting around the fact that I'm very self-conscious of negative publicity.

"I don't care about that," I tell her bluntly. "He's not here now, because when I left..." I can't finish. I can't say the words because I'm ashamed that I didn't answer him. I've known I still love him. I know damn well I do, and I did then. I just didn't want to admit it.

"You upset him?" Kat says, taking a guess.

"I knew I might not see him again… and I still didn't say it back. He said I love you, and I didn't say it back."

"It's just words," Kat says, "Actions are what count. And if you love him, go for him. Fix it. You can always fix it." She's full of so much confidence. So much conviction, I have to believe her although part of me wonders if she's telling me what she's telling herself when it comes to her own relationship.

"Go to him," Maddie says sweetly.

"Don't you want him?" Kat presses when I don't respond, too caught up in my own thoughts.

Had I known the truth, I never would have gotten close, but he didn't give me that chance. He pulled me in and drowned me before I realized I couldn't breathe. I'll forever be his. All the sins and secrets could never tear us apart. We both have them. But if we have each other… they don't matter.

Maddie nods her head in agreement. "Just because you're fighting over something that happened before this doesn't mean anything." Her voice is firm. "He needs you."

And I need him. We always have, both in our own way.

All three of us turn our heads to the door as I hear it open with a loud thud. My heart hammers in my chest, pounding harder and harder as I see him. Mason.

The breath leaves my lungs and I nearly fall off the stool at the sight of him.

He doesn't look at me or even in this direction as he closes the door and tucks the keycard into his pocket. He slips off his boots easily, as if he belongs here and it's only natural.

As if he hadn't kept me waiting here for him for hours.

When he finally looks up, something breaks in me. The walls crumble, and I want to run to him. To climb off the stool and embrace him.

To thank him for taking the fall. For protecting me. For loving me even if he brought all this hell along with him. To check him over and make sure he's okay.

But I'm frozen in place. Paralyzed by the sight of him. He rolls his broad shoulders before tossing the jacket over the sofa and finally looking up at me. His steel gray eyes pierce through me, questioning only for a moment before turning his attention to the other two women.

Kat's hand squeezes mine briefly before she whispers, "Do you want us to get out of here?"

"Yeah," Maddie answers for me. "We'll see you tomorrow?" Maddie asks with wide eyes.

I nod my head, but still I can't speak. I can't answer either of them. He's here. All I can do is be thankful that he's here.

He's standing right there, only inches away from me. I can still feel the coldness from the outdoors around him. But it doesn't belong to him in the least. His tanned skin is pink on his cheeks and the tip of his nose. My fingers itch to reach out to him, to touch him and pass the chill of the air and feel his hot skin.

I'm vaguely aware of Kat and Maddie leaving, the sounds of keys jingling and each saying hello and then goodbye to Mason.

He gives them a tight smile and nods, his deep voice sending a soothing wave through me as he shoves his hands in his pockets and watches them leave.

As soon as the door shuts, he looks back at me, consuming me the way he does with his full attention as comes to the bar, close to me. Close enough to touch.

I lick my lips and scoot forward on the stool, my left knee brushing his right. "Mason," I say, whispering his name with a reverence I'm not sure he hears or recognizes, but his eyes look the same way they did months ago when I first left him. Raw and vulnerable. Emotional.

He can hide a lot of things from me, and I won't deny that because it's the absolute truth. But I can see the pain and love in his gaze when he looks at me like this.

I know that's real. He can't ever hide that from me.

"Jules," he says and Mason's voice is low. Too low. Panic drifts into my veins. It courses through me as he reaches out to run his fingers down my hair before resting his large hand on my thigh. His thumb runs back and forth in soothing strokes, but there's something about the way he's looking at me, something off about his body language. Something I don't like.

"I never should have put you through all this, Jules."

My heart clenches, feeling so constricted that I can't fathom the amount of pain I'm feeling. He's letting me go. He gave me hope, walking through the door. *No! No! Go back to the hope. We have hope. We don't have everything but we have hope, don't we?* The words tangle over themselves in the back of my throat.

"I never should have," he says then swallows before continuing, "I never should have killed him. I'm sorry." All I can do is shake my head slightly as I listen to Mason. It was a mistake, an unforgivable sin. An act that ruined my life. But he had his reasons. I can't deny that it was wrong, but so much was wrong. The pieces fell, and there was blood on everyone's hands.

"I was a different man then. I didn't know you yet, and I can't ever take it back." Mason pulls his hand away, and the warmth and comfort of his touch vanishes, replaced by a sudden chill.

"I fell in love with you and I'd do anything to keep you, but I know you don't want that.

I hate myself as much as you hate me."

He starts to turn away from me. To leave me like I've wanted since I learned the truth, but my body comes to life, my blood a mix of anxiety and depression. I grip Mason's hand as I stumble off the stool, the damn thing nearly toppling over.

"Don't you dare leave me," I say. My voice comes out raw as tears threaten to spill from my eyes. I refuse to take my hands from his to wipe under my eyes.

Never.

He's as much mine as I am his. I refuse to let him go.

His expression changes as he registers my words. "Don't you ever leave me again," I tell him with a strength formed from panic. *Please, please God, don't let him deny me.*

"I need you." The hot tears fall to my lips and I try to swallow, but it hurts too much. Everything hurts as I stand before the man I love, knowing it's wrong. Knowing he broke me, ruined me and then showed me how fucked up love can be. The only cruel thing left for him to do to me would be to leave me like this. To throw me away after everything we've been through.

"There's hope, isn't there?" I say. "I love you," I whisper with complete conviction.

Just as I part my lips to confess every emotion in me to him, he crashes his lips against mine, filling my chest with a warm flow of desire and completion. My lips are hard at first, caught off guard, but I'm quick to mold them to his, spearing my fingers through his hair as his hand splays at the small of my back, both of us deepening the kiss, both of us wanting more.

"Mason." I moan his name as he breaks the kiss, my eyes still closed as our hot breath mingles between us.

"Just hold me. I love you," I tell him and bury my head into his hard chest. He wraps his strong arms around me as his warmth consumes me and kisses my hair over and over. This is where I belong, I know it is.

"I love you," he says and it's all I need.

I love Mason. And he loves me.

epilogue

Julia

Deceit is pretty,
The truth is better than the lie.
Its beauty lurks in darkness,
It's gorgeous in ways you can't deny.

Although the tale is strange,
Not the ever after for you and me.
It's broken and imperfect,
And the way fate meant it to be.

Y BRUNETTE HAIR LOOKS NEARLY BLACK WHEN it's wet. The brush makes a loud thud as I set it down and reach for my makeup bag.

Looks can be so deceiving, can't they?

We have a beautiful home, seemingly the perfect life and many days, that's all I see. It's all I saw with Jace too, but that was a sham and a lie and I realize now that I knew the truth well back then. I was happy with the image, but the truth was something I hid; I wanted it that way.

What I have with Mason is the opposite. Although no one can see the truth, I know what we are. Raw and broken, but together, we're whole.

The world will never know what it took for the two of us to come out of this alive. No one will ever realize how much strength there is between us. We're unbreakable. Shattered to pieces, but healed together with a scar that's so much stronger than what was once there.

It's not a fairytale, but it's a happily ever after suited for us both. It gives me chills when I look back at the past, but I don't do that often. It's much better to look ahead, at the true happiness and comfort we give each other. At the full life of trust and faith that's been forged between us.

My phone pings with another text from Kat. And then another.

She finally told me what's happening with her and Evan.

He's still your Evan, I answer and stare at my phone, waiting for her response.

If anyone ever heard my story, maybe they'd say what I did was wrong. That crawling back to Mason after knowing what he did, is simply unforgivable.

Even my closest friends. I don't think they would understand. No one would.

Love is inexplicable. It makes you do crazy things. Love is blind… that's a saying for a reason, isn't it?

I know, Kat writes back. *He's still the man I married. Dangerous in ways I don't like to think about. I did this to myself. I knew better than to fall for him.*

My heart hurts for her when she messages again before I can respond: *I only wish love were enough to fix this…*

It is. I'm desperate to write that back to her. But there are pieces to their story I'm missing. Pieces that will come out one way or another…

ABOUT THE
author

Thank you so much for reading my romances. I'm just a stay at home mom and avid reader turned author and I couldn't be happier.

I hope you love my books as much as I do!

More by Willow Winters
www.WillowWintersWrites.com/books